'I don't apologise and I always *get* I want you. You should be ~~flat~~ Bastien told her without hesitation.**

'I'm not flattered. I'm shocked and disgusted at your lack of scruples!' Lilah told him angrily, her blue eyes bright with condemnation. 'You're trying to take advantage of this situation and play on my affection for my family.'

'I will use any advantage I have and do whatever I have to do to win you,' Bastien stated, his wide, beautifully shaped mouth firming as he stalked fluidly closer to tower over her. 'You're the glittering prize here, Delilah. Doesn't that thrill you?'

Lilah stiffened even more. 'No, of course it doesn't.'

'It would thrill most women,' Bastien told her drily, staring down at her with burnished dark golden eyes that sent an intoxicating fizz of awareness and frightening tension shooting through her every limb. 'A woman likes to be wanted above all others.'

'I very much doubt that you're *capable* of wanting one woman above all others,' Lilah retorted sharply.

'Sexual satisfaction is extremely important to me,' Bastien parried, studying her with cool gravity. 'I don't feel any need to explain that or apologise for it.'

Introducing Lynne Graham's fabulous new duet,
full of prestige, power and passion!

These are two alpha males
you just *won't* be able to put down.

The Notorious Greeks

...and the women they claim!

Whether it's the boardroom or the bedroom,
Leo and Bastien Zikos are masters of all they survey.
Until they each meet a woman who has the temerity to
deny them the one thing they most desperately crave…

In a true battle of wills,
Lynne Graham whisks you away to
glamorous destinations and epic tales of love in:

The Greek Demands His Heir
August 2015

The Greek Commands His Mistress
September 2015

Introducing Lynne Graham's fabulous new duet
full of prestige, power and passion!
These are two alpha males
you just *won't* be able to put down.

THE GREEK
COMMANDS
HIS MISTRESS

BY
LYNNE GRAHAM

Published in Great Britain 2015
by Mills & Boon, an imprint of Harlequin (UK) Limited,
Eton House, 18-24 Paradise Road, Richmond, Surrey, TW9 1SR

ISBN: 978-0-263-25076-3

Harlequin (UK) Limited's policy is to use papers that are natural,
renewable and recyclable products and made from wood grown in
sustainable forests. The logging and manufacturing processes conform
to the legal environmental regulations of the country of origin.

Printed and bound in Spain
by CPI, Barcelona

Lynne Graham was born in Northern Ireland and has been a keen romance reader since her teens. She is very happily married, with an understanding husband who has learned to cook since she started to write! Her five children keep her on her toes. She has a very large dog, which knocks everything over, a very small terrier, which barks a lot, and two cats. When time allows, Lynne is a keen gardener.

Visit the author profile page at millsandboon.co.uk for more titles

CHAPTER ONE

'IT'S OVER, REBA,' Bastien Zikos pronounced with finality.

The stunning blonde he was addressing flashed him a pained look of reproach. 'But we've been great together.'

'I've never pretended that this is anything more than it is...*sex*,' Bastien traded impatiently. 'Now we're done.'

Reba blinked rapidly, as though she was fighting back tears, but Bastien wasn't fooled. The only thing that would reduce Reba to tears would be a stingy pay-off. She was as hard as nails...and he was no more yielding. Indeed, when it came to women he was tough and cold. His mother, an eighteen-carat-gold-digging promiscuous shrew, with a polished line in fake tears and emotion, had been the first to teach her son distrust and contempt for her sex.

'You got bored with me, didn't you?' Reba condemned. 'I was warned that you had a short attention span. I should've listened.'

Impatience shivered through Bastien's very tall, muscular frame. Reba had been his mistress, and terrific entertainment in the bedroom, but it ended now.

And he had given her a small fortune in jewellery. He took nothing for free from women—not sex, not anything.

Bastien turned on his heel. 'My accountant will be in touch,' he said drily.

'There's someone else, isn't there?' the blonde snapped.

'If there is, it's none of your business,' Bastien told her icily, his dark eyes chilling in their detachment as he glanced back at her, his lean, extravagantly handsome features hard as iron.

His driver was waiting outside the building to ferry him to the airport for his scheduled flight north.

A very faint shadow of a smile softened the tough line of Bastien's mouth as he boarded his private jet. *Someone else?* Maybe…maybe not.

His finance director, Richard James, was already seated in the opulent cabin. 'Am I allowed to ask what secret allure—evidently known only to you—exists in this dull northern town we're heading to, and about the even more dull failed business enterprise you have recently acquired?'

'You can ask. I don't promise to answer,' Bastien traded, flicking lazily through the latest stock figures on his laptop.

'Then there *is* something special at Moore Components that I haven't yet picked up on?' the stocky blond man prompted ruefully. 'A patent? A new invention?'

Bastien dealt the other man a wryly amused glance. 'The factory is built on land worth millions,' he pointed out drily. 'A prime site for development close to the town centre.'

'It's been years since you played asset-stripper,'

Richard remarked in surprise, while Bastien's personal staff and his security team boarded at the rear of the cabin.

Bastien had started out buying and selling businesses and breaking them up to attain the maximum possible profit. He had no conscience about such things. Profit and loss was a fact of life in the business world. Trends came and went, as did contracts. Fortunes rose and fell as companies expanded and then contracted again.

Bastien was exceptionally gifted when it came to spotting trends and making millions. He had a mind like a steel trap and the fierce, aggressive drive of a male who had not had a wealthy family to give him his breaks. He was a self-made billionaire, who had started out with nothing, and he took great pride in his independence.

But just at that moment Bastien wasn't thinking about business. No, indeed. Bastien was thinking about Delilah Moore—the only woman who had ever rejected him, leaving him tormented by lust and outraged by the frustrating new experience. His ego would have withstood the rebuff had she been genuinely uninterested in him, but Bastien knew that had not been the case. He had seen the longing in her eyes, the telling tension of her body when she was close to him, had recognised the breathy intimate note in her voice.

He could forgive much, but unquestionably *not* her deceitful insistence that she didn't want him. Fearlessly and foolishly judgemental, she had flung Bastien's womanising reputation in his face with as much disdain as a fine lady dismissing the clumsy approaches of a street thug. In reaction, Bastien's rage had burned, and now, almost two years on, it was still smouldering at the lack of respect she had demonstrated—not to mention her lies and her sheer nerve in daring to attack him.

And now fortune had turned the tables on Delilah Moore and her family. Bastien savoured the fact with dark satisfaction. He didn't believe she would be hurling defiance at him this time around…

'How is he?' Lilah asked her stepmother in an undertone when she spotted her father, Robert, standing outside in the backyard of her small terraced house.

'Much the same…' Vickie, a small curvaceous blonde in her early thirties, groaned at the sink, where she was doing the dishes with a whinging toddler clinging to one leg. 'Of course he's depressed. He worked all his life to build up the firm and now it's gone. He feels like a failure, and being unable to get a job hasn't helped.'

'Hopefully something will come up soon,' Lilah pronounced with determined cheer as she scooped up her two-year-old half-sister Clara and settled her down with a toy to occupy her.

When life was challenging, Lilah was convinced that it was best to look for even the smallest reason to be glad and celebrate it. Just then she was busy reminding herself that, while her father *had* lost his business and his home, their family was still intact and they all had their health.

At the same time Lilah was marvelling at the reality that she had grown so close to the stepmother she had once loathed on sight. She had assumed that

Vickie was another one of the good-time girls her father had once specialised in, and only slowly had she come to recognise that, regardless of their twenty-year age gap, the couple were genuinely in love.

Her father and Vickie had married four years earlier and Lilah now had two half-siblings she adored: three-year-old Ben and little Clara.

Currently Lilah's family were sharing her own rented home. With only two small bedrooms, a cramped living room and an even tinier kitchen, it was a very tight squeeze. But until the council came up with alternative accommodation for her father and his family, or her father found a paying job, they didn't have much choice.

The impressive five-bedroom home that her father and his wife had once owned was gone now, along with the business. Everything had had to be sold to settle the loans her father had taken out in a desperate effort to keep Moore Components afloat.

'I'm still hoping that Bastien Zikos will throw your dad a lifeline,' Vickie confided in a sudden burst of optimism. 'I mean, nobody knows that business better than Robert, and surely there's a space somewhere in the office or the factory where your father could still make himself useful?'

Lilah resisted the urge to remark that Bastien was more likely to tie a concrete block to her father's leg and sink him. After all, the Greek billionaire had offered to buy Moore Components two years earlier and his offer had been refused. Her father should've sold up and got out then, she thought regretfully. But the business had been doing well and, although tempted by the offer, the older man had ultimately decided that he couldn't face stepping down.

It was no consolation to Lilah that Bastien himself had forecast disaster once he'd realised that the firm's prosperity depended on the retention of one very important contract. Within weeks of losing that contract Moore Components had been struggling to survive.

'I'd better get to work,' Lilah remarked in a brittle voice, bending down to pet the miniature dachshund pushing affectionately against her legs in the hope of getting some attention.

Since her family had moved in Skippy had been a little neglected, she conceded guiltily. When had she last taken him for anything other than the shortest of walks?

Thoroughly unsettled, however, by her stepmother's sanguine reference to Bastien Zikos as a possible saviour, Lilah abandoned Skippy to pull on her raincoat, knotting the belt at her narrow waist.

She was a small, slender woman, with long black hair and bright blue eyes. She was also one of the very few workers still actively employed at Moore Components now it had gone bust. The Official Receivers had come in, taken over and laid off most of the staff. Only the services of the human resources team had been retained, to deal with all the admin involved in closing down the business. Engaged to work just two more days there, Lilah knew that she too would soon be unemployed.

Vickie was already zipping Ben into his jacket, because Lilah left the little boy at nursery school on her way into work.

It was a brisk spring day, with a breeze, and constantly forced to claw her hair out of her eyes, Lilah regretted not having taken the time to put her hair up long before she dropped her little brother off at the school. Unfortunately she had been suffering sleepless nights and scrambling out of bed every morning heavy-eyed, running late.

Ever since she had learned that Bastien Zikos had bought her father's failed business she had been struggling to hide her apprehension. In that less-than-welcoming attitude to the new owner, however, Lilah stood very much alone. The Receivers had been ecstatic to find a buyer, while her father and various resident worthies had expressed the hope that the new owner would re-employ some of the people who had lost their jobs when Moore Components closed.

Only Lilah, who had once received a disturbing glimpse of the cold diamond-cutting strength of Bastien's ruthlessness, was full of pessimism and thought the prospect of Bastien arriving to break good news to the local community unlikely.

In fact, if ever a man could have been said to have *scared* Lilah, it was Bastien Zikos. Everything about the tall, amazingly handsome Greek had unnerved her. The way he looked, the way he talked, the domineering way he behaved. His whole attitude had been anathema to her and she had backed off fast—only to discover, to her dismay, that that kind of treatment only put Bastien into pursuit mode.

Although Lilah was only twenty-three she had distrusted self-assured, slick and handsome men all her life, fully convinced that most of them were lying, cheating players. After all, even her own father had once been like that—a serial adulterer whose affairs had caused her late mother great unhappiness.

Lilah didn't like to dwell on those traumatic years, when she had begun to hate her father, because it had seemed then that he could not be trusted with any woman—not her mother's friends, not even his office staff. Mercifully all that behaviour had stopped once her father met Vickie, and since then Lilah had contrived to forge a new and much closer relationship with her surviving parent. Only now Robert Moore had settled down was his daughter able to respect him again and forgive him for the past.

Bastien, on the other hand, was not the family-man type, and he had always enjoyed his bad reputation as a womaniser. He was an unashamed sexual predator, accustomed to reaching out and just taking any woman who took his fancy. He was rich, astute and incredibly good-looking. Women fell like ninepins around him, running to him the instant he crooked an inviting finger. But Lilah had run in the opposite direction, determined not to have her heart broken and her pride trampled by a man who only wanted her for her body.

She was worth more than that, she reminded herself staunchly, as she had done two years earlier— *much* more. She wanted a man who loved and cared about her and who would stick by her no matter what came their way.

Being powerfully attracted to a man like Bastien Zikos had been a living nightmare for Lilah, and she had refused to acknowledge her reaction to him or surrender to the temptation he provided. Yet even now, two years on, Lilah could still remember her first sight of him across a crowded auction room. Bastien…tall, dark and devastating, with his glorious black-lashed tawny eyes.

She had been there to view a pendant that had once belonged to her mother and which Vickie, unaware of Lilah's attachment to the piece, had put up for sale. Lilah had planned to buy it back quietly at auction, preferring that option to the challenge of telling Vickie that she had actually been pretty upset when her father had so thoughtlessly given all her late mother's jewellery to his then live-in girlfriend.

And the first person Lilah had seen that day had been Bastien, black hair falling over his brow, his bold bronzed profile taut as he examined something in his hand while an auction assistant in overalls stood by an open display cabinet. When she had been directed to that same cabinet she had been hugely taken aback to see that Bastien had had her mother's very ordinary silver sea horse pendant clasped in his lean brown hand.

'What are you doing with that?' she'd asked possessively.

'What's it to you?' Bastien had asked bluntly, glancing up and transfixing her with breathtaking dark brown eyes enhanced by lush, curling black lashes.

In that split second he had travelled in her estimation from merely handsome to utterly gorgeous, and her breath had tripped in her throat and her heart had started hammering—as if she stood on the edge of a dangerous precipice.

'It belonged to my mother.'

'Where did *she* get it from?' Bastien had shot at her, thoroughly disconcerting her.

'I was with her when she bought it at a car boot sale almost twenty years ago,' Lilah had confided. although she'd been startled by his question, not to mention the intensity of his appraisal.

'My mother lost it in London some time around then,' Bastien had mused in a dark, deep accented drawl that had sent odd little quivers travelling down her spine. He had turned over the pendant to display the engraving on the back, composed of two letter As enclosed in a heart shape. 'My father Anatole gave it to my mother Athene. What an extraordinary coincidence that it should have belonged to *both* our mothers.'

'Extraordinary...' Lilah had agreed jerkily. as disturbed by his proximity as by his explanation. He'd been close enough that she'd been able to see the dark stubble shadowing his strong jawline and smell the citrus-sharp tenor of his cologne. Her nostrils had flared as she'd taken a hasty step backwards and cannoned into someone behind her.

Bastien had shot out a hand to steady her before she could stumble, long brown fingers closing round her narrow shoulder like a metal vice to keep her upright.

Lilah had jerked back again, breathless and flushed, heat flickering in places she had never felt warm before as her gaze had collided with the tall Greek's stunning eyes.

'May I see the pendant before it goes back in the cabinet?' she had asked curtly, putting out her hand.

'There's not much point in you looking at it. I'm planning to buy it,' Bastien had imparted drily.

Lilah's teeth had snapped together as though he had slapped her. 'So am I,' she had admitted grudgingly.

With reluctance Bastien had settled the pendant into her hand. Her eyes had prickled as she looked at it, because her mother had loved the fanciful piece and had often worn it in summer. The pendant reawakened a few of the happier memories of Lilah's childhood.

'Join me for coffee,' Bastien had urged, flipping the pendant back out of her hand to return it to the hovering assistant.

Lilah had dealt him a bemused look of surprise. 'It would hardly be a-appropriate,' she'd stammered. 'Not when we're both going to bid on the same lot.'

'Maybe I'm sentimental. Maybe I would like to hear about where the necklace has been all these years.'

Bastien had dangled that unlikely assurance in front of her like a prize carrot and she had caved in to coffee, feeling that to do otherwise would be rude and unreasonable.

And so her brief acquaintance with Bastien Zikos had begun, Lilah recalled unhappily. Hurriedly she blanked out the memories of that short week she never, *ever* allowed herself to think about, far too well aware of how mortifyingly long it was taking for her to forget meeting Bastien Zikos. Yet she had never had any regrets about turning him down—not then and not since, even when the most cursory internet search of Bastien's name always revealed the never-ending parade of different beauties that it took to keep Bastien happy. Quantity rather than quality was what Bastien went for in women, she had often thought, while telling herself that she had made the only decision she could…even if he still hated her for it.

As Lilah walked through the factory gates, saddened by the lack of vehicles and bustle that had used to characterise the once busy site, her mobile phone rang. Digging it out, she answered it. It was Josh, whom she had gone to university with, and he was suggesting she join him and a few friends for a night out. Every six weeks or so they met up as a group, went for a meal and out to see a film. One or two of the group were couples, the others simply friends. Josh, for example, was recovering from a broken engagement, and Lilah's last boyfriend had dumped her as soon as her father's business had hit the skids.

'Tomorrow night?' Lilah queried, thinking about it and liking the idea, because evenings in her crowded little house were currently far from relaxing and the idea of getting out was attractive. 'What time?'

Her friends would take her mind off things, she reflected gratefully, and stop her constantly fretting about a situation she had no control over. Unfortunately for Lilah an instinctive need to fix broken things and rescue people and animals ran deep and strong in her veins.

From the main office on the top floor, Bastien watched Delilah Moore cross the Moore Components car park with laser-sharp attention. She was still the most beautiful creature he had ever seen, he acknowledged, angry that that should *still* strike him as being the case. There had been a lot of women in his bed since he had met Robert Moore's daughter, but none of them had held his interest for very long.

Bastien still saw Delilah in the same light as he had first seen her, with her silky black curling cloud of hair falling almost to her waist and her sapphire-blue eyes electrifyingly noticeable against her creamy, perfect skin. Even wearing worn jeans and scuffed biker boots she'd had that casual effortlessly elegant look which some women had no matter what they wore.

Then, as now, he had told himself impatiently that she wasn't his type. With a single exception he had always gone for tall curvy blondes. Delilah was tiny, and very slender—the complete opposite of voluptuous. He just couldn't explain what made her so appealing to him, and that annoyed Bastien because *anything* he couldn't control or understand annoyed him.

This time around, he would get close enough to see all her flaws, he promised himself grimly.

'The new boss is in the building!' carolled Lilah's colleague Julie as soon as she walked into the small office the two women shared.

Halfway out of her coat, Lilah froze. 'When did he arrive?'

'The security guard said it was barely seven… talk about an early start!' Julie gushed admiringly. 'Mr Zikos has brought a whole team with him—I think that's hopeful, don't you? He is seriously good-looking too.'

Lilah's coat finally made it on to the hook. Her slender spine was rigid. *'Really?'*

'Absolutely beautiful…like a male supermodel. Maggie made coffee for him and even *she* agreed,' Julie said, referring to the office cleaner and tea lady, a known man-hater, who was hard to impress. 'But Maggie said it isn't his first visit. Apparently he was here a couple of years back?'

'Yes, he was. He was interested in buying this place then.'

'You *knew* that? You've seen him *before*?' Julie exclaimed in consternation. 'Why didn't you mention it?'

'With all that's been going on, it didn't seem important,' Lilah muttered, sitting down at her desk and closing her ears while Julie lamented her lack of interest in the new owner of Moore Components.

A young man with a neatly clipped beard entered their office an hour later. 'Miss Moore?' he asked, stopping in front of Lilah's desk. 'I'm one of Mr Zikos' team—Andreas Theodakis. Mr Zikos would like to see you in his office.'

Lilah lost colour and tried and failed to swallow, scolding herself for the instantaneous fear that washed through her. Of course Bastien wasn't going to harm her in any way. Why did even the thought of him charge her with near panic?

As she mounted the stairs she breathed slow and deep to compose herself. Bastien would want to crow, wouldn't he? He had got the business at a knockdown price and the Moore family had lost it, exactly as he had predicted. Rich, powerful men probably liked to boast whenever they got the opportunity, she reasoned uncertainly. For, really, her brain cried, what did *she* know about rich, powerful men? After all, Bastien was the only rich and powerful man she had ever met.

He was using her father's office, and it felt exceedingly strange to Lilah to be entering such a familiar space and find her father absent. Her eyes flickered super-fast over Bastien without pausing, as she registered that no other person was to be present for their meeting. Was that a good sign or a bad one?

'Mr Zikos,' she framed tightly.

'Oh. I think you can still call me Bastien,' he derided, studying her while wondering how on earth she could look so good in a plain black skirt of indeterminate length and a shapeless camel sweater.

Curly black hair lay in tumbled skeins across her shoulders. It was still the same length. He would have been vexed had she had it cut shorter. But, no, it was unchanged, and there was still something strangely fascinating about that long, long black hair that had ensnared his attention the instant he first saw it. And something equally memorable about the striking contrast between her bright blue eyes and her pale porcelain-fine skin.

Forced to look at him properly for the first time, Lilah froze, willing her rigid facial muscles to relax, ensuring that she betrayed no reaction to him. It was an exercise she had become adept at using in self-defence two years earlier. Her breath rattled in her throat, as if she had been dropped unexpectedly into a dark and haunted house where she was surrounded by unseen threats.

Bastien stood about six foot four inches tall, a clear twelve inches bigger than she was, which meant she could easily get away with focusing on his blue silk tie. But the glance she had got at him as she'd entered the office was still etched on her brain—as if it had been burned there in lines of fire with a red-hot poker. Whether she liked it or not, Julie had hit it right on the nail: Bastien *did* have a supermodel look, from his sculpted high cheekbones, classically arrogant nose and strong jawline to his full, incredibly kissable lips. Uncomfortable warmth washed up over her skin and she reddened, gritting her teeth, because she knew that she was blushing and that he would notice. *Why* would he notice? Because Bastien never missed a trick.

'Take a seat, Delilah…' Bastien indicated one of the armchairs beside the coffee table in one corner of the spacious panelled room.

'It's Lilah,' she corrected, and not for the first time.

He had always insisted on calling her by her full name—that name with its biblical connotations, which had caused her so much embarrassment from primary right up through to secondary school.

'I prefer *De*-lilah,' Bastien purred, with all the satisfaction of a jungle cat who had been lapping cream.

Lilah sank down in the chair, her slender spine too rigid to curve into the support of the seat. Her entire attention was locked on to Bastien and she clashed unwarily with his truly spectacular eyes. Tawny brown, golden in sunshine, literally mesmerising and surrounded by the most fabulous velvety black lashes, she reflected dizzily, plunged into one of the terrifying time-out-of-time lapses of concentration and discipline which Bastien had frequently inflicted on her two years earlier.

'I can't think why you would want to see me,' Lilah told him quietly, just as the door opened and Maggie bustled in with a tray of coffee and biscuits.

Lilah jumped up and immediately removed the tray from the older woman's grasp. Maggie had chosen to work well beyond retirement and, although she would never have admitted the fact, Maggie now found it difficult to carry heavy trays.

'I would've been fine,' Maggie scolded.

Lilah settled the tray of fancy silverware and fine china which her father's secretary had kept for VIPs down on the table. Maggie departed. Lilah poured the coffee and sugared Bastien's before she had even thought about what she was doing.

'You can't think why I would want to see you?' Bastien queried, unimpressed by the claim. 'How very modest you are…'

Suspecting him of mockery, Lilah flushed and extended his coffee to him. He reached for the cup and took a sip of the black, heavily sweetened coffee, smiling when he discovered that she had got it right.

Striving to play it cool and composed, Lilah lifted her own cup and saucer—but that smile…oh, *that* smile…was flipping up the corners of his beautiful mouth, transforming his lean, dark forbidding features with an almost boyish grin. Helplessly she stared, sapphire-blue eyes widening.

'Today,' Bastien drawled lazily, 'you are a very influential young woman, because it is in *your* power to decide what happens next to Moore Components.'

Lilah kept on staring at him, literally locked into immobility by that astonishing assurance. 'What on earth are you talking about?'

CHAPTER TWO

BASTIEN STUDIED HER, inordinate satisfaction glittering in his dark deep-set eyes. He had waited a long time for this particular moment and it was giving him even more of a kick than he had hoped.

'I have a few options to put before you. The fate of Moore Components is now entirely in your hands.'

Lilah set her coffee down with a jarring rattle of china and leapt upright. 'Why the heck would you say something like that to me?' she demanded.

'Because it's the truth. I don't lie and nor do I back-track on promises,' Bastien asserted levelly. 'I assure you that what ultimately happens to this business will be solely *your* responsibility.'

Still frozen in place, Lilah blinked rapidly while she battled to concentrate. 'I don't understand. How can that be?'

'You're not that naïve,' Bastien drawled with a curled lip. 'You *know* I want you.'

'*Still?*' Lilah gasped in astonishment at that declaration, because after all two years had passed since their last meeting, and even six months on she would have expected Bastien barely to recall her name, never mind her face.

The faintest scoring of colour had flared across Bastien's high cheekbones and he parted his lips, even white teeth flashing. *'Still,'* he confirmed, with forbidding emphasis.

Lilah didn't understand how that was possible. How could he still find her attractive after all the other women he had been with in the intervening months? It didn't make sense to Lilah at all.

It was not as if she was some staggeringly beautiful woman who regularly stopped men dead in the street. Admittedly she had never had a problem attracting men, but retaining their interest when she wasn't prepared to slide casually into bed with them had proved much more of a challenge. In fact, most men walked away fast sooner than test her boundaries, choosing to assume that she was either devoutly religious or desirous of a wedding-ring-sized commitment before she would share her body.

Lilah dropped back into the seat she had vacated, her brain buzzing with bewildered thoughts. How could Bastien's continuing physical desire for her have anything to do with the business and its prospects? And how could he still find her attractive when he had so many other more sophisticated women in his life? Was it simply the fact that Lilah had once said no to him? Could a male as clever as Bastien be that outrageously basic?

'I don't want to keep you all morning, so I'll run through the three options.'

'Three…options…?' Lilah queried even more uneasily.

'Option one—you choose to walk away from me,' Bastien extended grimly, shooting her a glance of warning that made her pale. 'In that event I sell the machinery in the factory and sell the site to a developer. I already have a good offer for the land and it would turn an immediate healthy profit…'

Lilah dropped her head, appalled at that suggestion. The town needed this factory for employment. The closure of Moore Components had already damaged the small town's economy. Shops and entertainment venues were suffering from a downturn. People were struggling to find work because there were few other local jobs, and many had already had to put their houses up for sale because they could no longer afford their mortgages.

Lilah was well-acquainted with the human cost of unemployment and had done what little she could in her HR capacity to offer her father's former workers guidance and advise them on suitable retraining schemes.

'Option two—you choose only to spend *one* night with me,' Bastien framed, impervious to the slight sound Lilah made as her lips parted on a stricken gasp of disbelief. 'I will then make the business function again for at least a year. It will cost me money and it will be a waste of time, because the factory requires sustained and serious investment to win and retain new contracts. But if that's the best I can get from you I'm prepared to do it…'

Lilah lifted her head and focused on Bastien's lean darkly handsome face in sheer wonderment. 'Let me get this straight. You are using Moore Components as a means of bargaining with me for my *body*?' she spelled out incredulously. 'Are you out of your *mind*?'

'Be grateful. If I *didn't* want you there would be

nothing at all to put on the table. But for you I wouldn't even have bothered coming up here. I simply would have sold the land,' Bastien informed her with lethal cool.

Lilah had great difficulty hinging her jaw closed again, because she was stupefied by the options he was laying out before her. 'You can't possibly want me that much,' she told him involuntarily. 'That would be crazy.'

'Obviously I'm crazy.' Bastien dealt Lilah a slow, lingering appraisal that began at her lush pink lips, segued down to the small pert breasts outlined by her sweater and glossed over her delicately curved hipline to her shapely knees and ankles. 'You have terrific legs,' he mused, fighting the sting of awakening interest at his groin with fierce determination.

Two years back Delilah Moore had kept him in a state of virtually constant arousal that had given him sleepless nights and forced him into cold showers. He was damned if he was going to let her have that much of an effect on him again! He wanted her and that was that—but their affair would be on his terms only.

Option two was probably the wisest choice for him, because once he had bedded her, her fascination would surely wane fast and he would tire of her as he had tired of all her predecessors. But although he was convinced that one night should completely exorcise her from his fantasies, he still didn't want to be forced to agree to that restriction.

Lilah yanked her skirt down over her knees, suddenly boiling up below her clothing, her whole skin surface prickling and reacting to his visual assessment with a rush of heat. He was such a very sexual male, she conceded in bewilderment. The atmosphere pulsed with astonishing tension and she hurriedly snatched her attention from him, recognising the swelling tautness of her nipples and the surge of ungovernable heat between her thighs as totally unacceptable reactions.

But she couldn't prevent those reactions—couldn't stop them happening around Bastien. On that level two years earlier Bastien had drawn her like a moth to a flame, because the wild, seething excitement he'd evoked in her had been incredibly seductive.

In a desperate attempt to regain control of her disordered thoughts, Lilah said with careful precision, 'I refuse to believe you're serious about this, Bastien. A man of your stature and wealth cannot possibly want a woman like me so much that he would make such a bargain.'

'What would *you* know about it?' Bastien cut in, whiplash-abrupt in that dismissal. 'I haven't reached option three yet.'

Outraged by his persistence, Lilah rose to her feet again. 'I refuse to listen to any more of this nonsense!'

'Then I sell this place today,' Bastien fired at her with cold finality as she walked towards the door. 'Your choice, your decision, Delilah. You're lucky I'm giving you options.'

Lilah was still and then spun round again, black hair sliding in a glossy fall across her shoulders. *'Lucky?'* she exclaimed in angry disbelief, her temper stirring as she thought about the contemptible offer he had made to her. Bottom line: Bastien Zikos was willing to do just about anything to get her into bed. Was she supposed to be *pleased* about that? Was it normal to feel as insulted as she did…as *hurt*? Why did she feel hurt?

'With my backing you can wave a magic wand here and be a heroine if you want to be,' Bastien imparted very drily. 'Option three—I do almost anything you want, up to and including employing your father as consultant and manager.'

That startling suggestion not only stopped Lilah's thoughts mid-track and froze her feet to the carpet, it also made everything else inside her head blur. For a split second she pictured her deeply troubled father restored to some semblance of his former confident, energetic self, able to earn again and provide for his family. What a huge difference that would make to Robert Moore!

'So *that's* what it takes to stop you walking out… you're a real Daddy's girl!' Bastien remarked with galling amusement. 'Are you ready to listen now, and stop flouncing around dramatically and asking me if I'm crazy? The answer to that is that I'm only crazy to have you in my bed…'

Colour blossomed below Lilah's skin and ran up to her hairline in a scalding surge. She could barely credit that he had said that without even a shade of discomfiture. But then she reckoned it would take something considerably more shocking than sex to embarrass a male as resolute and dominant as Bastien. 'All right…for my father's sake I'll agree to hear you out,' she conceded with flat reluctance.

'Then *sit*!' Bastien indicated the chair.

It occurred to Lilah that Bastien had spoken to her just then as she spoke to Skippy when the dog was playing up.

Raising a wry brow at his disrespectful mode of addressing her, she sat down again. 'Option three?' she reminded him succinctly.

'You become my mistress and stay with me for as long as I want you.'

'Keeping a mistress is an astonishingly old-fashioned concept,' Lilah remarked, to mask the reality that inwardly she was knocked sideways by that proposition.

Bastien shifted a broad shoulder in a careless shrug. 'In my world it's the norm.'

'I assumed sex slavery of that sort ended about a hundred years ago.'

'But then you don't have a clue what the role entails,' Bastien said drily, watching her while picturing her slender body sheathed in decadent silk and lace and diamonds purely for his private enjoyment.

The image gave him both a high and a hard-on.

'In return for your agreement to become my mistress I will set this business up and invest in it. As the owner of a network of companies I can easily provide contracts to keep the factory busy. I will instruct your father to rehire his former workforce. After all, skilled employees are difficult to replace. With my full financial support, virtually everything could go back to the way it was before Moore Components lost that crucial contract.'

Lilah was floored by those comprehensive assurances. Now she understood Bastien's jibe about her having the opportunity to play the heroine and wave a magic wand. *Everything back the way it was!* How many times in recent months had she longed for that to happen and for everyone to be content again instead of stressed, broken and unhappy? Countless times.

Bastien was a very powerful, enormously wealthy male, and perhaps for the first time she fully appreciated that reality—because she knew it would take thousands and thousands of pounds to get the factory up and running again, never mind build the business up to survive in the long term. It would be a hugely expensive challenge, but it would turn around the lives of *so* many people, Lilah reflected with a sinking heart.

'Like Tinker Bell, you're quite taken with the offer of a magic wand?' Bastien quipped with brooding amusement as he watched her expressive face intently. 'I suppose your response will depend on how much of a do-gooder you are. So far you're ranging fairly high in that list of good works now that you have your whole family living with you. You're keeping them too, aren't you?'

Lilah was furious that he should have access to such facts about her personal life, and the label of 'do-gooder' offended her. 'I'm *not* a do-gooder.'

'By my estimation you are,' Bastien countered drily. 'You've saved your wicked stepmother from living in emergency accommodation and you also raise funds for abandoned dogs and starving children.'

Lilah stood up again in a sudden motion. 'How on earth do you know so much about me?'

'Obviously I've kept an eye on developments here.'

'My stepmother is *not* wicked,' Lilah added uncomfortably. 'How do you know my family are staying with me? How do you know about the volunteer work I've done for the dog sanctuary?'

'I had to check you out before I came up here,' Bastien pointed out impatiently. 'If you'd got married or picked up a boyfriend since we last met there would have been little point in my approaching you. I don't like to have my time wasted.'

Lilah's chin lifted. 'I *did* have a boyfriend!' she bit out resentfully.

'Not for very long. He dropped you the minute your father's business went down.'

Angry words brimmed on Lilah's tongue, but she swallowed them whole because she wasn't going to sink to the level of arguing with Bastien over someone as unworthy of her defence as Steve, her ex-boyfriend.

Ironically, Bastien's reading of Steve's behaviour exactly matched her own. Steve had turned out to be very ambitious. He had started dating Lilah when Moore Components was thriving and had tried to persuade her father to take him on as a junior partner. It mortified her that Bastien should know about the revealing speed and timing of Steve's defection.

Rigid with self-control, Lilah lifted her head high. 'I can't believe that you really mean those options you outlined. They're immoral.'

'I'm not a very moral man,' Bastien told her without hesitation. 'I don't apologise for what I want and I always *get* what I want…and I want you. You should be flattered.'

'I'm not flattered. I'm shocked and disgusted at your lack of scruple!' Lilah told him angrily, her blue eyes bright with condemnation. 'You're trying to take advantage of this situation and play on my affection for my family.'

'I will use any advantage I have and do whatever I have to do to win you. Of course whether or not you choose to accept one of my two preferred options is entirely your decision,' Bastien pointed out, his wide, beautifully shaped mouth firming as he stalked fluidly closer to tower over her. '*You're* the glittering prize here, Delilah. Doesn't that thrill you?'

Lilah stiffened even more. 'No, of course it doesn't.'

'It would thrill most women,' Bastien told her drily, staring down at her with burnished dark golden eyes that sent an intoxicating fizz of awareness and frightening tension shooting through her every limb. 'Most women like to be wanted above all others.'

'I very much doubt that you're *capable* of wanting one woman above all others,' Lilah retorted with sharp emphasis. 'Women seem to be very much interchangeable commodities to you, so I really can't understand why you should have a fixation about *me*.'

'It's *not* a fixation,' Bastien growled, dark eyes hard, strong jawline squared.

'Oh, for goodness' sake—call a spade a spade, Bastien!' Lilah countered in exasperation. 'At least look at the lengths you're willing to go to to *make* me do what you want…does that strike you as *normal*?'

'Sexual satisfaction is extremely important to me,' Bastien parried, studying her with cool gravity. 'I don't feel any need to explain that or to apologise for it.'

Lilah felt like someone beating her head up against a brick wall. Bastien didn't listen to what he didn't want to hear. He went full steam ahead, like an express train racing down a track. He saw what he wanted and he went for it, regardless of reason and the damage he might do.

'Delilah… I would treat you well…' Bastien murmured huskily.

'What you've suggested…it's out of the question—*impossible*!' she exclaimed in a furious outburst of frustration. 'Not to mention downright sleazy!'

Bastien lifted a lean tanned hand and scored a reproving fingertip along the strained line of her lush lower lip. 'I am never, *ever* sleazy…' He positively purred. 'You have a lot to learn about me.'

Subjected to even that minor physical contact, she felt her whole skin surface break out in enervated goose bumps and jerked back a hasty step.

'What I've learnt today, just listening to you, is more than enough,' she stressed in biting rejection. 'You talk as if you're playing some amusing game with me, but what you're proposing is offensive and unthinkable. And nothing you could hope to offer would persuade my father to accept a job that would literally sell me to the highest bidder as part of the deal!'

Bastien scanned her flushed and furious face and the sapphire-blue eyes shooting defiant sparks at him. 'Only an idiot would suggest that you tell your father the truth and nothing but the truth,' he derided. 'All you would need to tell your family is that I have offered you your dream job, which will entail a lot of foreign travel and an enviable lifestyle.'

With a reflexive little shudder at that Machiavellian suggestion, Lilah snapped, 'My goodness, you have absolutely everything worked out!'

'But will you take the bait?' Bastien breathed in a roughened undertone. 'You have until ten tomorrow morning to make your decision and choose an option.'

'You haven't given me even *one* reasonable or fair option,' Lilah condemned bitterly.

'If you don't give me your answer tomorrow I *will* sell,' Bastien warned her with chilling bite.

Her narrow spine went poker-straight with the force of her resentment and her slender hands knotted into fists. It was far from being the first time she had been in Bastien's company and had longed to knock his teeth down his throat.

In the smouldering silence, Bastien released his breath in a hiss of impatience. 'It doesn't have to be like this between us, Delilah. We could discuss this over dinner tonight.'

Lilah flung him a shaken and furious look over her shoulder as her perspiring hand worked frantically at the doorknob. 'Dinner? You've got to be joking! Anyway, I'm already booked,' she fibbed, refusing to give him the idea that she sat in every night.

'To see who?' Bastien demanded, pressing a hand against the door to prevent her from opening it.

'That's none of your business.' Refusing to fight for control of the door, Lilah stood back and folded her arms defensively. 'Nothing I do is any of your business. You may own Moore Components, but that's the only thing you own around here.'

Dark eyes glittering brilliant as stars, Bastien flung the door wide for her exit. 'I wouldn't be so sure of that, *koukla mou.*'

Lilah hurried downstairs and straight into the cloakroom, needing a moment before she returned to work and faced Julie and her curiosity. She was shaking and sweating, and she held her trembling hands below the cold tap while snatching in a deep sustaining breath, praying for self-control.

Unfortunately Bastien had struck her on her weakest flank. The very idea that she could rescue her family from their current predicament had turned her heart inside out with hope and desperation. And what about all the other people whose lives would be transformed by the opportunity to regain the jobs they had lost? Jobs in a revitalised business which would be much more secure with Bastien's backing? All their former workers would be ecstatic at the idea of the factory reopening.

But Bastien Zikos had put an incredibly high price on what that miracle would cost Lilah in personal terms. It was too much to think about, she thought weakly, anger still hurtling through her, tensing her every muscle. How could he *do* that? How could he stand there in front of her and outline such demeaning options? A one-night stand…or a one-night stand which ran and ran until he got bored? Some choice! What had she ever done to him to deserve such treatment?

Her temples thumped dully—a stress headache was forming. She was stressed, out of her depth and barely able to think straight, she acknowledged heavily. Hadn't she felt very much like that when she was first exposed to Bastien's soul-destroying charm?

Of course that charm had not been much in evidence just now, during their office meeting, she conceded bitterly. It had, however, been very much in evidence when Bastien had taken her for coffee at the auction house two years earlier.

After a casual exchange of names and information

Bastien had taken out his business card to show her that his company logo was, in fact, a seahorse. The awareness that he also had a strong family connection to the pendant had made Lilah relax more in his company. Noting his sleek gold Rolex watch, and the sharp tailoring of his stylish suit, she had recognised the hallmarks of wealth and suspected that it was highly unlikely that she could hope to outbid him at auction.

She had teased him about the amount of sugar he put in his coffee and a wickedly sensual smile had curved his lips, sending her heartbeat into overdrive. Oh, yes. At first sight she had been hugely, hopelessly attracted to Bastien and had hung on his every word.

'You still haven't explained one thing,' Bastien had mused. 'If you value it so much, why is the pendant being sold at auction?'

She had explained about the jewellery her father had given her stepmother. 'Now Vickie's having a big clean-out, and I didn't want to risk upsetting her by admitting how I felt.'

'If you don't ask, you don't get,' Bastien had censured drily. 'Not that I'm complaining. Your delicate sense of diplomacy has worked in *my* favour. If the necklace hadn't gone on sale I wouldn't have known where it was. I've been trying to track it down for years.'

'I suppose you remember your mother wearing it?' she remarked.

'No, but I remember my father giving it to her,' Bastien had countered rather bleakly, his dramatic dark eyes veiled while his beautiful mouth had tightened unexpectedly. 'I was about four years old and I honestly believed we were the perfect family.'

'Nothing wrong with that,' she had quipped with a big smile, trying to picture him as a little kid, thinking that he had probably been very cute, with a shock of black hair and brown eyes deep enough to drown in.

'Irrespective of what happens at the auction tomorrow, promise that you will have dinner with me tomorrow evening,' he'd urged, and had invited her to his hotel.

'I'm still planning to bid,' she warned him.

'I can afford to outbid most people. Dinner?' he'd pressed again.

And she had crumbled, like sand smoothed over and reshaped by a powerful wave.

Bastien hadn't made the connection between her and Moore Components, and it had been a big surprise for both of them when her auction disappointment had been followed by an unexpected meeting with Bastien in her father's office the next day. Dinner at Bastien's hotel had been replaced by dinner at her father's home, to which she had been invited as well.

When a phone call had claimed Robert Moore's attention he had asked his daughter to see Bastien out to his car.

'If you're expecting me to congratulate you on your win, you're destined for disappointment,' Lilah had warned Bastien on their way down the stairs. 'You paid a ludicrous amount for that pendant.'

Bastien laughed out loud. 'Says the woman who bidded me up to that ludicrous amount!'

Lilah reddened. 'Well, I had to at least *try* to get it. Why are you seeing my father?' she had asked abruptly as they came to a halt in the car park.

'I'm interested in acquiring his business and he

wants some time to think my offer over. You work here. *You* could be my acquisition too,' Bastien had said huskily, sexily in her ear, making the tiny hairs at her nape stand up while an arrow of heat shot straight down into her pelvis.

Unsettled by the strength of her reaction to him, Lilah had stiffened. 'I don't think so. I don't think Dad will sell up either—not when he's riding the crest of a wave.'

'That's the best time to sell.'

Bastien had dealt her a dark, lingering appraisal that had made her toes curl even as her gaze widened at the sight of the limousine that had rolled up to collect him. She'd been impressed but troubled by the obviously large difference in their financial status and had resolved to look him up on the internet as soon as she got the time.

'I wish your father hadn't invited us to his family dinner.' Bastien had sighed. 'I was looking forward to having you all to myself at my hotel.'

Unease had filtered through Lilah. He was coming on very strong, and while initially she'd been delighted by that, she was unnerved by the suspicion that he might be expecting her to spend the night with him. An impulsive move like that would have been way outside Lilah's comfort zone.

But at the same time still being a virgin at the age of twenty-one had not been part of Lilah's life plan either. She just hadn't met anyone at university who had attracted her enough to take that plunge. Lilah didn't give her trust easily to men, and by the end of first year, after standing by and watching friends commit too fast to casual relationships that had ended in tears and recriminations, she had decided that she would definitely hold off on sex until she met a man who cared enough about her to be prepared to wait until she was as ready for intimacy as he was.

'Bastien's really into you in a big way,' Vickie had whispered in amusement after dinner at her father's comfortable home that evening. 'He watches your every move. And although I prefer men to be more grey round the edges, he *is* gorgeous.'

Before Lilah had been able to call a taxi, Bastien had offered to run her home. Within seconds of them getting into the limo Bastien had reached for her with a determined hand and kissed her with a hungry, sensual ferocity that had set her treacherous body on fire. She had pulled back, trying to cool the moment down, but Bastien had ignored her.

'Spend the night with me,' he'd pressed, his thumb stroking her wrist where her pulse was racing insanely fast.

'I hardly know you,' she had pointed out hastily.

'You can get to know me in bed,' Bastien had quipped.

'That's not how I operate, Bastien,' Lilah had murmured, reddening with discomfiture. 'I would need to know you really well before I slept with you.'

'*Diavelos*… I'm only here for another forty-eight hours!' Bastien had ground out incredulously, studying her as though she was as strange and incongruous a sight as a snowball in the desert.

'I'm sorry. I can't change the way I am,' Lilah had told him quietly as the limousine drew up outside the terraced house where she lived.

'You're my polar opposite. I don't get to know

women really well. To be brutally honest, sex is the only intimacy I want or need,' Bastien had breathed in a driven undertone.

'We're like oil and water,' Lilah had mumbled, hurriedly vacating his car and heading indoors, to heave a sigh of relief as soon as the door was closed behind her.

In the aftermath of that uneasy parting tears had burned her eyes and she'd been immediately filled with self-loathing. She was guilty of having woven silly romantic dreams about Bastien. Hadn't she just got what she deserved for being so naïve? He was only interested in a night of casual sex—nothing more. It wasn't a compliment…it was a slap in the face—and a wake-up call to regain control of her wits.

Although Lilah had initially been attracted by Bastien's stunning good looks, she had been infinitely more fascinated by his strong personality, and the seemingly offbeat way his brain worked. That same night she'd sat up late, looking Bastien up on the internet, and the sheer number of women she'd seen pictured with him had shaken her almost as much as his reputation for being a womaniser. Bastien Zikos slept around and he was faithless.

At first Lilah had been appalled by what she had discovered, but there had also been an oddly soothing element to those revelations. After all, what she had found out only emphasised that she could never have any kind of liaison with Bastien: he didn't do relationships…and she didn't do one-night stands.

Sinking back to the present, Lilah was dismayed to register that her eyes were swimming with tears. She blinked them back and freshened up, writing off her far too emotional frame of mind to the shocks Bastien had dealt her. She hated the way that Bastien always got to her—cutting through her common sense and reserve like a machete to make his forceful point.

'You were a long time upstairs with the boss,' Julie commented as Lilah dropped back behind her desk.

'Mr Zikos wanted to discuss his plans for the business,' she said awkwardly.

'Oh...*wow*!' Julie gushed, fixing wide, speculative eyes on Lilah's flushed and taut face. 'You mean he's planning to keep Moore Components open? He's not just going to sell up?'

Lilah cursed her loose tongue. 'No, his selling up is a possibility too,' she backtracked hastily, fearful of setting off a round of rumours that would raise false hopes. 'I don't think he's actually made a final decision yet.'

With a regretful sigh, Julie returned to work. But Lilah found that she could not concentrate for longer than thirty seconds. Aftershocks from her meeting with Bastien were still quaking through her.

He might as well have taken the moon down from the sky and offered it to her, she reflected in a daze. Her family were suffering—just like everybody else caught up in the crash of Moore Components. The little half-brother and half-sister so dear to Lilah's heart no longer had a garden to play in, and their more elaborate toys had been disposed of because there was no room for such things in Lilah's little house. Her father was suffering from depression and taking medication. The day the factory had closed the bottom had dropped out of his world. Without work, without his business, Robert Moore simply didn't know what to do with himself.

Lilah blinked back stinging tears. In spite of the troubled years, when her parents had been unhappily married, Lilah still loved her father very much. She had only been eleven years old when her mother had died very suddenly from an aneurysm. Her father had been very much there for her while she was grieving, but he was also a very hard worker, who had soon returned to work, slaving eighteen hours a day to build up his business.

Now, shorn of his once generous income and humbled, he felt less of a man—and at his age, with a failed business under his belt, who was likely to employ him? Although Lilah had told herself that she shouldn't be thinking about it, she could not resist picturing her father returning to work with a new spring in his step.

She blanked out the thought.

Was she really prepared to become a mistress?

Bastien's sex slave?

An extraordinary little chirrup of excitement twisted through Lilah and she was seriously embarrassed for herself. She was pretty sure Bastien wouldn't be expecting a virgin. But what did that matter? It was not as though she was seriously considering his sordid options, was it?

Still mentally far removed from work, she sank back two years again into her memories and recalled the flowers Bastien had sent her the morning after that family dinner and her rejection of what little he'd had to offer her. He had shown up on her doorstep the following evening as well, displaying a persistence that had taxed her patience. When he had tried to persuade her to join him that night for dinner she had lost her temper with him.

Why had she lost her temper?

Remembering why, Lilah paled and then flushed a painful pink. Utterly mesmerised by Bastien, she had already started falling for him. Being rudely confronted with the reality that he was a stud, who only wanted her for sex, had been hurtful and demeaning. *That* was why she had lost her temper. She had been angry with herself because somehow he had contrived to tempt her with that single erotically charged kiss and had made her question her own values. She had resented his power over her and she had flung her knowledge of his bad reputation in his teeth and called him a man whore.

Lilah was still secretly cringing from that memory as she walked home after work. Attacking Bastien had been wrong. He was what he was, and she was what she was. They were very different people. Insulting him had been ill-mannered, pointless and immature. His dark eyes had glittered like black ice, the rage in his stunning gaze filling her with fright. But he had done nothing, said nothing. He had simply turned on his heel and got back into his opulent limousine to drive away.

A few weeks later an unexpected gift had arrived for her at work. She had unwrapped an almost exact replica of the seahorse pendant Bastien had won at auction. The only difference between it and the original was that the new piece lacked the engraved initial As on the back. Only Bastien could have had it made for her and sent it to her. That he had given the pendant to her in spite of the way she had spoken to him had shocked Lilah, and made her feel as if she didn't know Bastien Zikos at all. She had asked herself then if she had imagined that dark fury in his eyes.

But now Lilah knew for a fact that she had not imagined Bastien's rage, and she suspected that what she was being subjected to was 'payback time' in his parlance.

CHAPTER THREE

IN THE MIDDLE of the night, tossing and turning without sleep, Lilah crept out of bed and went downstairs to make herself a cup of tea.

Vickie was already there, seated at the kitchen table. 'Great minds, eh?' she framed round a huge yawn.

'You couldn't sleep either?' Lilah stated the obvious.

'It's the constant worrying that keeps me awake,' her father's wife opined ruefully while Lilah boiled the kettle. 'Some of the parents I was talking to at Ben's school said Bastien Zikos was at Moore Components today… I was surprised you hadn't mentioned it.'

Lilah stiffened defensively. 'I didn't see the point.'

'I hate asking you this…but I was thinking…maybe if you get the chance you could ask Bastien if he has an opening for your father anywhere?' Vickie said hopefully.

Lilah reddened. 'If I get the chance,' she echoed, feeling incredibly guilty for not telling the truth.

Bastien had been right on that score. No one would thank her for telling a truth that no one wanted to hear. And the truth was that she *could* wave a magic wand

and fix everything for everybody. How could she live with that knowledge and stand by doing nothing? How could she live with seeing her father slumped in a chair, staring into space? It was all very well to be furious with Bastien, to take offence and walk out. but at the end of the day she had to be practical. He had, after all, offered her a miracle.

Everything back the way it was.

Hanging on to her virginity at all costs seemed a little pathetic in such dire circumstances, didn't it? And, whether she liked it or not, she had always been attracted to Bastien. How could she hold out and justify herself when so many positive outcomes would result from her agreement? Bastien's interest in her would be short-lived as well: his past history spoke for him. He never stayed long with a woman. She would get her life back again quickly and probably never come back home, she acknowledged unhappily. When Bastien got bored with her she would look for a job in London and make a fresh start.

Lilah dressed for work with more care than usual, braiding her black mane of hair into submission and choosing a black pencil skirt and a silky cream blouse to wear.

The mere thought of finding herself in bed with Bastien brought her out in a cold sweat and turned her tummy over, so she refused to think about it. Sex was a rite of passage, she told herself impatiently. She was no different from any other woman and would soon become accustomed to it. No doubt practise had made Bastien most proficient in that department, and it was probably safe to assume that she wouldn't find sharing a bed with him too unpleasant. Of course she wasn't going to *enjoy* any of it either. Sex shorn of any finer feelings was a physical rather than mental exercise and she would detach herself from the whole experience, she told herself soothingly.

Detachment, after all, would hardly be a challenge when she hated Bastien with every fibre of her being. His options had taught her to hate him. Before yesterday he had simply been the womaniser who had once bruised her tender heart and whom she couldn't ever have. Now he was the ruthless lowlife forcing her to seal a bargain with her body as if she was a whore.

A little shudder racked her at that view and she breathed in slow and deep, strengthening herself for what lay ahead. She was about to make a devil's bargain, but she was darned if she would show an ounce of weakness in front of Bastien.

When she walked into the office, Julie gave her a curious appraisal. 'Mr Zikos has phoned down to ask for you already. I explained that you're never in before nine because you leave your kid brother at nursery on the way.'

'Thanks,' Lilah breathed, hanging up her coat with a nervous hand.

Bastien had said ten o'clock, but he was clearly jumping the gun. Of course he had no patience whatsoever, she reflected ruefully. He tapped his feet and drummed his fingers when forced to be inactive for any length of time. He was edgy, bursting with frenetic energy, always in need of occupation.

She smoothed her skirt down over her hips as she mounted the stairs. Her hands weren't quite steady and she studied them in dismay. Why was she getting herself into a state? Hadn't she already decided that sex would be no big deal and not worth making a silly fuss over? It wasn't as though Bastien was going to spread her across the office desk and have his wicked way with her this very day…was it?

Her face burned, her stomach performing a somersault at that X-rated image. She wanted Bastien to do the deed in pitch-darkness and complete silence. She didn't want to have to look at him or speak to him. She wished there was some way of having sex remotely, without any need for physical contact, and it was on that crazy thought that she entered what had once been her father's office.

With a single gesture Bastien dismissed the team hovering attentively round him and set down the tablet he had been studying.

'You've asked for me but it's not ten yet,' Lilah pointed out thinly. 'It's only ten minutes past nine.'

Bastien straightened, brilliant dark golden eyes lancing into hers in direct challenge. 'My internal clock says it's ten,' he contradicted without hesitation.

'Your clock's wrong.'

'I'm *never* wrong, Delilah,' Bastien traded thickly, his long-lashed gaze roaming over her as intently as a physical caress. 'Lesson one on how to be a mistress: I keep you around to stroke my ego, not dent it.'

Lilah froze where she stood, wide sapphire eyes travelling over him with a hunger she couldn't control. She scanned the exquisitely tailored designer suit that delineated every muscular line of Bastien's broad-shouldered, lean-hipped frame as he stood there facing her, with his long, powerful legs braced. Something clenched low in her body when she clashed with his gaze and her legs felt strangely hollow.

Her attention welded to his darkly handsome face, she stopped breathing, reacting with dismay to the treacherous stirrings of her own body. Her breasts swelled, constrained by the confines of her bra, while the sensation at her feminine core made her press her thighs together hard.

'I'm no good at stroking egos, Bastien,' she warned him.

Bastien dealt her an unholy grin. 'I've got enough ego to survive a few dents,' he asserted. 'Where do you think your true talents will lie?'

'You've taken my answer for granted, haven't you?' Lilah exclaimed. 'I haven't said yes yet, but you're convinced I will.'

'And am I wrong?' Bastien traded.

Her teeth gritted together. 'No, you're not.'

'So, are you going for option two or option three?' Bastien enquired lazily, leaning back against his desk in an attitude of relaxation that infuriated her.

Option three, option *three*, Bastien willed Delilah to tell him. That would be the most profitable option for him. He would sell the current site, relocate the factory to the outskirts of town and in doing so take advantage of several lucrative government grants aimed at persuading companies to open up in areas of high unemployment. For him it would be a win-win situation, because he would gain Lilah, an immediate profit to cover all outlay *and* a cost-efficient business.

'You have no shame, have you?' Lilah hissed, like oil bubbling on too high a heat.

'Not when it comes to you,' Bastien agreed. 'It's the only way I'm ever going to get you, because you're stubborn and contrary and you have a very closed little mind.'

'I am none of those things,' Lilah rebutted angrily.

'Stubborn because the minute we saw each other we were destined to be together but you immediately fought it. Contrary because you feel the same way about me as I do about you—instantaneous lust—but you deny it. And a closed mind because you believe a life of self-denial is innately superior to mine.' A wolfish smile slashed Bastien's lean strong face. 'I can't wait for the moment when you realise that you can't keep your hands off me.'

Lilah gave him a look of withering scorn. 'You'll get old waiting for that.'

Straightening up to his full commanding height, Bastien strolled forward, fluid as a predator tracking prey. 'Don't keep me in suspense. Option two? Or option three?'

'*Three*... Although I should warn you, you've picked the wrong woman.'

'Three...' Bastien's accent made a three-course meal of the word as he savoured it with immense satisfaction. 'In what way are you the wrong woman?'

Lilah shifted uneasily from one foot to the other. 'I haven't got the experience you'll probably expect,' she told him stiffly, deeply disturbed by his increasing closeness and fighting the revealing urge to step back out of reach.

'I've got enough experience for both of us,' Bastien purred, dark eyes flashing gold as he stared down at her. 'Are you trying to tell me that you haven't indulged that side of your nature very often?'

'Haven't indulged it at all,' she countered curtly, lifting her chin, standing her ground, refusing to feel embarrassed. 'I'm a virgin.'

Bastien actually backed away a couple of feet, his lean chiselled features setting into rigid angles of shock while his eyes flared more golden than ever below the thick canopy of his black lashes. 'Is that a tease?'

Lilah gave him a grim glance. 'No, it's not. I just thought I should warn you in case it's a deal-breaker.'

'Are you telling me the truth?' Bastien prompted in a roughened undertone, prowling closer again and circling her like a stalking panther. 'You're a *virgin*?'

Colour ran up below her pale cheeks but she held his fierce gaze. 'Yes.'

'If you're telling me the truth it's not a deal-breaker—it's the biggest turn-on I've ever had,' Bastien confessed, thoroughly shocking her with that assurance.

Bastien was disturbingly conscious that for once he was not uttering a mere soundbite for effect. He had never been with a virgin. When he was a teenager his partners had all been older, and when the age range of his lovers had begun to match his own maturity he had never dallied or even *wanted* to dally with a sexually innocent woman. For a start, he had never been attracted to young, immature girls. In addition he did very much like sex, and he had no time for those who would stick limits on a physical outlet he saw as both natural and free.

Yet something strange was happening to his views

while he looked at Delilah, because he was discovering that when those same limits were applied to her and her innocence he was happy with the idea…and even happier at the prospect of becoming her first lover. He didn't understand why he felt that way, because he had never been a possessive man, and nor had he ever been remotely unsure of his own skills in the bedroom and afraid of comparison.

A frown settled between his brows while he attempted to penetrate the mystery of his own gratification at her announcement—until the obvious answer came to him. What he found appealing had to be the sheer novelty of the experience she offered him…*of course* she would be something different, something new, something fresh!

'That's disgusting,' Lilah told him furiously. 'How can you admit something like that?'

Uncomfortably aroused by his thoughts, Bastien wanted to reach for her and demonstrate exactly how he felt, but he knew it wasn't the right moment. The nervous flicker of her bright blue eyes, her very restiveness, warned him that if he gave her sufficient ammunition she would take off in a panic like a hare bolting for its burrow.

'I will want you to sign a confidentiality agreement,' he told her levelly, sticking strictly to practicality. 'That's standard. It means that you will never be able to talk about our association in public or in private.'

Her nose wrinkled with distaste. 'I hardly think I would *want* to talk about it,' she said drily, fighting the nerves leaping in her stomach.

'In return I will purchase a suitable house for your father and his family.'

Lilah squared her slight shoulders. 'No, you will not. I don't want my family to be suspicious about my supposed job with you, and if you splash around too much cash they will definitely be suspicious. Give my father employment and he'll take care of his own family without any further help from *you*,' she told him with quiet pride.

'I'll want you to fly down to London with me to-morrow.'

Her eyes flew wide. *'Tomorrow?'*

'I'll call your father in to see me today and share the good news. I'll inform him that you're joining my personal staff. You can go home early to pack and you can dine with me at my hotel tonight.'

'I have a prior arrangement to meet friends.'

'To do what?' Bastien demanded impatiently.

'To eat out and see a movie.'

Bastien compressed his wide, sensual mouth. He wanted to tell her that in the near future she would do nothing without his permission. It was astonishing how much pleasure that belief gave him. But he didn't need to crack the whip right here and now, did he? She would be his soon enough and he would share her with no one—not friends, not family, no one.

Was that what could be described as a 'posses-sive' thought? His skin chilled at the suspicion. No, the thought was born of the reality that he had had to wait so long for Delilah that he wanted and indeed expected to receive one hundred per cent of her at-tention. He was not and never would be a possessive man, he assured himself with confidence. Even so, now that Delilah was officially set to become part of his life, in a way no other woman had ever been, he would ensure that she was protected by telling one of his security team to keep an eye on her from a discreet distance.

Lilah watched as Bastien unfurled his cell phone, stabbed out a number and spoke at length in Greek—short, staccato phrases that sounded very much like instructions.

'My driver will take you home now,' he informed her smoothly. 'And wait to collect your father and bring him back here to see me.'

Lilah hovered, because he made it all seem so bloodless and impersonal. Nothing she had said had changed his outlook about what he was doing. He neither regretted nor questioned his callous methods. He wanted her and he didn't care what he had to do to get her. The passion that had to power such an unapologetic desire for her body shook Lilah.

He closed a hand round hers and entrapped her without warning. 'Evidently I won't see you now until tomorrow, when we meet on my plane. It's probably just as well that you're seeing friends tonight. It takes the focus off us,' he pointed out with grudging appreciation. 'It will be more comfortable for all of us that way.'

'Certainly for you…if it keeps my father in the dark,' Lilah gibed.

'Do you honestly think I care about his opinion?' Bastien countered thickly. 'We're single adults. What we do in private is our business.'

Long dark fingers closed round her other hand, tugging her closer, fully entrapping her.

'Our business alone,' Bastien repeated thickly, lowering his arrogant dark head to hers and teasing along the tense line of her full lower lip with the blunt edge of his teeth, before soothing it with his tongue in a provocative caress that caught her unprepared and sent liquid heat to pool in her pelvis.

'We're at *work*, for goodness' sake!' Lilah protested in a rattled undertone.

'It's just a kiss,' Bastien husked, delving between her parted lips with his tongue and plunging deep with an unashamed hunger that roared through her like a bush fire.

Her knees locked and her legs swayed and she grabbed his forearms to steady herself, fingers clenching into the fabric of his suit jacket in consternation.

Just a kiss.

A little voice reminded her that in the near future she would have to give him a great deal more than a kiss. His mouth hardened on hers, hot and demanding, and a sensation like an electric shock tingled through her, awakening her body as nothing else had ever done. Her nipples pinched into tight buds of sensitivity; the secret flesh between her legs pulsed with sudden dampness. It was a wanting—a fierce wanting unlike anything she had ever felt before—and she was appalled by the response he was wringing from her treacherous body.

A lean hand clamped her spine to force her closer, and against her stomach she felt the hard swell of his erection even through the barrier of their clothing. A surge of burning heat that was very far from revulsion engulfed her and her face burned even hotter as he set her back from him with controlled force.

'I shouldn't start something I can't finish,' Bastien quipped.

Desperately flailing for something...*anything*...to distract her from the attack of self-loathing waiting to pounce on her, Lilah paused on her way to the door. 'Is it all right if I bring my dog with me tomorrow?'

'No pets. Leave the dog with your family.'

'I can't. My stepmother isn't comfortable with dogs. He's very small and quiet,' Lilah assured Bastien, lying through her teeth because Skippy wasn't remotely quiet once he got to know people.

Bastien frowned. 'Write down its details. I'll arrange for a specialist transport firm to handle the travel arrangements,' he pronounced after a considered pause. 'But once the animal arrives in France keep it away from me.'

'France?' she repeated in consternation.

'We're going to France the day after tomorrow.'

Lilah tottered back downstairs, shattered by the way she had succumbed to that single kiss. How could Bastien still have that effect on her? She hadn't been prepared for that. Perhaps naively she had assumed that her disgust at the unholy agreement he had offered her would protect her. But it hadn't.

Bastien had bought her acquiescence with a job for her father and the promised long-term prosperity of the reopened factory. Didn't he see how wrong that deal was? That reducing her body to the level of something to be traded like a product made her hate him? Didn't that matter to him?

But why should it matter to him? she questioned heavily as she informed Julie that she was leaving early. Bastien only wanted sex. He wasn't interested in what went on inside her head or how she felt about him. He didn't care... And neither should *she* care, she told herself defiantly. Being oversensitive in Bastien's radius was only going to get her hurt and humiliated. He wouldn't give her the kind of polite or gracious pretences that would allow her to save face. There would be no frills in the way of romance or compliments. He wasn't about to dress up their connection by making it about anything more than sex.

Later that same evening, in the wake of a whirlwind of embarrassingly untruthful explanations on the home front and a great deal of packing, Lilah emerged from the cinema with Josh—a tall, attractive man in his twenties, with brown hair and green eyes—and two other couples, Ann and Jack and Dana and George. There was nothing like a good fright or two to dispel tension, Lilah acknowledged wryly as she laughed at something Ann said about the horror movie they had watched.

'You're making a wise move on the career front,' Josh told her. 'Doing HR at Moore wasn't stretching you. Working for an international businessman will offer you much more experience.'

A shamefaced flush lit Lilah's face, because her friends had swallowed her lies about going to work for Bastien hook, line and sinker—just as her family had. 'I suppose so...'

'Very bad timing for me, though.' Without warning Josh reached for both her hands. 'You're leaving just when I was about to ask you out on a *real* date.'

'What?' Lilah's voice was shrill with surprise.

Josh grinned down at her, ignoring Jack's mocking wolf whistle. 'I mean, you must have wondered at least once what it would be like if we got together.'

Lilah grimaced, not knowing what to say to him. Because she never *had* wondered.

Josh edged her back against the wall behind her. 'Just one kiss,' he muttered.

Lilah stiffened, wondering why she felt like a stick of rock with 'Property of Bastien Zikos' stamped all the way through her. 'No, Josh,' she said, her hands braced against his chest.

But because she couldn't bring herself to actively push him away he kissed her, and she felt much as a shop window mannequin might have felt…absolutely nothing. Because while she liked Josh, and enjoyed his company, she had never fancied him.

'While you're away think about the possibility of *us*,' Josh urged, stretching an arm round her to guide her towards his parked car.

'I don't think so,' Lilah responded, wondering if there was a kind way of telling a man that you didn't fancy him in the slightest and knowing that there wasn't, and that the best response was probably for her just to pretend that absolutely nothing had happened.

'Awkward…' Ann mouthed, her eyes rolling with sympathy.

When Lilah walked back into her living room she was surprised by the expression of sincere happiness on her father's face. But she knew that even before she had reached home that afternoon Bastien had phoned her father, and the older man had already put on a suit by the time the car bringing his daughter home had arrived. When Lilah had gone out to meet her friends her father had still been out, presumably still with Bastien, which had worried Lilah.

'Everything all right, Dad?' she questioned anxiously.

'Better than that,' the older man assured her with vigour, and informed her that Bastien had hired him to act as manager at Moore Components—a role which he was very happy to take on.

'I'm beginning to understand how Bastien has become so very rich so fast,' the older man remarked in wry addition. 'He's very astute, and he spotted a break that would benefit Moore when no one else did.'

'What? *What* did he spot?' Lilah prompted with a frown.

'Bastien recognised that the council has recently rezoned the town's plans to open the door for further development. He's selling the current site for a *huge* amount of money and relocating the factory to the Moat Road, where he'll qualify for all sorts of lucrative government grants when he reopens for business. It's an incredibly smart move.'

'Good grief!' Lilah gasped, shock and temper bubbling up inside her at the belated awareness that Bastien had cut a very good deal with her in *every* way. Not only was he getting *her*, parcelled up like a gift, but he was also evidently on course to make a big profit too! And that realisation absolutely enraged Lilah.

CHAPTER FOUR

LILAH BOARDED BASTIEN'S private jet with her head held high. No, she wasn't about to show the shame she felt, and she wasn't anyone's victim—least of all Bastien's. This was *her* choice, she reminded herself doggedly. Bastien might have laid out those hateful options but *she* had made the choice, and she was still happy with what her sacrifice had achieved for her family.

Her father was managing the business he loved. For the moment he and Vickie would stay on in Lilah's little house, because it was affordable and within easy reach of Ben's school. Lilah thought her father and stepmother probably couldn't quite credit that life had changed for the better again. Having so recently lost everything, they were afraid of another disaster.

Lilah had had tears in her eyes when she'd parted from her little brother and sister that morning, for she had no idea when she would see them again. Did a mistress get time off from her role? Would she have any rights at all?

Bastien rested his arrogant dark head back to survey Delilah as she walked into the cabin. His mouth took on a sardonic curve when he saw her. She wore a drab, dated black trouser suit and had braided her hair again, concealing her every attraction to the best of her ability. But Bastien was hard to fool. She couldn't conceal the supple elegance of her delicate build or the healthy youthful glow of her fair skin and bright blue eyes, and when the jacket of her suit flapped back, revealing a sheer white shirt that hugged her small pouting breasts like a second skin, the fit of his trousers became uncomfortably tight.

Tonight, he thought impatiently, would finally rid him of the almost adolescent state of arousal she inflicted on him. A virgin, though… Was that really the truth? Didn't that deserve a certain amount of considerate staging?

Since when had he been considerate? Bastien asked himself irritably as Delilah attempted to walk past him towards the back of the cabin, where his staff were seated. His hand snapped out to close round her wrist and bring her to a halt.

'You sit with me,' he told her flatly.

Her full pink mouth tightened.

'Take off that ugly jacket. Let down your hair,' Bastien instructed.

Lilah froze. 'What will you do if I say no?'

'Rip off the jacket and yank out the hair tie for you,' Bastien traded without hesitation.

Warm colour flooded Lilah's cheeks and feathery lashes lowered over her eyes, because she was insanely conscious of his staff watching from the other end of the cabin. They were clearly wondering what she was doing on board and were now about to have their curiosity satisfied. She shrugged out of the jacket stiffly and reached up to tug at the tie anchoring her braid. Her hand was shaking as she loosened her hair.

Rage and mortification gusted through her as she dropped down into the seat beside Bastien, glossy black curls fanning in tousled disarray across her shoulders and brushing her flushed cheekbones.

'And just like that you look gorgeous again, *koukla mou*.'

'Is it going to be like this with everything? Your way or the highway?' Lilah pressed in a strangled hiss.

'What do *you* think?'

'That I once thought you were enough of a man not to need to control a woman's every move!'

His lean, darkly handsome features slashed into a sudden, entirely unexpected grin, his pride untouched by that crack. 'The trouble is…I *enjoy* controlling you.'

Lilah snatched in a much-needed gulp of oxygen. He sent her temper zooming from zero to sixty in the space of seconds. She had never considered herself quick-tempered until she met Bastien, but he literally set her teeth on edge almost every time he spoke.

'Why would you even want a woman who doesn't want you? Or is that what it takes to turn you on?'

That was a suggestion that deeply affronted Bastien, for the merest hint of aversion to him from a lover would have repulsed him.

He turned round to face her more directly, his dark eyes flaming gold as ingots, and closed a hand into the fall of her hair to hold her still. 'No, *you're* what it takes to turn me on…but, believe me, you can make very angry.'

'Is that a fact?' Lilah whispered tauntingly, tilting her chin, blue eyes gleaming.

In a searing movement of sensual intimidation Bastien crushed her soft mouth under his, driving her lips apart for the stabbing penetration of his tongue. She wasn't able to breathe, but then at that moment she didn't *want* to breathe. Her head was swimming, her body stinging with wild awareness, and a roaring hunger was awakening like a hurricane deep down inside her.

For a count of ten energising seconds Bastien thought about carrying her into the sleeping compartment and sating himself on her. But he would hurt her. He knew he was too hyped up for control. Besides, it was only a short flight to London and the jet would be landing soon.

He pulled back from her, positively aching from the throbbing force of his desire. 'You *do* want me,' he contradicted thickly, scanning her wildly flushed face and swollen, reddened mouth with satisfaction. 'You did from the first, *koukla mou.*'

Lilah whipped her attention away from him again and stared into space. *Well, you asked for that,* she told herself crossly, wondering why she always felt such a driving need to try to shoot Bastien down in flames. Unfortunately, in spite of all her efforts to ground him, he kept on soaring heavenward like a rocket.

Even so she was being confronted by a truth that she couldn't bear to examine. From the very first glimpse she had got of Bastien she *had* wanted him, and the hunger he had awakened in her was both primitive and terrifying. It truly hadn't mattered who he was or even what he was like, because her body had instantly seethed with a life of its own, wanting to connect with his, and her brain had swum with new and disturbing erotic images.

She hadn't known attraction could be that immediate or that powerful, and had certainly never suspected that it could overwhelm all restraint and common sense. Even worse, she was painfully aware that, had Bastien employed a more subtle approach and less honesty, he most probably would have succeeded in seducing her into his bed.

The cabin crew served drinks, the glamorous blonde stewardess syrupy sweet and persistent in her determination to serve and flirt with Bastien at the same time. He ignored her behaviour as if it wasn't happening, neither looking directly at the woman nor responding to her inviting chatter.

'Where are we going?' Lilah asked once the jet had landed.

'I'm taking you shopping, and tomorrow we head to Paris. I have a business meeting there.'

'Shopping?' she queried in surprise.

Bastien shrugged a broad shoulder and said nothing. Lilah caught the stewardess studying her with naked envy and thought, *If only you knew the truth.*

But what *was* the real truth? Lilah asked herself as the limo whisked her and Bastien through the crowded streets of London. She had given her word and Bastien had already delivered on his promises, which meant that he owned her body and soul for the foreseeable future. And that interpretation cast her as a complete victim, Lilah acknowledged ruefully—until she admitted the reality that one glance at Bastien's exquisitely chiselled features and tall athletic physique reduced her to a melted puddle of lust and longing. He was incredibly attractive—and, taking into account his reputation as a legendary womaniser, a very large number of women agreed with her.

They were met at the door of a world-famous store and conveyed upwards in a lift, surrounded by a posse of attendants composed of a stylist, a personal shopper and sales assistants. Clearly Bastien had already stated his preferences, and they were shown into a private room where he was ushered into a seat. Lilah hovered, watching the approach of a tray of champagne, and then she was steered into a changing room, where an astonishingly large selection of clothing awaited her.

Surely trying on loads of clothes for Bastien's benefit wasn't the *worst* thing that could have happened to her? But if making her model the clothes he wanted her to wear was a deliberate ploy to annoy her, he had played a blinder. The demeaning concept of swanning around in clothing personally picked by Bastien set her teeth on edge.

With a flush on her cheeks, she stepped back into the room clad in a blue silk dress that clung to her like cling film.

Bastien kicked back in his comfortable chair, very much in the mood to enjoy himself. His burnished gaze rested on Delilah and the oddest sense of contentment settled over him. Amusement tilted his handsome mouth when she teetered dangerously in the very high heels she clearly wasn't accustomed to walking in. The dress was rubbish: far too revealing. The only place Delilah would be encouraged to show that amount of flesh was in his bedroom and nowhere else.

He moved a dismissive hand and awaited the next

outfit, a pale pink jacket and skirt that was cute as hell against her cloud of blue-black hair and bright blue eyes. There might not be much of her, Bastien conceded, but what she lacked in curves she more than made up for in class, and with a delicacy that he considered incredibly feminine. The first time he had seen Delilah she had put him in mind of a flawless porcelain doll—until he'd noticed how expressive her face was: an ever-changing fascinating vista of what she was feeling and thinking. And what he liked most about her face was that he could read it as easily as a child's picture book.

'I'm not modelling underwear for you,' she warned him in a biting undertone.

Disconcerted, Bastien froze and lifted his arrogant, dark head to meet her bright eyes head-on, finally recognising the blaze of anger banked down there. 'Not a problem,' he assured her lazily. 'We'll save that show for the bedroom, *glikia mou.*'

Lilah's cheeks blazed with sudden livid colour. 'No, that's not me,' she parried abruptly. 'If that's what you want, you've picked the wrong girl!'

'You're perfect for me,' Bastien assured her levelly.

'Well, that's not a compliment I can return,' Lilah replied tartly. 'After all, it's obvious that we're a match made in hell. You want a dress-up doll that does exactly what's it's told and I won't do that.'

Bastien rose lithely to his feet and looked down at her from his commanding height with unreadable dark eyes. 'That's not what I want.'

'You want all the imperfections airbrushed away. You want obedience. Clearly you want a woman with submissive traits, and yet I don't have a submissive bone in my body! In fact, I'm more likely to *argue* with people who make unreasonable demands,' Lilah shot back at him in angry frustration. 'You're the king of unreasonable demands, Bastien. So, what are you doing with *me*?'

'You're misinterpreting everything I've ever said to you,' Bastien told her drily.

'Am I?' Lilah rolled her bright blue eyes, unimpressed by that accusation. 'You're such a control freak that you even want to choose the clothes I wear.'

'That's untrue,' Bastien incised. 'You're more like a jewel I want to see polished up and placed in the right setting. I don't want to see you wearing cheap clothes... I want to see you shine—'

'Bastien!' Lilah broke in helplessly, hopelessly confused by his attitude. He only wanted to have sex with her. He had been brutally honest about that reality. What did the clothes she wore have to do with a hunger that basic? Why on earth did he care what she wore?

She had paraded around for his benefit in one outfit after another. A vast wardrobe was being assembled for her use. She was stunned by that reality as well. For goodness' sake, was Bastien planning to keep her for the rest of her life—and his? How would she ever wear even a quarter of these clothes while she was with him? This was a male who was famed for barely lasting a month with one woman. Yet she had been equipped with countless wardrobe choices— indeed, everything a woman could conceivably want for every possible occasion and every season. Late afternoon had already stretched well into evening to encompass the shopping trip.

'We'll go back to the hotel now for dinner,' Bastien proposed, as if no dispute had taken place.

Lilah returned to the changing cubicle and selected a skirt and top from the rack to put on. She was being torn in two. On one level she wanted to fight Bastien, but on another she wanted to give him what he wanted to keep him happy. After all, how much was her own pride really worth when she could still clearly recall her father's renewed energy and hope?

What Bastien had given could easily be taken away again, she reflected fearfully. By giving her father a job, Bastien had revitalised the older man's drive and confidence. She should be grateful, she told herself urgently, but it was no use—she was too idealistic for such practicality. Unlike Bastien, she wanted sex to come packaged with romance and commitment.

Bastien took her back to an exclusive hotel and a very spacious suite. There were two bedrooms, and in the doorway of the first, Bastien paused to say, 'This is your room. I like my own space.'

Relieved by the news that she would not have to share a bedroom and surrender *all* privacy, Lilah watched as the hotel staff carted in the boxes and bags containing her brand-new wardrobe as well as a sizeable collection of designer luggage.

Bastien turned to grasp the phone extended to him by one of his personal assistants. Lean, strong face intent, he began talking urgently in French while raising an impatient hand to summon his team. As he spoke he strode to the desk in the large reception room, where a laptop had already been set up for his use.

His attention had drifted away from Lilah at supersonic speed. She watched his staff move into action, unfurling phones and tablets to follow Bastien's instructions. One name was mentioned repeatedly—Dufort Pharmaceuticals.

She kicked off her high heels and switched on the television in the far corner of the room. The fancy evening meal she had expected to eat in Bastien's company did not materialise. Instead, about an hour later waiters arrived with trolleys of buffet food to feed staff more interested in standing upright to eat than sitting down.

'Delilah!' Bastien called across the length of the room. 'Eat…you must be hungry by now.'

'Starving,' she admitted, padding over to him barefoot to grasp the plate he extended, daunted by the sheer size of him when she stood next to him without her shoes.

'A promising business deal has come up,' Bastien confided, studying her casually tousled hair and teeny-tiny bare toes, admiring the lack of vanity that allowed her to relax to that extent in his presence. She didn't care about impressing him, and he respected her innate sense of self-worth.

'I guessed that…' Lilah hid her amusement, delighted not to be the sole focus of his attention.

Ebony brows pleating, Bastien watched Delilah curl up on the sofa to return to the reality show she was watching. She was simply accepting that business came first for him without either taking offence or angling for a greater share of his attention. Yet, watching her relax back into the sofa and start eating with appetite, Bastien wondered if *he* should be the one taking offence—because it really wasn't a compliment that she should be so unconcerned by his preoccupation.

Becoming bored after an hour, Delilah switched off the television and crammed her feet back into the shoes she had kicked off to stand up. It was too early for bed and she was restless.

'Where are you going?' Bastien asked as she moved towards the door.

'For a walk. I need a break.'

Delilah was stepping into the lift when, to her surprise, one of Bastien's security team joined her.

'Is Bastien scared I'm going to run away?' she gasped in frustration, recognising the young man.

'I'm afraid you're stuck with me.' Her companion sighed. 'My instructions are not to let you out of my sight.'

'What's your name?' she asked.

'Ciro.'

'I'm Lilah,' she responded with a rueful smile, knowing that it wasn't fair to take her irritation out on Ciro, who was only guilty of doing his job.

A pianist was playing in the low-lit bar on the ground floor. Sitting down, Lilah ordered a drink. Ciro retreated to a table by the wall and left her in peace. Wishing she had thought to tuck a book into her bag, Lilah decided to catch up on her phone calls instead.

She rang her father first. Robert Moore talked non-stop to his daughter about Bastien's plans for the business and the advantages of the new location Bastien had picked for the firm. Lilah followed up that call with one to Vickie, learning that her dog, Skippy, had been picked up on schedule by a transport firm that morning.

She was replacing her phone in her bag when a

blonde woman sat down without warning in the seat opposite her. Lilah looked up in disconcertion.

'You're staying here with Bastien Zikos, aren't you?' the woman pressed with a smile.

Lilah's brows pleated. 'Why are you asking me that?'

'I'm Jenny Gower and I write for the women's page on the *Daily Pageant*,' the blonde told Lilah cheerfully, setting a business card down in front of her. 'That's my number. Feel free to call me any time you'd like a chat. Bastien's a real favourite with our readers and we like to keep up to date with his latest ladies.'

The woman was a reporter, Lilah realised in dismay. 'I've got nothing to say to you,' she said uncomfortably.

'Don't be shy. We pay generously for even little titbits.'

Without warning Ciro appeared at her elbow and intervened. 'Lilah…you're talking to a journalist.'

Lilah stiffened. 'We're not actually talking. I was just about to leave.'

And with that last word Lilah finished her drink and left the table.

'Mr Zikos loathes gossip columnists,' Ciro warned her with a grimace. 'I'll try to avoid mentioning the fact that you were approached.'

When Lilah returned to the suite Bastien was in the act of dismissing his staff for the night. 'I was planning to come down and join you,' he informed her.

Lilah flinched and coloured, focusing on Bastien with her heart in her mouth.

Annoyance flared in Bastien when he recognised the apprehension flashing in her gaze. Women didn't shrink from him; they *wanted* him. She must've been telling the truth about her inexperience, he concluded grimly. Only ignorance could explain such an attitude. It was surely past time that he showed her that she had nothing to fear from him.

'Would you like a drink?' he asked lazily, strolling closer.

'No, thanks,' she said jerkily.

Bastien crossed the room and scooped her right off her feet. Loosing a startled gasp, she wriggled like an electrified eel, strands of coconut-scented hair brushing his cheek as she moved her head back and forth.

'Relax,' he urged.

'Are you *kidding*?' Lilah exclaimed.

'You said you were a virgin. You didn't tell me that you were a hysterical one,' Bastien derided.

Lilah froze in his arms as though she had been slapped. She *was* overreacting, she acknowledged ruefully. Obviously Bastien was going to touch her, so his move shouldn't have sent her into panic mode.

'I'm *not* hysterical,' she protested, dry mouthed.

'You could've fooled me,' Bastien traded, settling down in an armchair with her slim body still firmly clasped to his broad chest.

'You startled me…you *pounced*,' Lilah condemned.

'And I'm not about to apologise for it,' Bastien husked, running down the back zip on her top and tugging it off her arms in one smooth movement.

'Oh…' Lilah gasped again, shocked to find herself stripped down to her bra without ceremony.

Bastien splayed a big hand across her narrow midriff to hold her in place while his mouth moved urgently across the pale skin at the nape of her neck.

Her heart hammered inside her tight chest and a tiny uncontrollable shiver racked her when his teeth grazed and nipped along the slope between her neck and her shoulder. It was a fiercely erotic assault, subsequently soothed by the skim of his tongue.

Her eyes flew wide, her pupils expanding as quiver after quiver of response gripped her. Suddenly even breathing became a challenge. Bastien closed his hands to her waist to lift her and turn her to face him, bringing her down again with her skirt hitched and her legs splayed either side of his hips.

His tongue plunged against hers in a deep, marauding kiss that made her tremble. Her bra felt too tight and the ache stirring in her pelvis was powerful enough to hurt. He kept on kissing her, forcing her lips apart with urgency and drawing her down on him so that she could feel the hard thrust of his erection between her spread thighs.

'Bastien… I—'

Dark golden eyes accentuated by a canopy of black velvet lashes held hers and silenced her. He truly had the most stunning eyes. Her mouth ran dry. Her mind was as blank as an unpainted canvas because she was reeling from the intensity of what he was making her feel.

She didn't even realise he had flicked loose her bra until he ran his hands up over her pert breasts to make actual skin-to-skin contact. Her usual alarm about her lack of size in the breast department had no time to develop, because his hands were already curving to the small pale mounds. With knowing fingers and thumbs he roughly tugged and chafed the pale pink sensitivity of her straining nipples. His touch sent hot tingles of longing arrowing through her limp body, heat and moisture gathering at the pulsing heart of her.

'You have such pretty breasts,' Bastien said thickly, bending her back over his supporting arm to capture a swollen stiff bud between his lips and torment it with attention. 'And so very sensitive, *koukla mou…*'

Her breath see-sawed back and forth in her throat while he rocked her over his lean, powerful body, ensuring that on every downward motion her tender core connected with the hard swell of his arousal. The tightening sensation in her womb increased to an un-bearable level. Long fingers skated over the taut fabric stretched between her legs, where she was excruci-atingly sensitive. He eased a finger below the lace edge of her panties. Excitement roared through her as he stroked and rubbed the tender bud of her clito-ris. Rational thought vanished, because her body was greedily craving every new sensation, living from one intoxicating moment to the next.

As he rimmed the tiny wet entrance to her body with a teasing fingertip and at the same time let his carnal mouth latch hungrily on to an agonisingly tender nipple, Lilah's every nerve ending went into screaming overdrive.

'Come for me, Delilah,' Bastien told her rawly.

And then there was no holding back the explosion of excitement that had risen to a high Lilah could no longer suppress. Within seconds she was crying out, shuddering and convulsing with the wild surge of pleasure Bastien's expert hands had released. Ex-hausted and drained in the aftermath, she let her head drop down against his shoulder, barely able to credit that her body could react so powerfully that it still felt as though she was coming apart at the seams. He smelt of expensive cologne, testosterone and clean musky male, and at that moment—astonishingly—it was the most comforting scent she had ever experienced.

The strangest sense of protectiveness crept through Bastien while Delilah clung to him. He licked his fingers, her unique taste adding another layer to his fierce arousal. He wanted more—so much more that he knew he dared not let himself touch her again until he had cooled down. Unfortunately he had never been a patient man, and he knew his own faults.

He stood up, cradling her slight body in his arms, and carried her through to her room, where he settled her down on the bed.

'I'll see you in the morning.'

Conscious of the cool air hitting her bare breasts, Lilah crossed her arms across her body with a defensive jerk and looked up at Bastien in astonishment as he switched on the bedside lamp. That was it? He wasn't joining her in the bed to finish what he had started?

Hot colour surged in her cheeks as she collided with glittering dark golden eyes. 'But—'

'Tonight was for you, not for me,' Bastien told her wryly, striding back to the door and then coming to a halt to glance back at her with a blindingly charismatic smile that mesmerised her into staring. 'You know the weirdest thing…?'

His lean, darkly handsome features were pure fallen angel in the shadowy light. 'No…' she whispered, almost hypnotised by the flawless perfection of his sculpted features.

'What we just did…' he mused, with a self-mocking

curve to his beautiful mouth. 'That has to be the most innocent experience I've ever shared with a woman.'

As the door thudded shut on his exit Lilah's brows lifted almost as high as her hairline. *Innocent?* How could such shattering intimacy be in any way innocent? What on earth was he talking about?

Her body was still aching and quaking as though it had come through a battle zone. She slid off the bed and staggered dizzily into the en-suite bathroom, challenged to place even one foot accurately in front of the other. There she studied her tousled reflection in disgust. Her hair was messy, her mascara smeared and she was half-naked.

With a groan of shame she stripped off the skirt and panties and stepped into the shower. But even beneath the cleansing, cooling flow of water her body tingled and burned with new awareness in the places Bastien had touched.

Lilah shuddered—and *not* in disgust—at the thought of him doing it again. That acknowledgement alone was sufficient to keep her tossing and turning half the night.

CHAPTER FIVE

'COULD I HAVE a quiet word, sir?'

Manos, Bastien's head of security, approached him as he was still working, close to midnight. The older man seemed uncomfortable.

'It relates to Miss Moore…'

And within the space of minutes Bastien's even-tempered mood had been destroyed by the information Manos put in front of him.

Having initially assumed that Delilah was simply another employee, Manos had only belatedly realised that the news that she had been seen consorting with another man might be of interest to Bastien.

Bastien was shocked. And then furious with himself for *being* shocked. After all, how many times had a woman let him down? Lied to him? Ripped him off? Faked emotions to impress him? Too many times to count, Bastien conceded, tight mouthed with cynicism, his lean, starkly handsome bone structure rigid. But as far as he was aware not a single one of his lovers had ever *cheated* on him.

Forewarned is forearmed, Bastien told himself forbiddingly. And if Delilah had been with another man as recently as the night before, he no longer wanted her, did he? Damn Security for not following her home to establish exactly how the evening had concluded!

Frustration building at this incomplete picture of events, Bastien clenched his fists, plunged upright and decided to go out. The frustration was fast becoming rage, in a vicious tide that came with a bitter backwash.

A virgin? Of *course* Delilah was not a virgin! How likely had that claim ever been? Obviously she had made up that story in an effort to make him feel guilty while she played the poor little victim. And he didn't do victims any more than he did relationships, did he? Delilah Moore was toxic for him. Hadn't he suspected as much two years earlier? When had he ever wanted one particular woman that much? Any hunger that particular wasn't healthy.

Bastien headed for an exclusive nightclub to find another woman for the night. He had to prove to his own satisfaction that he was not remotely concerned by what he had learned about Delilah. She was not special in any way, he told himself furiously, downing his third drink in fast succession. She was like every other woman he had ever met: immediately... *easily*...replaceable.

In the club, Bastien was surrounded by beautiful women eager to attract his attention. He waited for one to give him a buzz, studying a blonde and deciding she was too voluptuous. A brunette who had eyes that were too close together. A redhead who laughed like a hyena. Another wore a hideous floral dress, and yet another had enormous feet.

Delilah's were the very first female feet Bastien had ever actually noticed, he acknowledged abstractedly. She had very small feet, with teeny-tiny toes and nails like polished pearls.

He settled into his fourth drink and wondered first of all why he was thinking about feet and then why he was still on his own. Why the hell was he suddenly being so fastidious? *Any* attractive woman would do. Hadn't he always believed that? He did not, *could* not, still want a woman who had cheated on him.

So what was he planning to do about Delilah?

Bastien registered that he wanted to confront her, and that strange urge deeply unsettled him. After all, he had always avoided high drama, and he had never, ever argued with the women who'd shared his bed. Why would he argue when women who annoyed him were instantly banished from his life, never to hear from him again?

He would send Delilah back up north, forget about her, cut his losses....

When the bedroom door opened abruptly Lilah was jolted awake. She sat up. Light was flooding the doorway to silhouette a powerful male figure. Instantly she knew it was Bastien, and instantly she was apprehensive.

The light was snapped on, momentarily blinding her, and Bastien strode in. His lean bronzed features were clenched ferociously hard, and his eyes, dark as eternal night, glittered above high lancing cheekbones. Her tummy performed a nervous dance and she backed up against the pillows with her knees defensively raised.

'I want a word with you.'

Bastien sent the door behind him thudding shut and her throat closed over convulsively.

A faint whiff of alcohol assailed her nose; he had been drinking. For the first time Lilah was appreciating that she knew very little about Bastien Zikos—basically only what she had read on the internet, none of which was reassuring. Did he drink a lot? Was he drunk now? Was he violent? Was such random temperamental behaviour the norm for him?

'Stop looking at me like that...' Bastien growled in frowning reproof, studying her from below the thick canopy of his black lashes.

Clutching the duvet to her with a nervous hand, Lilah breathed out. 'Like what?'

'As if you're scared!' Bastien grated accusingly. 'I have never hurt a woman in my life.'

A tentative half smile stole some of the tension from Lilah's triangular face. 'You just walked in... You startled me... I was fast asleep,' she explained, struggling to excuse herself rather than tell him the truth.

And the truth was that Bastien *was* scary. He was very tall, very muscular, much larger and stronger than she was in every way. Moreover, although he had the hauntingly beautiful face of a fallen angel, his dark eyes currently had a piercing, chilling light that utterly intimidated her.

'I want you to tell me where you were and who you were with last night,' Bastien bit out harshly, taking up a brooding stance at the very foot of the bed. 'Don't leave anything out.'

'I was out with a group of friends,' Lilah almost whispered, wondering why on earth he could be demanding such an explanation. 'We went for a meal and then to the cinema.'

'Do you normally kiss your male friends and then climb into a car to go home with them at the end of the night?' Bastien asked grimly.

Her eyes widened and flickered in dismay, colour warming her pale face. 'How do you know there was a kiss?'

Bastien was watching her face, recognising the embarrassment and the sudden flash of resentment there but seeing not a shred of guilt. 'I had one of my security team watching you last night. He lost track of you after you got into the guy's car.'

'Oh…' It was the only thing Lilah could initially think to say, because she was hugely disconcerted by the idea that someone Bastien employed had been following her round before she'd even left her home town. How dared he invade her privacy like that? 'You had no right to have anyone watching me.'

'From the moment I let you into my life I had that right. Did you spend the night with him?'

Battling to keep her temper over that far-reaching declaration of his rights over her, Lilah swallowed hard. 'No, I didn't. Josh dropped me straight home. There was one kiss, Bastien, nothing more.' She frowned at him, dismayed by the depth of his distrust. 'He's never kissed me before, and I wasn't expecting it. He was just trying it on.'

'You didn't try to stop him.'

'He's a friend and we had an audience.' Lilah grimaced. 'I didn't want to make a big scene of rejecting him in front of everyone. It would have made us all feel horribly uncomfortable.'

Bastien studied her, torn between belief and disbelief. His lean, strong features remained hard and set, his tawny eyes veiled by his lashes. The silence lay there, thick as a swamp between them.

'You were too generous. You're mine now,' Bastien told her in a raw, gritty undertone. 'I will not tolerate any other man touching you.'

'Bastien...I don't want anyone following me around, spying on me.'

'It goes with the territory. It's for my peace of mind and your protection.'

'I don't need protection.'

'That's my decision,' Bastien decreed, snapping off the light in a sudden movement that made her flinch.

'Bastien...?' Lilah whispered.

A powerful silhouette, he hovered. 'What?'

'Sometimes you really, really annoy me.'

'That cuts both ways.'

Bastien studied her slight figure in the bed and then strode into the room to flip back the duvet and scoop her up into his arms.

'What are you doing?' she gasped in consternation as he strode into the room next door to hers.

Bastien thrust back the sheet on his bed and settled her on the mattress. 'I want you where I can see you,' he told her curtly.

'You told me that I was getting my own room,' she reminded him breathlessly.

'For what remains of tonight, I've changed my mind.' Removing his jacket, he cast it on a chair, a lean, strong band of muscle flexing below his shirt. 'I'm going for a shower,' he extended, without any expression at all.

Lilah curled up in a ball on one side of the bed, too tired and wrung out to agonise or argue. So that was that? There was to be no further discussion?

Bastien had assumed that she had slept with Josh last night. Did he believe that she hadn't? Did she care whether he believed her or not?

He was so…so…*volatile*. She hadn't been prepared for that—had assumed that deep down inside he was cold as ice and detached. She had been wrong. In addition, only a few hours ago she would have been overcome with embarrassment at the prospect of facing Bastien again. At least she would've been until Bastien himself had dismissed what they had shared as 'innocent', which had certainly clarified matters as far as she was concerned.

Years of standing back and protecting herself while other people dabbled in sex had, she had decided ruefully, made her prudish and naive. As far as Bastien was concerned nothing worthy of note had yet happened between them. Why else would he have called an episode that had shocked her 'innocent'? And if *he* wasn't disturbed or embarrassed by it why should *she* be?

The arrival of a lavish breakfast tray awakened Lilah the next day. She glanced at the dent in the pillow next to her own and marvelled at the reality that she had fallen asleep with Bastien beside her and, in spite of his presence, slept like a log.

She was tucking into a chocolate croissant and covered in crumbs when Berdina, one of Bastien's personal assistants, arrived to tell her that Bastien was in a meeting and that after a brief appointment with

Bastien's lawyer she would be flying to Paris with Bastien in a couple of hours.

While wondering why she was to meet with a lawyer, Lilah packed her new wardrobe and picked out a stylish electric blue coat and fine dress to wear. These designer clothes were props, to support the role that she was being well paid to play, Lilah told herself firmly. Bastien was reopening Moore Components and re-employing the workforce—including her father. That was her payoff. That was why she was with Bastien in the first place.

She needed to remind herself of that reality on a regular basis. There was nothing complicated about their agreement. Bastien had made it all completely straightforward, hadn't he? He wanted her and he had worked out exactly what it would take to persuade her to surrender to his demands. He had proved that she had a price, and she doubted she would ever be able to forgive him for being right about that.

When she emerged from the bedroom the lawyer was waiting to present her with the confidentiality contract that she had agreed to sign.

The older man settled the slim document on the table and Lilah sat down to read it. He drew her attention to various clauses and handed her a pen. It was fairly standard stuff, and after adding her signature she passed the document back.

Porters had arrived to pick up her luggage, and she vacated the hotel in Berdina's company.

'We're lunching with François and Marielle Durand in Paris,' Bastien informed Lilah the instant she sat down opposite him on board his sleek, opulent jet. He wore a charcoal-grey suit, superbly tailored to his lean, powerful frame, and his white shirt framed his strong bronzed jaw.

'Who are they?' Lilah asked curiously.

'Marielle is an ex, now married to François. Including you in the arrangement will make it a more relaxed meeting,' Bastien opined with smooth assurance as coffee was served.

His admission that Marielle Durand was a former lover sent Lilah's interest hurtling into the stratosphere.

'This is for you...' Bastien tossed down a credit card on the table between them. 'While I'm taking care of business this morning you will go shopping, and I'll pick you up when it's time for lunch—'

Lilah studied the credit card with a sinking heart and pushed it away several inches. 'I don't want to spend your money,' she told him tightly.

'I didn't give you a choice. Spending my money goes with the territory and I expect you to do it,' Bastien decreed, flicking the card back towards her with the tip of a forceful finger.

Lilah reminded herself that she didn't have to buy anything and put the card in her clutch bag for the sake of peace. It had not escaped her notice that Bastien's staff watched her every move, visibly curious about her connection with their employer. That interest implied that, from the outside at least, her relationship with Bastien appeared unusual in some way.

She lifted her chin and collided unexpectedly with Bastien's smouldering dark golden eyes. Her temperature rose and her heartbeat thundered, the tip of her tongue sliding out to moisten the dryness of her full lower lip. She was helplessly recalling the expert stroke of Bastien's fingers over the most intimate part of her body and reddening to the roots of her hair.

'*Se thelo…* I want you…' Bastien breathed thickly.

Lilah couldn't have found her voice to save herself. Hot colour inflamed her pale complexion, her eyes widening she gazed back at him, taken aback by his candour.

A long, tanned forefinger skimmed down the back of her hand where it rested on the tabletop. 'I've never waited as long for any woman as I've waited for you. Of course I'm hot for you. Last night only whetted my appetite, *koukla mou.*'

As he touched her Lilah tore her gaze from his and yanked her hand back out of reach. 'You weren't *waiting,*' she told him with tart emphasis, before she could think better of it. 'Over the past two years you've been with one woman after another.'

A winged ebony brow climbed. 'Keeping count, were you?' Bastien quipped.

'Why would *I* care what you do?' Lilah traded, hot cheeked.

'I don't want you to *care* about me in any way,' Bastien countered without hesitation, his stunning dark eyes welded to her expressive face. 'This is sex, nothing more.'

Lilah lifted a delicate brow. 'What else could it be?'

Walking through the airport in Paris with Bastien, she was disconcerted to move beyond the barrier and suddenly find a phalanx of cameras aimed at them. Dismay gripped her, because the last thing she wanted was to be publically outed as Bastien Zikos's latest 'hottie'.

In an effort to lessen that risk she stepped away from Bastien and endeavoured to act more like an employee than a lover. The cameras continued to flash regardless. Questions were shouted, asking who she was in both French and English. They, like the photographers, were ignored.

Her colour fluctuating, Lilah climbed into the limo outside the airport accompanied by Berdina, who was to act as her guide on the shopping trip, and Ciro, who was with her for security. By that time Lilah was worrying that her family or her friends would see photos of her with Bastien in the papers and become suspicious that she was doing more than simply working for him.

But once the affair was over would that really matter? she asked herself ruefully.

The car whisked them to the Avenue Montaigne, where a whole range of designer shops were located.

While Berdina's attention was elsewhere Lilah looked up Marielle Durand on her phone. Photos of a slender exquisite blonde cascaded across the screen and Lilah swallowed hard. Marielle had been a famous model before her marriage.

Her thoughts abstracted, Lilah prowled through Louis Vuitton, Dior and Chanel and browsed, before obeying the letter of the law in Ralph Lauren and flourishing Bastien's credit card to buy Bastien a new tie. He couldn't complain now, could he? She had bought something.

Bastien joined her at noon. 'Where are your shopping bags?' he demanded.

Lilah extracted the small package from her clutch and handed it to him. 'For you.'

Bastien frowned at her. 'For...*me*?'

'You said I had to spend your money, so I did.'

Bastien unwrapped the gold silk tie and studied it in astonishment. 'You bought me a tie?'

'I won't need anything new to wear this century, after the amount of stuff you bought in London,' Lilah pointed out.

'That wasn't the point of the exercise,' Bastien traded harshly. 'The point is that, for once, I wanted you to do *exactly* as you were told.'

'Sorry, sir, I'll have to try harder,' Lilah quipped.

'Have you always found it this hard to follow instructions?'

'When *you're* issuing them...yes,' she admitted ruefully.

'You should *want* to please me,' Bastien told her as blue eyes bright as sapphires met his critical gaze.

With her dark hair framing her triangular face and her eyes sparkling above her neat little nose and her full rosy mouth, she looked amazingly fragile and feminine—as well as fizzingly alive.

'Why?'

'It puts me in a better mood.'

While Lilah tried to imagine Bastien's moods influencing her in any way, the limo nosed back into the traffic.

The Durands lived in an imposing eighteenth-century townhouse on Ile Saint-Louis. A maid ushered them into an airy salon, where introductions were performed and drinks were served.

Keenly aware of Marielle Durand's scrutiny, Lilah struggled to relax. Marielle was even more beautiful in the flesh than she had looked in her photographs, and Lilah was surprised to realise that the other woman was English.

Bastien surprised Lilah by closing his hand over hers to keep her close while he chatted to François. The conversation was solely in French, until Marielle addressed Lilah in English and asked her about her home town. Relieved not to be forced to stumble out any more stock phrases in her schoolgirl French, Lilah relaxed a little over the light lunch that was being served.

Over a glass of wine, the beautiful blonde invited Lilah to walk round the garden with her.

'How long have you been with Bastien?' Marielle asked with unconcealed curiosity, as soon as the men were out of earshot.

'Only a few days,' Lilah admitted wryly. 'Am I allowed to ask when you…?'

'Years and years ago—soon after I first made my name in the modelling world. He was probably my most exciting affair,' the other woman confided with an abstracted laugh. 'I adore my husband, but I've never felt anything like the excitement I once felt around Bastien. He's a heartbreaker, though, too damaged to ever trust his heart to one woman and settle down.'

'Damaged?' Lilah queried with a frown.

'Oh, I don't know any details, but I've always been certain he must come from a challenging background. No man's that hard to hold, and no man finds it that impossible to trust a woman without good reason,' Marielle opined. 'He was too complicated for me.'

And then Lilah made a discovery that disconcerted her: she *liked* complicated—actually *enjoyed* the challenge of wondering what made Bastien tick. He was like no other man she had ever met. Incalculably clever, impatient, volatile and unpredictable. He was an unashamed workaholic, evidently unfulfilled by the huge achievements he had already made. What had made him like that... *Who* had made him like that? What drove him? And why did she care?

'You charmed the Durands very effectively,' Bastien pronounced on their journey back to the airport. 'You don't have a jealous bone in your body where I'm concerned, do you?'

'Why would I?' Lilah parried, quickly overcoming her surprise at that unexpected stab. 'I can't think you'd welcome a possessive woman.'

That was certainly true, Bastien acknowledged grudgingly, and yet when he had glanced out through the patio doors standing open to the sunlight to see Delilah smiling and laughing, seemingly on the very best of terms with Marielle, he had been surprisingly riled by Delilah's complete indifference to his past history with the beautiful blonde.

The faintest colour warmed Lilah's cheeks, because although she had not been jealous or possessive she *had* felt uncomfortable in Marielle's company—and positively nauseous at the knowledge that Bastien had been sexually intimate with her hostess.

'Where are we going now?' she asked, purely to change the subject.

'I have a chateau in Provence...'

CHAPTER SIX

THEY LEFT THE airport in a rough terrain vehicle, with Bastien at the wheel and his security team following in another car.

The glorious Provençal light was beginning to fade, softening hard edges with shadow. They drove through rugged hills with deep gorges and fertile valleys. The hilltops were scattered with picturesque fortified villages with narrow meandering streets and sleepy shuttered houses. As the landscape grew increasingly spectacular the land became lusher. Ancient vineyards cloaked the sloping hills with ranks of bright green vines, while orchards of peaches, pears, nectarines and cherries flourished on stone terraces.

'Did you inherit the chateau from your family?' Lilah finally asked, unable to stifle her curiosity because Bastien had not offered a shred of further information.

'I'm not from a rich family,' Bastien told her drily. 'My mother was a waitress born in an Athens back street. My father is a small-time property developer who is, admittedly, married to a very wealthy woman. Regrettably, he was never married to *my* mother.'

'Oh…' Lilah responded after an awkward pause.

'When you mentioned your father giving your mother the sea horse pendant, and you thinking that you and your parents were the perfect family, you gave me a very different impression of your background.'

'What I meant was that back then I was still young enough to be ignorant of exactly what their relationship entailed.'

'And what *did* it entail?'

'My father, Anatole, is married to another woman. My mother was his mistress. She once admitted to me that she deliberately chose to become pregnant with me because she believed my father would divorce his wife for her if she gave him a child,' Bastien volunteered in the driest of tones. 'Unhappily for her, her scheme failed—because my father's wife had already conceived my half-brother, Leo, who is only a few months older than I am. My mother was extremely bitter about *that* development.'

'And she *told* you that?' Lilah pressed in consternation.

His beautifully shaped mouth quirked. 'Athene wasn't the maternal type, and she never did overcome her resentment at having the responsibility and expense of a child she no longer had any use for.'

Lilah compressed her full lips, the skin around her mouth bloodless from the force of will it took for her to remain silent in the face of what he was telling her. She was shocked, but she didn't want to admit it, sensing that Bastien would ridicule her revulsion at his mother's callous candour. But no child should know he was unwanted, she thought painfully. No child should have to live with the demeaning knowledge that he had only been conceived to be used as a piece of emotional blackmail in his mother's battle to win a wedding ring from his father.

'No comment? I felt sure you would have several moralising remarks to make.'

'Then you were wrong. I know that all children don't grow up in a picturebook-perfect world,' Lilah breathed tautly. 'Otherwise my father would have loved my mother and stayed faithful to her…'

'He *wasn't*?' Bastien shot her a disconcerted look from frowning dark eyes. 'You're very close to your father. I naturally assumed…'

'My parents weren't happily married. There were always other women in my father's life, and constant upsetting scenes in my home. He didn't love my mother. They'd been together since they were teen-agers, though, and everyone expected him to marry her—so eventually he did,' she proffered ruefully. 'It was a long time before I understood that succumb-ing to that social pressure had made him feel trapped in their marriage. He's a different man with my step-mother.'

'Did your father's infidelity contribute to your judgemental view of me as a "shameless man whore"?' Bastien shot at her, throwing her completely off bal-ance.

Lilah flushed to the roots of her hair at having her own insult flung back at her two years after the event and when she'd least expected it. 'Of course not… However, you *are* a womaniser, Bastien.'

'But *not* a man whore. I have never been unfaith-ful to a lover,' Bastien asserted levelly. 'I have never taken indiscriminate sexual partners either. While my values may not be the same as yours, I *do* have standards.'

Mortification had claimed Lilah and it was eating her alive. She closed her hands together tightly on her lap. 'I lost my temper that night. I shouldn't have made such personal and disparaging comments to someone I barely knew,' she conceded, hoping that her admission would close the subject.

'Is that an apology?'

Lilah breathed in so deep that her narrow chest swelled.

'I mean,' Bastien mused, and his deep, dark, Greek-accented drawl was as rich as molasses, 'I did only ask you to dine with me and spend the night. I didn't assault you or abuse you.'

Lilah lost her battle with her temper and flung her hands up in a violent demonstration of exasperation. 'All right…all *right*… I'm sorry with bells on! Are you satisfied now?'

Bastien stole an amused glance at the glittering brightness of her eyes above her pink cheeks. 'What would a virgin know about a man whore's lifestyle anyway?' he derided.

Staring rigidly out through the windscreen as the vehicle turned between tall stone pillars to drive down a lane lined on both sides with very tall stately trees, Lilah rolled her eyes. 'Maybe I read a lot of raunchy books…'

Amused against his will, Bastien bit out a rough-edged laugh. She was in the wrong and she knew it—but she still wouldn't back down the way other women did with him. He enjoyed her stubborn streak and the challenge of making her toe the line.

Lights came on as Bastien parked and killed the engine. 'Welcome to the Chateau Sainte-Monique.'

Wall lamps in the form of iron lanterns illuminated the old building, accentuating the warm honey-coloured stone of the façade and the very Provençal violet-blue shutters at the many windows. Gravel interspersed with formal beds of flowers and trees ornamented the frontage.

Lilah climbed out of the car and accompanied Bastien to the entrance. 'So, when did you buy this place?'

'About three years ago. The owner was an elderly countess, whom I met during the course of a land development deal. The first time I saw the chateau I made her an offer, but it was months before she finally agreed to sell. The renovation took another year. I come here when I want to relax and when I can work from home. I stayed here all last month,' Bastien admitted smoothly.

A middle-aged man in a crisply ironed white shirt and bow tie opened the door and greeted them with a smile.

'Stefan and his wife, Marie, take care of everything here,' Bastien informed Lilah after making an introduction, and a lean hand resting at the base of her spine guided her indoors.

The interior was breathtaking. The hall had a chequerboard black-and-white marble floor and surprisingly modern furniture. A huge stone staircase curved up from the ground floor.

Their luggage was being brought in behind them, and Bastien was heading for the stairs, when Stefan opened a door and a familiar little bark of eagerness froze Lilah in place. Stefan grinned as a brown, silky little bundle of flying flapping ears and wriggling body flew at Lilah with a noisy burst of excited barking.

'Yes…yes, I missed you too,' Lilah admitted, crouching down to scoop up the miniature dachshund. She separated him from one of the beloved squeaky toys he liked to carry around in his mouth and attempted to calm him before she put him down again.

As the dog snatched up the toy again and hurtled across to Bastien, Lilah warned him. 'Just ignore Skippy. He'll get the message and leave you in peace…that's what Vickie always did with him. She prefers cats.'

Skippy nudged the toe of Bastien's shoe with his nose, his beady little eyes pleading. Bastien sidestepped the animal to stride on up the stairs, and Lilah watched in dismay as Skippy hurtled in his wake. Stefan moved forward to intercept the little dog, seemingly aware that his employer was not animal-friendly.

Lilah followed Bastien upstairs into a spectacular atmospheric bedroom furnished with a mixture of antique and contemporary pieces. Oyster-coloured silk festooned the windows and tumbled down in opulent swathes from the wrought-iron crown holder above the big bed.

'This is an amazing place,' Lilah whispered, impressed beyond words by the splendour of her surroundings.

'The maids will unpack for you. I'll see you downstairs for dinner in an hour,' Bastien imparted as a man brought in her luggage and two young women in uniform arrived to move the cases into the dressing room visible through an open door.

Lilah hovered uncertainly.

'Dress up...' Bastien lowered his handsome dark head to murmur huskily in her ear. 'Dress up for dinner so that I can enjoy *undressing* you later, *glikia mou.*'

Banners of self-conscious colour brightened Lilah's porcelain-pale complexion as she turned her head to stare up at him. She collided with brilliant dark eyes that glittered like stars in the low light—stunning eyes, ringed by spiky lashes of velvet black. She was mesmerised. He curved long flexible fingers to the side of her face and brought his mouth crashing down on hers.

That kiss was a taste of heaven and a taste of hell in one package. It was heaven because she couldn't get enough of that hot, hungry mouth on hers and hell because she hated the response she couldn't suppress. He released her, staring down at her for a split second in silence, and then swung on his heel and walked out.

Lilah drifted into the marble bathroom, her fingers creeping up to brush her tingling swollen lips, shame and guilt rising like a dark, choking cloud inside her. It would be cruel if he made her *like* having sex with him, she thought wildly. Or would it? Surely that could only be foolish pride talking?

Her rational brain scolded her for the melodrama Bastien could somehow infuse into her very thoughts. Common sense told her that simply accepting that their intimacy was inevitable would make the experience much more manageable for her. After all, she wasn't a masochist, was she?

Sex was supposed to be enjoyable, she reminded herself. But from listening to friends talk about their experiences she knew it often wasn't that great. Once she had done the deed with Bastien she would probably wonder what all the fuss was about, she reflected wryly, because, after all, sex had to be the most ordinary pursuit in the world.

Stripping, she went for a shower, retrieved her cosmetics to do her face and finally returned to the bedroom wrapped in towels. In the dressing room she flicked through the formal wear now hung for her perusal. *Dress up*, Bastien had urged. Humour sparkling in her eyes, she pulled a ballgown from the rail and fanned it out on the bed. It was over the top and theatrical, rather like the chateau, and when she had modelled it she had noticed Bastien's dark golden eyes blaze like banked-down fires.

Bastien stood in the hall, watching Delilah descend the stairs with the glossy grace and dignity of a queen. The dress was amazing—a glistening sheath in peach that hugged her slender body to just below the waist before it flared out into thousands of layers of net that swept the stone steps. Her black hair tumbled in a mane down her back, strands rippling round her triangular face to highlight her bright blue eyes. The tightening swelling at his groin was so instant he didn't even question his reaction.

He stretched out a lean-fingered brown hand to greet Lilah as she reached the foot of the stairs, his arrogant dark head thrown back, smouldering dark golden eyes locking to the full pink pout of her lush mouth. He closed his fingers round hers.

'In that dress you take my breath away,' he told her.

Her mouth ran dry as she met his gaze and her

small breasts swelled below the skin-tight bodice as she gulped in oxygen. She hadn't expected that blunt compliment, didn't know how to deal with it.

He walked her through an airy salon, with an ancient stone carved fireplace and sleek blue sofas, out on to a tiled terrace where a candlelit table awaited them.

'I'm really hungry,' Lilah confessed as a manservant moved forward to pull out a chair and lingered to whisk a napkin across her lap.

'You should enjoy the meal. Stefan's wife, Marie, is my cook, and she was a chef in a Michelin-starred restaurant in Paris before they came to work for me,' Bastien remarked while the wine was poured.

'You have a huge staff here…you live like a king,' Lilah commented helplessly as soon as they were alone.

'I do when I have the time to enjoy the chateau— which is rarely,' Bastien qualified drily. 'When I'm travelling on business I eat out or cook for myself.'

'You can *cook*?' Lilah said in surprise.

'Of course I can. I'm not spoilt. I've never been spoilt. But I do appreciate the best things in life.'

'Is your mother still alive?' she asked abruptly as the first course was served.

Bastien studied her in silence, black brows drawing together in a frown. 'You're very curious about my life.'

Lilah shrugged her lightly clad shoulder. 'Why wouldn't I be?'

Bastien set down his glass. 'My mother died in a car accident when I was a child and I had to go and live with my father.'

Lilah toyed with the artfully presented courgette flowers topping the tiny onion tart on her plate. 'And how was that?'

'Hideous,' Bastien admitted grimly. 'Anatole's wife, Cleta, hated me on sight. I was the living proof of her husband's infidelity. As for my half-brother… Leo was an adored only child and suddenly I turned up. Naturally he resented me. But there were some advantages to my new home,' he conceded, his dark eyes veiled with mystery, his beautiful mouth compressing.

'Such as…?' The sliver of onion tart Lilah had selected was melting in her mouth.

Bastien frowned at her continuing interest. 'It was a fresh start for me in many ways. I was able to see Anatole regularly and I went to a much better school.'

'Obviously you're close to your father,' Lilah commented, relieved to hear that hint of indulgent warmth in his dark drawl when he referred to his parent, because really it was brutally obvious to her that Bastien had been cursed by the most utterly miserable childhood.

'Yes. I'm very fond of Anatole. He may have been a push-over for the wrong women, but as a father, when I needed him, he was the very best,' Bastien stated with quiet pride.

Relief filled Lilah that there had been someone loving in Bastien's life, and she wondered why the idea of nobody having cared for him as a child should disturb her so much. His answers to her questions, however, had given her a certain insight into what had made him so tough and unyielding.

'But that's enough about my life, *glikia mou*,' Bastien continued, smooth as glass. 'Tell me about Josh Burrowes.'

Thrown off balance in her turn, Lilah stiffened, her spine straightening. 'There's nothing to tell. We were on the same course at uni. He's one of my friends.'

Bastien lounged back in his seat as their plates were cleared and the main course served. 'But obviously Josh wants to be something more. You should've told him the truth.'

Lilah's delicate bone structure tightened. 'I gave my friends the same story you suggested I use with my family. I said you'd offered me a job.'

Bastien rested his shimmering dark gaze on the voluptuous promise of her pink lips as she savoured the tender lamb on her plate. 'But you should have come clean for Josh's benefit and told him that you are *mine*.'

Her small white teeth gritted as if she had trodden barefoot on a stone. 'I am *not* yours, Bastien.'

'You *are*,' Bastien purred in immediate contradiction, his accented drawl vibrating through her slender taut frame. 'I know it every time I look at you. No hunger this powerful is one-sided.'

Lilah concentrated on her meal, deeming silence the most diplomatic response. She was very, *very* attracted to him, she admitted inwardly, but no way did she owe him that amount of truth.

As she studied him a snaking curl of warmth stirred low in her pelvis and something tightened even deeper inside her, making her shift uneasily in her seat. The hard, masculine lines of his compellingly beautiful face and the suppressed ferocity of his stunningly intense eyes welded her attention to him.

The first time she had seen Bastien she had known

that she had never seen a more beautiful male speci-
men, and in the two years that had since passed that
fact remained the absolute truth. Bastien was gorgeous. She knew it and he had to know it too.

Perspiration beaded her short upper lip, and as a
member of staff stepped up to the table to refresh their
wine glasses she finally dragged her attention from
Bastien and breathed in deep.

'Stefan's wife is a fantastic chef,' she remarked,
after savouring the first mouthful of a roasted pear
dessert served with chocolate sauce and then pushing the plate away in defeat. 'But I can't find room
for another bite…'

'Coffee?' Bastien prompted.

'No, thanks…' Lilah tensed as he rose fluidly out of
his seat and strolled, jungle-cat-graceful, towards her.

'I react like a teenager around you,' Bastien murmured thickly. 'I can't wait one minute longer.'

Lilah pushed her hands down on the table-edge and
levered herself upright, the layers of her dress spilling out round her in peach abundance. *Time to pay
the piper*, she thought crazily.

Bastien didn't immediately touch her. Instead he
lowered his dark head and circled her mouth almost
teasingly with his own, touching delicate nerve-
endings that screamed with awareness to send pulses
of heat shooting down through her. Her head swam a
little…her knees wobbled.

With a guttural sound low in his throat, Bastien
swept her up in his arms.

'I was so angry with you last night when I heard
about you kissing Josh,' he told her unexpectedly as
he carried her up the stone staircase, contriving that

feat as easily as if she weighed no more than a child. 'Don't let another man touch you in any way while you're with me.'

Her senses still drowning from that extraordinarily intoxicating kiss, Lilah looked up at him with dazed blue eyes and blinked. 'Not much risk of that.'

'Why not? You're a beauty. I saw it... *Josh* saw it,' he grated in harsh reminder.

'But you see things in me that I don't,' she muttered uncomfortably, thinking of the conventionally beautiful fashion models he generally took to his bed.

In comparison, *she* was an aberration. Each and every one of her predecessors that she had seen had been tall, blonde and classically lovely, with Marielle the perfect example of that ideal. Lilah, however, was small and kind of skinny. She had certainly been way too skinny and small in the bust and hip department for any of the boys to look at while she was at school, at an age where having curves had seemed so very important.

'I know that I want you,' Bastien spelt out. 'Everything else fades in the face of that.'

'Everything?' Lilah questioned in disbelief

'Everything...' Bastien husked, breathing in the coconut scent of her shampoo, the faint aroma of the cosmetics she had applied, the fragrance that was uniquely and alluringly hers. And those eyes, he savoured, those sapphire-blue eyes that shone like jewels...

He settled her down on the bed in her room, and the hunger driving him spooked him more than just a little as he looked down at her. That hunger would fade as soon as he'd had her, he told himself cynically, and in all likelihood even the sex would be a disappointment. How could it be otherwise when she had no experience? She couldn't possibly be a truly sensual woman, his rational mind assured him. No truly sensual woman could have stayed untouched as long as she had. She might light up when he looked at her, move in his arms as though she were a sensually aware woman, but it was unlikely that she would have much to offer.

He plucked off her shoes, resisting a decidedly warped urge to stroke those tiny feet of hers. Her virginity was unsettling him, Bastien decided, desperate to suppress the strange thoughts and reactions assailing him. But if she was telling him the truth—and he had to believe it *was* the truth—she would be more his than any other woman had ever been. And for some peculiar reason he liked that idea, he acknowledged in bewilderment. He *really* liked that idea.

'What are you thinking about?' Lilah whispered awkwardly as he ran down the zip on her dress.

'Sex. What else?'

'So I asked a stupid question…deal with it,' Lilah cut back without skipping a beat.

Above her head, an unholy grin slashed Bastien's firmly modelled mouth. He eased the dress off a slight white shoulder and rolled the sleeves down her slim arms, completely attuned to the rising tempo of her breathing.

'I'm not going to harm you,' Bastien breathed with husky assurance. 'Not in any way.'

'I've heard it can hurt,' Lilah told him stubbornly.

'You make the prospect of having sex with me

sound like some form of medieval torture,' Bastien growled.

'I'm going to shut up now. Zipping my mouth,' Lilah spelt out jerkily.

Bastien tugged off the dress and tossed it in a careless heap on the carpet.

'I saw the price tag on that dress, Bastien. You can't treat it like that…it's indecent!'

Bastien flung back his handsome dark head and laughed out loud. 'I thought you were zipping it? Keep quiet…you're making me nervous.'

'What have *you* got to be nervous about?' Lilah demanded in wonderment.

She was finding it a huge challenge not to simply dive below the sheets. There she was, with her body on display, skinny as a rail, clad only in little pale pink lacy pieces of lingerie, and she was being forced to pose like some pantomime seductress on a silk-clad bed. Goosebumps rose on her exposed skin.

Bastien slid a hand into his pocket and withdrew a jewel box. 'This is for you.'

Lilah sat up and took the opportunity to hug her knees, covering up her all-too-bare body as best she could. 'I don't want gifts, Bastien.'

'You will wear it to please me, *koukla mou*. The first time I saw you I wanted to see you in diamonds.' Bastien flipped open the lid on an exquisite shimmering diamond pendant on a chain. He removed it from the box and clasped it round her slender neck.

Taken aback, Lilah didn't move a muscle as he put the pendant on her, feeling the diamond settle cold and heavy against her chilled skin. Bastien stepped back from the bed to remove his jacket and unbutton his shirt, but the whole time his attention was fixed to her.

Lilah met dark golden eyes, tawny as a lion's, and her skin blazed as though he had set her on fire, all sense of being cool in temperature and cold with nerves instantly evaporating. Beneath his bronzed skin he flexed washboard abs and well-developed pectoral muscles, which made her stare for a second or two. He was what a friend had once described as 'built'—powerfully masculine in every way.

She glanced away as his long, tanned fingers reached for the waistband of his trousers, cursing her shyness, her awful self-consciousness with her own body, never mind his. He tossed some foil packets down by the bed, and the nape of her neck prickled.

He came down on the bed still in his boxers, and with the flick of a finger unfastened her wispy bra and pulled it away. She felt her nipples bead, tightening into pointed peaks, and then all of a sudden, or so it seemed to her in her heightened state of nerves, he was laying her down against the pillows and touching those agonisingly sensitive buds with his mouth and his fingers.

A little shudder racked her, and then another. Sensation was breaking through her defences as her breasts tingled and swelled, responding to his attention.

'At least put out the light!' she exclaimed.

'You're beautiful. I need to look at you.'

'I don't want you looking,' she gritted between clenched teeth.

'Close your eyes and pretend I'm not,' Bastien suggested.

Sniping back at him became an impossibility while he was tracing a trail down her slender body with his mouth—kissing here, licking there, discovering the areas of her midriff that responded to his blatant teasing with wild enthusiasm and then slowly shifting down to more intimate areas. His fingers tugged at the waist of her knickers and she stopped breathing. She felt his breath on her...*there*...where it shouldn't be. He found the most achingly sensitive place of all with his clever fingers, and her hips jerked and her breath hitched and she closed her eyes, blocking out the bedroom while becoming even more insanely aware of Bastien's every move.

'You're really practised at this, aren't you?' Lilah commented gruffly.

'We're not about to pursue that subject.'

'No... *Oh!*' A strangled exclamation broke involuntarily from her lips as he stroked his tongue across the little nub of nerve-endings at the apex of her thighs.

With a strangled groan, Bastien came up over her again and crushed her parted lips under his, his tongue plunging only once, but deep, into the moist interior of her mouth, somehow igniting a ball of heat in her pelvis. Startled blue eyes flew wide and clashed with gold circled by lush black lashes.

'Oh...' Bastien said for her, with a wolfish grin that made her tummy flip in a somersault.

Feeling like a child who had foolishly stuck her hand in the fire, Lilah closed her eyes again circumspectly. He punished her by returning to his former activity, his fingertips grazing the inside of her slender thighs, where she had never been touched, and every single point of contact tingled and fired hot, like a burn. He used his mouth on her clitoris and it felt unbearably good, with sensation firing through her on all cylinders as the little tickles and prickles of uncontrollable pleasure mounted and she could no longer stay still. Her neck extended and her hips shifted and rose.

Bastien was touching her so gently. She had not imagined that he could be gentle in bed—had, in truth, been braced for passion, aggression and impatience. He slid a finger into her tight sheath and then another...tender, subtle, tormentingly pleasurable. Her blood was pounding in her veins, her heart was racing, and her whole body was damp with perspiration because everything she was feeling had swiftly become so shockingly intense.

She gave up on the losing battle to resist and opened her mouth on a gasp of reaction. Indeed, she was all reaction now, as waves of response coursed through her in an unstoppable tide. Every tiny caress and exploration he executed engulfed her in another wash of sensation. A tight feeling nestled at the heart of her and she shifted impatiently up towards Bastien, fighting the hollow sense of tortured frustration he had awakened without even fully grasping what it was.

'Bastien!' she exclaimed.

Burnished golden eyes assailed hers. 'Tell me you want me.'

'You know I do!' she flared, with a bitterness she couldn't hide.

'You always did, didn't you?' Bastien grated.

'What do you want? A trophy?' Lilah gasped.

'You *are* my trophy,' Bastien told her, his skilled fingertips moving with expert precision at her tender core and setting off a chain reaction inside her.

The mushroom of heat penned inside Lilah suddenly surged up, with a force that blindsided her and overflowed. Out of her control, her body bucked and twisted and convulsed as the paroxysms of a powerful climax rippled through her slender frame.

Bastien ripped open a foil packet with his strong white teeth. He didn't want to hurt her, he didn't want to harm her in any way, but now she was as wet and receptive as she would ever be. He dragged a pillow under her to tip her hips up more and settled between her spread thighs.

The pleasure Bastien had meted out was like a powerful drug that took time to wear off. Lilah was still in a daze when she felt the pressure of Bastien's entry stretching her tender flesh. Apprehension made her stiffen, a heartbeat before the sharp sting of his full possession made her catch her breath on a huff of dismay. He withdrew, hooked her legs higher and thrust into her yielding body again. This time there was no pain—only the amazing sensation of his fullness inside her.

'It's not hurting,' she told him in relief.

A sheen of perspiration dampened Bastien's lean, handsome features—for such care, such temperate precision, had not come without cost. '*Se thelo*…you feel unbelievable, *hara mou*.'

He rolled his hips in a wicked snaking motion that sent extraordinary sensation flooding through Lilah's pelvis, and her eyes went wide with surprise. As he began to move, the first jolt of excitement careened through her without warning, and then the heat and pressure at the heart of her began to build again. It was a little like hitching a ride on a comet, she thought dizzily, with new responses released and overwhelming her.

Hunger sank talon claws of need into her very bones. Her heart slammed against her ribcage. Her body thrummed and pulsed with rippling darts of pleasure that only stoked her rising hunger. And then the intensity climbed to an unbearable height and pushed her over into the intoxicating grip of wave after wave of sweet, drowning pleasure.

It was over...it was done, Lilah reflected in a daze, crazily conscious of the crash of Bastien's heart against hers, the brush of his hair against her cheek, the dampness of his big, powerful body against hers, the sheer weight of him and the incredible intimacy of their position. Well, she had no complaints, she conceded thoughtfully. In fact, he had made the experience amazing.

In the process of rebooting, after the longest, hottest climax in his considerable experience, Bastien breathed again. He rolled off her and caught her back into his arms, pressing a kiss to her brow without even thinking about it...

And then the thinking kicked in hard. What the hell was he doing? What the hell was he playing at? He didn't *do* touchy-feely—never had and never would. True, she had just given him a pleasure he was finding hard to match in his memory, and he already knew he wanted her again. But it was in the way an alcoholic knew he wanted a drink.

The comparison jarred, but it worked its magic, and Bastien pulled away from the strangely tempting pleasure of having her small, slender body lying against his. He sprang out of bed and headed for the bathroom.

'I'm a restive sleeper and I prefer my own space,' he told her carelessly. 'I'll be sleeping in the room next door.'

Lilah could feel herself freeze with regret and discomfiture. Yet such separation was what sex without caring was like, she scolded herself. It was a bodily thing—not a mental thing. Bastien didn't feel any deep connection with her. He had satisfied his lust for the moment and that was that: he had leapt out of bed and straight into the shower. She could already hear it running.

Had she expected a warmer conclusion to their intimacy?

Well, if she had expected that she was an idiot. After all, wasn't this exactly why she had lost her temper with Bastien two years back? He had only offered sex when she had wanted more, and that had hurt—hurt her pride, hurt her heart too. Wasn't it time she was honest about that? She had started falling for Bastien Zikos the first moment she'd laid eyes on his fallen angel face and stunning eyes.

Of course she hadn't known him in any way, so it had been infatuation rather than love, but his magnetic attraction had called to her on every level. And resisting it, recognising that he could only make her unhappy, had cut deep and filled her with disappointment. But it was the truth and it remained the truth, Lilah conceded ruefully. Bastien skated along happily on the shallow side of life, taking pleasure where he chose, discarding women whenever he got bored... and now she was one of those passing fancies—a sexual whim.

She shifted in the bed, and the ache between her

thighs made her wince and grimace. Once she had said no to Bastien, and evidently that had put a price beyond rubies on her head because he wasn't used to the word *no* and evidently couldn't live with it.

Stop thinking these negative thoughts—stop it, she screamed inside her head, shifting on the pillow as if to clear it. It would be better to concentrate on the positive—think of the factory up and running again, her father back in his office and her little half-siblings secure because their parents were no longer worried sick about how to pay their bills. That was a *good* picture, she told herself soothingly.

And what about all Moore's former employees? Her father had mentioned that he'd be calling a meeting on site today, to discuss the relocation of the factory and the planned reopening. That news would make a lot of people very happy.

Indeed, only a very sad, total loser would sit feeling sorry for herself when she was surrounded by so many positive reminders of what sacrificing her pride had achieved. And she *wasn't* a loser, she told herself angrily, and she *wasn't* going to make a big dramatic deal out of what couldn't be changed. So she had had sex with Bastien—that was all it had been and she could live with that reality.

Sliding out of bed, she walked naked into the dressing room and extracted a robe, knotting the sash at her waist with impatient hands.

As she walked back towards the bathroom, Bastien emerged from it, lean bronzed hips swathed in a towel. Crystalline drops of water sprinkled his hair-roughened chest and his thick black hair curled back damply from his brow.

Seeing her out of bed, he frowned. 'I thought you'd be sleeping.'

'No. I need to shower.' To wash his touch and the memory of it away, Lilah thought frantically, colliding with smouldering golden eyes framed by velvet dark lashes and feeling her heart skipping an entire beat. A shadow of faint black stubble accentuated his hard masculine jawline and his beautifully modelled sensual mouth.

As Delilah attempted to sidestep him, Bastien shot out a hand to enclose her wrist and force her to a halt again. 'You were amazing, *glikia mou*,' he husked.

Mortification drummed up hot below Lilah's skin, but she lifted her tousled head high. 'It wasn't as bad as I thought it would be,' she admitted prosaically, tugging her wrist free to continue on past into the bathroom.

Taken aback, Bastien blinked. How to damn with faint praise, he reflected grimly, thrusting open the communicating door between the bedrooms to stride into his own. And how very typical of Delilah to sting him like a wasp.

Well, what else had Bastien expected from her? Lilah asked herself as she washed. Compliments?

She had told him the truth, even though she knew that she hadn't been strictly fair. He could have been more selfish and less careful with her in bed. To give credit where it was due, he *had* made an effort not to hurt her. Unfortunately his consideration in that respect could not eradicate the ugly fact that Bastien Zikos had blackmailed her into his bed. Yes, she had made the choice to accept his unscrupulous deal, but he could not expect her to start treating him like a much-appreciated and personally chosen lover, could he?

Lilah fell into an exhausted sleep, but Bastien was awakened by a phone call at an ungodly early hour of the following morning and given the kind of news that wrecked both his day and his mood.

CHAPTER SEVEN

'DELILAH!' BASTIEN GRATED from the doorway. 'Get up—I need to talk to you…'

Wondering what she had done to deserve such a rude awakening, Lilah opened her eyes only wide enough to peer at the pretty miniature alarm clock adorning the bedside cabinet. It was barely seven in the morning.

Blinking rapidly, in an effort to get her brain functioning again, she swallowed back a yawn and struggled to focus on Bastien's tall, powerful figure by the door that appeared to communicate between her room and his. 'What's wrong?' she asked sleepily.

'We'll discuss it when you get up,' Bastien framed darkly, glittering dark eyes settling on her with chilling distaste. 'I'll see you downstairs in five minutes.'

Exasperated, Lilah rolled her eyes. In mega-bossy mode, Bastien infuriated her—and she refused to be ordered round like an unruly schoolgirl. On the other hand, something bad had clearly happened, and he evidently thought she was involved in it in some way—because why else would he have looked at her as if she had just crawled out from under a stone? Even so...he expected her downstairs within *five minutes*? In his dreams!

Scrambling out of bed, she went into the dressing room and searched through innumerable drawers to find her own humble clothing, from which she selected denim shorts and a simple white tank top to deal with the early-morning heat she could feel in the air. Following a quick shower and the application of a little light make-up, Lilah stalked downstairs in flat canvas shoes, ready for whatever Bastien might choose to throw at her.

With a noisy scrabbling of his claws on the hallway tiles, Skippy hurled himself at Lilah's knees. Stefan informed her that Bastien was waiting for her in his study and directed her down a corridor. Breakfast, he added helpfully, would be served out on the terrace.

Bastien was lodged by the window of a large, imposing book-lined room with his broad back turned towards her. Muscles flexed beneath the taut, expensive fabric of his jacket. He swung round, and she was irritated that she immediately noted that his dark designer suit acted as a superb tailored frame for his wide shoulders, narrow hips and long, powerful thighs.

Hard, dark golden eyes zeroed in on her, and involuntarily, Lilah paled at the intensity of that tough, questioning scrutiny.

Mouth curling, Bastien scanned her appearance in the worn shorts and casual top, neither of which had featured in her officially sanctioned new wardrobe. The adolescent outfit combined with her long, tumbled hair and only a touch of make-up made her look very much like a teenager. Admittedly, though, an incredibly pretty teenager.

Pretty…an old-fashioned word which didn't belong in his vocabulary, Bastien reflected in exasperation at his lack of concentration. *Hot* would be a more appropriate word, and from the top of her curly dark head down to her pert breasts, tiny waist and slim sexy legs and the very soles of her tiny canvas-shod feet, Delilah looked amazingly hot.

He tensed, reluctant to embrace that thought, but his body was already doing that for him, reacting with libidinous enthusiasm to her presence.

'What's this all about?' she asked in apparent innocence.

In answer, Bastien crossed the room and lifted his tablet from the desk top. *'This!'* he bit out wrathfully.

Lilah moved closer to stare at the British newspaper headline depicted on the screen.

Dufort Pharmaceuticals to join Zikos stable?

'I still don't know what you're talking about,' Lilah pointed out, although she had the vaguest recollection that she *had* heard that company's name mentioned during Bastien's deliberations with his staff that first evening in the hotel in London. Unfortunately, since she had not really been listening, she had not the foggiest idea why Bastien was so annoyed.

'Someone leaked confidential information to the press that night in London…and I believe it was *you!*' Bastien breathed with raw emphasis.

Lilah's spine snapped straight as an arrow, her blue eyes rounding with disbelief as she tipped her head back to look him in the eye. *'Me?'* she spluttered incredulously. 'Are you nuts?'

His cool, sculpted mouth hardened. 'You're the only person who left the suite during my discussions with the team that evening. According to my sources, someone tipped off the press halfway through that evening. The bodyguard accompanying you saw you making several phone calls. You also had contact with a journalist.'

Her soft mouth had fallen open in shock, because she could barely credit what she was hearing. How dared he accuse her of being some sort of business spy when he had shared a bed with her the night before? How *dared* he?

Her colour rose even higher when she recalled that he had actually slept apart from her, and she replied curtly, 'I can't believe you're serious. Why would you suspect me of stealing confidential information? Why would anyone want to leak it?'

'The tip that I'm planning to buy Dufort Pharmaceuticals is worth hundreds of thousands of pounds on the open market.'

'But I didn't leak it. I didn't discuss it with anyone,' Lilah remonstrated. 'Why would I have? Apart from anything else, I'm not interested in that information and I wasn't really listening to what you and your staff were talking about… I was watching TV.'

'You were present throughout. You heard *everything,*' Bastien reminded her obdurately.

'At least four members of your staff were present as well! Why are you picking on *me*?' Lilah demanded in a furious counter-attack.

'I have absolute faith in my personal team.'

'I'm delighted to hear it, but obviously your faith is misplaced in at least *one* of them,' Lilah pointed out thinly. 'Because I can assure you that *I* didn't sell any information about your business dealings to anyone.'

'I don't trust you,' Bastien admitted harshly, because he had looked at the evidence from every angle and the conclusion that Delilah had sold the information made the most sense.

Lilah set the tablet back down on the table. 'Well, I'm not playing the fall guy, here, so you have a problem. I suggest you stop wasting time suspecting me of doing the dirty on you and search out the real mole. Why would you suspect me anyway? I've got too much to lose in this situation.'

'How?' Bastien gritted, unimpressed, and particularly outraged because he had wakened to the phone call forewarning him of the press release with a powerful craving to enjoy her small slender body again.

'You gave my father a job, which means a lot to him. I wouldn't do anything to jeopardise his continuing employment,' Lilah argued vehemently. 'I'm not an idiot, Bastien. If I betrayed your trust you wouldn't stick to our agreement.'

His hard mouth set into a grim, clenched line, Bastien said nothing. He could not count on her loyalty. She was a woman, not an employee, and she might well want to punish him for the choice he had offered her. That gave her a good motive, and she had certainly had the opportunity that night to pass on news of his acquisition plans for Dufort Pharmaceuticals.

Worst of all, the damage was done now that the facts were out in the public domain. Either he paid through the nose to acquire a company which was no longer the bargain it had been or he decided to back off altogether.

'You have cost me a great deal of money,' Bastien told her harshly.

'You don't *listen*. You haven't listened to a single word I've said in my own defence, have you?' Lilah accused, her eyes flaring an almost other-worldly blue with suppressed rage. 'But I'll say it one more time… *not guilty*. I didn't gossip about your business plans or pass them on to anyone who could profit from knowing about them. I made two separate phone calls after leaving the hotel suite—one to my father and the other to my stepmother. On neither call did I mention your business discussions. The journalist who approached me was a gossip columnist, *not* a financial reporter…' Her voice trailed off as she studied his lean, darkly handsome face, which was shuttered and forbidding. 'You're *still* not listening to me…'

Seething resentment was flaming up through the temper which Lilah was struggling to keep under control. Her hands closed into punitive fists. Even before she had answered his charges she had clearly been judged and found guilty, which was hideously unfair.

'Tell me, do you distrust *all* women or just me?' she slammed.

'Women are very clever at establishing a man's weaknesses and playing on them,' Bastien countered.

'And your only weakness is protecting your profit margins?' Lilah folded her arms defensively and breathed in slow and deep. 'What you really need, Bastien, is a proper challenge.'

The lush black lashes enhancing his gorgeous eyes

lifted, to reveal glittering dark gold chips full of stark enquiry. 'Meaning…?'

'All bets are off between us until you find out who *did* betray your trust and you clear my name.'

'*Diavelos*…what are you trying to say?' Bastien demanded curtly.

'No sex until you sort this out,' Lilah told him in the baldest possible terms. 'I refuse to sleep with a man who thinks I'm some sort of thief and fraudster.'

Dark colour accentuated the exotic line of Bastien's supermodel cheekbones. 'That is *not* what our agreement entails and nor is it an accurate version of what I said to you.'

'Stuff the agreement!' Lilah flung back at him wildly. 'You can't make the kind of accusation you just made and then act like it shouldn't make a difference to me. You check out every employee who was there that night, and anyone else who knew about your interest in that company, you find out who sold you down the river…and then you *apologise* to me.'

Bastien sent her an incredulous glance, dark eyes flashing the purest gold, pride and anger etching taut hard lines into his lean, darkly handsome features. 'Apologise?'

'Yes, you *will* apologise—even if it *kills* you!' Lilah launched at him full volume, all control of her temper abandoned in the face of such wanton provocation. 'You have deeply insulted me, and I refuse to accept that kind of treatment. And, by the way, you can keep this…' Digging the diamond pendant out of her pocket, Lilah set it down on the table. 'I didn't ask for it, I don't appreciate it, and I will not wear it again unless you apologise to me!'

'Are you finished?' Bastien demanded wrathfully. 'I don't *do* apologies.'

'Fortunately it's never too late to learn good manners!' Lilah stated without hesitation, before turning on her heel with Skippy following close behind like a shadow.

She walked out to the shaded terrace for the breakfast Stefan had promised her.

She was trembling when she collapsed down limply into a seat by the table, but she didn't regret a word she had said to Bastien. She had to be tough to deal with him or he would roar over her like a fireball and burn her to ashes in his wake. Bastien had questioned her integrity, and Lilah was proud of her integrity. She was no angel, but she didn't lie, cheat or defraud, or go behind people's backs to score or make a profit, she thought angrily.

It shook her that he could misjudge her to such an extent even after they had become lovers. And that she should even *have* that thought warned her that she was still being very naïve the nature of their relationship. Their bodies had connected—*not* their minds. Bastien did not know her in the way she had always assumed her first lover would know her. But did that excuse him for assuming on the flimsiest of evidence that she would sneakily sell confidential information about his business plans?

She was already convinced that Bastien did not hold a very high opinion of women—at least not those who shared his bed. She shuddered as she remembered the cold, heavy feel of that brilliant glittering diamond at her throat the night before. Did he believe that expensive gifts of diamonds would excuse bad behaviour? Had other women taught him that?

Nibbling little bites of a chocolate croissant and sipping fresh tea, Lilah tried to be realistic about Bastien. He was incredibly good-looking and incredibly rich…and incredibly good in bed, she affixed, hot-cheeked. For many women his wealth alone would be sufficient to excuse almost all character flaws. Not that it would bother Bastien that *she* was unwilling to overlook those flaws, Lilah reflected ruefully, because Bastien was only interested in sex.

And every time she came back to that salient fact it was like crashing into a solid brick wall, which concluded all further speculation.

Having eaten, she asked Stefan for a bottle of water and went off to explore, with Skippy bouncing in excitement round her feet. She could not contemplate sitting around in the chateau submissively, as if she was waiting for Bastien to vindicate her or justify her very existence.

The gardens surrounding the chateau were typically French and formal, lined with precise low box hedges and sculpted topiary set off with immaculate paths, weathered urns and gravel. She balanced like a dancer to walk the edge of an old stone fountain, sending shimmering water drops down into the basin below.

From above, Bastien watched her from a window in the huge first-floor salon. Delilah was larking about like a leggy child, while repeatedly throwing that damned stupid squeaky toy for her even sillier yappy little dog. Delilah outraged his sense of order—

because he did not like the unexpected, and in every way she kept on tossing him the unexpected.

He was willing to admit that she was not behaving like a guilty woman. At the same time he knew women who could act the most legendary Hollywood stars off the screen. His own mother had always put on an impressively deceptive show for his father, who had adored Athene to the bitter end.

But while Anatole had been easily fooled Bastien had always had a low opinion of human beings in general, and he preferred hard truths to polite lies and social pretences. He had also learned that the richer he became, the more people tried to take advantage of him, and he was always on the watch for false flattery and sexual or financial inducements.

In fact, when anyone injured Bastien he hit back twice as hard to punish them and teach them respect. He was not weak. He was not foolish. He was not forgiving. That had been his mantra growing up, when he had had to prove to his own satisfaction that he was stronger than the feeble but kindly father he loved. No woman would ever make a fool out of Bastien Zikos as his mother had made a fool out of his father.

His mother, Athene, had ridiculed his father, calling him 'Mr Sorry', because every time Anatole had visited his mistress and his son he had invariably been grovelling and apologising for something, in a futile effort to keep the peace in the double life of infidelity he led. That was why Bastien was unaccustomed to making apologies of any kind. To his way of thinking, apologies stank to high heaven—of weakness, deceit and cowardly placation.

But at that precise moment Bastien was shocked

to acknowledge that he had not thought through the likely consequences of choosing to confront Delilah immediately about the newspaper leak. Shouldn't he have kept his suspicions to himself until he had established definitive proof? Why the hell had he lost his temper with her like that? Loss of temper meant loss of focus and control, and invariably delivered a poor result. That was why he never allowed himself to lose his temper. Yet on two separate occasions now he had gone off like a rocket with Delilah. Naturally she was playing the innocent and offended card— what else could she do?

'I'll check out every member of your team,' declared Manos, his chief of security, in receipt of his employer's instructions. 'I'm aware that Miss Moore had the opportunity, but somehow she doesn't seem the type.'

'*Is* there a type?' Bastien asked drily, his attention locked to the sway of Delilah's shapely derrière in those tight, faded shorts and the slender perfection of her thighs below the ragged hems.

His fingertips tingled at the idea of trailing those shorts off her slender body and settling her under him again. He cut off that incendiary image and hoped she wasn't planning to leave the grounds dressed in so provocative an outfit.

His strong white teeth gritted. His continuing sexual hunger for Delilah had made her important to Bastien in a way he utterly despised. If she realised how much he was still lusting after her she would use it against him—of course she would. He much preferred the immediate boredom that usually settled in for him after a fresh sexual conquest. He needed to move on, he told himself urgently. He needed to move on from Delilah Moore in particular...*fast*.

The morning flew past while he worked, furiously trying to counteract the damage done by this morning's news report. He went downstairs for lunch and discovered that he had the terrace all to himself, Delilah having opted to have a simple snack in her room. His teeth gritted again and he studied Skippy, lying in a panting heap in the shadows. She had evidently roved far enough around the estate to totally exhaust the dog, which admittedly had pitifully short, stumpy legs.

After a moment's contemplation of the miniature dachshund's lolling pink tongue, Bastien emptied some fruit out of a bowl and poured water into it before putting it down for the animal. Skippy lurched up and drank in noisy gulps. After trotting back indoors, he reappeared with his squeaky toy in his mouth and laid it tenderly at Bastien's feet...where it was ignored.

Full of restive energy, Lilah paced her room. Was she supposed to be a prisoner at the chateau? She refused to sit around and wait as if she had no existence without Bastien to direct her every move.

Recalling the pretty little village of Lourmarin, which they had passed through shortly before their arrival, she decided that what she really needed was an afternoon of sightseeing. Having washed the dust off her canvas-shod feet, she pulled on a white sun dress and sandals before heading downstairs to find Stefan and ask if it was possible for her to visit the village.

Within minutes a car drew up outside to collect

her, and she skipped down the steps, smiling at Ciro as he slid in beside the driver.

Bastien was disconcerted when he discovered that Delilah had left the chateau. He hadn't expected that. Frustration at the childish avoidance tactics she was using on him coursed through him, and he had Manos check with her driver. He set out for Lourmarin in a short temper.

What *was* it about Delilah? She was a lot of trouble, demanding so much more effort and attention from him than other women did. *Why* was he allowing her to wind him up? And why did he still want her, regardless of how much she annoyed him?

It was market day in Lourmarin, and Bastien's disposition was not improved by a lengthy search for a parking spot.

When he tracked Delilah down he heard her laughter first, and even that contrived to annoy him— because two years had passed since *he* had last heard her laugh. In addition, although he hated gigglers, there had always been something incredibly infectious about Delilah's giggles. He saw her seated on a café terrace, her white dress spilling round her, black hair framing her animated face as she laughed and chattered to Ciro, at one point even touching the younger man's arm with a familiarity that set Bastien's teeth on edge.

Ciro, not surprisingly, wore a slack-jawed expression of masculine admiration.

'Delilah…'

The sound of that deep, dark drawl banished the pleasure of Lilah's sun-drenched surroundings and stiffened her spine as much as if a poker had been attached to it. She lifted her head and fell into the smouldering golden sensuality of Bastien's intent scrutiny. His dark-fallen-angel face was grim, but nothing could detract from the sheer beauty of it, nor the mesmeric potency of his gaze.

'Been looking for me?' she quipped, setting down her glass of wine. 'I doubt that your presence here is an unlucky coincidence.'

In answer, Bastien reached down to close a hand over hers and used that connection to literally lift her upright out of her chair. 'Thanks for looking after her for me, Ciro. We're heading home now.'

'You're making me feel like I shouldn't have gone out,' she whispered thinly as he walked her away.

'No, what you shouldn't have done is flirt with Ciro,' Bastien told her drily.

'I wasn't *flirting* with him!' Lilah snapped back in irate protest, practically running to keep up with his long stride as, with one strong hand gripping hers, he cut through the clumps of pedestrians and dragged her in his wake. It didn't help that almost two glasses of wine had left her head swimming a little…

'He should know better than to get that close to a woman who's mine,' Bastien added grittily, hanging on to his temper by a hair's breadth and ready to grab her up into his arms and bodily carry her back to the car at the first sign of rebellion.

'I'm *not* yours!' Lilah fired back at him with ringing vehemence. 'I simply agreed to sleep with you until you got bored…that's all!'

As that startling statement rang out, Bastien watched curious heads swivel in their direction and compressed his sensual mouth. 'You're shouting.

Would you like a megaphone to share that confession further afield?' he demanded in a tone of incredulous reproof.

'I wasn't shouting,' Lilah hissed with a furious little shrug of her slight shoulders, her bright blue eyes remaining defiant. 'I was merely pointing out the basic terms of our agreement. It was a devil's bargain but I've stuck to *my* side of it. The least I deserve from you in return is respect and consideration.'

'When do *I* qualify for some respect?' Bastien enquired with honeyed scorn.

'When you do something *worthy* of respect,' Lilah slammed back without hesitation.

Unlocking the Ferrari, Bastien scooped Delilah up and stowed her in the passenger seat, impervious to her vocal complaints. He wanted to shout at her. For the first time since his childhood, anger and frustration had reached a peak inside him and he actually wanted to shout. Evidently Delilah really was toxic for him, challenging his self-discipline and making him react in unnervingly abnormal ways.

'And why are you dragging me back to the chateau anyway?' Lilah queried truculently as he swung in bedside her. 'You should be avoiding me like the plague right now.'

In slow motion, Bastien twined his fingers slowly into her long black hair to turn her face up while his other hand framed a delicate cheekbone to hold her steady. The crash of his mouth down on hers felt as inevitable to him as the drowning heat of the summer sun in the sky.

Lilah jerked, as if he had stamped her with a burning brand. Her hand rose of its own volition and delved

into his luxuriant black hair, fingertips roaming blissfully over his well-shaped skull. Hunger coursed
through her like a hot river of lava, scorching and
setting her alight wherever it touched.

She had never felt hunger like it. In fact, it was as
if Bastien's lovemaking the night before had released
some dam of response inside her that could no longer be suppressed. The resulting ache between her
legs and the sheer longing to be intimately touched
physically hurt.

Long fingers eased below the hem of her dress and
roamed boldly higher.

In a sudden movement Lilah pulled back and
slapped her hand down on top of Bastien's to prevent
him from conducting a more intimate exploration.
'No,' she told him shakily.

Bastien swore long and low in Greek, the pulsing
at his groin downright painful. He wanted to yank her
out of the car, splay her across the bonnet and sink into
her hard and fast. He gritted his teeth, rammed home
his seat belt and drove out onto the narrow twisting
road that snaked down the mountain.

The screaming tension inside the car made Lilah's
mouth run dry. It was his own fault. He should never
have touched her, she thought piously, pride making
her ignore the hollow dissatisfaction of her own body.
But then *every* time Bastien touched her he shocked
her, she conceded grudgingly, because somehow he
always made her desperate to rip his clothes off.

Mortified, she dragged her attention from him and
stared out of the car, mouth swollen and tingling.

Manos was waiting for Bastien when he returned.
Delilah took the opportunity to race upstairs.

Bastien did not want an audience as he learned that preliminary enquiries had revealed damning facts about one of his personal staff. Andreas Theodakis had taken a smoke break that evening in London, and had been seen using his phone out on the balcony. Furthermore, a colleague had volunteered the news that Theodakis was a gambler. Bastien knew then in his gut that in all likelihood Andreas had tipped off the business press about the Dufort Pharmaceuticals deal.

'I should have confirmation for you one way or another by the end of tomorrow,' Manos concluded.

Bastien had a stiff drink and brooded over the information. No way was he saying sorry when Delilah had made such a big deal of him humbling himself. Indeed, he cringed at the prospect.

He dined alone at his desk, burying himself in work—as was his habit when anything bothered him.

A scrabbling noise made him glance up from the screen, and he frowned at Skippy, who must have sneaked in when Stefan had delivered Bastien's meal. The miniature dachshund was engaged in using a briefcase on the floor as a springboard to the chair on the other side of Bastien's desk. Skippy made it up on to the chair and then with a sudden tremendous leap reached the desk top, whereupon he trotted towards Bastien, his long ears flapping, and dropped his squeaky toy beside Bastien's laptop.

With a sigh, Bastien scooped up the dog before it skidded off the desk and broke its legs, and settled it on the floor. Then, lifting the toy with distaste, he flung it—sending Skippy into a race of panting pleasure.

'I will only throw it once,' he warned the animal.

Unable to get back to work, he walked out onto the balcony and groaned out loud as he paced in the warm evening air. His muscles were stiff.

Banishing Skippy, who was showing annoying signs of wanting to follow him, Bastien went down to the basement gym in an effort to work off some of his tension. A marathon swim, followed by a long, violently cathartic session with the punch bag, sent Bastien into the shower.

All he needed was a good night's sleep and a clear head, he told himself urgently when he was tempted to approach Delilah. He did not need or want *her*...

Lilah sat up late in bed, reading, and fell asleep with the light on, wakening disorientated at around three in the morning. On her way back from the bathroom she thought she heard someone cry out, and she went to the window and brushed back the curtain to look down at the moonlit garden below. Nothing stirred... not even the shadows.

When the sound came again she realised that it had come from Bastien's room, and she crossed the polished wooden floor to listen behind the communicating door with a frown etched between her brows.

The sound of a shout galvanised her into opening the door. Bastien was a dark shape, thrashing about wildly in the bed, and choked cries interspersed with Greek words were breaking from him.

There was no way on earth that Lilah could walk away and leave him suffering like that. He was having a nightmare, that was all, but it was clearly a terrifying one.

She hovered uncertainly by the side of the bed,

and then closed her hand firmly round a sleek tanned muscular shoulder to shake it.

'Wake up, Bastien…it's just a dream,' she told him gently.

CHAPTER EIGHT

ARMS FLAILING AND eyes wild, Bastien reared up and closed a hand round her throat, dragging her down to the bed on top of him as he struggled to focus on her.

'Bastien…it's Lilah!' she gasped, in stricken dismay at the effect of her intervention. 'You were stuck in a bad dream. I was trying to wake you up.'

'Delilah…' Bastien framed dazedly, shifting his tousled dark head in confusion, his eyes glittering dark as night in the faint light emanating from her room. He blinked. 'What are you doing in here?'

'You were having a really bad nightmare,' she repeated as she levered herself away from him and settled on the empty side of the bed. The dampness of perspiration sheened his lean dark features and he was still trembling almost imperceptibly. 'What on earth has got you that worked up?'

'I put my hand round your neck… Did I hurt you?' Bastien demanded, switching on the bedside light and tipping up her chin to examine the faint red fingermarks marring her slender white throat. '*Diavelos*, Delilah… I'm sorry. I could have seriously injured you. You should never have come near me when I was like that. I'm very restless. That's why I always sleep alone.'

'I'm fine… I'm fine… I was worried about you,' she admitted.

'Why the hell would you be worried about a guy who doesn't treat you with respect or consideration?' Bastien prompted grimly.

'I was really concerned about you,' Lilah countered, ignoring that question because she could not have answered it even to her own satisfaction. 'What on earth were you dreaming about?'

His lean dark features were shuttered. 'Believe me, you don't want to know.'

In an abrupt movement that took her by surprise, he pulled her backwards into his arms. Little tremors were still running through his big powerful frame.

Lilah released her breath in a bemused hiss. 'Try to relax,' she urged him, aware of the shattering tension still holding his muscles taut in his big body.

'Don't try to mother me, *glikia mou*,' Bastien growled warningly, resting back against the pillows and breathing in slow and deep before exhaling again. 'That's not what I want from you.'

'Well, you're not getting anything else,' Lilah warned him bluntly.

At that tart response unholy amusement quivered through Bastien's lean, powerful frame and he laughed out loud.

'So, what was the dream about?' she prompted again.

In the low light, Bastien rolled his eyes and laced his fingers round her abdomen as she relaxed back against him. 'I was getting beaten up… It's something that happened when I was a child.'

Taken by surprise, Lilah twisted round in the circle of his arms and lifted her head to look directly at him. 'When you were a *child*?'

'I walked in on my mother, in bed with her drug-dealing boyfriend. She didn't intervene. She was terrified that I would accidentally let it drop to Anatole that she had other men because Anatole paid all our bills.'

Lilah frowned down at him in disbelief. 'For goodness' sake—what age were you?'

He shrugged a broad shoulder. 'Five…six years old? I really don't remember. But I almost died because Athene didn't take me to hospital until the next day—and then not until she had coached me to say that I'd fallen down the stairs.'

'Damaged'—that was how Marielle Durand had labelled Bastien. And for the first time Lilah truly saw that in him, recognising the angry defensive pain in his eyes. His mother had neither wanted nor loved him, and by the sound of it had been a cruel and selfish parent.

Lilah recognised his discomfiture under her continuing scrutiny and she looked away, twisting round to give him back his privacy. Her eyes were smarting with tears, though.

As a teenager she had felt so sorry for herself when her father had been bringing a string of different women home for the night and she'd had to occasionally share the breakfast table with strangers. In retrospect, though, she was realising that she could have suffered much worse experiences, and that no matter how much her father's sex-life had embarrassed her he had always looked after her and loved her.

Bastien had not been so lucky.

'I don't know why I told you that,' Bastien breathed in a harsh undertone.

'Because I'm very persistent when I want to know something,' Lilah declared, with deliberate lightness of tone. 'And because you're shaken up.'

'I don't *get* shaken up,' Bastien asserted predictably.

'Of course not,' Lilah traded, tongue in cheek.

Without warning Bastien sprang off the bed, carting her with him.

'What—?'

'I need a shower,' he ground out.

'I'll go back to—'

'You're not going anywhere,' Bastien contradicted, striding into the en-suite bathroom and straight into the spacious shower with her still in his arms.

'Bastien…what on earth…?' she exclaimed in angry disbelief as he elbowed a button and warm water cascaded down on her from all directions, instantly plastering the nightdress she wore to her body.

Bastien knew he was acting like a mad man, but he was on automatic pilot and he didn't care—because his hunger for Delilah at that moment was overwhelming. He hauled her dripping body up against him and closed his mouth hungrily to the luscious soft pink enticement of hers, long fingers stroking her wet hair back from her face.

Lilah's hands closed over his broad shoulders, clenching there to steady herself as the hot, demanding intensity of the kiss took her by storm. His tongue delved deep into the moist interior of her mouth, plundering a response from her.

She recognised the force of his need, suspecting that Bastien was not in control the way he usually was. Rather than dismaying her, that suspicion excited her beyond bearing—because Bastien was generally so controlled that he unnerved her. In fact, the unashamed passion he was unleashing now was much more to Lilah's taste, and it went to her head even more strongly than the wine that afternoon.

Her hands skimmed down over his lean, strong torso. She could feel the hard urgency of his erection against her midriff, and before she could even let herself think about what she was about to do she had dropped to her knees. The warm water teemed down, somehow separating her from the world and from all the anxious self-judgement that kept her from experimenting. For the first time ever she felt free to do simply as she liked. As she liked and as she wanted. And she was proud of that inner spur of passion for the first time.

Slender fingers roved up over Bastien's hair-roughened muscular thighs, and she was smiling at his sudden ferocious tension as she bent her head—all woman, all feminine power.

Bastien groaned, threw his head back against the tiles and arched his hips to facilitate her, making no attempt to hide his pleasure as she worked magic with her mouth and her tongue and her agile fingers.

His potent reaction gave Lilah a high. For once she was in charge, and what she lacked in experience she more than made up for with creativity and enthusiasm.

Allowing himself to be out of control in any way

was a dark and seductive novelty for Bastien. And when he could no longer withstand the hot, all-encompassing pleasure of her mouth, he bent down and hauled her up to him, bracing her against the tiles as he hitched up her nightdress and clamped her slim thighs to his waist. He plunged into the glorious tight wet heat of her body with a raw groan of masculine pleasure.

Still tender from her first experience the night before, Lilah felt every inch of Bastien's smooth hard length as he surged inside her. Her arms wrapped round his neck for support, her head falling back as he withdrew and surged deep again. Excitement engulfed her in a heady rush, her heart slamming inside her chest, her breath hitching and breaking in her throat.

So sensitive was she that as Bastien increased the tempo and hammered into her the pleasure swelled to an almost painful intensity. The rising heat within her finally soothed the hollow ache of tormenting hunger, and she gasped and moaned in delight. Her hips writhed against the cold tiles as she reached a climax too powerful to restrain and it swept her over the edge, sending intoxicating explosions of blissful sensation rippling through her quivering length as she sagged in Bastien's powerful hold.

By the time she had floated down from that dizzy peak of satisfaction Bastien was trailing off her sodden nightdress and wrapping her in a towel.

'You didn't say sorry…this wasn't supposed to happen between us…' Lilah mumbled in limp reminder as she reclaimed her wits.

'I jumped to conclusions. I was wrong. It appears that one of my staff *was* responsible for the leak to the press,' Bastien shared with taut reluctance as he grabbed up another towel to fold it round her dripping hair.

'Told you so,' Lilah remarked ungraciously.

'I lost my temper with you. I don't *do* that,' Bastien growled half under his breath in explanation. 'When anger is in control, mistakes are made.'

'So you're saying sorry?' Lilah whispered, weak as a kitten as he laid her down on the soft firmness of his bed and pulled a sheet over her cooling skin.

Bastien didn't answer. He didn't do apologies, but he was quite happy for her to assume that he had apologised. He was intent on her, still worked up in an unsettling way he didn't understand. She made him feel alive, crazily *alive*, and for some reason he hadn't had enough of her yet. One taste of her had only made him hunger for more.

He framed her face with long dark fingers, rejoicing in the silky softness of her skin and the rosy purity of her features. He savoured her swollen pink mouth with his own, revelling in the taste of her and the thundering race of his heartbeat as the hunger raged through him again like a tempest.

Bastien kissed with the same wild potency with which he made love, Lilah reflected dizzily, and the pulse of heat was awakening in her pelvis again as his tongue tangled with hers and flicked the ultra-sensitive roof of her mouth in a teasing assault that made her push up against him. Desire shimmied through her like an electrical storm, lighting up every place he touched, from the peaks of her straining nipples to the infinitely delicate damp flesh between her thighs.

'I still want you, *glikia mou*,' Bastien grated, and his stunning dark golden eyes were bright with lingering wonder at that anomaly as he ran his mouth down hungrily over the sweet mounds of her small breasts, licking and tasting and nipping to make her slim body writhe frantically.

As he reached the heart of her arousal and dallied to torment her with every carnal caress he had ever learned she gasped his name over and over again, and he very much liked the sound of his own name on her lips.

Lilah had not believed he could make her want him again so soon, when her body was still heavy with fulfilment, but somehow he'd pushed her to the raw, biting edge of feverish need again, and the first plunge of his powerful male heat inside her felt gloriously necessary.

Her spine arched, wild torrents of joyous sensation cascading through her quivering body as he pushed back her thighs and rose over her, pounding into her tight depths with driving hunger. She thrashed under him, every nerve-ending electrified by the pagan rhythm of his hard thrusts and the inexorable climb towards another climax. When it came, she hit a peak and shattered like glass, shocked by the white-hot intensity of excitement exploding inside her.

She fell back against the pillows, utterly drained of energy, while Bastien groaned long and low and shuddered with pleasure.

Bastien drank in the scent of Delilah's shampoo as he struggled to get his breath back. Her silky hair had the sweet fresh perfume of a summer meadow. Her arms were still wrapped around him and he lifted his tousled dark head to drop a brief but appreciative kiss on her brow.

'You're an unbeatable cure for a nightmare, *glikia mou*,' he husked with wicked amusement, rolling free of her to head for the bathroom.

The minute he arrived there he realised too late what was missing. He had not used a condom—not that last time or the time before it in the shower.

It was a very dangerous oversight that chilled Bastien and made him want to punch something hard in angry self-loathing. The shower beat down on him while some of the worst memories of his life engulfed him and he shuddered, knowing what he must do, knowing that this time around he would not dare to walk away and simply hope for the best.

Delilah needed to know that, whatever happened, her future and that of any child she had would be totally secure.

A towel knotted round his lean brown hips, he strode back into the bedroom and proceeded to disconcert Lilah with what she deemed to be inappropriate questions.

'Why on earth are you asking me such things?' she demanded tautly, her colour high from embarrassment.

'We've had sex twice without a condom,' Bastien told her grimly. 'I'm regularly tested and I'm clean, so there is no risk of an infection. I'm merely trying to calculate the odds of conception.'

Lilah's whole body turned cold at the threat of an unplanned pregnancy. She hadn't noticed the lack of contraception—had been as lost in passion as he must have been. That acknowledgement stung, because she knew how important it was to take precautions and protect herself from such consequences.

Ashamed that she could have been so reckless and immature as to overlook such necessities, she answered his questions about her menstrual cycle and watched his frown steadily darken.

'Obviously you could conceive. You're young, fertile...naturally there's a good chance.' His beautiful mouth compressed hard. 'We'll get married as soon as I can get it organised.'

'*Married?*' Lilah parrotted in a strangled shriek, sitting up in bed with a sudden jerk, her eyes awash with disbelief as she stared back at him.

His unfathomable dark eyes glittered. 'You need to know that whatever happens I'm there for you, and a wedding ring is the only security a man can offer a woman in that situation.'

'People don't rush off and get married simply because of a contraceptive oversight,' Lilah whispered shakily. 'That would be crazy.'

'I know exactly what I'm doing. My first child was aborted when I was only twenty-one,' Bastien explained, shattering her with that flat statement of fact. 'I refuse to risk a repeat of that experience.'

Lilah was poleaxed. 'But...but I—'

'So we'll get married. And if it transpires that we have no reason to *stay* married we'll get an equally quick divorce,' Bastien assured her smoothly, as though such a fast turnaround from marriage to divorce would be the most natural development in the world.

'But we can't just get married on the off-chance that I might be pregnant,' she muttered incredulously.

'If you have conceived we'll be married and you'll be less tempted to consider a termination,' Bastien pointed out with assurance. 'We don't need to publicise our marriage in the short term, or drag anyone else into our predicament. We'll have a private wedding.'

Stunned, Lilah flopped down flat again, exhaustion rolling over her like a hefty blanket. It was all too much to take in. The shocking revelations of his past and the sheer impossibility of their future.

'We'll argue about it in the morning,' she countered in a daze. 'You're thinking worst-case scenario.'

'No, I've already *lived* the worst-case scenario,' Bastien contradicted with an edge of derision. 'And that was losing the child I wanted because the woman concerned decided that she didn't.'

Lilah winced, recognising the edge of bitterness in his dark deep drawl. She wondered who that woman had been, while marvelling at how much Bastien was revealing about himself. He had a deep, sensitive side to his nature that astonished her. For the first time she wondered what it had felt like for him—a man who wanted a child with a woman when the woman did not feel the same. Her heart ached for him. Clearly he had grieved that loss, but he had also interpreted the termination as a personal rejection and a humiliation, which struck her as even more sad.

Without comment she watched him stride lithely back to his own room, utterly unconcerned by his nudity. But why would he be concerned? an inner voice asked. When you were *that* perfectly built and physically beautiful you had to be aware of the fact.

She stretched out in the big bed, wondering why

she wished he had stayed…wondering why what he had told her had left her feeling bereft and unsettled.

Had he loved the woman who had chosen not to have his child? Why did it bother her that Bastien might once have cared deeply for another woman? Evidently back then Bastien had not been quite as emotionally detached and untouchable as he was now. He had cared…he had been hurt. Why did that touch something deep down inside her and wound her? It couldn't be jealousy… It couldn't possibly be jealousy.

She didn't care about Bastien in the smallest way, Lilah assured herself agitatedly. Bastien Zikos was simply the man she'd slept with to fulfil her side of their agreement to be his mistress. That was all he wanted from her. And all she had ever wanted from him was that he reopen the factory and re-employ her father.

Honesty urged Lilah to admit that she *was* lying to herself. Two years earlier, when she had first met Bastien, she had very quickly begun developing deep feelings for him—but his sole reaction to *her* had been superficial and sexual. And nothing had changed since then, she reminded herself doggedly. Even if she was pregnant—even if she agreed to marry him—nothing would change between them. If she hadn't got to Bastien on a more meaningful level when they first met it was extremely unlikely that anything more would develop the second time around.

But how dared he simply assume that if she had conceived she would automatically want to consider a termination? He had no right to make that assumption—no right to try and take control of that decision either.

Too tired to lie awake agonising about what might never happen, Lilah ultimately dropped off to sleep.

The next morning that entire conversation with Bastien about getting married seemed surreal to Lilah. She was still deep in her bemused thoughts when she went downstairs for breakfast.

Bastien watched Delilah cross the terrace, a lithe, slim figure in a turquoise playsuit that showcased her tiny waist and long slim legs. She looked very young, with her black curls rippling loose round her shoulders. He watched her sit down and settle anxious sapphire-blue eyes on him.

Clad in tailored cream chinos and a black T-shirt, Bastien was casually seated on the low wall bounding the terrace, with a cup of coffee in his hand. His bronzed sculpted features smooth shaven, his lean, powerful body fluidly relaxed, he exuded poise, sophistication and an absolute charisma which stole Lilah's breath from her lungs.

A tiny muscle low in her pelvis clenched and her face coloured hotly as she became uncomfortably aware of the damp flesh between her thighs.

'I've been thinking, and I believe you're worrying about something that's unlikely to happen. It's not always that easy to get pregnant,' Lilah told Bastien quietly, keen to distract him from looking at her too closely because Bastien was far too astute at reading women. 'It took my stepmother months to conceive.'

'I'm not about to change my mind about marriage as a solution, Delilah,' Bastien warned her, secretly amused and impressed that she lacked the avaricious streak that would have made many women grab at the chance to marry him. 'While the arrangements are being made—there's a lot of paperwork involved in getting married in France—we'll continue here as normal. My lawyers are drawing up a pre-nup as we speak—'

Lilah poured her tea and groaned. 'You're really serious about this…'

'It may not seem immediately obvious to you in our current relationship,' Bastien remarked in a roughened undertone, watching her nibble at a croissant with unconscious sensuality and gritting his teeth as he hardened in response, 'but if you do prove to be pregnant I have a lot to offer as a husband and a father…'

Who was she? Lilah immediately wanted to know. Who was the evil witch who had made Bastien feel worthless at the age of twenty-one when he had been little more than a boy?

'I know that, Bastien,' she said quietly. 'Who was the woman who had the termination?'

Bastien grimaced. 'This long after the event, there is no need for us to discuss that.'

Lilah tilted her chin. 'If you want me to marry you in these circumstances I have a right to know the whole story.'

'Her name is Marina Kouros. She's the daughter of a wealthy businessman.'

'Greek?'

'Yes. She hung out with my half-brother, Leo. I knew she had a thing for him, but he saw her only as a friend.'

Lilah winced when he described that connection. 'Complicated…'

'Nothing I couldn't handle at the time, I thought.

I was very confident with women even at that age,' Bastien admitted bleakly. '*Too* confident, as it turned out. Of course I was infatuated with Marina. We had a one-night stand but I wanted more. I didn't see it at the time, but she was using me to try and make Leo sit up and take notice of her.'

'You were *brothers*. It was wrong of her to come between you like that,' Lilah opined.

'To be fair, Marina didn't intend to cause trouble, and Leo and I have never been close. I also know why she went for the termination behind my back,' he admitted tautly. 'I was illegitimate and penniless— hardly a winning package for a wealthy socialite. Unfortunately when Leo heard the rumours that I had got her pregnant she lied to save face with him and pretended that I had bullied her into the abortion clinic. He's held that against me ever since.'

'That's *so* unfair,' Lilah breathed angrily.

Bastien shrugged a broad shoulder. 'Very little in my life has been fair,' he derided softly. 'That's why I prefer to make my own luck and my own fortune. I don't owe anyone anything and that's how I like it, *glikia mou*.'

'But *I* would prefer not to risk having an unnecessary marriage and divorce in my relationship history,' Lilah told him quietly. 'I think we should wait and see if we have anything to worry about first.'

His dark golden eyes hardened. 'Not this time.'

'Even if I have conceived I don't think I'd choose a termination,' Lilah added.

Bastien sprang upright and set down his coffee cup, an aggressive edge to his movements. 'We'll do this my way. We'll get married.'

Lilah stood up. 'It's not the course of action I would choose, Bastien.'

'I don't care. This is an amendment to our original agreement,' he declared without hesitation. 'Deal with it.'

Lilah turned away from him, angry and stressed.

'You'll have a few days to think your position over,' Bastien told her. 'I have to make a trip to Asia, to check out some trouble at one of my manufacturing plants.'

Taken aback, Lilah turned. 'How long will you be away?'

'About a week.'

Lilah had a second cup of tea while Bastien talked on the phone in a foreign language. *Deal with it*, he had told her. An amendment to their original agreement? Was he *threatening* her? Would continuing refusal to marry him on her part be treated as a breach of that agreement? Did she dare push it?

What, after all, *was* she planning to do should Bastien's fears prove correct and she found herself pregnant? Her skin turned clammy with anxiety. If she was pregnant she would want Bastien's support every step of the way, she reflected ruefully. Maybe, just maybe, she was fighting the wrong battle…

CHAPTER NINE

I<small>T WAS A</small> beautiful dress. Exquisitely simple in shape, it flattered Lilah's slender figure, with long tight lace sleeves, a boat-shaped neckline and a slimline skirt. Her wedding gown, she acknowledged in lingering astonishment as she studied her reflection. It was her wedding day, and she still couldn't believe that she was actually about to marry Bastien Zikos.

The whole of the previous week had been taken up with marriage-orientated activity. Accompanied by one of Bastien's personal assistants, a fluent French-speaker, she had undergone an interview at the local *mairie*—the mayor's office, where the ceremony would take place. A whole heap of personal documents had been certified and presented on her behalf to fulfil the legal requirements, and forty-eight hours later, following a meeting with a lawyer at the chateau to protect her interests, she had signed a pre-nuptial agreement. Bastien had made liberal provision for her in the event of a divorce, offering a far more generous settlement than she thought necessary.

'Look on it as compensation,' Bastien had advised her on the phone, when she had protested the size of that settlement. 'You didn't want to marry me, but you're doing it.'

It wouldn't be a *real* marriage, she told herself soothingly as she clasped the diamond pendant round her throat. And wasn't that just as well? Bastien had been away for seven days and she had missed him almost from the moment of his departure. How was that possible? How could she miss the male she had believed she hated, who had persuaded her into a morally indefensible sexual relationship?

Lilah walked to the window and breathed in slow and deep, struggling to calm herself. She had *not* become attached to Bastien, and she had *not* fallen for him. She was just wildly attracted to him. She had also begun to understand him better as she'd come to appreciate his tough childhood and the experiences which had made him the hard, aggressive character that he was.

She wasn't *excusing* anything he had done, was she? No—she remained fully aware of Bastien's every flaw, and was therefore completely safe from getting attached to him, she assured herself soothingly.

A knock sounded on the bedroom door. It was time for her to leave. Manos smiled at her as she emerged from the room, rich fabric gliding in silken folds round her legs. Bastien had had a whole rack of designer wedding gowns sent to her and she had been taken aback, having assumed that they would be bypassing all such frills.

'No, this should look like a normal wedding,' Bastien had decreed.

Yet how could it look or feel normal when neither of them had any family members present?

Lilah felt absurdly guilty that she was about to get married without her father's knowledge.

Bastien was waiting in the hall. Clad in a superbly tailored pale grey suit, he looked breathtakingly handsome. When she met his long-lashed dark golden eyes her heart thudded and her pulses quickened, and she could feel heat rushing into her cheeks.

'You look fantastic,' he husked, closing a hand over hers as she reached the bottom step.

'When did you get back?'

'At dawn. I slept during the flight,' he shared, just as Stefan presented Lilah with a small bunch of flowers and she thanked him warmly.

They came to a halt in the stone front doorway as a photographer stepped forward to capture them on film.

'I wasn't expecting him,' Lilah admitted out of the corner of her mouth.

'This is not a moment we can easily recapture,' Bastien declared.

'But who's going to be interested?' she whispered helplessly.

'Our child will be interested in our wedding day,' Bastien countered.

'But…' Her lips clamped shut on a rush of denial as the photographer asked her to relax and smile.

She was convinced that there wasn't going to be a pregnancy, or a child, but she could see that Bastien had already decided otherwise.

A limousine whisked them to the *mairie*, a sleepy creamy stone building sited behind the war memorial in a small village. It was a civil ceremony, conducted by a middle-aged female official. Lilah held her breath as Bastien slid a gold ring on to her finger and she performed the same office for him, albeit more clumsily, all fingers and thumbs in her extreme self-consciousness as she thought about what the gesture actually meant: Bastien was her husband now.

When they emerged back into the sunshine the photographer was waiting, and she laughed and smiled, suddenly grateful that the unsettling ceremony was over and she could forget about it.

She was climbing back into the limo when a sports car shot to a sudden halt at the other side of the road and a woman called, *'Bastien?'*

Bastien stepped back from the limo and swung round as a lithe blonde scrambled out of the sports car and ran to greet him. She wore only a chiffon wrap, which was split to the waist at either side to show off her fabulous legs and brief leopard print bikini pants.

Lilah smoothed her gown over her knees and watched as the blonde kissed Bastien on both cheeks and he returned the greeting. The woman chattered, her slim hands moving expressively in the air. Very French, very chic, Lilah conceded, deliberately looking away from the encounter. Bastien's dealings with other women were none of her business.

Her tummy flipped, her chin coming up. No, that couldn't be true *or* acceptable. She was Bastien's wife now, and that had to make a difference.

'Who is she?' Lilah enquired when Bastien finally joined her and the limo moved off again.

'Chantal Baudin—one of my neighbours,' Bastien divulged carelessly.

'You've slept with her…haven't you?'

The instant those provocative words leapt off Lilah's tongue she was shocked by them, because she hadn't even known that that question was in her head.

'On several occasions over the years since I bought the chateau,' Bastien revealed, as cool as ice water in tone. 'She's a model.'

'What else would she be?' Lilah traded drily, while colour flared over her cheekbones like a revealing banner, because she felt as though an evil genie had taken over both her brain *and* her tongue.

'We were ships-that-pass-casual,' Bastien qualified very quietly. 'Not that that's any of your business.'

Lilah's shot a stubborn look at him, sapphire-blue eyes bright and defiant. 'Oh, it's my business *now*,' she assured him without hesitation. 'For as long as you remain married to me you have to be a one-woman man.'

A line of colour flared over Bastien's exotic cheekbones and his dark golden eyes smouldered. 'That sounds suspiciously like a warning.'

'It was. Do you expect *me* to stay away from other men?' Lilah asked dangerously.

'Of course,' Bastien breathed, in a harsh uncompromising undertone.

'Well, let's not be sexist about it—the rule cuts both ways. While we're married, your wings are clipped,' Lilah pronounced with satisfaction.

'Presumably you intend to ensure that the sacrifice of my sexual freedom is worth my while?' Bastien purred, black lashes dropping low over his gaze.

Lilah clashed with expectant dark eyes, brilliant as stars in a black sky, and her tummy performed a somersault while damp heat gathered at her feminine core. She shifted uneasily on the seat, uncomfortable with the potent physical effect Bastien had on her. Even when he annoyed her he could still make her want him. One glance at those high cheekbones and those stunning eyes and she melted into a puddle of longing.

Lunch awaited them on their return to the chateau. The table had been set with white linen, lace and rose petals, and Lilah stiffened in dismay when she saw it because it was very bridal and romantic. But the meal was superb, and Bastien's businesslike account of how he had dealt with the problems at his Asian manufacturing plant relaxed Lilah again.

Bastien studied Delilah, ultra-feminine and lovely, in a dress that merely enhanced her petite proportions, wondering if she was pregnant. He wanted a child, he acknowledged. Perhaps it was simply that he was *ready* for a child and for a change in lifestyle. But would he have felt that way with any woman other than Delilah?

'I should get changed,' Lilah murmured over coffee.

'*I* want to take off that dress.'

Lilah coloured. 'It's the middle of the day, Bastien.'

'My libido is not controlled by the clock. In any case, we're newly married and anything goes,' Bastien pointed out smoothly as he rose from his chair.

But Lilah refused to think of them as a married couple, thinking it wiser to regard their current relationship as simply an extension of their original arrangement. In other words, barring the ring on her wedding finger, she was still Bastien's mistress and his desired entertainment between the sheets. It would be very unwise, she thought, to start thinking of herself as occupying any more important or permanent role in Bastien's life.

Lean brown fingers closed over hers and she walked upstairs with him, her slender body taut with anticipation. She listened to the faint buzz of his mobile receiving messages and suppressed a sigh. Bastien never, ever switched his phone off, and it set her teeth on edge.

Bastien glanced at his phone and frowned when he saw the text. Chantal was making a nuisance of herself. He had told her that he was not alone at the chateau and she should have taken the hint that he wasn't available. Perhaps he should have mentioned that he had just got married, but why telegraph that news when there might be no need to do so? After all, if Delilah *hadn't* conceived he would soon be alone and free as a bird again, he reminded himself. And that was what he wanted, wasn't it? What he had always wanted: freedom without rules or ties.

Obviously he still had to get Delilah out of his system. Surely one more week would do that? Although he grudgingly admitted to himself that he did not *like* the prospect of parting with her. Why did the thought feel like a threat?

And then the sure knowledge hit him like a bombshell, blowing apart everything he had believed he knew about himself. He didn't *want* to let Delilah go. He wanted to *keep* her.

Struggling to rationalise that aberrant urge, he ran down the zip on her dress very slowly and eased her smoothly out of its concealing folds. Her porcelain-pale skin showed to advantage against the defiantly unconventional scarlet bra and panties she sported.

For some reason he had expected to find her wearing blue underpinnings, in line with that old bridal rhyme about something old, something new. He scanned her slender legs, but there was no garter to be seen either.

'Something blue?' he queried.

'It wasn't a real wedding, so I didn't see the point of bothering with tradition,' Delilah explained cheerfully.

Exasperation and annoyance shot through Bastien, who had assumed that she would be more sentimental. 'It felt real enough to me.'

'It's not real when you've already planned the divorce *before* you get married,' Delilah told him with vehement conviction.

'No man of my wealth marries without a pre-nup. And I won't be divorcing you if you're carrying my child,' Bastien pointed out, lifting her up to seat her at the foot of the bed, while wishing she would stop talking about divorce.

'I just don't think that it's very likely...that I'll be pregnant,' she extended, feeling insanely bare in her flimsy underwear while he remained fully dressed.

'Time will tell,' Bastien traded, easing off her silk sandals. 'And I do have an entire week to concentrate on getting you pregnant.'

Her bright blue eyes flew wide. 'What on earth do you mean?'

'Now that we're married it would be silly to start taking precautions again,' Bastien pronounced.

'Not to *my* way of thinking. If there is a decision still to be made on that score I don't think I want to *plan* to have a baby with a womaniser,' Lilah told him tartly.

Bastien shrugged free of his jacket and pitched it on to a chair before tugging at his tie. Whatever it took, he was determined to keep her. 'If you give me a baby I can promise that you'll be the only woman in my life.'

Lilah was hugely disconcerted by that offer, coming at her out of nowhere. 'You want a baby that much?'

But only with *her*, Bastien completed inwardly. She had first-rate qualities which he had noticed from the first. She wasn't greedy, dishonest or manipulative, like so many of the women he had known. In addition she was loyal, and kind to those she cared about, and she was a curiously attractive combination of downright old-fashioned sensible and mulishly spirited. Add in her looks and sex appeal and Delilah Moore-Zikos inhabited a class all of her own...

Not that he was planning to share that high opinion with her, though. Particularly not when she talked as though she was indifferent to both him and the prospect of a baby. But he didn't believe that. Like him, Delilah tended to hold back, judging a situation before she bared her soul or committed to a path of action.

Having reached his decision at a speed which slightly stunned him, Bastien curved long fingers to her slim shoulders. 'I want a baby with *you*.'

'But that pre-nup—'

'*Thee mou*...think outside the box,' he urged. 'I will settle down with you if you give me a child.'

Lilah went pink. 'And why would you think that I would be interested in *that* outcome?'

Bastien elevated an ebony brow. 'Aren't you?'

'Are we bargaining again, Bastien?'

Lilah was so tense she could hardly breathe. The unthinkable was happening: Bastien Zikos, the legendary womaniser, was offering her fidelity and a real marriage.

'Negotiating?' he countered.

'I may not even be able to *get* pregnant,' Lilah countered with quiet practicality.

'If and when that happens we'll deal with it, *glikia mou*,' Bastien told her levelly. 'I don't expect an easy ride. Nothing worthwhile is ever easy.'

Her heart swelled like a balloon inside her chest at that forthright opinion, which perfectly matched her own. Tears lashed the back of her eyes and she blinked them back furiously to focus on the beautiful burnished golden shimmer of his gaze.

'In that case, I'll… I'll give it a go,' she responded jerkily, afraid of the way she was laying herself open to getting hurt again, but desperately wanting to give him another chance.

Another chance to smash her heart to smithereens? Another chance to walk away from her without a backward glance and console himself with other women? How likely was it that Bastien could settle down into marriage? Did she dare risk bringing a child into so potentially volatile a relationship? And why was she even considering doing so?

Stealing a glance at his lean, darkly handsome face, she felt her breath hitch in her throat. The freedom of choice was suddenly cruelly wrenched from her, along with much of her pride. The reason she so badly wanted to give Bastien another chance was that she had fallen hard for him two years earlier and had struggled to fight feelings almost stronger than she was. Sadly, now that she was actually in Bastien's life and wearing his ring on her finger, she was weaker, more open to hope and dream fulfilment and love.

And that was the most basic truth, which she could no longer ignore or deny. She *loved* Bastien Zikos—had fallen like a giant stone the very first time he had settled those gorgeous dark eyes on her and smiled.

'You look so serious,' Bastien censured as he trailed off his shirt to reveal the torso that starred in her every fantasy. He was so wonderfully well-built, and he worked at staying fit—a reality etched in the lean hard sheet of roped muscle framing his pectoral muscles and abdomen.

Lilah's mouth ran dry. He brought his mouth down on hers, nibbling sexily at her full lower lip, swiping the upper with the tip of his tongue to gain entry to the intimate space beyond. A ball of heat mushroomed inside her when his tongue flicked against her own. Her hands spread on his chest, fingertips grazing hair-roughened skin and smoothing down to feel him jerk with sensitivity when she found the hard thrusting length of him.

With a hungry groan he lifted her up and brought her down again on the bed, arranging her over him with careful hands.

'I want you,' Bastien growled, dark eyes shooting golden sparks over her warmly flushed face.

'You sound so aggressive,' Lilah scolded as she obediently bent forward for him to unclasp her bra.

'It's been a week.' He swore bitterly. 'An endless, frustrating week.'

Strong hands pulled her down to him, to enable

him to close his lips round a pouting pink nipple. He hauled her close to him and rolled her over.

'Didn't *think* I was going to get to stay on top,' Lilah muttered with helpless bite.

His broad chest rumbled with amusement. 'Some day very soon…but not today,' he agreed in a roughened undertone.

Employing every sensual skill he had acquired, Bastien worked his way down over Delilah's slim squirming body, revelling in each sound that revealed her enjoyment. As her hips bucked in climax and she cried his name he smiled and flipped her over, lifting her up on to her knees.

He slid against her damp flesh to tease her, and then when she complained in frustration he sank into her, hard and deep.

Lilah moaned, her head still swimming and her body still sensitised, floating on the aftermath of extreme pleasure. Extraordinarily conscious of Bastien's every slight movement, Lilah felt her heart race and her pulse quicken with exhilaration. Intense excitement controlled her as he ground his hips into hers, quickening his pace until all she was conscious of was the wild, feverish climb of pleasure. As the ascent to satisfaction consumed her spasms of potent sensation coursed through her quivering body and then rose to an irresistible peak, leaving her thrashing in explosive convulsions of delight.

'I'll never move again,' she whispered limply in the aftermath.

'I'll move you,' Bastien husked, turning her round in the circle of his arms, his breath fanning her cheek, his body hot and damp against hers.

The scent of his skin enveloped her and she smiled up at him.

'I do hope you appreciate that you're not getting out of this bed for the rest of the day?' Bastien purred. 'But I'll make up for it tomorrow. I'm taking the rest of the week off. You will have my full attention, *kardoula mou*.'

Lilah rubbed her face against a broad brown shoulder, gloriously relaxed and feeling amazingly happy. She loved him, and he was with her, and his entire attention was on her. For the moment that was enough. And for the first time she didn't feel like Bastien's mistress—she felt like his wife, and it felt good.

A week after their wedding day Lilah woke suddenly during the night to register that Bastien had got out of bed and was pacing naked while he spoke Greek into his phone, his lean strong features stressed and taut. He waved a hand to silence her when she mouthed a query and she had to be patient, even though she didn't *feel* patient, lying back against the pillows and wondering what had happened to put that look of concern on his beautiful face.

So much had changed between them in the course of a week. Bastien had let down some of his barriers and was sharing a bed with her every night. Only once had he had another bad dream, and wakening to find her leaning over him had put more exciting pursuits into his mind, she recalled, her body heating at that wickedly erotic memory.

By day they had explored the chateau grounds before ranging further afield. They had gone to a jazz concert in the vineyards near Vaison-Ventoux-en-

Provence. They had strolled round vibrant markets, walked through narrow cobbled streets to enjoy coffee in shaded squares with softly flowing fountains. The hilltop villages were wonderfully picturesque, and the views spectacular.

He had bought her a gorgeous leather handbag in a workshop, and laughed heartily at the colourful pottery hen she had bought for Vickie, questioning that she could really *like* her stepmother and still buy her such a thing.

On several evenings they had dined out in local restaurants, although truthfully they had yet to eat anywhere that could compete with the superb food Marie served at the chateau. Some nights they made love until dawn…some afternoons they didn't get out of bed until the need to eat drove them out. His insatiable hunger for her was mercifully matched by hers for him, and with his encouragement Lilah had become more adventurous.

The only little niggle at the back of her mind, that had prevented her from totally relaxing, was the question of how Bastien was likely to react if she *didn't* prove to be pregnant. After all, was it really her he wanted, or was he merely giving way to a long-suppressed desire to become a father?

He could become a father with almost any woman, couldn't he? Lilah didn't like to think that her being in the right place at the right time was all that had prompted Bastien to seek a more lasting relationship with *her*. In any case, in another few days she would know whether or not she had conceived. And even if she had it was perfectly possible that she would still never tell Bastien that she loved him for fear of making him feel trapped, she thought ruefully.

'What's wrong?' she asked as Bastien cast aside his phone and paced restively back across the room.

'That was my brother, Leo,' he explained grimly. 'My father's in hospital in Athens with a suspected heart attack. Leo says there's no need for me to go, because he'll keep me posted, but…'

'Naturally you want to be there,' Lilah slotted in.

'But equally naturally Leo and his mother don't want me there.'

'How is *that* natural?' Lilah pressed, immediately defensive on Bastien's behalf. 'Anatole is as much your father as your brother's.'

'I may have lived with my father's family for years, but I was never part of that family,' Bastien pointed out drily. 'I'm never a welcome visitor. Leo's mother Cleta—my father's wife—hates me.'

Lilah compressed her lips. 'After the number of years that have passed since your mother's death, and the years you lived in her home with Anatole, that's very definitely *her* problem—not yours,' she pronounced with conviction. 'Don't let *anyone* make you feel as though you don't have the right to see your own father. You're his son too.'

The fiery gleam that illuminated Bastien's dark eyes only accentuated the worried frown stamped on his lean bronzed face. 'I do want to see him. We'll fly out as soon as I can get it organised.'

CHAPTER TEN

BASTIEN AND LILAH drove straight to the hospital from the airport. Lilah hung back a little as they entered the waiting room, because at first glance it seemed to be filled with people. Anatole was still having tests, and only close family would be allowed to visit him. The target of a slew of stares as she entered the room, Lilah flushed and acknowledged that she might be married to Bastien but she did not *feel* like a member of his family.

A small, curvy older woman, improbably dressed in a purple brocade evening coat and matching dress, and more diamonds than Lilah had ever seen outside a shop window, shot a look of derision at Bastien. 'How *dare* you bring one of your whores to the hospital?' she spat.

The very tall black-haired male standing to one side of this shrew stiffened and said something in Greek, while Bastien curved a strong arm to Lilah's tense spine.

'May I introduce my wife, Delilah? This is Cleta Zikos, my father's wife...and my brother Leo and his wife, Grace.'

'Your *wife*?' the pretty redhead exclaimed in an

unmistakable English accent as she surged forward. 'When did you get *married*?'

'Recently,' Lilah responded, grateful that Leo's wife seemed warm and friendly in comparison to his brother, who seemed stunned by the news, and Anatole's sour-faced wife, who had merely grimaced, making it clear that any attachment of Bastien's—married or otherwise—was not welcome.

Annoyance rippled through Lilah at the disturbing awareness that after his mother's death Bastien had spent *years* living in Cleta Zikos's home. Evidently Cleta had never tried to treat Bastien as a stepchild, but had preferred to despise him for the reality that his late mother had been her husband's mistress.

Bastien's brother, Leo, stepped forward to congratulate them. 'Never thought I'd live to see the day,' she heard him quip, half under his breath.

Apart from their similar height and build, the two men did not look obviously related. The awkwardness between them was apparent as they engaged in stilted chat, slipping into Greek, presumably to discuss their father's condition.

Grace settled a hand on Lilah's sleeve and urged her over to some seats at the far wall. 'So, tell all, Delilah,' she urged. 'Leo was convinced that Bastien would stay single for ever.'

'Everyone but Bastien calls me Lilah,' Lilah shared with a rueful look.

'We are both married to very stubborn individuals,' Grace said with a grin. 'Neither one of them gives an inch in a tight corner.'

Lilah glanced up as another woman arrived and

Cleta Zikos rushed up to welcome the tall, shapely brunette with a flood of Greek.

'Who's that?' she asked her companion.

'Marina Kouros—an old friend of the family.'

Bastien's first love, Lilah registered, her heart performing a heavy thud inside her chest.

Clearly Bastien had had good taste, even at the age of twenty-one, because the lively chattering brunette was a classic beauty. She watched Marina stiffen and pale, her animation taking a dip when she belatedly appreciated that Bastien was present. She didn't smile at him and he didn't smile at her. They exchanged a stiff nod of acknowledgement, but Lilah fancied that Bastien looked at his former lover longer than was necessary, and a twist of green jealousy shivered through her.

What was that old cliché about a man never forgetting his first love? Her attention roved down to Marina's hand, which bore no rings, indicating that the woman was still single.

'I propose that you, me and Marina take a break for coffee at our home,' Grace suggested. 'None of us are going to be allowed in to see Anatole anyway. Cleta, I would invite you, but I know you won't leave the hospital until you've seen your husband.'

'I'll pick you up later,' Bastien told Lilah quietly, clearly content for her to depart.

'I'd be happy to stay,' she told him.

His dark golden eyes skimmed her troubled face. 'I don't need support, *hara mou*.'

That was a matter of opinion, Lilah reflected ruefully, avoiding Cleta's haughtily resentful glance and Leo's cool, curious regard. In such company Bastien stood very much alone, and she hated that it was like that for him. But then in such a dysfunctional family circle he had *always* been alone, she thought unhappily. Bastien was still treated like the illegitimate son—the outsider to be resented and kept at a distance.

Not unnaturally, Bastien had eventually learned to live like that—never getting too close to people, steering clear of messy human emotions as best he could because he had seen far too many unpleasant displays of turbulent emotion while he was growing up.

'How do you get on with your mother-in-law?' Lilah asked Grace as the three women stepped into a lift.

'I don't see much of her. Her life revolves round Anatole. She's a bit of a cold fish,' Grace volunteered with a grimace.

Lilah pressed her arm against her breasts. They were sore, aching and tender, but she occasionally suffered from such discomfort before her menstrual cycle kicked in. On the other hand, she was already late... She was planning to do a pregnancy test the following morning, but was convinced it would be a waste of time because she just couldn't imagine that she would be pregnant.

She rested back against the wall of the lift, feeling incredibly weary, and noticed that Marina was staring at her.

'I was surprised to hear that Bastien had got married,' she admitted baldly.

'He rushed me into it,' Lilah responded coolly, studying the woman whose one-night stand with Bastien almost ten years earlier had caused such lasting and damaging repercussions.

'He must've been scared of losing you,' Grace opined.

'Very little scares Bastien,' Lilah said wryly, thinking of how she and Bastien had started out at daggers drawn, and of how quickly her feelings had changed.

Obviously she had no resistance when it came to Bastien. Love had been softening her up for a serious fall from the beginning, she reckoned ruefully, feeling nausea stirring in her tense tummy because she felt so ridiculously uncomfortable in Marina's presence.

Lilah was experiencing a volatile cocktail of jealousy and resentment, and telling herself that she was not entitled to those reactions wasn't helping. She hated knowing that Marina had once shared a bed with Bastien, hated the fact that Bastien had wanted Marina first, and hated even more the reality that Marina could have had him but had instead chosen to throw him away, while at the same time lying about him to poison his relationship with his only sibling.

'You're very quiet,' Grace commented in the limousine.

'I napped during the flight but I'm still very tired,' Lilah confided with an apologetic smile.

'When did you first meet Bastien?' Marina asked.

'Over two years ago.'

'He's quite a guy,' Marina remarked, in a tone that Lilah took exception to because it oozed intimacy to her sensitive hearing. 'A lot of women will envy you.'

Including you? Lilah wondered, thinking that the brunette might well have come to live to regret rejecting Bastien once he had become rich and successful, and as such much more socially acceptable.

It dismayed Lilah that she should feel so angry with Marina and so very protective of Bastien.

Leo and Grace lived in a palatial town house. A nanny brought their daughter, Rosie, to meet them. The toddler was adorable, and Lilah relaxed in little Rosie's presence—but only until she began wondering how Bastien would react to her not being pregnant. After that disappointment would he still want to stay married to her? Or would that single disappointment be sufficient to knock the gloss off his belief that he wanted to keep her as his wife? Rich, powerful men didn't deal generously with disappointments because they met with very few.

A chill ran down Lilah's spine as she sipped her tea and tried to think cheerfully of returning to the life she had left behind.

'I was hoping that you and Bastien would join us for dinner some evening while you're in Athens,' Grace shared. 'Break the ice a bit.'

'I think it would take an ice pick,' Lilah confided ruefully.

'Bastien's not the family type. He's a natural loner,' Marina remarked.

Lilah stiffened angrily and her bright blue eyes sparked. 'Bastien might be closer to his brother if *you* hadn't soured their relationship by lying about what happened between you and Bastien ten years ago,' Lilah condemned, the stream of recrimination racing off her tongue before she could even stop to think about what she was saying.

In response to Lilah's outburst the most appalling

silence spread. Marina had turned the colour of ash, and Grace was staring at Lilah in wide-eyed consternation.

'I… I don't know what to say,' Marina responded, and as a deep flush highlighted her cheeks her guiltiness was obvious to Lilah.

'But I do. Delilah…time for you to leave.'

A deeply unwelcome voice sounded from behind the sofa she was sitting on. Lilah's head swivelled and she focused on Bastien in shock. The fact that he had heard what she had said to Marina was stamped on his lean darkly handsome face and in the threatening golden blaze of his eyes. She had embarrassed him by prying into his past and he was absolutely furious.

Her cheeks warm, she stood up and encountered a sympathetic glance from Grace.

'I'm sorry. I put my foot in it…trod where I shouldn't… whatever you want to call it,' Lilah muttered in a rush as soon as she was in the car with him.

'We'll discuss it when we get back to the apartment.'

'How's your father?' she asked.

'They think he's had a minor heart attack. He's going to have to change his lifestyle—eat less, exercise more,' he breathed curtly. 'Cleta's staying with him. I'll go back to see him later.'

Lilah stole a glance at his grim bronzed profile and cursed the misfortune that had led to Bastien overhearing her attack on his former lover. She knew she was in the wrong. She should have minded her own business. Should never have embarrassed Grace like that in her home. And now Bastien was furious with her.

She gritted her teeth, angry that she had spoken on impulse and without sensible forethought, but not sorry that she had told Marina what she thought of her behaviour.

His apartment was a penthouse, furnished in contemporary style and full of airy space, glass, metal and stone.

Lilah slung her bag down in the main reception room and sat down heavily. 'Say what you have to say,' she urged apprehensively, her nerves worn to a thread by the enforced wait.

Bastien settled burning golden eyes on her. 'What the *hell* got into you? I told you something private and you used it as a weapon to attack Marina. It was none of your business. You embarrassed me and you embarrassed Grace.'

'Well, if I embarrassed Marina, I'm not sorry,' Lilah fired back. 'She deserved what I said. And I didn't specify what I was talking about in any way, so I doubt if I embarrassed anyone.'

'Is that all you've got to say to me?' Bastien raked back at her rawly. 'You dug up something very confidential from my past. I can't *believe* that I even told you now. I should've known a woman couldn't be trusted.'

'Oh, don't throw any of that prejudiced nonsense at me!' Lilah warned him, equally rawly. 'It just got to me when Marina walked in all smiles and charm, acting as if she was a friend of the family.'

'She *is* a friend!'

'Not of yours, she's not!' Lilah flung back feelingly. 'She's caused a whole lot of trouble between you and your brother and you shouldn't have let her lies stand unchallenged. Your pride makes you your own worst enemy, Bastien!'

'I can't believe we're even having this conversation. Nothing that happened between Marina and I or Leo and I is anything to do with you. Where the hell do you get the nerve to interfere?'

'Maybe…just maybe…I was trying to do something for you.'

'You had no right to upset Marina like that.'

'*Marina?*' Lilah gasped as if he had punched her, because she was suddenly desperately short of breath, pierced to the heart that he should be more concerned about his former lover's feelings than about her.

'Yes—Marina,' Bastien repeated curtly. 'Of *course* she was upset. I saw her face. She knew instantly what you were referring to. You can't have thought this through, Delilah.'

Lilah was wounded by the angle the conversation had taken and fighting to hide the fact from him. Bastien was standing there, all lean, powerful and poised and devastatingly beautiful, and he was defending another woman to her face. He was *her* husband but he wasn't on her side.

Her tummy flipped, leaving her struggling against a sickening light-headed sensation.

'The termination caused Marina considerable distress,' Bastien delivered in a grim undertone. 'She made her choice, but I don't doubt that the decision cost her. That's the main reason why I didn't persist in arguing my case with Leo. Marina doesn't deserve to have that distressing experience raked up again. So she lied and played victim to look more sympathetic in

Leo's eyes? OK…that was wrong. But *Leo* is the one who chose to believe her story and disbelieve mine.'

Belated guilt pierced Lilah and she felt more nauseated than ever. On one score Bastien was correct. She had not thought through the implications of what she was throwing at Marina. But she was not a naturally unkind or unfeeling person. She knew she should never have referred to so private a matter. She had been cruel, and the shame of that reality engulfed Lilah like a suffocating blanket.

She blundered upright, desperate simply to escape Bastien's censorious gaze and lick her wounds and her squashed ego in private.

She swayed as the room telescoped around her in the most disturbing way. Her head was swimming and her skin was clammy and cold. Not a sound escaped Lilah's lips as blackness folded in behind her eyelids and she flopped down on the rug in a faint.

For a split second Bastien stared at Delilah, who had dropped in a heap on the rug, and then he plunged forward to crouch and gather her up, his brain obscured by the most peculiar fog of something that felt like panic but which he refused to acknowledge as panic. He wasn't the panicking type—never had been, never would be.

He dug out his phone to ring his brother's home and ask for Grace. Leo, mercifully, asked no questions, but Grace more than made up for that omission.

Grace told him quietly and succinctly what to do and Bastien followed her instructions, furious that he had once disdained to take a first aid course, assuming he would never feel the need for such training.

By the time he'd come off the phone and was carrying Delilah down to the main bedroom she was showing signs of recovery. Her lashes fluttered, her head moved, and a faint hint of colour began to lift the drawn pallor of her complexion.

Only then did Bastien dare to breathe again. He smoothed a shaking hand over Delilah's brow to brush back her tumbled dark hair. He had never felt so scared in his life. That knowledge shook him up even more. He had shouted at her, condemned her. And why had he done that?

Maybe I was trying to do something for you, Delilah had said, and the sheer shock value of those words was still reverberating inside Bastien. When had anyone *ever* tried to do anything to improve his life? When had anyone *ever* tried to protect him from the consequences of his own behaviour?

Delilah had been trying to *protect* him.

He swallowed hard. He didn't need anyone's protection. Nobody had protected him as a child or as an adolescent—neither his mother nor his father—and Bastien had learned never to look to other people for support. But Delilah had blundered headfirst into a difficult and delicate situation in a clumsy and futile attempt to straighten out his non-relationship with his only sibling.

Admittedly he had noticed how his wife had pokered up by his side when she'd seenhow the Zikos family treated him. Delilah, he registered in a daze, *cared* about him—in spite of the methods he had used to ensnare her, in spite of all the mistakes he had made.

He snatched in a ragged breath and studied her in wondering appreciation.

'My goodness—what happened?' Lilah mumbled, blue eyes opening to fix on Bastien's lean darkly handsome face. 'Did I faint? I've never done that in my life! I'm *so* sorry.'

'You were upset—and when did you last eat?' Bastien pressed, pushing her back against the pillows when she tried to get up. 'Lie there for a while. Are you feeling sick?'

Lilah grimaced. 'Only a little… It's fading.'

'I'm really sorry I shouted at you,' Bastien said abruptly, a lean brown hand closing over hers, and he was astonished at how easily the apology emerged.

'You weren't shouting.'

'I'm not in a good mood. I was stressed about Anatole and feeling guilty about him,' Bastien admitted, disconcerting her with that confidence. 'I love my father, but I've never been able to respect him, and… and that makes me feel like a lousy son.'

Lilah squeezed his fingers uncertainly. 'No, I think it means you're adult enough to appreciate that he's not perfect and love him anyway…which is good.'

'Do you have a comforting answer for *everything* bad that I feel?' Bastien groaned, searching her anxious features with appreciative golden eyes.

'I doubt it, but you were right about Marina. Dragging that up was cruel… I'm afraid I didn't see it from her point of view, only yours, and I also felt jealous of her, which was even less excusable.' Lilah loosed a heavy sigh. 'I'm ashamed of myself for being so insensitive.'

'You were thinking of me and of my relationship with Leo,' Bastien said. 'But why on earth would you feel jealous of Marina? It's nearly ten years since I was with her—when we were both young and foolish.'

Lilah breathed in deep. 'I'm jealous of anyone you've ever been with. There—I've said it. I've got a possessive side I didn't know I had.'

'Like me,' Bastien cut in unexpectedly. 'I am irrationally jealous when it comes to you, and I've never been like that with any other woman. I couldn't even stand seeing you laughing and chattering with Ciro.'

'*Seriously?*' Lilah prompted, wide-eyed at that confession.

'I've been acting like a madman since I got you back into my life. Unfortunately for you I like my life much better with you in it. In fact, simply waking up in the morning to find you beside me makes me happy,' he bit out with bleak reluctance.

'It…it does?' Lilah was hanging on his every word, wondering why he was talking in such a way. 'Are you still going to be happy if I'm not pregnant?'

'*Diavelos*…what difference should *that* make?' Bastien was bemused. 'If it's not meant to be it's not meant to be and we'll handle it…that is if you want to stay with me…'

Lilah lifted up off the pillows and wrapped both arms round his neck, burying her face against his shoulder, drinking in the familiar scent of his skin in a storm of relief that felt both emotional and physical.

'Of *course* I want to stay with you.'

'There's no "of course" about it,' Bastien countered wryly as he unhooked her arms and gently settled her back against the pillows. 'I railroaded you into my bed and then into marriage, employing every piece of blackmail I had to put pressure on you.'

Lilah treated him to a troubled appraisal. 'I know… I know you're extremely imperfect and that you've done dreadful things. I know you manipulated me. But… I still love you. I shouldn't, but I can't help loving you…'

Bastien's throat thickened as if he had been slugged in the vocal cords. 'I don't deserve your love.'

'No, you don't.' Lilah was quick to agree with him. 'But it seems I love you anyway.'

'Which is fortunate, because I'm not going to turn perfect any time soon, and it's probably best that you see all the flaws upfront—so that you know what you're getting in me,' Bastien told her uncomfortably.

Both of his hands closed slowly round hers to hold them in a grip of steel.

'But I love you too—so much more than I ever thought I could love anyone. In short, I'm absolutely crazy about you…so crazy I thought it was *normal* to waste two years plotting and planning to acquire your father's business and gain enough power over you to acquire you as well.'

Lilah blinked rapidly. '*Crazy* about me?'

Bastien lifted one hand to his mouth and kissed it almost awkwardly. 'Can't-live-without-you crazy,' he extended in a driven undertone. 'It doesn't matter if you're pregnant or not pregnant, or even if you can never get pregnant. I just want and *need* you in my life to make it feel worthwhile.'

'Even though I go interfering in things that are none of my business?' she whispered, scarcely able to believe what she was hearing, while her heart was taking off inside her like a rocket ship.

'That was just you, taking a typical caring approach to sorting my life out,' Bastien informed her forgivingly. 'You know, in my whole life nobody has ever stood up to defend me or try to protect me until you spoke up today. And when I thought about that... *that* was the crucial moment when I finally realised how much I love you and why.'

Lilah was gobsmacked. 'It *was*?' she whispered.

'I've probably been in love with you since you called me a man whore and slammed that door in my face two years ago...' Bastien groaned. 'I've certainly been pretty much obsessed with *you* ever since then.'

'Obsessed while sleeping with other women?' Lilah derided gently.

'And I couldn't settle for five minutes with *any* of them. Don't blame me for that when you weren't willing to take a chance on me back then.'

Moisture stung the backs of her eyes and she blinked rapidly. 'I wasn't brave enough to dream that something more lasting might come from what seemed to be a very shallow sexual interest.'

'Ouch...' Bastien groaned again, looking pained. 'The minute I had you in my life everything changed, *hara mou*. You make me feel things. And when you're not around... I feel dead, as if I have nothing to look forward to or work for.'

A tear trickled down Lilah's cheek. 'Oh, Bastien...' she mumbled in a wobbly voice. 'You're making me cry. I love you so much, but I'm terrified you'll wake up some day and feel trapped.'

'Every woman who came before you made me feel trapped or bored. You do neither.'

His dark golden eyes burnished with warmth and appreciation, Bastien leant down and claimed a kiss—

a slow, deep kiss that said everything he couldn't find the words to say. She was the woman he hadn't even known he was looking for, waiting for. Her image had been locked in his head for two long years, ensuring that no other woman could please or hold him.

The kiss wakened Lilah's body, sending little tingles into her tender breasts and down into her pelvis. The sound of a doorbell could not have been less welcome to either of them.

Bastien lifted his head. 'I'd better see who that is… Don't get up.'

Lilah slid her legs off the mattress as soon as he had left the room and sped back to the main reception room to reclaim her bag. On her return she passed through the hall, and realised that their visitor was Leo.

When Bastien frowned at her, for being out of bed without permission, Lilah smiled valiantly at both men and muttered, 'I'm going back to lie down, Bastien.'

In fact, she took her bag straight into the en-suite bathroom and removed the pregnancy test she had purchased some days earlier. She had to know one way or the other, she reflected ruefully. Had she not been so fearful that their relationship would be damaged by a negative result she believed she would have done the test sooner. But Bastien's assurances had removed that worry. Furthermore, that fainting fit had roused Lilah's suspicions, because she had never fainted before.

The couple of minutes she had to wait for the result of the test seemed to last an unnaturally long time. When she finally straightened from her seat on the side of the bath she froze, because she saw the result straight away. It had an electrifying effect on her and she wrenched open the bathroom door to yell.

'Bastien? *Bastien?* We're *pregnant!*' she gasped from the bedroom doorway, reddening in dismay when she registered Leo's presence, because she had totally forgotten that Bastien was not alone.

Leo was startled enough by her announcement to break into a grin. He gave Bastien a very masculine punch on the arm and wrenched open the front door for himself, departing at speed to leave them alone.

'Pregnant?' Bastien queried with a frown of uncertainty. 'But I thought you were convinced that you weren't.'

'The symptoms were misleading,' Lilah told him primly. 'Well? You're not saying anything… What do you think? How do you feel?'

'I think I'm in shock. I'm a husband, and now I'm going to be a father, and…' Bastien's beautifully shaped mouth slanted into a wide, brilliant smile as he moved towards her. 'I couldn't be happier.'

Lilah padded towards him 'Even though it's not what you originally signed up for?'

'I signed you up in an open-ended contract…or didn't you notice that? I *never* promised to let you go, and believe me, I won't now,' Bastien warned her. 'You're my wife, and you're going to have my baby, and I'll never let either of you go.'

'We won't want to be without you,' Lilah swore, rising on tiptoe to close her arms round him. 'I love you so much, Bastien.'

Bastien stared down at her with wondering pleasure. 'I know—and I don't know why.'

'Because you're very loveable,' she pointed out.

Bastien was still bewildered, but he decided that it would be insane to question a miracle. He had done everything wrong and she had forgiven him. She cared about him—*really* cared. When had anyone ever truly cared about him?

His eyes suspiciously bright, Bastien lifted his wife with reverent hands and laid her back down very gently on the bed. 'You need to rest,' he said with conviction.

'No, I need *you*,' Lilah countered, her hand snatching at his to keep him close.

Bastien hung back a step. 'If I join you on that bed, I'll—'

His wife grinned at him, her heart racing, body thrumming. 'Do you think I don't know that? I'm throwing down a red carpet and a welcome mat.'

'In that case…' A wolfish smile tilted his beautiful mouth and he shed his jacket with fluid grace, all power and satisfaction. 'Your wish is my command.'

'Since when?' Lilah quipped, unimpressed by that unlikely claim.

'Since you told me that you love me.'

'I do…' Lilah sighed, breathing in the scent of him like an addict.

Bastien smoothed her hair back from her cheekbone, his burnished dark golden eyes brilliant. 'I really do love you, Delilah…'

Lilah put her sultry mouth to his and slow-burning heat rose inside her, as potent as the happiness she was barely able to contain. Her future was filled with Bastien and the promise of a family, and she was overjoyed by the knowledge.

EPILOGUE

Three years later

LILAH SMOOTHED DOWN her print sundress and studied the sapphire and diamond eternity ring Bastien had given her to celebrate their son's birth. Nikos was a lively toddler, with a shock of black hair and his mother's bright blue eyes. He was also a wonderfully affectionate child, and revelled in the attention he received from his father, who was determined to give his son a secure and loving childhood.

So much had changed during the past three years. Their home base was a London town house, but whenever they needed some downtime from their busy lives they flew out to the chateau in Provence.

The big house was the perfect base for family get-togethers, and Lilah's father, stepmother and siblings were regular visitors. Robert Moore was still running Moore Components, which had gone from strength to strength, expanding to facilitate the number of orders it was receiving.

Within weeks of Anatole's heart attack Bastien and Lilah had celebrated a second wedding in Provence—

a church ceremony, attended by all their family, and followed by a lively party at the chateau.

For a while afterwards Lilah had worked with Bastien as one of his PAs, and that had enabled the couple to spend more time together—particularly when he was travelling a lot. Since their son's birth, however, Bastien had consolidated the various elements of his business empire to enable him to travel less and spend more time with his family.

Grace and Leo had also become steady visitors. It had taken a long time, but Leo and Bastien had finally bonded as the brothers they were. Marina had told Leo the truth about the termination, and Leo had come to see Bastien to mend fences the same day on which Lilah had discovered she was pregnant.

Prompted by Grace and Lilah, who got on like a house on fire, the two families had enjoyed several vacations together, both on Leo's yacht and at the chateau.

Following his heart attack Anatole had lost a good deal of weight, in order to improve his health. He adored his grandchildren, and was a regular visitor to both London and Provence, but his wife, Cleta, almost never accompanied him on those visits. The pleasure Anatole received from seeing his sons finally treat each other like brothers had touched Lilah's heart.

'Sorry I'm late…' Bastien groaned from the doorway, already in the act of peeling off his shirt to head for the shower. 'Nikos and Skippy caught me on the way in and I've been playing ball. Leo has taken my place, even though Rosie has told us that kicking balls is "a stupid boy thing".'

Lilah laughed, because Grace's daughter was extremely clever for her age and often amused the adults with the things she came out with.

She crossed the room to help Bastien unbutton his shirt. 'Happy birthday,' she told him softly. 'Fancy some company in the shower?'

'Is that my birthday present?' Bastien asked hopefully.

Lilah stripped off her dress where she stood, reaching round to unhook her bra. 'No, it's just a surprise. You've been away for three days and I missed you.'

'Missed you too,' Bastien groaned, dropping his shirt to reach for her warm slender body. 'You'll get your hair wet.'

'I'll put it up…'

Lilah moaned under the urgent onslaught of his passionate kiss, sensible matters like her appearance dwindling in importance when it came to reconnecting with Bastien.

'I told Leo we'd be a while,' Bastien confessed.

'Fancied your chances, did you?'

'Always, *hara mou*,' Bastien husked, fighting free of his clothes without once letting go of his wife.

And the passion that never failed to enthral them when they had been apart reigned supreme until they lay in the lazy aftermath, wrapped in each other's arms and catching up on stray bits of news while simply revelling in being together again.

'I love you,' Lilah sighed.

'I love you more,' Bastien murmured, ever competitive.

* * * * *

'In a moment we will leave the chapel,' Luca told her. He hesitated. **'When we step outside it will be necessary for me to kiss you.'**

She blinked at him. 'Necessary for you to…? Why?'

Athena had the most incredible eyes. The thought came unbidden into Luca's mind. 'There's no time to explain now. The press are outside, and it's vital that we make them believe our marriage is real.'

'Real?' She knew she probably sounded witless, but she couldn't take in what he had said about needing to kiss her.

'All you have to do is kiss me back,' Luca said impatiently, when she stared at him as if he had grown a second head. 'It shouldn't be too much of an ordeal. You seemed to enjoy it when I kissed you in Zenhab.'

So he hadn't forgotten that kiss. Her mind flew to the palace gardens and she remembered vividly the whisper of the fountains and the silver gleam of the moon, the scent of orange blossom and the gossamer-soft brush of Luca's lips on hers.

He opened the chapel door and Athena's thoughts scattered as she was blinded by an explosion of flashbulbs. Luca slid his arm around her waist and drew her close to his body—so close that she could feel his powerful thigh muscles through her dress; his hard, masculine frame was a stark contrast to her softness.

'Remember, this has to look convincing,' he murmured as he lowered his face towards hers.

Dear Reader,

I am intrigued about the way sisters can share a close relationship and yet so often have very different characteristics. This is certainly true of Athena Howard, whose story is told in *A Bride Worth Millions*, and her older sister Lexi, who features in *Sheikh's Forbidden Conquest*.

Awkward Athena wishes she was more like daring helicopter pilot Lexi, who met her match when she fell in love with Sultan Kadir Al Sulaimar. Athena is not the academic daughter her parents had hoped for, but at least they approve of her engagement to English aristocrat Charles Fairfax. It's set to be the society wedding of the year—but hours before the ceremony Athena discovers that Charles only wants her to be his convenient wife to hide a shocking secret!

Desperate to escape from her wedding, Athena falls— literally—into the arms of Luca De Rossi, whom she met previously at Lexi's wedding to Kadir. Athena is attracted to Luca, but a traumatic event when she was a teenager has resulted in her being wary of men.

Luca must marry before his thirty-fifth birthday, so he offers Athena a marriage deal: he will pay her one million pounds to be his temporary bride. Athena has secret plans for how to spend the money—and Luca has a devastating secret of his own!

I enjoyed writing about these two sisters—and the gorgeous men who claimed their hearts!

With love

Chantelle

A BRIDE
WORTH MILLIONS

BY
CHANTELLE SHAW

MILLS & BOON

Published in Great Britain 2015
by Mills & Boon, an imprint of Harlequin (UK) Limited,
Eton House, 18-24 Paradise Road, Richmond, Surrey, TW9 1SR

© 2015 Chantelle Shaw

ISBN: 978-0-263-25076-3

Harlequin (UK) Limited's policy is to use papers that are natural, renewable and recyclable products and made from wood grown in sustainable forests. The logging and manufacturing processes conform to the legal environmental regulations of the country of origin.

Printed and bound in Spain
by CPI, Barcelona

Chantelle Shaw lives on the Kent coast, and thinks up her stories while walking on the beach. She has been married for over thirty years and has six children. Her love affair with reading and writing Harlequin Mills & Boon® began as a teenager, and her first book was published in 2006. She likes strong-willed, slightly unusual characters. Chantelle also loves gardening, walking and wine!

Books by Chantelle Shaw

Mills & Boon® Modern™ Romance

The Chatsfield

The Bond of Brothers

Irresistible Italians

After Hours with the Greek

Visit the author profile page at millsandboon.co.uk for more titles

For Rosie and Lucy, best sisters and best friends!

CHAPTER ONE

'I'VE BEEN THINKING.'

'Really?' Luca De Rossi could not disguise the scepticism in his voice as he glanced at the blonde in bed beside him. Giselle Mercier was exquisite, and she was an inventive lover, but Luca doubted that the French model with baby-blue eyes and a penchant for expensive jewellery was about to announce that she had discovered a solution for world peace, or a cure for cancer.

His suspicions were confirmed when she held up her left hand so that the enormous diamond on her third finger was set ablaze by the early-morning sunbeams streaming into the penthouse.

'Yes. I've been thinking that I don't want to get married at a registry office. I want our wedding to be in a church, or even a cathedral.'

Giselle glanced towards the window and the view of the elegant spires of the Duomo—Milan's magnificent cathedral.

'And I want to wear a wedding dress. Think what a fantastic publicity opportunity it would be for De Rossi Designs,' Giselle purred when Luca frowned. 'The press would go mad for pictures of a wedding gown designed by the creative director of DRD for his bride.'

'There will be no press coverage of our wedding,' Luca said tersely. 'You seem to be forgetting that our marriage will be a temporary arrangement. I only require you to be my wife for one year. After that we will divorce and you will receive one million pounds—as we agreed.'

Giselle threw back the sheet to reveal her naked, golden-tanned body, and hooked one lissom thigh across Luca's hip. 'Perhaps you'll decide that you don't want a temporary marriage,' she murmured. 'Last night was amazing, *chéri*. I think we could have something special…'

Luca muttered something ugly beneath his breath as he swung his legs over the side of the bed. It was true that the sex last night had been good—albeit in the vaguely uninspiring way that sex always was with any of his mistresses. But it meant nothing to him. Just as it always meant nothing.

He didn't know why Giselle had suggested that their relationship could be in any way 'special'. They had made an arrangement that suited both of them and he could not conceal his impatience at her attempt to try and change the rules.

He strode across the room and stared moodily out of the window, while his mistress ran her eyes hungrily over his bare buttocks and muscular thighs. In the sunlight, Luca's thick black hair, which had a tendency to curl at his nape, gleamed like polished jet. His broad shoulders were tanned a dark bronze, the same as the rest of his body, even his buttocks, which made Giselle wonder if he sunbathed in the nude.

She had never had a lover as skilful and tireless as Luca De Rossi. No wonder the tabloids dubbed him the 'Italian Stallion'! He was as famous for his affairs with the countless female celebrities who wore his designs to red-carpet events as he was for his undeniable artistic talent and his flair for designing clothes that flattered women whatever their shape.

Luca was sinfully sexy and filthy rich. He was also in urgent need of a wife, so that he could keep his ancestral home: Villa De Rossi—a palatial house on the shores of Lake Como. It was something to do with the terms of his grandmother's will. Luca had to be married by his thirty-fifth birthday or the villa, which had been owned by the De Rossi family for three hundred years, would be sold.

Giselle did not understand all the details and did not particularly care. The important thing was that Luca had asked *her* to be his bride. The deal included an amazing pay-off, as well as lots of other perks—such as the diamond solitaire ring that Luca had promised she could keep when they went their separate ways.

But Giselle had no intention of going anywhere. It had occurred to her that, even though a million pounds was more than she was ever likely to earn from modelling, it made sense to hang on to her soon-to-be husband for as long as possible. After all, if he was willing to pay her one million pounds for one year of marriage then even Giselle's poor grasp of mathematics could work out the amount she should receive after two or three years of being Luca's wife. And of course if they had a child then Luca would have to pay maintenance and school fees.

Really, the future looked very promising, Giselle decided.

'Luca…' she said huskily. 'Why don't you come back to bed?'

Luca ignored the invitation. A familiar sense of frustration at the situation he found himself in made his blood boil, and he felt a strong urge to smash his fist through the window. He rested his brow against the glass and looked down on Corso Vittorio Emanuelle II, Milan's famous shopping precinct.

Despite the early hour, people were already milling

in the glass-domed walkways where all the top fashion brands, including De Rossi Designs, had boutiques. The fashion label that Luca had created fifteen years ago had become a global success, and the iconic DRD logo was a byword for haute couture and high-end ready-to-wear clothes that complemented the exclusive leather shoes, handbags and accessories that De Rossi Enterprises—founded eighty years ago by Luca's great-grandfather Raimondo—was famous for.

It was thanks to Luca that the family business had been saved from the brink of bankruptcy and now enjoyed an annual sales revenue of over a billion pounds. But he had never received praise or thanks from his grandparents when they had been alive, Luca reflected bitterly.

He walked back over to the bed, frowning when he saw the soft expression in Giselle's eyes. The last thing he wanted was for her think that she was in any way special to him, or that their relationship could become permanent. He had met her days after he had learned of his grandmother's will, when he had been reeling from shock and consumed with rage.

Giselle had been just another blonde at a party, but when she had tearfully confided that she had been dropped from her modelling contract, and was worried about how she would be able to afford the rent on her flat, Luca had seen a way to resolve both their problems. He had money, but he needed a wife. Giselle needed money and she had agreed to his marriage deal.

It was as simple as that, and he did not need her to complicate things with messy emotions that he was incapable of reciprocating.

'The jewellers who sold you my diamond ring have a matching necklace on display in the window.' Giselle arranged herself on the pillows so that her breasts tilted forward provocatively. 'It would be nice to have the set.' She pouted when Luca ignored her attempt to pull him down onto the bed. 'Why are you getting dressed? It's the weekend and you don't have to go to work today, do you?'

Luca forbore from pointing out that he hadn't built up his successful fashion label at the same time as running De Rossi Enterprises by working weekdays, from nine till five. Twenty-four/seven was nearer the mark. For the past fifteen years he had slogged his guts out to restore the De Rossi brand, but he faced losing everything he had achieved if he did not give in to his grandmother's outrageous attempt to blackmail him from beyond the grave.

Nonna Violetta had wanted him to marry, and marry he would, Luca thought with a grim smile as he stared down at his bride-to-be. But it would be a sham marriage, a business deal, and the only reason he intended to go through with it was because it would allow him to give Rosalie the special care she needed.

'I have to go to England,' he told Giselle as he pulled on his trousers, followed by a shirt and jacket.

The superb tailoring of the suit he had designed himself emphasised his lean, six-feet-plus frame, and the shirt moulded his powerful abdominal muscles.

'I've been invited to a society wedding,' he said drily.

Giselle's pout switched from sexy to sulky. 'You could take *me*. Who is getting married?'

'Charles Fairfax is someone I know from school. He's marrying the sister-in-law of my good friend Sultan Kadir of Zenhab.'

'You're friends with a *sultan*?' Giselle's eyes widened. 'I bet he's mega-rich. Will I meet him when I'm your wife?'

Not if he could help it, Luca thought to himself. Kadir Al Sulaimar was his closest friend, and would understand his reasons for marrying Giselle. But the truth was that

Luca felt uncomfortable about his fake marriage. He was a world-weary cynic, but when he had acted as best man to Kadir at his wedding to his beautiful English wife, Lexi, nine months ago, Luca had witnessed the intense love between the couple and had briefly felt envious of something that he could never have.

'Who is this sister-in-law of the Sultan that your friend Charles is marrying?' Giselle flicked through the pages of a gossip magazine that she had brought with her because Luca only kept boring books at the penthouse. 'Is she a celebrity?'

'Unlikely.' Luca had a vivid recollection of Athena Howard's sapphire-blue eyes, her oval-shaped face, and the determined chin that hinted at a stubborn streak in her nature. In Zenhab he had felt curious because Athena shared no physical resemblance with her sister. Lexi, with her silvery-blond hair and slender figure, had been a breathtakingly beautiful bride, but her sister and chief bridesmaid had faded into the background.

Luca had simply been carrying out his duties as best man when he had stood beside Athena for the wedding photographs and later led her onto the dance floor. She was petite in stature, and the top of her head had only reached his mid-chest. Following Zenhabian tradition she had worn a headscarf during the wedding ceremony, but at the private reception Luca had been surprised to see her long braid of dark brown hair—until she had explained that Lexi was her adoptive sister and they were not related by blood.

A memory slipped into Luca's mind of the perfume that Athena had worn at the wedding—an evocative fragrance of old-fashioned roses that had stirred his senses as they had walked together in the palace gardens. Stirred rather more than his senses, in actual fact, he recalled ruefully.

He could not explain to himself why he had kissed Athena Howard, or why the memory of that brief kiss still lingered in his subconscious.

Giselle's petulant voice pulled him from his thoughts. '*Why* can't I come to the wedding with you? Anyone would think you were trying to avoid being seen with me.'

'That's not true, *cara*. But I can't turn up at a wedding with an uninvited companion.'

The hard gleam in Giselle's eyes warned Luca that damage limitation was needed. His fiancée had been blessed with beauty at the expense of brains, but she was well aware that his thirty-fifth birthday was two weeks away. He felt a surge of impotent fury that everything that mattered to him lay in the hands of a brainless bimbo. It wasn't Giselle's fault, he reminded himself. She was the solution—not the cause of his problems.

'While I'm away, why don't you visit the jewellers and buy that diamond necklace?'

He dropped a credit card onto the bed and Giselle snatched it up.

'I might as well get the matching earrings, too.'

'Why not?' Luca murmured drily.

So what if his bride-to-be had an avaricious streak a mile wide? he thought five minutes later, as he walked out of the building and climbed into the chauffeur-driven car waiting to take him to the airport. What were a few diamonds when he would soon have everything he wanted?

Inexplicably, the memory of a pair of sapphire-blue eyes slid into his mind. He gave an indifferent shrug. Later today Athena Howard would become Mrs Charles Fairfax. He had only agreed to attend the wedding as a favour to Kadir.

Luca frowned, thinking of the phone call he'd received from the Sultan of Zenhab.

'Lexi is upset that we can't fly to England for her sister's wedding because the baby is due any day. We'd both be grateful if you would attend the wedding in our place and try and talk to Athena. Lexi is worried that her sister is making a mistake by marring Charles. You and I both know from our schooldays that Charlie Fairfax is a charmless oaf,' Kadir had reminded Luca. 'But if Athena seems happy then you won't need to hang around. However, if you detect that she's having doubts about the marriage...'

'What do you expect me to do?' Luca had demanded.

'Stop the wedding from going ahead,' Kadir had replied succinctly. 'I don't know how, exactly, but I'm sure you'll think of something.'

She did not look so much like a meringue as a cream puff, Athena decided as she studied her reflection in the mirror in her bedroom at Woodley Lodge, the country house of Lord and Lady Fairfax. But it was too late now to wonder why she had allowed herself to be persuaded to choose this crinoline-inspired wedding dress with a skirt so wide that she could be mistaken for the White Cliffs of Dover. The puffed sleeves broadened her top half, while the enormous skirt with its layers of white satin ruffles accentuated her lack of height and made her look dumpy.

'You'll be marrying into the aristocracy in front of five hundred guests,' her mother had reminded Athena when she had tentatively remarked that a simpler style of dress might suit her better. 'You need a dress that will make you the centre of attention.'

Butterflies performed a clog dance in Athena's stomach at the prospect of five hundred people looking at her as she walked down the aisle. Please God, she prayed she didn't do something embarrassing like trip on her long skirt and annoy Charlie.

She hoped he was in a better mood than he had been the previous evening. She had felt awful when she'd spilt red wine on the cream velvet carpet in the sitting room. Lady Fairfax had said that it didn't matter, although she'd compressed her lips into a thin line, but Charlie had made a fuss and had said she was like a bull in a china shop.

Athena bit her lip. Sometimes Charlie said quite hurtful things—almost as if he didn't care about her feelings. During the past year that they had been engaged, she had tried her best to be a gracious and elegant hostess at the dinner parties he had asked her to organise. But she would be the first to admit that she was clumsy—especially when she was nervous—and she always seemed to do something wrong that earned Charlie's criticism.

Heaven knew what he would say when he heard of her latest catastrophe. While inserting the contact lenses she wore because she was short-sighted she had dropped a lens—the last of her disposable lenses as it turned out—down the plughole of the sink, which meant that she would have to wear her glasses to the wedding.

Athena glanced longingly out of the window at the cloudless September sky. It was a beautiful day, and she would love to be outside, but she'd had to spend hours having her hair styled in an elaborate 'up-do', which required dozens of hairpins and so much hairspray that her hair felt as rigid as a helmet. And a make-up artist had applied a heavy foundation to her face which made her feel as though she was wearing a mask. Dramatic eye make-up and a cherry-red shade of lipstick certainly made her noticeable.

The person in the mirror did not look like her. Somewhere in all the wedding preparations Athena Howard had turned into someone she didn't recognise, she thought ruefully.

She tried to reassure herself that the sick feeling in the

pit of her stomach was just pre-wedding nerves. But her sense of panic would not go away. Her legs felt as if they had turned to jelly and she sank down onto the edge of the bed.

Why was she about to get married in a four-thousand-pound dress that did not suit her? That amount of money would keep the orphanage she supported in India running for months. She thought of the House of Happy Smiles in Jaipur, which was in desperate need of funds, and wished that instead of paying for an expensive wedding the money could have been donated to the fundraising campaign she had set up for the orphanage. She didn't want an extravagant wedding—she would have been happier with a small event—but what she wanted didn't matter.

It was typical of her that she had tried so hard to please everyone—her parents, Lady Fairfax and Charlie—that she had ignored the voice inside her head warning her that she was making a mistake. It had taken a phone call from her sister last night to make her confront her doubts.

'Do you love Charles Fairfax with all your heart? And does he love you?' Lexi had asked her. 'If you can't say yes to both those questions you should cancel the wedding.'

'I can't cancel it!'

The tension Athena had felt during her conversation with her sister gripped her again now. Through the window she could see the huge marquee on the lawn. Dozens of waiters in white jackets were scurrying to and fro, carrying trays of glasses for the champagne reception which was to take place after the four o'clock wedding ceremony at the village church. Later in the evening there would be a banquet for five hundred guests, followed by a firework display.

Charlie had said that three members of the House of Lords who were friends of his father's were on the guest list, as well as a minor member of the royal family. Calling off the wedding at this late stage was not an option. It was all her parents had talked about for months, and her father, for the first time in Athena's life, had told her that he was proud of her.

Lexi's words played in Athena's head. *'Do you love Charles Fairfax with all your heart?'*

A picture flashed into her mind of Lexi and Kadir on their wedding day. A huge state celebration befitting the Sultan of Zenhab and his bride had been followed by a private ceremony at the palace for close family and friends. The couple's happiness had been tangible, and the adoration in Kadir's eyes as he had looked at his wife had been deeply moving.

Charlie had never looked at *her* like that, Athena thought, unconsciously gnawing on her lip until she tasted blood. His eyes had never blazed with fierce possession, as if she was the most precious person in the world and the absolute love of his life.

She and Charlie had a different relationship from Lexi and Kadir, she told herself. Charlie worked long hours in the City, and it wasn't his fault he was often tired and tetchy.

Because he stayed at his London flat during the week, and she lived at her parents' house in Reading, they had only seen each other at weekends since they had got engaged. Either she had stayed at Woodley Lodge when Charlie had visited his parents, or she had gone to his flat in London. But even there they were rarely alone, because his friend Dominic always seemed to be around.

Sometimes Athena gained the impression that she was in the way, and that Charlie would rather go to his club with Dominic than spend time with her.

And then there was the subject of sex—or rather the lack

of it. She had never been able to bring herself to tell Charlie what had happened to her when she was eighteen—it was too personal, too shameful, and she never wanted to speak about it. And she had felt relieved when Charlie had said he was happy to wait until they were married before they slept together because he wanted to do things 'properly'. But lately she had been concerned about the lack of sexual spark between them.

Lexi and Kadir had barely been able to keep their hands off one another at their wedding, she remembered. Lexi had confided that she was sure that her baby, which was due any day now, had been conceived on her wedding night.

Charlie's kiss lacked a vital ingredient—but Athena would never have known it if Kadir's best man had not kissed her. She closed her eyes and tried to try to block Luca De Rossi's handsome face from her mind. But his sculpted features—the slashing cheekbones, aquiline nose and the faintly cynical curve of his mouth—had haunted her subconscious since she had met him in Zenhab.

She had heard of his reputation as a playboy and assumed she would not find any man who thought that women had been put on earth solely for his pleasure appealing. So it had been a shock when one smouldering glance from Luca's amber-gold eyes had turned her insides to molten liquid. She had never met a man as devastatingly sexy. He had stirred feelings in her that she had not known existed—or perhaps she had simply done a good job of suppressing her sensuality since she was eighteen, she thought ruefully.

She hadn't expected Luca to kiss her when they had walked together in the palace gardens in the moonlight, and she certainly had not expected that she would respond to the sensual magic of his lips and kiss him back. She had pulled out of his arms after a few seconds, assailed with guilt as she had frantically reminded herself that she was engaged to Charlie. Back in England she had tried to forget about the kiss, but sometimes in her dreams she relived the incandescent pleasure of Luca De Rossi's lips on hers...

What was she doing? *Why* was she thinking about a kiss she had shared with a notorious playboy she was never likely to meet again when all her thoughts should be on the man she was set to marry in two hours' time?

Athena jumped up from the bed and paced up and down the bedroom. Of course one kiss with a notorious playboy nine months ago had meant nothing. But deep down hadn't it made her realise that there was something missing from her relationship with Charlie? She had ignored her misgivings because the wedding preparations had already been well under way, and by marrying the future Lord Fairfax she had felt she was making up for her parents' disappointment that she was not the brilliantly academic daughter they had hoped for.

She had convinced herself that she was doing the right thing, but now she felt as though iron bands were crushing her ribs, and she couldn't breathe properly as her feeling of panic intensified and solidified into a stark truth.

She did not love Charlie with all her heart.

She had been flattered when he had shown an interest in her, and frankly astounded when he had proposed. Her parents had been over the moon that she was going to marry a member of the landed gentry. She remembered that at her engagement party Lexi had warned her that she shouldn't marry to earn their parents' approval. She had assured her sister that she loved Charlie, but she had been fooling herself—and probably Lexi, too, Athena thought bleakly.

She took a shuddering breath and ordered herself to

calm down. Perhaps if she spoke to Charlie he would be able to reassure her that he loved her and that everything would be all right. It was supposed to be bad luck for the bride to see the groom before the wedding on the day, but she *had* to see him and be reassured that she was simply suffering from a bad case of nerves.

Charlie's bedroom was in a private wing of the house. As Athena hurried along the corridor she almost collided with the Fairfaxes' dour butler, Baines.

'Master Charles gave strict instructions that he does not want to be disturbed while he is changing into his wedding attire,' Baines told her in a disapproving tone.

Usually Athena felt intimidated by the butler, but she resisted the urge to slink away back to her room and said coolly, 'Thank you, Baines, but I must see my future husband.'

The butler looked as though he wanted to argue, but then he nodded his head stiffly and walked away.

She paused outside Charlie's room and took a deep breath. Just as she was about to knock she heard voices from the other side of the door.

'This is the last time we can be together for a while. I'm going to have to play the role of devoted husband for the next few months.'

'I guess so,' a second voice drawled. 'It will be unbearable for both of us. You say that Athena wants to try for a child straight away?'

'Oh, she's mad keen to have a baby.' Charlie laughed. 'She'll be an ideal brood mare, because to be honest she's not overly bright or ambitious for a career. I'll need a few drinks before I bed her, but with any luck she'll get pregnant quickly and I won't have to touch her again because all she'll be concerned about is the sprog—leaving you and I free to carry on where we left off.'

Athena's hand was shaking so much that she could barely grip the door handle. Had Charlie been joking? Why had he said such horrible things about her to the other person in his bedroom? She recognised the second voice—but it *couldn't* be who she thought…

She turned the handle and flung open the door with such force that the heavy oak creaked on its hinges.

'Athena!'

Charlie's startled shout reverberated around the room, before fading to leave a deafening silence that was broken by his best man's amused drawl. 'Well, that's let the cat out of the bag.'

'I don't understand—' Athena choked.

But of course she *did* understand—even though she was 'not overly bright'. Charlie's top hat and cravat were scattered across the floor, together with the grey morning suit that he was to wear to the wedding, and he was in bed with his friend Dominic. The best man was also naked—apart from his top hat, which was perched at a jaunty angle on his head.

'For God's sake, Athena, what are you doing here?' Charlie sprang out of bed and hastily thrust his arms into a silk dressing gown.

How ironic that this was the first time she had seen her fiancé's naked body, Athena thought, swallowing down her hysteria.

'I needed to talk to you.' Her earlier doubts about marrying Charlie were nothing compared to the shock she felt now, at seeing him with his best man. 'Charlie…I…I've realised that I can't marry you. And this…' her gaze flew to Dominic '…this confirms that I was right to have second thoughts.'

'Don't be stupid—of course you have to marry me,' Charlie said sharply as he walked over to her and caught hold of her arm. 'You can't back out of the wedding now. My mother would have a fit. And think about how upset *your* parents would be,' he added cleverly, going directly for her weak spot. 'It will be all right, Athena,' he said, in a more conciliatory tone. 'Dom and I…' He shrugged. 'It means nothing…it's just a fling.'

'No, it isn't. I heard the two of you when I was outside the bedroom. What I don't understand is why you asked me to marry you when you know you're—' she broke off helplessly.

'Gay,' Charlie finished for her. He gave a mocking laugh. 'That's why I need a wife—to give me an air of respectability. There's still discrimination against gay men working in the City, and if I came out it would wreck my career. It would also devastate my father if he found out. The shock, so soon after his heart surgery, could finish him off. But if I marry and provide an heir I'll keep the parents happy and my inheritance safe—coincidentally.'

'But you can't live a lie for the rest of your life—and nor can you expect me to,' Athena said shakily. 'I realise it will be hard, but you need to be honest about who you are.'

Despite her shock, she felt some sympathy for Charlie's situation—especially as she knew his father was frail after undergoing a heart bypass operation. But she felt hurt that Charlie had expected her to provide a cover for his true sexual preference.

'I'm sorry, but I won't marry you.'

'You *have* to.' Charlie gripped her arm harder to prevent her from leaving the room.

She shook her head. 'I realised this morning that I don't love you, and I see now that you have never loved me. Let me go, Charlie.'

'You *need* to marry me.' Desperation crept into his voice. 'You want children. Who else do you think will want to marry a twenty-five-year-old virgin with a hang-up about sex?' Charlie said viciously.

Athena paled. 'Please don't be nasty, Charlie. Can't we at least end this as friends?'

His face was mottled red with anger. 'You silly bitch. If you refuse to marry me you'll ruin *everything*.'

She had to get away. From somewhere, Athena found a burst of strength to tear herself out of Charlie's grasp. As she fled from the room his voice followed her down the corridor.

'I didn't mean it. Come back, Athena, and let's talk. We can work something out.'

She ran into her bedroom and closed the door, leaning back against the wood while her chest heaved as if she had just completed a marathon.

Charlie and Dominic! Why hadn't she guessed? There had been signs, she realised, but she had simply thought the two men were good friends. No wonder Charlie had said he was happy to wait until they were married before they slept together. He had sensed that she had inhibitions about sex and he had used her—only asked her to marry him so that she would be a smokescreen to hide his relationship with Dominic.

Her stomach churned. What was she going to do? What reason could she give for calling the wedding off, even supposing she found the courage to walk downstairs and face Lord and Lady Fairfax? She would not expose Charlie's secret relationship with Dominic. He had done an unforgivable thing by trying to trick her into marriage, but it was against her nature to betray him. It was up to Charlie to be honest with his parents about his private life.

Oh, God, what a mess!

She stared at the phone, feeling tempted to call her sister. Lexi would know what to do. But it wouldn't be fair to worry her when she was so close to giving birth, and Athena knew that her sister *would* worry about her. Although Lexi now lived far away, in the desert kingdom of Zenhab, the bond between the sisters had grown stronger since Lexi had married Kadir and become utterly confident of his love.

Voices sounded from out in the corridor, and when Athena opened her door a crack she saw her parents emerging from the guest bedroom across the hall. Her father looked elegant, in top hat and tails, and her mother was wearing a spectacular wide-brimmed hat covered in lilac silk roses.

'Who would have guessed that our daughter will be related by marriage to *royalty*?' Veronica Howard said excitedly.

'*Distantly* related,' her husband pointed out. 'According to the *Encyclopedia of Genealogy* Lord Fairfax is a seventh cousin twice removed of the royal family. But, yes, Athena has certainly done well.'

Athena quickly closed the door. Tears filled her eyes. She couldn't bear to disappoint her parents again, as she had done on many occasions—such as when she had failed to get into university. She was the only Howard not to study at Oxford, as her father had said so sadly.

But the alternative was to continue with the wedding and marry Charlie even though she had discovered the truth about him.

There was another option. *You could disappear*, whispered a voice in her head. It would be cowardly, her conscience argued. But she felt trapped in a truly appalling situation and in her despair all she wanted to do was run away.

She could still hear her parents' voices out on the landing. Her only escape route was via the window, but her bedroom was on the second floor, overlooking a gravel path at the side of the house. Although the walls of the house were covered in ivy, and the thick, gnarled stems looked strong enough to support her weight...

Without giving herself time to think, she did at least remember to grab her bag, containing her phone and other essentials that she had packed for when she and Charlie flew to their honeymoon in the Seychelles. She wouldn't need the daring black lace negligee she had bought for her wedding night now, she thought bleakly.

From the window the ground did not look too far away, but when she climbed out onto the windowsill and grabbed hold of the ivy, the drop down to the gravel path seemed terrifyingly distant. It had been a stupid idea, she acknowledged. She froze with fear, unable to haul herself back through the window, but too afraid to climb down the ivy.

Oh, dear God! She looked down and instantly felt dizzy and sick with terror.

'Let go and I'll catch you.'

The voice from below was vaguely familiar, but Athena couldn't place it. She couldn't do anything but cling to the twisting vines that were beginning to tear under her weight. Suddenly the ivy was ripped away from the wall—and she screamed as she plummeted towards the ground.

CHAPTER TWO

WOLF'S EYES—amber irises flecked with gold and ringed with black—were watching her intently, Athena discovered as her eyelashes fluttered open. She saw heavy brows draw together in a frown above an aquiline nose.

'Athena.' The voice was as rich and dark as molasses, and the sexy accent sent a tingle down her spine. 'You must have fainted. Is that how you came to fall out of the window?'

The concern in the voice penetrated Athena's hazy thoughts. She blinked, and focused on the darkly masculine face centimetres from hers.

'Luca?'

She was suddenly aware that his strong arms were holding her. Her mind flashed back to those terrifying minutes when she had clung to the ivy growing on the wall. She remembered the sensation of falling, but nothing more.

'I caught you when you fell,' Luca told her—which explained why she wasn't lying on the gravel path with multiple fractures to her limbs.

The fact that her rescuer was Luca De Rossi was yet another shock to add to a day from which she fully expected to wake up and find had been a nightmare.

He certainly felt real. She became aware that her cheek was resting against his broad chest, and she could make out the shadow of dark hair beneath his white shirt. The spicy sent of his aftershave stirred her senses and reminded her of that moonlit night in the Zenhab palace gardens, his dark head descending as he brushed his lips across hers.

Heat unfurled deep inside her and her face flooded with colour. 'What are *you* doing here?' she mumbled.

'I'm a wedding guest. I knew Charles Fairfax at Eton and he sent me an invitation.' Luca frowned. 'My name must be on the guest list.'

'I've never seen the guest list.' Tears, partly from the shock of falling, filled Athena's eyes. 'Can you believe that? I don't even know who has been invited to my own wedding.'

Luca had caught Athena before she'd hit the ground, so he knew that she could not be concussed, but she still wasn't making any sense. He controlled his impatience and set her down on her feet. She swayed unsteadily. Her face was as white as her dress.

The designer in him shuddered as he studied the abomination of a wedding dress. A skirt that wide should theoretically have worked well as a parachute when she'd fallen out of the window, he thought sardonically.

He glanced up at the window ledge and his mouth compressed as he imagined the serious injuries she might have sustained if he hadn't caught her.

'It was stupid to stand beside an open window if you were feeling faint.'

'Stupid' summed her up, Athena thought bitterly. She remembered how Charlie had described her as 'not overly bright' and her insides squirmed with humiliation.

'I didn't faint. I climbed out of the window because I need to get away.' Her voice rose a notch. 'I *can't* marry Charles!'

Over Athena's shoulder Luca watched a group of waiters struggling to carry a huge ice sculpture of a swan into

the marquee. In another part of the garden cages containing white doves were being unloaded from a van, so that
they could be released during the reception. The wedding
promised to be a circus and the woman in front of him
looked like a clown, with a ton of make-up plastered over
her face and that ridiculous dress. He barely recognised
her as the unassuming, understated Athena Howard he
had met in Zenhab.

'Here.' He handed her the pair of spectacles that had
sailed through the air just before she had landed in his
arms.

'Thank you.' She put them on and blinked at him owl-
ishly.

'I don't remember that you wore glasses in Zenhab.'

'I usually wear contact lenses, but I've been so busy for
the last few weeks with the wedding preparations I forgot
to order a new supply.'

Athena felt swamped by a familiar sense of failure and
inadequacy. It was true that she was forgetful. 'If only
you were not such a daydreamer, Athena,' had been her
parents' constant complaint when she was growing up. 'If
you stopped writing silly stories and concentrated on your
homework your maths results might improve.'

Thinking about her parents made Athena feel worse
than ever. She had never been able to live up to their expectations. And then she pictured Charlie and Dominic in
bed together and shame cramped in the pit of her stomach that she wasn't even capable of attracting a man—
certainly not a man like Luca De Rossi. The thought slid
into her head as she studied his sculpted facial features
and exotic olive colouring. He was watching her through
heavy-lidded eyes and his lips were curled in a faintly
cynical expression that made him seem remote but at the
same time devastatingly sexy.

A van with the name of a fireworks company on its sides drove up to the house. She remembered Charlie had said that Lord and Lady Fairfax had spent thousands of pounds on a lavish firework display as a finale for the wedding reception. The sight of the van escalated her feeling of panic.

'I have to get away,' she told Luca desperately.

Luca recalled Kadir's instruction to stop the wedding if Athena had had second thoughts. The fact that she had risked her neck to escape marrying Charlie Fairfax was pretty conclusive evidence that she had changed her mind.

'I parked my car next to the gamekeeper's lodge. If we leave now we might get away without anyone noticing.'

Athena hesitated, and glanced up at Charlie's bedroom window in the far corner of the house. She thought she saw a movement by the window, but it must have been a trick of the light because when she peered through her glasses again there was no one there. She was gripped with indecision. Should she go with Luca, a man she had only met once before but who was a good friend of her brother-in-law? Or should she stay and face the emotional fireworks that were bound to explode when she announced to Lord and Lady Fairfax and her parents that the wedding was off?

'What are you waiting for?'

Luca's impatient voice urged her to turn and follow him along the path. Moments later he halted by a futuristic-looking sports car which, despite its long, sleek body, had a tiny, cramped interior.

'I won't fit in there,' Athena said, looking from the car to her voluminous wedding dress.

'Turn around.' There was no time for niceties, Luca decided as he lifted the hem of her skirt up to her waist and untied the drawstring waistband of the hooped petticoat beneath her dress.

'What are you *doing*?' Athena gasped when Luca tugged the petticoat down and she felt his hands skim over her thighs.

She blushed at the thought of him seeing the sheer stockings held up by wide bands of lace. He held her hand to help her balance while she stepped out of the petticoat. Without the rigid frame her dress was less cumbersome and she managed to squeeze into the passenger seat. Luca bundled her long skirt around her and slammed the door shut.

Thank heavens she wasn't wearing her veil, Athena thought, stifling a hysterical laugh that turned to a sob. It was bad enough that the elaborate bun on top of her head was being squashed by the low roof.

Her thoughts scattered when Luca slid behind the wheel and fired the engine. He gave her no time to question her actions as he accelerated down the driveway.

Heaven knew how fast they were travelling. Trees and hedges flashed past as they raced along the narrow country lanes and Athena closed her eyes as she imagined Luca overshooting a bend and catapulting the car into a field.

'Where do you want to go?'

She did not reply because she had no idea what she was going to do next. Her priority had been to escape from the wedding and she had not planned any further ahead.

'Do you want me to take you home? Where do you live?'

Luca groped for his patience *and* the gearstick. Although the skirt of Athena's wedding dress had deflated without the hooped petticoat, the car was still filled with yards of white satin. *Dio*, he could do without being landed with a runaway bride when he had enough problems of his own.

The text message he had received from Giselle announcing that she wanted to get married in Venice had left him feeling rattled. He had arranged a civil wedding ceremony at the town hall in Milan. As soon as the legal formalities were done he would get Villa De Rossi and the security he so desperately wanted for his daughter, and Giselle would get a million pounds.

Why did women always have to complicate things? Luca thought irritably. More worryingly, why was Giselle trying to make something of their sham wedding, which as far as he was concerned could never be anything but a business arrangement?

'I can't go home. I live with my parents, and I don't think they will want to see me once they find out what I've done,' Athena said in low voice.

'Do you have a friend you could stay with for a while? Maybe someone you work with who will help you out?'

She had grown apart from her old friends since she had moved into Charlie's social circle, Athena realised. And although she had tried to get to know his friends she had never felt accepted by the City bankers and their sophisticated wives.

'I don't have a job,' she admitted.

And without an income she had no means of supporting herself, she thought worriedly. The few hundred pounds in her savings account was not enough for her to be able to rent somewhere to live while she looked for a position as a nursery assistant.

'If you don't work, what do you do all day?' Luca drawled.

He thought of Giselle, whose sole occupation seemed to be shopping. It was funny, but when he had met Athena at Kadir and Lexi's wedding she hadn't struck him as one of the vacuous 'ladies who lunch' brigade. Actually, she had seemed rather sweet, although she was not his type. He went for blondes with endless legs and a surfeit of sexual confidence—not petite brunettes with eyes big enough to drown in.

He hadn't planned to kiss her when he had walked with her in the palace gardens during the evening reception at Kadir and Lexi's wedding. It must have been the effect of the bewitching Zenhabian moon, Luca thought derisively. Athena had given him a shy smile, and for some inexplicable reason he had brushed his mouth across hers.

He had felt her lips tremble and for a crazy moment he had been tempted to deepen the caress, to slide his hand to her nape and crush her rosebud mouth beneath his lips. His arousal had been unexpectedly fierce, and her soft, curvaceous body had sent out an unmistakable siren call. But the sparkle of an engagement ring on her finger had caught his eye and he'd abruptly bade her goodnight before returning to the palace.

Imagination was a funny thing, he brooded. He could almost taste Athena on his lips, and he recognised her perfume—that delicate fragrance of old-fashioned roses that filled the car and teased his senses.

'Over the past few months I've attended courses on French cookery and flower arranging and learning how to be a perfect hostess, so that I could arrange dinner parties for Charlie's business clients,' Athena said stiffly. At least she would never have to stuff another mushroom now she was not going to be Charlie's wife.

She caught her breath when Luca slammed on the brakes as they approached a sharp bend in the road. Coming towards them was a fleet of silver saloon cars decorated with white ribbons—obviously heading for Woodley Lodge to drive the bride and groom and other members of the wedding party to the church.

Her heart juddered. *Oh, God! What had she done?* Had Charlie broken the news to his parents that the wedding was off and the reason why? What would her parents think when they heard that she had run away?

She remembered her mother's hat, covered in lilac silk roses, the pride in her father's voice, and suddenly the dam holding back her emotions burst. Tears poured in an unstoppable stream down her cheeks and she sniffed inelegantly, feeling more wretched than she had ever felt in her life.

'Here,' Luca said gruffly, pushing a tissue into her hands.

He had never seen a woman cry so hard before. He was used to crocodile tears when one of his mistresses wanted something. Women seemed to have an amazing ability to turn on the waterworks when it suited them, he thought sardonically. But this was different. Athena was clearly distraught and he felt uncomfortable with her raw emotions.

He reached into the glove box and took out a hip flask. 'Have a few sips of brandy and you'll feel better.'

'I never drink spirits,' she choked between sobs.

'Then today seems a good day to start,' he said drily.

Athena did not like to argue—especially when she glanced at Luca's hard profile. She took a cautious sip of brandy and felt warmth seep through her veins.

'You're probably wondering why I've decided not to marry Charlie.'

'Not particularly. Kadir asked me to make sure you were happy, and if not to stop the wedding. I'm not interested in the reason why you've changed your mind.'

'Kadir asked you to stop the wedding?'

Luca glanced at her, and was relieved to see that the brandy had brought colour back to her cheeks. 'Lexi was sure you were making a mistake, and Kadir would do anything to prevent his wife from worrying—especially when she's about to go into labour.'

He had done what he had been asked to do, Luca

brooded. But neither Kadir nor Athena seemed to have planned further than halting the wedding. He could not abandon her, but the only place he could think of taking her was back to his hotel. Perhaps she would get a grip on her emotions there and then take herself out of his life so that he could concentrate on his own pre-wedding problems with Giselle.

Athena took another sip of brandy and felt herself relax a little. She had a headache from crying and she closed her eyes, lulled by the motion of the car...

The strident blare of a horn woke her, and she was confused when she saw that they were in a traffic jam. A glance at her watch revealed that she had slept for forty minutes.

Her memory returned with a jolt. She had run away from her wedding—dubbed by society commentators as 'the wedding of the year'. Luca De Rossi had helped her to escape in his sports car. For some reason the sight of his tanned hands on the steering wheel evoked a quiver in her belly. A picture flashed into her mind of those hands caressing her, his dark olive skin a stark contrast to her pale flesh.

She swallowed. 'Where are we?'

'London, Mayfair, to be exact. I've brought you to my hotel to give you time to decide what your plans are.' Luca handed her another tissue. 'You might want to clean yourself up before we go inside.'

Athena had recognised the name of the exclusive five-star hotel that overlooked Marble Arch and Hyde Park. Her heart sank when she pulled down the car's sun visor to look in the vanity mirror and saw her face streaked with black mascara and red lipstick smudged across her chin like a garish Halloween mask.

She did her best with the tissue, and when Luca had

parked in the underground car park and they'd taken the lift up to the hotel's opulent reception area, she shot into the ladies' cloakroom to avoid the curious stares of the other guests, who were clearly intrigued to see a tearful bride.

In one of the private cubicles she ran a sink of hot water and scrubbed the make-up off her face. Her elaborate bun had slipped to one side of her head, and she began the task of removing the dozens of hairpins before brushing her hair to get rid of the coating of hairspray. She gave a start when her phone rang from the depths of her bag, and the sight of her mother's name on the caller display caused her stomach to knot with tension.

Out in the hotel lobby, Luca tapped his foot on the marble-tiled floor and tried to contain his impatience as he waited for Athena to emerge from the cloakroom. Long experience of women warned him that she might be in there for hours while she reapplied her make-up. While he was waiting he reread the latest text message he had received from Giselle.

I have decided to ask my four young nieces to be brides-maids at our wedding and I've seen the most adorable dresses for them to wear.

The message included a photo of a sickly-sweet child dressed in a shepherdess costume. Luca ground his teeth. *Bridesmaids!* Giselle was pushing his patience to its limit. And another text revealed that she knew she had the upper hand.

I hope you will be amenable, chéri, because I'm sure I don't need to remind you that you will be thirty-five in two short weeks.

The warning in Giselle's second text was clear. *Do what I want, or...* Or what? Luca thought grimly. It was unlikely that his bimbo bride would give up a million pounds over an argument about bridesmaids, but he dared not risk upsetting her when he was so close to his goal.

His phone rang and he frowned when he saw that the caller was the other thorn in his side: his grandmother's brother, Executive Vice President of De Rossi Enterprises, Emilio Nervetti.

'This continued uncertainty about who will head the company is affecting profits.' Emilio went straight for the jugular. 'I intend to ask the board to support a vote of no confidence in your leadership. Under the terms of my dear sister Violetta's will, two weeks from now you stand to lose your position as chairman unless you marry before your birthday—which you show no signs of doing.'

'On the contrary,' Luca said curtly. 'My wedding is arranged for next week—*before* I turn thirty-five. My marriage will allow me to continue in my role as chairman of De Rossi Enterprises, and after I have been married for one year I will not only secure the chairmanship permanently, but also the deeds to Villa De Rossi, and the right to use the De Rossi name for the fashion label I created.'

For a few seconds an angry silence hummed down the line, before Emilio said coldly, 'I am sure the board members will be relieved to know that you intend to give up your playboy lifestyle for a life of decency and sobriety. But I'm afraid I cannot be so confident. You inherited your mother's alley-cat morals, Luca. And God knows what genes you inherited from your father—whoever he was.'

Luca cut the call and swore savagely beneath his breath. His great-uncle's dig about his parentage was expected, but it still made him seethe. Emilio had only been given a position on the board of De Rossi Enterprises because his sister—Luca's grandmother—had married Luca's grandfather. *He* was the rightful De Rossi heir, Luca thought grimly, even though his grandparents had disapproved of him.

Luca's grandfather, Aberto De Rossi, had lacked the vision of his father, founder of De Rossi Enterprises, Raimondo De Rossi. But at least Aberto had been a steady figure at the head of the company. With no son to succeed him Aberto had given his daughter Beatriz a prominent position on the board—with disastrous results.

Beatriz had been too busy with her party lifestyle to take an interest in running the company, and her scandalous private life had brought disrepute to the De Rossi brand name and resulted in falling profits.

Eventually Aberto had run out of patience with his daughter and had named his illegitimate grandson as his heir—with the stipulation that Luca could only inherit with his grandmother's agreement, and only after her death. Aberto had also voiced his reservations about Luca's decision to study fashion design alongside a business degree.

However, at the age of twenty Luca had presented his first collection at New York Fashion Week and received critical acclaim. The launch of his fashion label, DRD, had restored the De Rossi brand to the prestige it had known under the legendary Raimondo. But, according to the terms of Luca's grandmother's will, he faced losing everything. All his hard work and achievements had meant nothing to Nonna Violetta—and he knew why.

He was a *bastardo*—the product of a brief union between his mother and a croupier she had met in a casino—and in his grandparents' eyes not a true De Rossi. He had inherited his talent for innovative design from his great-grandfather, but Luca had been a shameful reminder to his grandparents that their only daughter had made the family a laughing stock.

Luca's jaw clenched. He had done everything he could to win his grandparents' approval, but it had never been enough to earn their love. And after Aberto had died, Violetta had become increasingly demanding, saying that Luca must marry and provide an heir. Presumably she had believed that an heir from the *bastardo* De Rossi was better than no heir at all, he thought bitterly.

His grandmother had threatened to use her casting vote with the board to have him replaced as head of the company. And even after her death she still sought to control her grandson by stipulating in her will that he must be married by his thirty-fifth birthday or the Villa De Rossi would be sold to a consortium that was eager to turn the house into a hotel. Luca would also be removed from his role as chairman of De Rossi Enterprises and barred from holding any other position within the company. And, although he owned DRD, he would lose the right to use the De Rossi name for his fashion label.

Luca's lip curled. Nonna Violetta's ultimate betrayal had been that threat to ban him from using the name he had been given at birth for his design business. It was a vindictive reminder that he had only been called De Rossi because his mother hadn't known his father's surname. Despite everything he had done to restore the fortunes of the company, to his grandparents when they had been alive, and to some of the board members of De Rossi Enterprises, he would always be a *bastardo*.

Anger burned in his gut, and with it another emotion he did not want to recognise. He had once assumed he had been hurt too often by his grandmother and no longer cared what she thought of him. But when he had heard the details of her will he had felt sick to his stomach.

He did not care so much if he lost control of De Rossi Enterprises, and he could always rename his fashion label—he might even enjoy the challenge of starting again and rebranding his designs, and he only wished he could stand at his grandmother's grave and laugh at her attempt to manipulate him. But there was one very good reason why he couldn't. Two reasons, he amended. The first was the Villa De Rossi and the second was his daughter Rosalie, whom he loved and was determined to protect at all costs—even if that cost was his pride.

His phone pinged, heralding another text from Giselle. *Dio*, he needed to return to Italy so that he could keep his future bride satisfied with sex until she had signed her name on the marriage certificate, Luca thought sardonically.

He glanced across the lobby and saw Athena walk out of the cloakroom. She looked younger without the heavy make-up, and now that her hair was loose he saw that it still fell almost to her waist and was not, in fact, a dull brown, but a warm chestnut shade that shone like raw silk.

As she came towards him he could see that she had been crying again. Behind her glasses her eyes were red-rimmed. He wondered if she was regretting her decision not to marry Charles Fairfax but reminded himself that he did not care.

Her wedding dress was drawing attention from the other hotel guests. He supposed he could take her up to his suite and ply her with the cups of tea that the British seemed to consume in great quantities in times of crisis, but he did not have the time or the patience to listen to her problems when he had enough of his own.

Another text arrived from Giselle. He would have to phone her—but while he did what could he do with Athena?

Luca spotted a waiter who worked in the hotel's cocktail bar. 'Miguel, this is Miss Athena Howard. Will you take her into the bar and make her a cocktail?' He smiled briefly at Athena. 'I have to make a phone call. I'll join you in a few minutes.'

To Athena's relief there were only a few people in the bar, and she was able to hide behind a large potted fern to avoid attracting more curious looks. She knew that one of her first priorities must be to buy some different clothes, but she did not relish the idea of walking along Oxford Street in her wedding dress.

'Have you decided what you would like to drink?'

'Um…' She stared at the cocktail menu. She certainly wasn't going to ask the waiter for a Sex on the Beach! 'Can you recommend something fruity and refreshing?'

'How about an Apple Blossom?'

It sounded innocuous enough. 'That would be lovely.'

The waiter returned minutes later with a pretty golden-coloured drink decorated with slices of lemon. Athena sipped the cocktail. It tasted of apples and something else that she could not place, and it was warming as it seeped into her bloodstream.

Her mind replayed the phone call from her mother.

Veronica Howard, typically, had not given her daughter an opportunity to speak, but instead had launched into a tirade about how Athena had once again let her parents down.

'How *could* you jilt poor Charles, almost at the altar, and run off with an Italian playboy who, I am reliably informed, changes his mistresses as often as other men change their socks? What were you *thinking*, Athena? Did you even stop to consider how mortified your father and I would feel when Lady Fairfax explained what you had done? Poor Charles is heartbroken.'

'Wait a minute… Luca isn't…' Athena had tried to interrupt her mother. 'How do you know about Luca?'

What she had meant was how did her mother know that Luca had helped her to run away from the wedding—but, as so often happened with Athena, her words had come out wrong.

'Charles watched you drive off with this Luca in his flash sports car,' Veronica had said shrilly. 'Apparently he'd had suspicions that you were seeing another man behind his back, but he hoped that once you were married you would be happy with *him*. You can imagine how shattered poor Charles was when he discovered *today* that you are having an affair with his old school friend.'

'I'm not having an affair with anyone. It's Charlie who—'

Athena had been tempted to tell her mother the true reason why she had refused to marry Charlie, but despite the callous way he had used her she had been unable to bring herself to betray his deeply personal secret.

'You need to persuade Charles to tell his parents the true situation,' she had told her mother.

'Actually, I *need* to go and talk to the photographer from *High Society* magazine and explain why they can no longer feature a five-page spread of your wedding in their next issue,' Veronica had said coldly. 'Your father and I will *never* live this down,' she'd snapped as a final rejoinder, before ending the call.

Athena finished her drink and the waiter immediately reappeared with another. She blinked away her tears as she sipped the second cocktail. Her parents—particularly her mother—had never listened to her, she thought miserably.

When she was a child they had ignored her requests to give up the tennis lessons and violin lessons, the ballet classes in which she had been the least graceful dancer—

more like an elephant than a swan, as the other girls had taunted her. It hadn't been until she'd left school, having scraped her exams, with the words *'Athena is an average student'* written on every school report and emblazoned on her psyche, that her parents had given up their hope that she would show late signs of academic brilliance.

Even when she had qualified as a nursery assistant—a job that she loved—they had kept on at her to reapply for university so that she could at least train to be a teacher. She believed she had been a disappointment to her parents all her life. It was partly for that reason that she had never told them she had been sexually assaulted by her Latin tutor when she was a teenager. She had always wondered if the assault had somehow been her fault, she brooded, as she drained her glass and took a sip of the second cocktail that the waiter had brought over to her—or was it the third?

If she had betrayed Charlie she would have had to admit to her parents the humiliating fact that her ex-fiancé preferred his best man to her. Was she *really* so unattractive that no man would want her, as Charlie had said? He had accused her of having a hang-up about sex, and the truth was that he was right, Athena acknowledged, swallowing a sob and gulping down the rest of her cocktail.

The waiter must have noticed her empty glass, because he arrived at her table with another drink. She had lost track of how many cocktails she'd had—and actually she didn't care.

Through the door of the bar she could see Luca De Rossi in the lobby, talking into his phone. He was drop-dead gorgeous, and she noticed every woman who walked past him paused to give him a lingering look. He seemed unaware that he was the centre of attention, but it was more likely that he was used to women staring at him, Athena thought ruefully. A man like Luca would not have to try very hard. One smile from his sensual mouth and most women would melt—like she had in Zenhab.

A memory slipped into her mind of him kissing her when they had been in the palace gardens. She had been watching the water droplets from the fountain sparkle like diamonds in the moonlight, but at the same time had been intensely aware of Luca standing beside her. When he had bent his head and brushed his lips over hers she had responded unthinkingly, beguiled by his simmering sensuality.

Why had he kissed her?

She watched him walk into the bar and stride over to where she was sitting. His charcoal-grey suit was expertly cut to show off his superb physique and his silky black hair was just a fraction too long, curling over his collar. He was dark, devastating, and undoubtedly dangerous—and it suddenly seemed imperative to Athena to find out the reason he had kissed her at her sister's wedding.

The room spun when she stood up, and the floor seemed strangely lopsided as she walked towards him. She felt oddly brimming with self-assurance—as if all her inhibitions had disappeared. Even Charlie's cruel taunt that no man would want a twenty-five-year-old virgin no longer hurt. Luca De Rossi, sex god and notorious womaniser, had kissed her once before, and it was possible—likely, even, she decided with a whoosh of confidence—that he wanted to kiss her again.

Perhaps inevitably, she tripped on the hem of her wedding dress, but Luca caught her in his strong arms as she had known he would. He was her hero and her handsome knight, she thought, giving him a beaming smile.

'I think I might be a bit tipsy,' she announced, trying to focus on him. 'Although I don't know why. All I've had to drink are a few lovely cocktails called Apple Bosoms.' She giggled. 'Oops, I didn't mean to say bosom.'

The word had come into her mind because while she had been admiring Luca she'd felt a tingling sensation in her breasts and her nipples had felt hot and hard beneath the stiff bodice of her wedding dress. 'I meant Apple *Blossoms*,' she said carefully, wondering why her tongue felt too big for her mouth. 'Anyway, the cocktails are made with apple juice.'

'And calvados and vodka,' Luca murmured as he attempted to unwind Athena's arms from around his neck.

At least she had stopped crying, but she had clearly had too much to drink, and her wedding dress was still attracting attention from the hotel guests who had come into the bar.

'I think I had better take you up to my room and order you some strong coffee,' he told her, keeping his tone light and hoping he could whisk her out of the bar without her causing a scene.

She swayed, and would have fallen if he had not caught her. *'Santa Madonna!'* he growled beneath his breath, his patience ebbing away fast. It was obvious that she could not walk, so he did the only thing he could and swept her up into his arms.

'I think that's a *very* good idea,' Athena said over loudly. 'Take me upstairs, Luca, and kiss me like you did in Zenhab.'

CHAPTER THREE

IT FELT AS though someone was using a pneumatic drill to bore into her skull. Wincing with pain, Athena forced her eyes open. Without her glasses her vision was blurred, but she was certain she did not recognise the elegant decor of eau-de-Nil walls and dusky blue furnishings.

Her mouth was parched. She carefully turned her head and made out a glass of water on the bedside table.

So she was in a bed. *But whose bed?*

Random memories came into her mind. Charlie and his best man Dominic in bed together… Her crazy idea to climb out of the window at Woodley Lodge and her terror when the ivy had given away and she had fallen…

Her brother-in-law Kadir's friend Luca De Rossi had caught her before she'd hit the ground. And Luca had helped her to run away from her wedding—at least he had driven her away in his sports car and brought her to his hotel. She had a vague recollection of being in a hotel bar and Luca saying that he would take her up to his suite and make her coffee.

Which meant that this must be Luca's room—and she must be…*in Luca's bed*!

Another piece of the jigsaw slotted into place. She remembered that Luca had undone the lacing at the back of her dress before lifting the wedding gown over her head. *Oh, God!* Her face burned as she recalled with excruciating clarity how she had stood in front of him in her underwear and said, 'Take me, Luca, I'm all yours.'

She thought he'd murmured, 'Lucky me,' in a dry tone. But she couldn't be sure, and after that her memory was blank.

Carefully she turned her head the other way on the pillow and was relieved to find that she was alone in the bed. But the tangled silk sheets seemed to suggest that a lot of activity had taken place between them.

Athena's heart juddered to a standstill.

Had she? Could she have had sex with Luca and not remember anything about it? He was a notorious womaniser, and she had literally thrown herself at him. Perhaps he had accepted her offer.

In a strange way it would be a relief if she'd lost her virginity without being aware of it, she thought, nibbling her lower lip with her teeth. She had allowed the incident that had happened years ago, with a university professor friend of her parents who had been giving her extra Latin tuition, to affect her for far too long. If she *had* had sex with Luca it couldn't have been too traumatic if she had no recollection of it.

She sat up and instantly felt very sick. The sheet slipped down and she saw she was wearing the white push-up bra that was part of the pretty bridal underwear set she had hoped would excite Charlie on their wedding night. Grimacing, she peeped beneath the sheet and discovered that the matching lacy thong was still in place, which suggested that her virginity was also intact.

'Good morning,' a gravelly voice said, followed curtly by, 'Although it beats me if there is anything *good* about it.'

Athena whipped her head round and instantly regretted moving so quickly as the room and her stomach lurched in unison. Luca was sitting in an armchair close to the bed. He was dressed entirely in black, and his tight-fitting sweater moulded his torso so that she could see the delineation of his powerful abdominal muscles beneath the fine wool.

Lifting her gaze higher, she noted that the night's growth of dark stubble on his jaw accentuated his raw sexual magnetism. His mouth was curled in an even more cynical expression than usual, and she felt unnerved by the assessing expression in his amber eyes. The fact that he was dressed seemed to indicate that he had *not* accepted her drunken invitation the previous night, but Athena was desperate for confirmation.

'If I spent last night in your bed, where did you sleep?'

His black brows snapped together, but his voice was deceptively soft as he drawled, 'Where do you *think* I might have spent the night?'

Her jerky glance at the rumpled sheets betrayed her. Luca's eyes narrowed and he swore. 'Are you suggesting that I took advantage of you while you were paralytic? Could you be *any* more insulting?'

She swallowed and rested her aching head against the pillows. 'I'm sorry…but I don't remember anything that happened after you brought me to your suite last night… and I need to know if you…if we…'

He moved with the speed of an attacking cobra as he sprang up from the chair and leaned over the bed, placing his hands on either side of her head.

'You are not in my bed. This hotel suite has two bedrooms. Let's get a few facts straight,' he said grimly. 'Number one—if we'd had sex I guarantee you would remember. Number two—I only make love to women who are conscious and capable of participating. Number three…'

Luca's wolf's eyes gleamed with a hard brilliance '…I dislike being manipulated, Miss Howard.'

'What do you mean?' she asked shakily.

His face was so close to hers that even without her glasses she could almost count his thick black eyelashes. The rigid line of his jaw warned her that his hold on his temper was tenuous. But despite his anger Athena did not feel the wariness that she usually felt with men. Far from it. She hardly dared to breathe as her senses reacted to the warmth emanating from Luca's body and the intangible scent of his maleness.

Molten heat washed over her entire body and pooled between her thighs. She was painfully aware of the ache in her breasts and her pebble-hard nipples chafing against her lacy bra cups. The intensity of her desire shocked her, yet deep down she felt relieved at this proof that she had normal sexual needs just like any other woman, and that the assault when she was a teenager had not destroyed her sensuality.

She pictured Luca lowering his body onto hers and pinning her to the mattress with his hard thighs. She imagined how it would feel to have her breasts crushed against his chest and her lips crushed beneath his mouth as he kissed her with fierce passion.

The urge to moisten her dry lips with the tip of her tongue was overwhelming. She saw his eyes narrow as he watched the betraying gesture, and she sensed from his sudden stillness that he knew she wanted him to kiss her.

He jerked upright, leaving her confused by her reaction to him and pink cheeked with embarrassment.

'*This* is what I mean,' he said harshly, dropping a pile of newspapers onto the bed.

Athena tried to ignore her pounding headache as she sat upright and peered at the headline on one of the papers. 'What does it say? I can't read it without my glasses. Thank you...' she murmured when Luca shoved her spectacles into her hand.

She put them on and drew a sharp breath as she saw clearly the newspaper headline and the photograph below it of Luca holding her in his arms in the hotel bar. She had her arms wrapped tightly around his neck and a silly grin on her face that in the cold light of day made her want to die of mortification.

'Bride Jilts Toff for Italian Playboy!' screamed the headline, followed by a paragraph explaining how The Honourable Charles Fairfax had been left heartbroken after his fiancée Athena Howard had run off with his old school friend from Eton College, famous fashion designer Luca De Rossi, an hour before their lavish wedding was due to take place.

'Oh, my God,' Athena said faintly. There were a hundred questions in her mind and she voiced the top one. 'How did the journalists know you had brought me to your hotel?'

'Drop the innocent act,' Luca growled. 'Obviously you tipped off the press about our location and told them this lie about us having an affair.'

'No... No, I *didn't*!' she stammered, suddenly realising that behind Luca's unreadable expression his anger was simmering like a volcano about to erupt. 'Why would I have done that?'

He shrugged. 'I don't know. Maybe you had a row with Charlie and wanted to hurt him. You used me as your stooge. I helped you to escape from Woodley Lodge because I believed your helpless *"I can't marry Charlie because I don't love him"* routine, and this is the thanks I get,' he said savagely as he picked up another newspaper with a similar sensational headline and screwed it up in his fist. 'I don't know why you did it. Who understands what goes on in women's minds?' Luca muttered.

His jaw clenched as he recalled his phone conversation with Giselle half an hour ago. The story about him stealing Athena from under his old school friend's nose had made the headlines in Italy as well as England, and Giselle had refused to be placated or to listen to him when he'd tried to explain that none of it was true.

'*Is* this Athena woman with you at your hotel in London?' Giselle had demanded.

He had been unable to deny it . 'Yes, but...'

The rest of his words had been drowned out by Giselle's shrill tones.

'You've made me look a fool to my family and friends. *Everyone* knew that you and I were supposed to be getting married, but a week before our wedding you've been caught with your pants down with your best friend's bride.'

'I have *not* been caught with my pants down,' Luca had said grittily, 'and neither is Charles Fairfax my best friend.'

At Eton, Charlie had been an irritating boy from a lower year who had hung around him and Kadir because Kadir was a sultan. Privately Luca had suspected that Charlie wasn't interested in women, and he'd been surprised to hear that he was getting married.

'And your family only know about our wedding,' he'd continued, 'because against my advice *you* told them. I said we should keep the news of our marriage of convenience a secret. I'm sure I don't need to remind you that you will be well paid for being my temporary wife.'

'You're damned right, I'll be well paid,' Giselle had said in a hard voice. 'I'm upping my price, *chéri*. I want two million, or the marriage deal is off.'

He had underestimated Giselle, Luca acknowledged. He had dismissed her as an airhead. But she understood that the closer it got to his birthday the more valuable she was. He was unlikely to find another woman prepared to marry him within the next two weeks and be his wife in name only.

Giselle had believed she was calling the shots, but Luca had had enough of being manipulated—first by his grandmother and now by a gold-digger. He had not lost his temper —that wasn't how Luca operated. But anyone who had crossed swords with him in the boardroom would vouch that behind Luca De Rossi's charming smile lay a heart made of ice and an implacable will that was second to none.

'I swear I didn't tell the newspapers that you and I are… involved.'

Athena's soft voice dragged Luca from the memory of his row with Giselle and the grim realisation that, although calling her bluff and telling her to get lost had been infinitely satisfying, he had blown everything.

'But I think I can guess who did.' Athena bit her lip. 'I suspect it was Charlie.'

'Why would Charlie tell the press that you'd jilted him and run off with one of the wedding guests?' Luca said impatiently. 'The story makes him look foolish in public. I remember at school he was a pompous oaf—he'll hate people believing that you dumped him for another man.'

'He has to put the blame on me to hide the fact that *he* is having an affair with…' Athena hesitated. She believed Charlie really had tipped off the press that she was at the hotel with Luca, but her innate sense of loyalty stopped her from revealing his secret relationship with Dominic. 'With someone else,' she finished flatly.

'Charlie is having an affair?' Luca's brows lifted in surprise.

Athena could be lying, he reminded himself. But he found he believed her. This morning she looked young and curiously innocent, with her face scrubbed of make-up and her long chestnut-brown hair rippling down her back. She had tugged the sheet right up to her chin, but not before he had glimpsed firm, round breasts that reminded him of plump peaches framed by a wispy white lace bra.

She kept darting shy glances at him from beneath the sweep of her lashes. But the sexy underwear that he'd seen last night when he had removed her wedding dress and put her into bed indicated that she was as sexually confident as he would expect of a woman in her mid-twenties who had been about to get married.

'When did you discover that Charlie was being unfaithful?'

'Just before I climbed out of the window.' Athena pushed a heavy swathe of hair back from her face. 'I knew I couldn't go ahead with the wedding. I panicked, and all I could think of was to get away. I thought Charlie would explain the truth about why the wedding was cancelled. I was horrified when my mother told me on the phone that Charlie had accused me of running off with you, but I never thought that he would lie to the *press*.'

She looked down at the lurid newspaper headlines and missed the flash of anger in Luca's eyes.

'Are you saying you already *knew* Charlie had accused you of having an affair with me?' Luca asked in a dangerous voice.

'Mum said that Charlie saw us drive off in your car. I assumed he had told his parents and mine that he'd suspected me of seeing another man in the weeks before the wedding. Of course you and I know he was lying…'

Her voice tailed off as Luca swore savagely.

'But now the story is in the newspapers and the whole damn world believes that you and I are lovers,' he grated. 'If you knew last night that Charlie had lied to the press, why the hell didn't you *say* so? I might have been able to stop the story from being printed.'

'I...I didn't think.' Her mother would say that was nothing new, Athena thought bleakly. And she did not actually remember much about the previous evening after she'd drunk several cocktails.

'I don't suppose there's any point telling the newspapers the truth about why I ran away. Charlie will deny it was him who was unfaithful and everyone will think I'm accusing him unfairly out of spite. We can only hope that the story will quickly be forgotten.' She gave Luca a hopeful look. 'I'm sure no one will pay much attention to gossip in the tabloids.'

Dio! Her chirpy optimism caused Luca to grit his teeth. She was either an incarnation of Mary Poppins, or a good actress—and his experience of women and the games they played made him favour the latter.

'The woman I was due to marry was *riveted* by the tabloid headlines,' he said sarcastically.

'*Due to marry?* You mean you're *engaged*?'

Athena's stomach swooped. She couldn't explain the hollow sensation she felt inside at Luca's revelation. He had a reputation as a womaniser, and she wondered what kind of woman had finally tamed him.

'Not any more—since Giselle read in the papers that I stole my old school friend's bride from under his nose and, according to at least one overly imaginative tabloid journalist, we spent last night having hot sex at my hotel.'

Luca cast a glowering look at the newspaper photo of him carrying Athena into the hotel lift. He hadn't noticed any photographer in the lobby, but he had been distracted when Athena had pressed her face against his throat and he'd felt her warm breath graze his skin.

It was possible that *she* had been aware of the photographer, he brooded. She might even have arranged for the press to be at the hotel. She'd admitted that she had discovered hours before her wedding that Charlie had cheated on her—perhaps she had decided to pay her errant fiancé back by being photographed apparently on her way to bed with her lover.

'*Oh, no!* That's *terrible* about your fiancée!' Athena's hand flew to her mouth and she dropped the sheet, exposing the sexy push-up bra that was nothing like her usual sensible underwear. Flushing hotly, she snatched the sheet back up to her chin.

'It's too late for modesty,' Luca told her impatiently. 'Last night you were so drunk that I had to take off your dress and put you into bed.'

'I'm sorry I've caused you so much trouble,' she said stiffly.

The idea that he had seen her almost naked body—the thong was *very* revealing—made her feel hot all over. But from Luca's grim expression she guessed he was thinking only about his fiancée's refusal to marry him.

The tense silence was broken by the sound of his phone. He glanced at the caller display and frowned. 'Excuse me—I have to take this,' he muttered, not even glancing at her as he strode out of the room.

Luca could feel his heart beating painfully hard as he walked through the interconnecting sitting room and into his bedroom. Maria never usually called him this early in the morning—unless something was wrong with Rosalie.

His daughter's nurse greeted him calmly, but Luca detected an underlying note of concern in her voice.

'Rosalie had a severe seizure earlier this morning, which lasted for approximately six minutes.'

'That long?' Luca swallowed. 'It must have put a huge strain on her heart. Were you with her when it happened?'

'I had just come on duty and taken over from the night staff. Because of the length of the seizure I called the doctor, and he has just left after checking Rosalie over. She seems fine, Luca. She's asleep now, and later I'll push her wheelchair out into the garden. You know how she loves to sit beneath the weeping willow tree.'

'I wish I had been there,' Luca said heavily. 'I *should* have been with her.'

Guilt clawed inside him that it wasn't always possible for him to be with his disabled daughter. He employed excellent staff to look after her, and Maria, who had been Rosalie's main carer since she had been diagnosed with a degenerative genetic disease ten years ago, adored her.

It would be Rosalie's thirteenth birthday in a few months, but she could not lead a normal life or enjoy the fun of being a teenager. Luca felt a familiar dull ache in his heart. His daughter's world was confined to Villa De Rossi and the rooms that had been adapted for her needs. One of her greatest joys was to spend time in the special garden he had created for her.

It was imperative for Rosalie's health and happiness that she remained living at Villa De Rossi. But unless Luca found a woman who was prepared to marry him before his thirty-fifth birthday he would lose the villa that was the only home his daughter had ever known. He could not imagine the trauma it would cause Rosalie if she had to be moved to a new house, away from familiar surroundings and the things she loved.

A nerve flickered in his jaw as he thought of his grandmother's vindictive last will and testament. His lawyers had picked over the details with a fine-tooth comb and had advised him that there were no grounds for him to challenge the will.

His only hope of keeping Villa De Rossi was to go

crawling to Giselle and agree to pay her whatever she demanded to marry him. Two million pounds was nothing compared to his daughter's wellbeing. It would stick in his craw to pander to a gold-digger like Giselle, but nothing was more important to him than his darling Rosalie, who was unable to walk or talk but whose beautiful smile was priceless.

Luca clenched his hands into fists. *What a mess!* He had been doing a favour for Kadir when he'd helped Athena to escape from her wedding, but in doing so his own marriage plans had been wrecked.

He walked into the sitting room and stopped dead. Athena was wearing her wedding dress—presumably because she had not brought any other clothes with her. And as he stared at her Luca was struck by the thought that fate had presented him with an alternative convenient bride.

He tried to push the crazy idea out of his mind as he strode over to the table where the hotel staff had set out breakfast. A pool of coffee was spreading across the white damask tablecloth and Athena was frantically trying to mop up the mess with a napkin.

'What the hell happened?'

'I'm so sorry. I knocked over the cafetière.' She grabbed another napkin and attempted to stanch the river of coffee, almost knocking over the milk jug. Luca's quick reactions allowed him to snatch it out of the way.

'Perhaps if you put your glasses on you would be able to see better,' he suggested.

'I'm wearing contact lenses. I can see perfectly well. I found a new pack of lenses in my bag. I'd forgotten that I *had* ordered some new ones before the wedding,' Athena explained. 'Charlie used to say that my mind has more holes in it than a Swiss cheese,' she said flatly.

She stared at the mess on the table. The breakfast had

looked so elegant until she'd poured herself a cup of coffee and the handle of the cafetière had slipped in her fingers.

'Charlie found my clumsiness very irritating. He called me hopeless, and he was right.'

'It's just spilt coffee—it doesn't matter,' Luca said, wondering why Athena's dejected voice made him feel strangely protective. 'I remember at school Charlie had as much charm as a pit of vipers. What made you decide to marry him?'

It was impossible for Athena to explain that she had felt unthreatened by the lack of sexual chemistry between her and Charlie. In the early days of their relationship she had been *relieved* that he hadn't pushed for anything more than a simple kiss at the end of the evening. Charlie had never tried to put his hands up her jumper. There had been no fumbling in his car—no need for her to push him away, her heart thumping with anxiety as memories of being assaulted by her Latin tutor made her, in the words of one disappointed ex-boyfriend, 'as frigid as a nun'.

Now, of course, she understood why Charlie had not pressured her for sex. It hadn't been out of respect for her. It had been because he had never been in love with her and had only asked her to marry him so that he could hide his relationship with the person he really loved—Dominic.

It was true she had realised she did not love Charlie either, but she was still hurt that he had intended to use her so callously, and she felt a resurgence of her old feelings of worthlessness.

'I believed that Charlie and I wanted the same things.'

Tears filled her eyes as she remembered how Charlie had said he wanted them to start trying for a baby as soon as they were married. She had never hidden the fact that she loved children and longed for a family. No wonder Charlie had decided she would be an ideal wife.

'He is very ambitious to do well at the bank, and I hoped to support his career and make a home for us.'

In other words Athena had hoped to enjoy a luxurious lifestyle provided by a wealthy husband, Luca thought derisively. She had told him she did not work. Perhaps she was looking tearful again now because she was regretting her decision not to marry Charlie and one day being able to sign her name as Lady Fairfax.

'Luca…' Athena turned away from the ruined breakfast table. It was one more thing to add to her weight of guilt. 'I feel terrible that your fiancée saw the story about us in the newspapers and has refused to marry you. It's partly my fault…'

'So you *admit* you tipped off the press that I'd brought you to my hotel?' Luca's temper soared.

'No!' Athena felt her insides knot with tension at Luca's explosion of anger. She hated confrontation, and whenever she and Charlie had argued she had always been the one to back down—just as she had with her parents. 'I've explained that I didn't tell anyone of our whereabouts. Charlie must have known the name of your hotel. Perhaps he phoned and found out that you had brought me here. But I do feel partly responsible because Kadir asked you to help me. I'm really sorry that your fiancée thinks we spent the night together. If I explained to her what really happened she might still be willing to marry you.'

Oh, Giselle would be willing—for the right price, Luca thought grimly. At the end of their phone conversation, when she'd realised that he wasn't going to concede to her demand for more money and was prepared to walk away, she had turned nasty and threatened to go to the media with the story of their marriage deal. He would be damned if he would allow her to manipulate him. It was bad enough that his grandmother was doing so from her grave.

'My relationship with Giselle is over for good,' he told Athena.

She looked visibly upset, which surprised Luca, for in his experience women rarely cared about anything other than themselves.

'I wish there was something I could do to help put the situation right,' she murmured.

The mellow September sunshine streaming through the window made Athena's hair gleam like silk. The chestnut tones were mixed with shades of gold through to dark auburn, Luca noted absently. He skimmed his gaze over her wedding dress—not with the critical eye of a designer this time, but with a view to fulfilling the terms of his grandmother's will.

'There *is* something you can do,' he said abruptly. '*You* can marry me.'

Athena's breath lodged in her throat. She knew she could not have heard him correctly. Luca De Rossi could *not* have just asked her to marry him. But even though she was certain she had misheard him, her heart was banging against her ribs.

'I'm sorry…could you say that again?'

'I want you to marry me.'

Oh, God! She felt a strange trembling sensation inside. Was it possible that Luca had been unable to forget, as she hadn't, the kiss they had shared in Zenhab nine months ago?

'We…we hardly know each other,' she stammered.

He frowned. 'Obviously I am not suggesting a *real* marriage.'

Obviously! Athena flushed with embarrassment that she had misunderstood him.

Luca's black hair was ruffled, as if he had been running his fingers through it, but the careless style only made him look even sexier. The sunlight highlighted his sharp cheekbones and the sculpted angles and planes of his face. He was the most handsome man Athena had ever seen, and she wondered how she could have been foolish enough to think he might be interested in someone as plain and ordinary looking as her.

'I didn't think you *were* suggesting a real marriage,' she said quickly. 'But I don't think it's a good idea for you to marry on the rebound as a way of paying your fiancée back for rejecting you. I realise you are probably heartbroken over Giselle…'

'I don't have a heart to break,' Luca drawled.

He had once. He had loved Jodie and it had hurt like hell when she had left him. He had no intention of repeating the great mistake of his youth. He did have a heart, but it belonged solely to his daughter.

He gave Athena an assessing look. Earlier, when he had leaned over the bed, he had sensed that she had wanted him to kiss her. A memory of when he had kissed her in Zenhab had stirred his desire, and he had been tempted to kiss her again. But then he had remembered that he suspected her of telling the press that he had helped her to run away from her wedding.

'I need to get married,' he said abruptly. 'But emotions won't be involved.'

He could see that had been the problem with Giselle. She had wanted more from him, and like every woman scorned, she had become spiteful when she'd realised that she meant nothing to him.

He looked into Athena's sapphire-blue eyes and dismissed the brief flicker inside him that he did not understand. 'I'm offering you a business deal. I'll pay you one million pounds if you will be my wife in name only for one year.'

CHAPTER FOUR

'ARE YOU THINKING what you could do with a million pounds?' Luca demanded as the silence stretched and Athena seemed to have been struck dumb.

She shook her head. 'I'm thinking that you are mad. Why do you *need* to get married?' He was wealthy, successful, and seriously gorgeous—it seemed bizarre that he had to pay someone to marry him. 'You have a reputation as a playboy. A lot of women would pay *you* to marry *them*,' she murmured.

'If I asked one of my mistresses I'd run the risk of them becoming emotionally involved.' He swept his gaze over her. 'I need to make it quite clear that there will be no point in you falling in love with me.'

Athena felt a spark of temper flicker inside her. Luca must *really* think she was pathetic if he felt he needed to warn her off him. 'If I was crazy enough to accept your marriage deal—which I'm not—I'm sure I would be able to restrain myself from falling in love with you,' she said curtly.

His brows rose, as if he was surprised by her sarcasm, and that infuriated her even more. She was tired of people walking all over her—but it was her own fault. She had spent her life trying to please people, but however hard she had tried she had never made her parents proud, and Charlie had neither loved nor respected her. It was time she grew a backbone—starting with telling this man who was too sexy for his own good what he could do with his outrageous marriage proposal.

The memory of the dismissive, faintly disdainful glance he had given her made her painfully aware of her short-comings. At least Charlie had *pretended* he wanted to marry her, she thought dismally. Luca hadn't bothered with niceties when he had offered to buy her as if she was a prize heifer at a cattle market.

'I'm sorry, but I don't—' she began, but he cut her off.

'You asked why I need to be married. The terms of my grandmother's will demand that I must marry before I am thirty-five or I will lose the house which has belonged to the De Rossi family for eight generations. I will also lose my place on the governing board of the family business—despite the fact that I restored the company's fortunes and saved it from bankruptcy,' Luca said harshly.

Athena succumbed to her curiosity. 'Why did your grandmother make such a horrible will? Didn't you get on with her?'

'She disapproved of me—and especially of my life-style.' He gave a humourless laugh. 'Although I believe that Violetta would have disapproved of me even if I had become a priest. I could do nothing right in her eyes.'

Athena had half turned away from him, but she caught the faint note of hurt beneath his sardonic tone and hesi-tated. She knew what it was like never to feel good enough, consistently to fail to meet the expectations of parents.

'What about your parents? Aren't they included in your grandmother's will?'

'My mother is dead.' Luca did not mention his father. He neither knew nor cared if the faceless, nameless man who had fathered him was alive or not. 'I am the only De Rossi heir. But if I don't produce a bride by my birthday, in two weeks' time, I will lose everything I have worked for over the past fifteen years.'

'I'm sorry,' Athena murmured for a second time. She felt guilty that Luca's fiancée had dumped him, but she couldn't marry him just to appease her conscience. 'I understand why you feel an urgency to marry, but what you're suggesting is…well, *wrong*—and immoral. Marriage should happen because of love, not financial gain.'

'So you were going to marry Charlie because you *loved* him, and the fact that the Fairfaxes are one of the richest families in England had nothing to do with your decision?' Luca said sharply.

'I thought I loved him. I didn't care about his money or his title,' Athena insisted, flushing when Luca gave her a disbelieving look. 'It's difficult to explain. My parents were so delighted when Charlie asked me to marry him… I just wanted to do something right, for once, that would make them proud of me. The wedding preparations snowballed and I couldn't bring myself to admit even to myself that I was making a mistake.'

'But the truth is that without a wealthy husband or a job you presumably do not have any means of supporting yourself.'

Luca forced her to face the reality of her situation.

'What would you do with one million pounds? Think about it,' he urged.

His voice softened and his sexy, smoky accent caused the tiny hairs on her body to stand on end.

'What do you wish for more than anything, Athena? Jewellery? Beautiful clothes? A house?'

His words circled in her mind. She wasn't interested in jewellery or designer dresses. But a house… She thought of the dilapidated building situated on an area of scrubland that housed fifty-four orphaned children. Rajasthan was one of the poorest areas of India, and the orphanage in Jaipur, which had been founded twelve years ago by a remarkable American woman called Cara Tanner, was built of crumbling bricks, with a tin roof that leaked during the monsoon season and made the house as hot as an oven in the summer.

The House of Happy Smiles provided food, shelter and hope to children who were utterly destitute. Athena had discovered the orphanage during a holiday to India with her parents, and the contrast between the luxurious hotel where she had been staying and the devastating poverty she'd witnessed in the slums of Jaipur had had a profound effect on her.

Since that day four years ago, when she had met Cara Tanner and learned of the work she was doing running the orphanage, which was dependent on charitable donations, Athena had set up a fundraising campaign in England, and she returned to the House of Happy Smiles to work as a volunteer as often as she could.

Cara had plans for the orphanage, which included building a properly constructed house for the children to live in and also a school, and employing teachers to give the children an education.

'It will cost hundreds of thousands of pounds to turn the Happy House into a proper home and school for abandoned children, and to pay for staff to care for them,' Cara had explained. 'That kind of money will take years of fundraising, but think how it would transform the lives of those kids who have nothing.'

Deep in thought, Athena walked over to the window and stared unseeingly down at the crowd of people standing outside the front of the hotel. Her training as a nursery nurse meant that she could look after the younger children at the orphanage. Her visits to Jaipur and the fundraising she organised back in the UK meant a lot to her, and she felt she was actually doing something worthwhile.

A million pounds could transform the lives of those orphaned children. Her heart gave a jolt as she imagined the plans for the new house that Cara had shown her coming to fruition. There would be six beds in each dormitory, with curtains around each one to give the children a sense of privacy. A nursery for the babies and toddlers would be filled with toys, and there would be colourful murals painted on the walls. And a school would be built, with proper classrooms and desks and books. The children could be taught to read and write and to develop the skills that would enable them to find good jobs.

A million pounds would set the orphaned children free from grinding poverty. And *she* could make that difference with the money Luca was offering her to be his wife in name only for a year.

She swung round to face him. Her brain was telling her she would be mad to accept his proposal, but her heart ached for children like Suresh, a seven-year-old boy who was unable to walk as a result of contracting polio, who had been found begging on the streets. The orphanage was the only home he had ever known.

One million pounds could transform a rundown shack into a true House of Happy Smiles and give Suresh and the other children a future.

'How would this marriage work?' she asked shakily. 'Where would I live?'

'I have a penthouse apartment in Milan, close to the famous shopping precinct, where I am sure you would be very comfortable. I only stay at the apartment occasionally, if business requires me to spend a few days in the city. I live mainly at Villa De Rossi. Occasionally I might need you to come to the villa and act as a hostess at dinner parties.'

She grimaced. 'I'm not very good at organising dinner parties. I always seem to forget something or spill something.'

'My staff will take care of all the arrangements. I don't do a lot of entertaining, but sometimes I have to invite the board members of De Rossi Enterprises to the villa.' Luca stared intently at Athena. 'So, what is your answer?'

She bit her lip, hardly able to believe that she was actually contemplating accepting his proposal. 'When...when would I be paid the money?'

'Five hundred thousand will be paid into your bank account when we marry, and you'll receive the other five hundred thousand after we have been married for a year.'

That would mean work on the new building for the orphanage could begin *soon*. She remembered Luca had said that he had to be married before his birthday in two weeks. But could she go through with a sham marriage?

She glanced at his sculpted features, softened slightly by that lush mouth, and something hot and fierce unfurled inside her.

He walked over to her, and swore when he glanced out of the window and saw the crowd on the street below. 'The damned paparazzi have caused enough trouble.' He glared at Athena. 'And so have you.'

Guilt swamped her. If Luca hadn't helped her escape from her wedding his own wedding to Giselle would still be on. 'I promise I didn't tell the press you brought me here.'

He didn't seem to hear her. 'You owe me, Athena.'

A nerve flickered in Luca's jaw as he thought of how Rosalie loved to watch the weeping willow tree in the garden of Villa De Rossi swaying in the breeze. He could not bear the thought of taking his daughter away from the few simple pleasures she had.

For a moment he considered telling Athena about Rosalie, in the hope of gaining her sympathy. But he still wondered if she had tipped off the press, and he did not trust her not to talk to journalists about his daughter. When Rosalie was younger he had often taken her out to the park or the zoo, but she had been terrified by the paparazzi, who followed him everywhere with their camera flashbulbs. His global fame as a fashion designer had made him a target for the press's interest.

Nowadays, Rosalie's disabilities meant that she was rarely well enough to leave home. Thankfully the media seemed to have forgotten about his daughter, and Luca was determined to protect Rosalie's privacy.

He pulled Athena away from the window and the prying lenses of the photographers. 'If I am not married two weeks from now I will lose everything I've spent the past fifteen years working for, and it will be *your* fault,' he said harshly.

She had a chance to do something worthwhile—something that mattered. What was a year out of her life if she could improve the lives of the orphaned children of Jaipur?

Athena drew a sharp breath. '*All right*, I'll do it. I'll marry you. But I want the one million pounds to be paid to me on the day of the wedding.'

That way she could give all the money to Cara Tanner to ensure that the project to build a new orphanage and school would be completed.

Luca frowned and she explained. 'If the money is in-stalments you might decide not to pay me the full amount at the end of the year.'

'But if I pay you the one million up front how do I know that you won't take the money and disappear?' he said grimly. 'I can only claim the deeds to Villa De Rossi after I have been married for a year.'

'I give you my word that I will be your wife in name for one year.'

Luca's brows lifted. 'You'll understand why I am suspicious of trusting the word of a woman who jilted the man she had promised to marry an hour before the wedding,' he drawled.

Athena blushed guiltily, even though she knew she could not have married Charlie after she had discovered the truth about him. But she was determined to stand her ground. The orphanage project would need to be fully funded before building work began, and she had to have all the money Luca had said he would pay her.

'I want a million pounds on the day I marry you or we don't have a deal.'

Luca's eyes narrowed on her flushed cheeks and resolute chin. 'I think I might have underestimated you. You're not as sweet and innocent as you look—are you, *mia bella*?'

It was lucky he didn't know that her knees had been shaking when she'd insisted that she wanted all the money upfront. It was the first time she had ever stuck up for herself, and Athena's feeling of euphoria was only slightly tempered by the knowledge that Luca would be shocked to know just how innocent she was.

She bit her lip, remembering Charlie's taunt. *'Who will want to marry a twenty-five-year-old virgin with a hang-up about sex?'* It was a good thing that Luca *did* only want her to be his wife in name. He had a reputation as a playboy and no doubt preferred his mistresses to be sexually experienced.

His dark good looks exuded a raw sensuality that both fascinated and repelled her. Briefly she found herself imagining what it would be like if Luca's marriage proposal was real and he wanted her to be his wife not just in name but in *every* way—including sharing his bed. As if that would ever happen, she mocked herself. In the unlikely event that Luca might find her attractive, she would not know how to respond to him, and she was sure he would be turned off by her lack of experience.

He should not be surprised that when it came to money Athena was as hard-nosed as every other woman he knew, Luca told himself. But he had to move fast—before she decided to up her price.

'Fine—you'll get all the money when we marry.'

He punched numbers into his phone and spoke in rapid Italian to his PA.

'My plane is waiting at the airport,' he told Athena when he'd finished the phone call. He frowned as a thought struck him. 'Do you have your passport with you?'

'Yes, but…'

'The hotel manager is arranging for us to leave the hotel through the kitchens, so that we can avoid the paparazzi out the front.'

She glanced down at her wedding dress. 'I need to buy some other clothes.'

'There is no time for you to go on a shopping spree now.'

Luca's jaw hardened. Nothing was going to stop him claiming the Villa De Rossi and everything that was rightfully his. All he had to do was get his ring on Athena's finger and her signature on the marriage certificate as quickly as possible.

It was hard to believe she was on a plane, Athena thought, looking around the cabin, which was more like a room in a house, furnished with cream leather sofas, a polished wood dining table and a widescreen television. She had only ever travelled economy class to India, sitting in a cramped seat for the nine-hour flight to Delhi. Luca's luxurious private jet belonged to another world, but she did not belong there. She belonged in his world even less than she had belonged in Charlie's.

She stared at her reflection in a mirror. Yesterday, when she had put on her wedding dress, she could not have known that she would still be wearing it twenty-four hours later, as she flew on Luca De Rossi's private jet to Italy so that she could marry him. Of course he only wanted her to be his wife in name, and in fact that was all Charlie had wanted, she now realised.

She had been so shocked when she'd found him in bed with Dominic. Her relationship with Charlie had been built on his lies. He hadn't suggested that they wait until their wedding night before they had sex because he'd been mindful of her feelings… No, Charlie had never desired her or loved her. And she had not loved him, she admitted. She had tried to convince herself she did to please her parents—and because she wanted children and Charlie had said he was keen to start a family.

Her wedding dress was a mocking reminder that her life for the past year that she had been engaged to him had been an illusion.

'The sleeves of your dress are wrong.'

Luca's voice broke into Athena's thoughts. Since the plane had taken off from London he had been working on his laptop, but now he stood up and came to stand behind her. He gathered a voluminous puffed sleeve in his hand.

'There's far too much material here,' he told her, studying her reflection in the mirror. 'You are not tall enough to wear big sleeves and a full skirt, and your curves need to be accentuated—not hidden by yards of material.'

'I know I'm short and unfashionably curvy,' she muttered. 'You don't need to point out my defects.'

'I don't consider breasts and hips to be "defects".'

His eyes met hers in the mirror, and something in his enigmatic expression made her heart lurch.

'The truth is that most men prefer women to have curves...' his voice was smoky '...especially Italian men.'

'Including you?' The question sounded too intrusive, and the atmosphere in the cabin suddenly felt too intimate. Athena laughed loudly. 'As you're a fashion designer, I thought you would favour stick-thin women.'

Tall, rangy blondes had always been his preference, Luca mused. He did not know why Athena's diminutive size evoked a primal masculine desire to protect her. She was tougher than she looked, and a sharp negotiator, he reminded himself. But her sapphire-blue eyes were big enough to drown in, and her waist-length chestnut-brown hair smelled of lemons and felt like silk against his skin as he pushed her hair over her shoulder.

Athena released her breath as Luca moved away from her, but moments later he returned to stand behind her.

His eyes met hers in the mirror once again as he ordered, 'Keep still.'

She gasped when she saw a pair of scissors in his hand, but before she could protest he began to cut through the puffed sleeves of her dress. 'Are you mad? Do you know how much this dress cost?'

She flinched as the scissors flashed near to her throat, but it soon became clear why Luca was regarded as one of the world's top designers. Within a few minutes he had cut away the sleeves, leaving narrow shoulder straps, and he had reshaped the neckline of the dress, taking it lower, to reveal just a hint of her cleavage.

'I need pins,' he murmured, although he was so engrossed in what he was doing that Athena was sure he had forgotten that she was not a tailor's dummy.

He opened a cupboard and swung out a table on wheels that held a sewing machine.

'I've created some of my best designs in the air,' he said when he noticed her startled expression. 'I like the fact that no one can disturb me and my imagination can flow. Why did you choose a dress that could double up as a parachute?'

He pulled the skirt against her hips, gathering up the excess material at the back.

'You see how much more flattering the dress looks when it moulds your hips? You have a beautiful body and you should make the most of your feminine figure.'

Her? Beautiful? He wasn't serious, of course, Athena told herself, thinking of her breasts, which were too full in her opinion and usually disguised beneath baggy tops. But Luca was a playboy—no doubt flattering women was second nature to him.

'How…how do you know what my body is like?'

Why was she asking him in that husky voice that was so unlike the way she usually spoke? she wondered. His hands were resting on her hips, and the warmth of his skin was burning through the satin dress. She was aware of him with every atom, every cell of her body, but she was confused by her reaction to him. Why didn't she feel tense, as she usually did when a man stood too close to her? The molten sensation in her pelvis was something she had never experienced before, and yet she understood that the ache between her legs was the ache of desire: primitive, raw, and shockingly intense.

'I took your dress off when I put you to bed last night,' he reminded her. 'Your underwear left little to the imagination—and I have a very good imagination.' His amber eyes glinted with amusement when she blushed.

'You should have been named after the Greek goddess Aphrodite.'

She stiffened, and in split second the warm blood in her veins turned icy cold and a familiar feeling of revulsion churned in her stomach. '*Don't* call me that,' she said sharply.

Come on, Aphrodite, goddess of love. Inside her head she heard the sound of her cotton blouse ripping, and her high-pitched cry as she tried to hold the torn material across her breasts.

'Athena!' Luca's deep voice dispelled the images in her mind. 'Are you feeling ill? You've gone white. Do you suffer from air sickness?' It was the only explanation he could think of for her sudden pallor, but it did not explain the haunted expression in her eyes.

She swallowed. 'I… I feel unwell. I guess I'm still paying for drinking too many cocktails last night.' Somehow she forced a faint smile. 'It was my first hangover, and I'm going to make it my last,' she said ruefully.

She was surprisingly unsophisticated, and Luca once again felt his protective instinct stir. It was that instinct that had caused all his problems, he thought darkly, remembering how he'd offered to help her run away from her wedding.

'You'd be best to sleep it off,' he said abruptly, pressing the buzzer to summon the stewardess. 'Tia will show you to the bedroom, and she will bring you a drink or anything else you want.'

It was becoming a habit to wake up in a strange bedroom, Athena mused when she opened her eyes. The portholes instead of windows were a reminder that she was on Luca De Rossi's plane and that she had agreed to marry him for one million pounds. It had seemed straightforward before she had fallen asleep, but was less so now that her hang-over had cleared and her brain was functioning.

It felt like a lifetime ago that she had fled from Wood-ley Lodge. Guilt surged through her as she wondered what had happened about all the wedding preparations. She pic-tured her parents explaining to the guests as they arrived that the wedding was cancelled because their daughter had jilted the groom.

Her wedding dress hanging on the back of the door was a painful reminder that she had made a mess of everything. But it was all she had to wear—and it was unrecognisable from the over-the-top dress that had not suited her, she dis-covered when she put it on.

Luca must have sewn his alterations into the dress while she had been asleep, and his new design, incorporating delicate shoestring shoulder straps instead of those big sleeves, and a fitted fishtail skirt that skimmed her hips and emphasised her narrow waist, flattered her hourglass figure.

There was a knock on the door, and when she opened it Luca stepped into the bedroom. He raked his eyes over her in a brooding appraisal that made her heart beat faster.

'I'm a genius,' he murmured. 'You look stunning in my redesigned dress—and very sexy.'

Athena blushed and stared at herself in the mirror. Luca was right: she *did* look sexy in the figure-hugging dress, with her hair tumbling around her shoulders. It was a long time since she had worn anything faintly revealing. Since the sexual assault when she was eighteen she had deliber-ately hidden her body beneath shapeless clothes, and she had stopped wearing make-up and experimenting with the way she looked.

She felt angry and sad that she had lost the years of her life that should have been fun. She had never flirted with boys after Uncle Peter had told her she gave off signals that she was hungry for sex.

She turned her head and found Luca was watching her. The predatory gleam in his eyes stirred something deep inside her, and suddenly she wished she was normal and didn't feel that anxious sensation in the pit of her stomach when she was in the company of a man.

Strangely, she did not feel anxious with Luca. She couldn't stop looking at him—as if her brain wanted to absorb every detail of his handsome face: the sharp lines of his slashing cheekbones and the sensual curve of the mouth that had once brushed across her lips when he had kissed her in the palace gardens in Zenhab.

'I'm not sure how long I dozed, but I expect we must be landing in Italy soon,' she said, desperate to shatter the inexplicable tension that she sensed between her and Luca.

'I came to tell you that you will need to wear a seat belt when we land. But we're not in Italy.' He dropped the news casually. 'The plane will make a brief stop-over in New York to refuel before we fly on to Las Vegas.'

CHAPTER FIVE

IT WAS DONE! He was legally married! Luca felt a mixture of triumph and relief as he escorted his new bride down the aisle of the wedding chapel in downtown Las Vegas. He had met the terms of his grandmother's will and nothing could prevent him from claiming his inheritance—which included the right to live at Villa De Rossi with his daughter.

He had felt a brief moment of guilt at Athena's shocked gasp on hearing that they were not on their way to Italy but to Las Vegas, but as soon as the plane had landed at McCarran International airport he had wasted no time and taken her to the Marriage License Bureau so that they could complete the necessary paperwork that would allow them to marry in the State of Nevada.

The next step had been to find a wedding chapel with availability to perform the wedding ceremony. Although it had been heading into the evening, many of the chapels had already been fully booked. Marriage was still a thriving industry in Vegas, Luca thought cynically.

Athena had looked increasingly tense as they had driven along the famous Las Vegas strip, and he had feared that she might change her mind at the last minute and refuse to go through with the wedding. But, although her voice had faltered during the brief ceremony, she had kept her side of the deal and married him.

The seats on either side of the aisle were empty apart from his PA, Sandro, and the stewardess from his plane, who had acted as witnesses at the wedding ceremony. The chapel was small, and its decor could only be described as tacky—the violently patterned carpet was stained and the chairs were made of plastic. At least there were flowers: white roses and lilies, whose sickly sweet perfume filled the air.

A lack of air-conditioning meant that the temperature inside the chapel was stifling—perhaps that was the reason why Athena was so pale. She looked as though she was about to faint.

As if she sensed his scrutiny, she turned her head towards him. Her eyes were huge sapphire pools and her face was white and strained. Something kicked hard in Luca's gut—the same feeling he'd had when he had slid the cheap ring he had bought at the airport onto Athena's finger. Her skin had been icy cold and her hand had trembled in his.

He had been unprepared for the fierce emotion that had gripped him when the wedding officiant had pronounced them man and wife. He had never expected to marry and had had good reason for his decision to remain single all his life. But he had been forced into this sham marriage.

As for his bride—tomorrow he would arrange for one million pounds to be transferred into Athena's bank account. She was his wife in name only and there was no reason why he should feel responsible for her, he told himself.

His wife! A nerve flickered in his jaw. The marriage was simply a formality. It meant nothing to him. Athena was a means to an end, and the only thing he cared about was his daughter's happiness and well-being.

As he led his bride towards the chapel doors, his PA stepped forward and spoke to him in a low voice. Sandro Vincenzi had worked for him for ten years, and the Vin-

cenzi family had served the De Rossi household for generations. Luca trusted his childhood friend as completely as
he trusted Sandro's sister Maria, who was Rosalie's nurse.

'Luca, a problem has arisen.'

'What kind of problem?'

'Social media is buzzing with a story that has broken in
the English newspapers. The English and European daily
papers have just been issued, and several of the tabloids
carry headlines about your relationship with Giselle.'

Luca shrugged. 'I assume Giselle has done a kiss-and-
tell. It's not the first time an ex-mistress has sold supposed
details of an affair with me for cash,' he said sardonically.

'It's rather more serious than that.'

Sandro showed Luca the online edition of one of the
newspapers that he had downloaded onto his smartphone.

Bartered Bride!
  *Luca De Rossi offered me a million pounds to
  marry him in a cynical bid to cheat the terms of his
  grandmother's will!*

Luca swore beneath his breath as he read the interview
Giselle had given, in which she revealed that he had asked
her to agree to a sham marriage so that he could claim his
inheritance.

  *But, in a shocking double betrayal, love rat Luca
  has dumped his faithful girlfriend and run off with
  his old school friend Charles Fairfax's fiancée.*
  *In a statement, French glamour-model Giselle
  Mercier sent a message to Luca's latest mistress,
  warning Athena Howard not to be fooled if her playboy lover proposes marriage.*
  'Luca isn't looking for love. All he wants is to

*con the board of De Rossi Enterprises into mak-
ing him chairman of the company by having a fake
marriage.'*

Luca thrust the phone at his PA. '*Dio*, I underestimated
Giselle. But I don't believe it is a problem. The story will
be forgotten in a few days.'

He glanced at Athena. She still looked pale and vulnerable, as if she was in shock, as she twisted the wedding
ring on her finger. Luca felt an uncomfortable twinge of
guilt, although he reassured himself that he had done nothing to feel guilty about.

'Miss Howard is aware of the reasons why I have married her,' he told Sandro in Italian.

'Giselle is only half the problem,' Sandro advised. 'Your
great-uncle Emilio has evidently seen the media coverage
and has released a statement announcing that in light of
Miss Mercier's story, the board of De Rossi Enterprises
will now be suspicious if you should marry before your
thirty-fifth birthday. Emilio is threatening that if you *do*
marry the board will try to prove that the marriage is a
sham, and will take legal steps to prevent you from claiming the chairmanship of the company and ownership of
Villa De Rossi.'

Luca shot another glance at Athena, thankful that she
could not understand Italian. At least he assumed she could
not speak his language. He frowned, realising that he knew
virtually nothing about her. But why should he? Their marriage was a business arrangement and he did not intend to
spend much time with her after he took her to Italy.

He ground his teeth as he thought of his great-uncle.
Luca knew that Emilio would do anything to get his great-
nephew removed from the board of De Rossi Enterprises.

But to have any chance of doing so Emilio would have to *prove* that his marriage to Athena was fraudulent.

'There is one more thing you should know,' Sandro said. 'Some American journalists have heard of the story breaking in the English media and somehow the information has been leaked that you are here in Las Vegas to marry Miss Howard.'

Athena wondered what Luca and his PA were talking about. She was curious about the fierce urgency in Luca's tone. She guessed he was speaking Italian. Perhaps she should try to learn the language, seeing that she would be living in Italy for a year. She grimaced as she remembered that she had not been any good at French at school, and even worse at Latin. But it was supposed to be easier to learn a language if you lived in the country where it was spoken, and if Luca spoke to her in Italian regularly it might help her to pick it up…

Her eyes were drawn to her husband. She could not quite believe that they were married. Luca did not look particularly happy, she noted. His sculpted features looked harder than ever and his mouth was drawn into a thin line, as if he was angry about something. She wondered if he wished he had married Giselle. He must have been devastated when his fiancée had broken off their engagement. And it was *her* fault, Athena thought guiltily. If she hadn't asked Luca to help her escape from her wedding, he could have married the woman whom she assumed he loved.

She tensed as he finished his conversation with his assistant and came to stand beside her. But her tension was not from the anxious feeling she usually experienced when she was around men. Her heart beat faster as she breathed in the spicy scent of Luca's aftershave, and her stomach muscles clenched when she lifted her eyes to his face and absorbed the masculine beauty of his chiselled jaw and above it the lush fullness of his mouth.

'In a moment we will leave the chapel,' he told her. He hesitated. 'When we step outside it will be necessary for me to kiss you.'

She blinked at him. 'Necessary for you to…? Why?'

Athena had the most incredible eyes. The thought came unbidden into Luca's mind. 'There's no time to explain now. The press are outside, and it's vital that we make them believe our marriage is real.'

'Real?' She knew she probably sounded witless, but she couldn't take in what he had said about needing to kiss her.

'All you have to do is kiss me back,' Luca said impatiently when she stared at him as if he had grown a second head. 'It shouldn't be too much of an ordeal. You seemed to enjoy it when I kissed you in Zenhab.'

So he *hadn't* forgotten that kiss. Her mind flew to the palace gardens and she remembered vividly the whisper of the fountains and the silver gleam of the moon, the scent of orange blossom and the gossamer-soft brush of Luca's lips on hers.

He opened the chapel door and Athena's thoughts scattered as she was blinded by an explosion of flashbulbs. Luca slid his arm around her waist and drew her close to his body—so close that she could feel his powerful thigh muscles through her dress, his hard, masculine frame a stark contrast to her softness.

'Remember, this has to look convincing,' he murmured as he lowered his face towards hers.

Athena's heart lurched as she realised that he hadn't been making some bizarre joke and was actually going to kiss her. She was aware of a fluttering sensation in the pit of her stomach, but it wasn't the horrible nervous feeling she'd had when her ex-boyfriends—she could count on one hand the number of men she had briefly dated after the incident with her Latin tutor—had tried to kiss her.

Time seemed to be suspended as she watched Luca's dark head descend. He slanted his mouth over hers and she discovered that the fluttering sensation in her stomach was not apprehension but anticipation.

He claimed her mouth with the supreme confidence of a man who had had more mistresses than he cared to remember. His lips firmly coaxed hers apart in a blatant seduction designed to make her capitulate to his mastery and warn her that resistance was futile. Luca was the ultimate charmer, and he knew exactly how to make a woman melt while he retained complete control.

For a moment Athena felt a familiar sense of panic—especially when he tightened his arms around her so that she could not escape. But the dark shadows in her mind receded as Luca continued to kiss her and she felt his tongue probe between her lips, seeking access to the moist interior of her mouth. She closed her eyes to blot out the flashing bright lights of the photographers' flashbulbs and sank into darkness and the sweet pull of desire that was stirring inside her.

Luca's tongue tangled with hers, and she dissolved, sliding her hands up to his shoulders to cling to him for support as she dismissed her inhibitions and kissed him with unrestrained passion.

He had asked Athena to kiss him convincingly and she was certainly complying, Luca thought. *Dio*, he was almost convinced himself that her passionate response was real and not just an act in front of the paparazzi. Her warm breath filled his mouth as she parted her lips beneath his. He could easily become addicted to the taste of her, he thought, to the softness of her mouth and the sweetness of her kiss that made his gut ache.

He had not expected to be so turned on that his body felt as if it was on fire. Athena was not doing anything more than kissing him. She wasn't running her hands over his body, or whispering artful suggestions in his ear the way he was used to women doing. There was something curiously innocent and unsophisticated in her kiss that he found incredibly erotic. He felt as though he was the first man to have awoken her sensuality, but he knew that could not be true because she had been engaged—and anyway he preferred sexually experienced women, he reminded himself.

He heard someone call out from the crowd of journalists gathered outside the wedding chapel, but did not catch what they said—and he did not care as he pulled Athena against him so that her soft contours were moulded to his taut body. His arousal was unexpected and painfully hard, and he heard her little gasp of shock as he rubbed his pelvis up against hers.

The voices and the camera flashbulbs disappeared and he was conscious only of Athena: the delicate rose scent of her perfume, the silky softness of her hair against his cheek and her incandescent sensuality that captivated him and made him long to remove the barrier of their clothes so that they were skin on skin, a man and a woman poised on the brink of fulfilling their sexual desires.

He drew her closer still, so that he could feel the erratic thud of her heart echoing the unsteady rhythm of his, and deepened the kiss, taking it to a level that was flagrantly erotic.

On the periphery of his mind Luca heard raucous laughter, and a voice called out, 'What do you say to the allegation that your marriage is a sham, Mr De Rossi?'

Someone else said loudly, 'It looks real enough from where I'm standing. Let them get to a hotel room before they combust. Will you and your wife be taking a honeymoon, Mr De Rossi?'

Luca felt a pang of reluctance as he lifted his lips from Athena's and turned his head towards the journalists. 'Of course Signora De Rossi and I will have a honeymoon. We are looking forward to spending a few days in Las Vegas.'

'Did you design your wife's wedding dress?'

'Certainly I wanted to create a gown that complemented Athena's beauty.' He returned Athena's startled look with a bland smile.

'Is it true that you only married Miss Howard to meet the terms of your grandmother's will?' someone called.

'I married Athena because...' Luca looked into Athena's sapphire-blue eyes and thought again how easy it would be to drown in their depths. 'Because she captured my heart when we met in Zenhab nine months ago, and I was determined to make her my wife,' he told the journalists. 'Now, if you will excuse us...?'

Athena was glad of Luca's arm around her waist as he led her towards the waiting limousine and the paparazzi surged around them. The sound of voices shouting questions and the glare of camera flashbulbs was disorientating. The chauffeur held open the door and she fell inelegantly into the car after Luca, almost landing in his lap. Hot-faced, she slid along the seat, and moments later the car pulled away from the kerb, chased by the photographers still snapping pictures.

'Why did you say all that rubbish about me capturing your heart?' she demanded. And why was there a little part of her that wished that what he had said to the journalists was true? Athena wondered. She and Luca were virtually strangers, but since her sister's wedding in Zenhab she had been haunted by the memory of his kiss, she admitted.

'It's important that the press believe our marriage is real,' Luca said tersely.

The man who had played the role of adoring husband outside the wedding chapel had disappeared, and his sculpted features were impossible to read.

'I don't understand.' Shock, jet lag, and the fact that her body clock was out of sync were having a detrimental effect on Athena's ability to think. 'Why would they think our marriage is a sham?'

Luca handed her his phone. 'I've downloaded the online edition of a tabloid newspaper currently being read by people in England while they eat their breakfast.'

She looked at the screen and gasped as she read the interview with Giselle Mercier. 'Why does your fiancée say that you offered her money to marry you?'

'Because it's true.'

'I assumed you were going to marry Giselle because you were in love with her, and that when she broke off your engagement you had to find a wife before your birthday in order to claim your inheritance.'

'I certainly wasn't *in love* with Giselle.' Luca's lips curled into a cynical expression. 'I accept that some people find true love...' he thought of Kadir and Lexi '...but for the majority of people love is simply a romanticised excuse for lust. And whilst I am happy to enjoy the latter, I have no inclination to fall in love.'

Athena felt a flicker of temper at his dismissive tone. 'One of the reasons why I agreed to marry you in name only was because I felt guilty that I had unwittingly been the cause of Giselle breaking up with you. I felt it was partly *my* fault that you would lose your inheritance if you didn't marry before your birthday.'

'Let's not forget the main reason you married me is because I'm paying you a million pounds,' Luca drawled.

Athena might have convinced herself that her motive for agreeing to be his wife was altruistic, but he didn't believe it for a second. She was as much of a gold-digger as Giselle, but the situation resulting from Giselle's story in the press meant that Athena was going to have to work a little harder for her money.

Anger surged through Luca, and with it another emotion —*desperation*. He was so close to achieving his goal. He did not care if he lost the chairmanship of De Rossi Enterprises, but he *had* to have the deeds of Villa De Rossi for Rosalie's sake. The degenerative disease his daughter suffered from was taking her from him, bit by bit, and in perhaps only a few more years it would claim her life. He would *not* allow the time that Rosalie had left to be disrupted by having to move her to a new house, away from the things she loved.

'Why were there journalists outside the wedding chapel?' Athena bit her lip. 'The pictures they took of us won't be printed in the newspapers in England, will they?'

'I hope so.' Luca's jaw hardened. 'After Giselle's stunt, my great-uncle Emilio—my late grandmother's brother— said that he and the board of De Rossi Enterprises will try to prove that my marriage to you is a sham. Their intention is to prevent me from claiming my inheritance. That's why it is vital that we convince the press—no, the world, and especially my great-uncle—that we married for conventional reasons. We are going to have to act like we are in love.'

He sighed impatiently when Athena looked blank.

'Pictures of us kissing on the steps of the wedding chapel will be a good start. For the only time in my life I will be happy to court the paparazzi. The more publicity we can get showing us as adoring newlyweds, the less chance my great-uncle will have to persuade the courts that our marriage is a fake.'

'You said our marriage would be in name only,' Athena said worriedly.

'In private it will be. But in public we must appear to be a blissfully happy couple.'

She shook her head. 'That wasn't part of the deal. I can't imagine what my family will think when they see photos of us and hear that we are married. I wasn't going to tell them that I'd married you. I planned to say that I was working abroad for a year. My parents will be horrified if I tell them about our deal.'

'You *can't* tell them of our financial deal,' Luca said sharply. 'No one can know the truth about our relationship except us. I can't risk the press finding out that we are married in name only. Your parents already think you and I are lovers because Charlie told them so. Convincing them that we are happily married shouldn't be too difficult.'

Athena gnawed on her bottom lip. 'I don't like the idea of lying to my family. You said that we would live quietly at your penthouse in Milan and few people would even know we are married.'

The limousine drew up at the entrance of a famous Las Vegas hotel and immediately a flurry of camera flashbulbs exploded outside the car window.

'Why have we stopped *here*?'

'My PA has booked us into the honeymoon suite. It's all part of the pretence that we are happily married.'

'I can't do this,' she said falteringly. 'I can't pretend to be in love with you.'

'If you want your million pounds, I'm sure you'll manage to give as convincing a performance as you gave outside the wedding chapel,' Luca said grimly. 'Keep thinking of the money, *mia bella*.'

He moved before she had time to register his intention, cupping her chin in his hand and dropping a hard kiss on her mouth that left her lips tingling. He had timed the kiss for the exact moment when the chauffeur opened the car door—much to the delight of the waiting paparazzi.

Athena would have liked to hurry into the hotel with her head down, but Luca clamped his arm around her waist and sauntered up to the front entrance, apparently totally relaxed as he smiled for the photographers.

'Can we have another shot of you kissing your wife, Mr De Rossi?'

He obliged, his eyes gleaming with a silent warning to Athena to play her part as he dipped his head and captured her mouth in a long, slow kiss that earned a few more cat-calls from the journalists.

He had missed out on a career as an actor, she thought dazedly. His performance as an adoring husband was so thorough that she simply melted against him, and her legs were trembling when he escorted her across the hotel lobby.

Her hope that Luca would take her to their suite, for some respite from the attention of the paparazzi and the other hotel guests, who were staring at her wedding dress, was dashed when they were greeted by the hotel manager, who personally showed them into the restaurant and explained that the head chef had prepared a special wedding dinner for them.

The elegant table, set with silver cutlery, crystal glasses and fine china, was a potential minefield for her. She was bound to knock something over or break something, and Athena kept her hands firmly in her lap.

'Would you like oysters, madam?'

'No, thank you.' She stopped the waiter just as he was about to place a plate of the unappealing-looking shellfish arranged on a bed of ice in front of her. Her stomach churned. 'I don't like oysters.'

The hotel manager who was hovering close to their table looked surprised. 'I understood that Mr De Rossi ordered oysters because they are your particular favourite?'

'Yes, darling,' Luca murmured. 'You love oysters, remember?'

'Oh…yes, of course I do, *darling.*' Athena flushed when the manager gave her a strange look. 'I *hate* oysters,' she muttered to Luca when they were alone. 'This is hopeless. How can we convince people that we are…in love when we don't know the first thing about one another?'

'We'll have to take a crash course in learning about each other.'

Luca sipped his wine and, noticing that the hotel manager was still looking at them curiously, reached across the table, clasped Athena's hand and lifted it to his mouth to press his lips against her fingers. He felt a tremor run through her and for a split second imagined that their marriage was real, and that after dinner they would go up to the honeymoon suite and he would remove her dress and the wispy scraps of lace underwear that he had been unable to forget since he had put her to bed in his hotel room in London.

'Tell me about yourself,' he instructed. 'I actually know more about your sister than I do about you. Lexi was an RAF helicopter pilot before she married Kadir, wasn't she? Did you consider joining the armed forces?'

Athena shook her head. 'Even when we were children Lexi was brave and bold, but I'm afraid I'm not. Lexi was adopted, but in fact she is far more like our parents than me. She is clever, and she did well at school, whereas I was an average student. Mum and Dad are both doctors and brilliant academics,' she explained. 'They named me after the Greek goddess of wisdom, but were hugely disappointed when I failed to get the grades to go to university to study medicine.'

'Did you *want* to be a doctor?'

'Not really. I didn't enjoy science, and I was useless at Latin—even though my parents paid for me to have extra lessons.'

Athena's stomach tied itself into a knot as she visualised her Latin tutor: Peter Fitch. He had been the same age as her father, and grey haired. He had worn grey flannel trousers and had had the air of respectability you might expect from a learned university professor.

Years after he had assaulted her she could still remember her absolute shock when he had commented on her breasts. She had felt uncomfortable rather than scared at first—until he had pushed her up against the door and grabbed at her blouse.

'You've gone very quiet.' Luca wondered why she had turned pale. Maybe it was the damned oysters. 'What are you thinking about?'

'I was thinking what a disappointment I've always been to my parents.' It wasn't far from the truth. She did not want to imagine how her parents would feel when they saw in the newspapers that she was married to Luca.

'What subjects were you interested in at school?'

'I loved art—particularly drawing. I would have liked to study fine art at university.'

'So why didn't you?'

'Oh, I wasn't good enough.'

'Did you apply to universities and get turned down?'

'Well, no, but my father said I was wasting my time doing silly drawings.'

She had buried her dream of becoming an illustrator and had revised like mad for her chemistry and biology exams—but she had still failed to get the grades required for medical school.

'How about you?' Athena asked Luca, keen to turn the spotlight away from her mediocre achievements. 'What made you decide to be a fashion designer?'

'Designing is in my blood. My great-grandfather founded De Rossi Enterprises when he began to design shoes for his wife after she complained that she could never find stylish shoes to wear with her evening gowns. Raimondo expanded to design handbags and accessories. To me it seemed a natural step to create clothes which reflected the De Rossi brand of cutting-edge style and exceptional quality.'

Unfortunately his grandparents had not shared his belief that the company needed to move into fashion design, including off-the-peg clothes to be sold on the high street, Luca brooded. He had fought constant battles with Aberto in his bid to expand the company into new global markets. But his instincts had proved right and De Rossi Enterprises, together with DRD, the fashion label he had created, were now in the top ten of Italy's most successful companies.

'Your parents must be proud of your success,' Athena said.

'My mother died when I was fifteen.'

'I'm sorry.'

It was not a throwaway remark. The compassion in her voice and in her eyes was genuine, Luca realised when he looked across the table and saw a gentle expression in her sapphire-blue gaze.

He shrugged. 'I didn't really know her. She had a wild lifestyle and was constantly flitting between her homes in Monaco and New York. Obviously I needed to be in one place to go to school, so she dumped me on my grandparents at Villa De Rossi.'

'I can't imagine your grandparents minded looking after you,' Athena murmured, thinking of the happy visits she had made to *her* grandparents' home when they had been alive. Unlike her parents, they had accepted her for who she was and had not put pressure on her to be cleverer or more studious.

'My grandparents bitterly resented me,' Luca said flatly.

The *bastardo* had been a shameful reminder of their daughter's often outrageous lifestyle. He hesitated, wondering why he found it easy to talk to Athena. The only time he really spoke to women was when he made small talk before taking them to bed, but something about the way she quietly listened, as if she was actually interested in what he had to say, made him relax his guard.

'In fact it was because of my mother that I wanted to be a fashion designer. I lived with her when I was younger, although I was mainly cared for by nannies, and I used to watch her getting ready to go out in the evenings. She would allow me to choose what dress she was going to wear, and her shoes and accessories. Even as a small boy I had a good eye for colour, and Mamma trusted my opinion.' He recalled the happiest moments of his childhood, when he had felt close to his mother. 'I felt proud that I had chosen what she wore when she went to grand parties. She was very beautiful.'

In the eyes of a young boy his mother had been like a fairytale princess, Luca mused. But one day she had disappeared out of his life and had gone to live with a lover who had not wanted a small child around. He had been sent to live with his grandparents, who had made it clear that they did not want him either.

His mother's desertion had hit him hard. It had been

an early lesson not to trust his heart—a lesson that had been reinforced years later when he had fallen in love with Jodie. She'd been a backpacker from New Zealand, who had been travelling around Europe and had taken a summer job in a village near to the Villa De Rossi. He had thought that Jodie would stay for ever—that their love would last for ever. But one day she'd disappeared from his life without warning, just as his mother had done, and Luca had realised that only a fool put his faith in love and the promises people made.

But there was another kind of love that he *did* believe in—the unconditional love of a father for his daughter. Jodie had not only deserted him, she had walked away from their daughter when medical tests had revealed the devastating news that Rosalie was suffering from a genetic brain disorder which would affect her development.

Luca's jaw clenched as he thought of his daughter who, since she was two years old, had been denied a normal life, and he felt the familiar, agonising sense of guilt that *he* was to blame for Rosalie's illness. Even though doctors had insisted that he must not feel responsible, he always would.

Despite her severe disabilities, Rosalie's smile lit up Luca's heart. His daughter was the reason why he had married a woman he barely knew, he brooded as he glanced at Athena and wondered how she was planning to spend a million pounds. They both had something to gain from their marriage and everything to lose unless they gave a convincing performance that they had married because they were in love.

CHAPTER SIX

'IF I HAVE to keep smiling I think my jaw will snap,' Athena muttered to Luca. 'How much longer are we going to stay in the casino? I want to go to bed.'

'Can you repeat that last statement in a louder voice, so that the paparazzi who have been stalking us all evening can hear you?' His eyes gleamed. 'Your eagerness for our wedding night is just the sort of thing to convince people our marriage is real.'

She was furious with herself for blushing, and with Luca for...well, for being Luca. For being drop-dead handsome and sexy and so charming that she was finding it impossible to resist his charisma.

'I'm sure we must have done enough to convince the press, seeing as you haven't left my side all evening and you keep kissing me,' she said tartly. 'You're like an octopus wrapping its tentacles around me, or in your case your arms, so that I can't escape.'

It was the first time in his nearly thirty-five years that he had been likened to an octopus, and it was not the most flattering comparison, Luca thought with a mixture of amusement and pique.

'I haven't seen much evidence that you've wanted to escape, *mia bella*,' he murmured. 'I have been impressed by your enthusiastic response when I've kissed you.'

He watched a rosy flush spread along her cheekbones

and suddenly felt as tired as Athena clearly was of keeping up the pretence that they were blissfully happy newlyweds in front of the paparazzi. Tomorrow's papers would undoubtedly publish photos of him and his bride staring adoringly into each other's eyes as they played craps and blackjack. The hotel's casino was jam-packed with tourists, which was why he had chosen it as a public arena in which to demonstrate that his marriage was the real deal.

Not that he had a problem with kissing Athena. He had found it surprisingly addictive to angle his mouth over hers and feel her soft, moist lips part, allowing his tongue to probe between them. He had spent the entire evening feeling so turned on that he hurt, and worse still was the knowledge that the only option ahead of him to alleviate the ache in his groin was to take a cold shower once he had escorted his bride up to the honeymoon suite.

'If you're tired we'll call it a night,' he said abruptly. 'You might as well play all your chips on one last spin of the roulette wheel. What are you going to bet on?' he asked as the croupier called for everyone to place their bets.

Athena put her stack of coloured chips on the board. 'I'll put everything on black, thirty-five. It seems to be a significant number, seeing that the reason we married is because you needed a wife by your thirty-fifth birthday.'

'Why don't you shout it out so that everyone in the entire room can hear you?' Luca growled.

'I'm sorry—I didn't think.' She cast a quick glance around and gave a sigh of relief when it appeared that her careless comment had gone unnoticed by the other people crowded around the roulette table.

The croupier spun the wheel and released the ball. Athena watched it half-interestedly. She had never gambled before, and after spending several hours in the casino still couldn't understand the attraction. Luca had teased her that with a million pounds behind her she could afford to place a few bets, but she did not want to risk losing a penny of the money that would pay for the new orphanage and school in Jaipur.

The white ball continued to rattle around the wheel and eventually came to rest—on black, thirty-five.

'You've won,' Luca told her when she stared in surprise at the roulette wheel. 'Thirty-five must be your lucky number.'

At least her winnings meant that she could buy some new clothes, Athena thought as she walked with Luca across the hotel lobby and was conscious of the curious looks her wedding dress still attracted from the other guests.

The honeymoon suite was on the thirty-fifth floor—although she did not believe in lucky numbers, she told herself. It was breathtakingly opulent, and she slipped off her shoes and walked barefoot across the thick velvet carpet as she explored the rooms—and discovered that one vital thing was missing.

'There is only one bedroom,' she told Luca when she went back into the sitting room and found him pouring himself a drink from the bar.

'I imagine there isn't much call for two bedrooms in the honeymoon suite,' he said drily.

'We can't stay here. We'll have to ask at Reception for a different suite, with two bedrooms.'

'And risk one of the hotel staff rushing to sell an exposé about our sleeping arrangements to the press? I think not.'

Luca noted Athena's anxious expression and felt a twinge of guilt for mocking her. She had played the part of his loving wife all evening, and it was not her fault that he had looked at the huge bed and visualised her naked, voluptuous, creamy-skinned body spread on the black silk sheets.

'I'll sleep on the sofa,' he reassured her. 'The suite *does* have his and hers bathrooms. I suggest you go and get ready for bed. You look…' The word *fragile* slid into his mind, and perhaps it was unsurprising considering the events of the past forty-eight hours since he had helped her to escape from her wedding to Charles Fairfax. 'You look tired,' he said flatly.

She did not feel tired, Athena thought twenty minutes later as she stepped into the pink marble sunken bath that was the size of a small swimming pool. She had used nearly the whole bottle of bubble bath provided by the hotel, and she sank into the foaming, scented water with a sigh of pleasure. The clock said it was one a.m. in Las Vegas, which meant it was morning in England, but she had slept for a few hours on the plane and her body felt strangely energised.

There was no mystery about why she felt more alive than she had ever done in her life, she mocked herself. She had spent all evening with Luca's arm wrapped firmly around her waist and his thigh pressed against hers, so that she had been aware of the muscled hardness of his athletic body. She knew that every time he had kissed her it had been a show for the watching paparazzi—so why had she trembled when he had brushed his lips over hers before deepening the kiss and stirring a passionate response that had shocked her?

She hadn't felt the knot of fear in the pit of her stomach that she'd felt in the past, when other men had kissed her. Charlie's chaste kisses had never made her feel apprehensive, she reminded herself. But since she had found him in bed with his best man she understood why there had been a complete lack of sexual chemistry between them. Her awareness of Luca did at least prove that the sexual assault years ago had not destroyed her sensuality. But she had buried normal feelings of passion and desire until Luca had kissed her outside the wedding chapel and awoken a yearning to satisfy the ache of need that throbbed deep in her pelvis.

The overnight bag that she had brought with her when she had escaped from Woodley Lodge contained her toothbrush and other personal toiletries—as well as the black negligee she had planned to wear on her wedding night with Charlie. The sheer black lace baby-doll nightgown barely covered any of her body, but it was all she had to sleep in.

Top of her shopping list tomorrow would be a pair of sensible pyjamas, Athena decided as she walked out of the en-suite bathroom into the bedroom—just as Luca entered the room through another door from the sitting room.

He must have showered, because his hair was damp, and he was wearing a black towelling robe loosely belted at his waist and gaping open over his upper body, so that she could see the whorls of black hairs that covered his chest. The skin visible beneath the mat of hair was dark bronze—the same as the bare legs revealed below the hem of his robe. The idea that he was naked beneath the robe made Athena feel quivery inside, and she could not stop staring at him.

'I came to get a pillow. I knocked but you didn't answer, so I assumed you were still in the bathroom.'

His voice was curiously husky, his accent more pronounced than usual and incredibly sexy, causing the tiny hairs on Athena's body to stand on end. Her heart lurched as he walked towards her and she saw the predatory gleam in his eyes. Her brain told her that he shouldn't be looking at her as he was doing—with a dark intensity, as if he was mentally undressing her.

It would not take him long, she thought ruefully, glancing down at her skimpy negligee and discovering that the darker skin of her nipples showed through the semi-transparent material.

'Luca…'

Did that breathless voice belong to her? She licked her dry lips with the tip of her tongue and watched him swallow convulsively. He was still coming closer, and she backed up until she bumped into the bed and couldn't go any further.

'What do you want?'

She remembered he had said he wanted a pillow, but he did not glance at the head of the bed, just kept his glittering gaze focused on her.

What did he want? Luca almost laughed at Athena's innocent question. As if she did not know, he brooded, noting how her pupils had dilated so that her eyes were almost completely black. The sexual tension shimmering between them was so acute he could almost taste it.

He knew he should not feel like this—as if his body was a tightly coiled spring, thrumming with frustration. It wasn't part of his game plan. When he had asked Athena to be his wife in name only he'd had no idea that he would be more turned on than he could ever remember by her petite but delightfully curvaceous figure, now inadequately covered by a wisp of black lace.

Everything had changed when he had kissed her on the steps of the wedding chapel, he acknowledged. Until that moment he had viewed her only as a means to claim his rightful ownership of the Villa De Rossi, which was so important to his daughter's happiness. But when he had taken Athena in his arms and her soft, voluptuous body had fitted so snugly to his, he had suddenly been aware of her as a desirable woman.

Their evening spent in the casino had been an exquisite form of torture as she had responded to his kisses with a sweet ardency that had driven him crazy—because he had known she was only acting for the benefit of the paparazzi.

But now they were alone in the honeymoon suite, and with no members of the press to impress there was no reason for Athena to catch her breath as he halted in front of her and ran his finger lightly down her cheek. He felt the tremor that ran through her and his body tightened in response as anticipation licked hot and hungry through his veins. There was nothing to stop him changing the rules of his game plan and making Athena his wife in every sense.

'I want you, *mia bella*,' he said softly.

If he had been able to think clearly he would have wondered about the flicker of wariness in her eyes, but Luca's thoughts were distracted by the betraying quiver of her lower lip.

'I want to kiss you,' he murmured as he cradled her cheek in his hand and brought his mouth down on hers.

Luca only wanted to kiss her. The knot of apprehension in Athena's stomach unravelled. That was all right. She did not mind him kissing her—didn't mind at all, in fact, she admitted as his lips gently teased hers apart and he explored their shape with his tongue.

He smelled of soap and spicy cologne, mixed with that subtle scent of maleness that so intoxicated her senses that without being aware of moving she swayed towards him and curled her arms around his neck. It seemed quite natural for him to lift her up and place her on the bed. Even when he knelt above her, his chiselled features accentuated in the golden glow of the bedside lamp, she was so absorbed by the feelings he was stirring in her, so entranced by the sharp, sweet throb of desire between her thighs, that the shadows from her past did not trouble her.

'You have beautiful hair,' Luca told her, threading his fingers through the long chestnut mane that felt like silk against his skin. 'And a beautiful body,' he growled as he trailed his lips down her throat before moving lower to the deep vee between her breasts.

His kisses scalded her skin, and the ache low in her pelvis grew more insistent as he slowly drew the straps of her negligee over her shoulders, peeling the wisp of black lace down so that, inch by heart-jolting inch, he bared her breasts. Athena held her breath as he cupped the pale mounds of firm flesh in his palms. She was not repelled by his touch, she discovered. She *liked* the feel of his hands caressing her.

'You are exquisite,' he said hoarsely.

His eyes blazed with a smouldering intensity and Athena realised that he wasn't joking—he really did think she was beautiful. He made her *feel* beautiful, especially when he rubbed his thumb pads over her nipples so that they instantly swelled to hard peaks and he gave a groan of appreciation. Her breasts felt heavy, and the tingling sensation in her nipples seemed to have a direct connection to the spiralling throbbing sensation between her legs.

Driven by instinct, she moved her hips restlessly, and felt a quiver of excitement as he slid his hand over her stomach and ran his fingers along the edge of the black lace knickers.

'*Mia bella* Aphrodite...' Luca stared down at Athena's creamy, perfect breasts with their rosy tips, and her glorious hair spread like a silken curtain across the pillows, and desire jack-knifed inside him. 'You should have been named after her—the goddess of beauty and pleasure,' he said thickly, anticipating the pleasure-filled night he was sure was ahead.

His words penetrated Athena's mind and the haze of sensual delight Luca had created began to fade as the warm blood in her veins cooled.

'*Don't* call me that.'

'*Let me touch you, Aphrodite. Do you wear low-cut tops to tantalise me with a glimpse of your breasts? Have you any idea how much I want to feel your firm, youthful flesh? Your body was designed for sex, and you're hungry for it, aren't you?*'

She looked up at Luca, but inside her head she heard the sound of her cotton blouse ripping, and her high-pitched cry as she tried to hold the torn material across her breasts. She heard her parents' friend Peter Fitch's panting breaths as he forced his hand inside her bra, his strong fingers pinching her flesh, hurting her, making her feel sick with fear when he shoved his other hand between her legs. This was *Uncle Peter*, whom she had known all her life. He shouldn't be touching her and saying horrible, disgusting things about what he wanted to do to her.

She looked at Luca but it was Peter Fitch's face she saw leering at her, sweat on his brow, his eyes glazed.

'No! Stop!' Panic ripped through her and she pushed frantically against the male chest leaning over her, while in her mind she fought against the hands ripping her blouse.

But it was *Luca's* chest that her hands were splayed flat against, she realised as the images in her head receded and the past turned into the present. It was *Luca* who was staring at her—not Uncle Peter.

She took a shuddering breath.

'No?' Luca drawled.

His voice was deceptively soft, but Athena sensed he was confused and frustrated by her sudden change from being warm and responsive to her curt rejection of him.

'What happened to make you change your mind?'

It was only natural that he wanted an explanation, she acknowledged. But his cynical tone annoyed her. He spoke as if it had been a foregone conclusion that they would have sex, but that had not been her intention when he had started to kiss her, and if anyone had changed their mind about the rules of their relationship it was him.

She could not tell him the real reason why she had pushed him away. The sexual assault had been humiliating, and although logically she knew it had not been her fault she had never forgotten Peter's accusation that she had deliberately led him on. The Latin tutor had insisted that she was wanton and eager for sex and that that was why she had worn a blouse that had revealed a hint of cleavage. Perhaps Luca believed that by wearing a sexy negligee she had sent out a message that she was available.

She bit her lip as logic once again pointed out that there was nothing shameful about a single, twenty-five-year-old woman living in the twenty-first century letting it be known that she was sexually available. The problem was *her* and her hang-ups. She wished she *could* let go of the past and make love with Luca. But now she was on dangerous ground—because Luca was a playboy and all he wanted was casual sex.

'When we made our deal you said our marriage would be in name only,' she reminded him. 'You also told me there would be no point in falling in love with you.'

His eyes narrowed. 'What does *love* have to do with what, up until a few minutes ago, you were as keen as me to enjoy? Why is it wrong to take pleasure in sex for no other reason than that we find each other attractive?'

Athena knew it would be pointless to deny his assertion that she was attracted to him after she had initially responded to him so enthusiastically.

'Sex wasn't included in the deal we made,' she muttered. 'You might be happy to indulge in casual sex, but for me making love is more than simply a physical act— it's a way of expressing the deep emotion of being in love.'

Having never had sex, she didn't know how she could be so certain of her feelings; she just *knew* that, for her, love and the act of making love were inextricably linked.

'Ah…' Luca finally understood.

Presumably if he offered to pay Athena more money she would turn back into the sexually responsive woman he'd thought—*damn it*, he'd *known* had wanted him as much as he had wanted her. The rubbish she'd spouted about sex needing to be an expression of love was ridiculous.

He still wanted her, he admitted as he stood up and looked at her lying on the bed. She had pulled her nightgown back into place, but her plump-as-peaches breasts were in danger of spilling over their lacy constriction and her pebble-hard nipples were clearly visible beneath the sheer material. *Dio*, she was small but perfectly formed— a pint-sized goddess.

He frowned as he remembered that the big freeze had happened after he had called her Aphrodite. He had almost thought she had seemed afraid. But afraid of what? Of *him*…? The idea made him feel uncomfortable. Maybe he *had* come on to her too strongly, but it hadn't been all one-sided, he reminded himself. The sexual awareness between them had been electrifying.

She sat up and pushed her hair back from her face. In the lamplight Luca caught the sparkle of tears on her lashes and something kicked in his gut.

'Athena?' he said softly.

'You said you needed a pillow…' She avoided looking at him as she handed him one.

He hesitated, feeling reluctant to leave her when she was clearly upset. 'What happened just now? Do you want to talk about it?'

And say what? Athena thought miserably. She felt ashamed—not about the sexual assault, but the fact that she had been unable to deal with what had happened to her when she was eighteen. She wished she could move on. At first when Luca had started to undress her and touch her breasts she had enjoyed his caresses—before ugly memories of the assault by her Latin tutor had intruded and her desire had been replaced with the feeling that she was dirty.

'Please go,' she whispered.

She held her breath when he did not move away from the bed, each passing minute stretching her nerves, until he sighed heavily.

'Goodnight, *piccola*. Try to get some sleep.'

The snick of the door closing told her she was alone. She wondered what *piccola* meant.

The unexpected gentleness in Luca's voice proved to be the last straw for her raw emotions, and she could not hold back her tears.

In the sitting room, the makeshift bed Luca had made on the sofa was comfortable enough, but he could not sleep. He wondered how many other bridegrooms had spent their wedding night relegated to the sofa in the honeymoon suite. Not many, he would bet. But this was not a real wedding night—just as his marriage was not real.

He should feel jubilant that he had found a way to meet the terms of his grandmother's will. And of course he was relieved that he would not have to move Rosalie away from Villa De Rossi. But he had barely given a thought to his position as chairman of De Rossi Enterprises, or the fact that his own design company, DRD, could now continue to use the De Rossi name.

His thoughts centred on his new wife. The muffled sound of crying he could hear from the bedroom tugged at his conscience. He remembered it was less than forty-eight hours since Athena had discovered her fiancé had been unfaithful. Perhaps she was heartbroken that her dreams of marrying Charles Fairfax had been shattered and that she was trapped in a sham marriage with *him* for a year.

Muttering a curse, Luca took his frustration out on the pillow and thumped it hard, before rolling onto his side and waiting a long time for sleep to come.

'Athena?' Luca knocked on the bedroom door a second time. After what had happened the previous night, when he had walked in and seen her wearing that sexy little negligee that had sent his blood pressure soaring, he wasn't going to risk entering the room without her permission.

She opened the door and he stared at her in surprise. The pink towelling robe provided by the hotel was at least five sizes too big for her and she looked as soft and sweet as a marshmallow. Without a trace of make-up, and with her glasses perched on her nose, she looked fresh-faced and wholesome. She was the complete opposite of the glamorous socialites Luca usually chose to be his mistresses, and he could not understand the powerful rush of sexual hunger that swept through him.

Last night he had vowed that, apart from having to pretend in public that they could not keep their hands off each other, when they were alone he would keep his hands very much to himself. It was disconcerting to admit that his will power was already being tested.

'I've arranged for some clothes to be sent over to the hotel from the Las Vegas DRD store,' he told her. 'You can't spend another day wearing your wedding dress.'

Athena followed him into the sitting room and looked along the rail of assorted outfits. 'They're not really my style,' she said, holding up a scarlet dress that she could tell would cling to her curvaceous figure. 'I tend to wear clothes that are less fitted and have a higher neckline.' *And preferably are not such an eye-catching colour,* she added silently, thinking of the mainly beige or navy skirts and blouses in her wardrobe in England. She glanced at the price tag on the dress and quickly hung it back on the rail. 'These are definitely *not* in my price range.'

Luca's brows lifted. 'You'll soon have a million pounds in the bank. I assumed you planned to spend a substantial amount of it on designer clothes. But I'll pay for any clothes you choose now.' He held the red dress against her. 'This will look fantastic on you. With your colouring you can carry off bold shades.'

'How do you know it will fit me?' Athena reluctantly took the dress from him.

'I have spent my entire adult life dressing women.' His eyes gleamed wickedly. 'And undressing them. I made a professional guess as to your size.' Helped by the fact that he had run his hands over her body last night and memorised the shape of her narrow waist and full breasts, Luca mused.

Athena had thought of another reason why the clothes Luca had chosen wouldn't be suitable. 'Tight-fitting dresses and skirts are no good for my line of work. I need to wear things that will allow me to move easily and even to roll around on the floor.'

He looked surprised. 'I thought you said you didn't work. What *is* your job anyway? Circus performer?'

She felt a sudden release from the fierce tension that had seized her when she had opened the door to Luca and been swamped by memories of how he had nearly made love to her last night.

Her lips twitched. 'I'm a qualified nursery nurse and I work with young children up to the age of about five years old. A lot of the time the job involves getting down on the floor to play with them. The nursery I worked at closed down a couple of months before I'd planned to marry Charlie. I told you—I used the time to go on cookery courses so that I would be able to give sophisticated dinner parties like the wives of his banker friends. Actually, most of the dishes I cooked were a disaster,' she admitted, thinking of her soufflés that had failed to rise and her mayonnaise that had curdled, whatever she did to it.

'You won't need to work while we are married—or after we divorce, if you invest your million pounds wisely.'

'Of course I'll work.'

She hesitated, wondering if she should tell Luca of her intention to give the money he was paying her to the orphanage project in India. Charles had been uninterested in her fundraising campaign for the street children of Jaipur, she remembered, and although her parents were supportive, Athena knew that they still wished she would focus more on furthering her career rather than her charity work.

But the orphanage meant a lot to her. She felt she was actually doing something worthwhile that could change the lives of homeless children, and she was afraid Luca would not understand her decision to give such a vast sum of money away to charity.

'I love being a nursery nurse,' she told him. 'I realise it may not be easy to find a job at a nursery in Italy, because I can't speak the language, but there might be a family that wants to employ an English-speaking nanny.'

She looked again along the rail of clothes and picked out a couple of dresses.

'I'll try these on, and *I'll* pay for them. You are already paying me a fortune. I won't allow you to buy my clothes.'

Five minutes later she walked back into the sitting room, feeling painfully self-conscious. The scarlet dress moulded her body like a second skin. 'It's too clingy,' she told Luca, 'and the shoes are too high.'

Luca swung round from the window and was powerless to prevent his body's reaction as his gaze encompassed Athena's hourglass figure shown off perfectly by the fitted dress. She was every red-blooded male's fantasy! And where had those legs come from? The three-inch stiletto heels accentuated her slim calves—and gave her a delightful wiggle when she walked, he noticed as she came towards him. She had swapped her glasses for contact lenses, and caught her hair up in a loose knot with stray tendrils framing her delicate face.

He swallowed. 'You look incredible.'

She bit her lip. 'You don't think the dress is a bit too...?'

'Too what?' He was puzzled by her doubtful expression. Hadn't she looked in the mirror and seen how gorgeous she was? How had he ever written her off as the plain Howard sister?

'Too revealing...' Athena mumbled.

'You have a beautiful figure and I think you should absolutely show it off.'

Luca silently acknowledged that the last part of that statement was a lie. He didn't want other men looking at Athena. He had discovered he had caveman tendencies, and would like to lock his wife away where only he could see her. Unfortunately the need to convince the board of De Rossi Enterprises that his marriage was not fake meant that he and Athena must court the attention of the paparazzi. His global fame as a top fashion designer guaranteed that pictures of him and his new bride wearing a sexy red dress would feature in newspapers around the world.

'I have something else for you.' He pulled a small velvet box from his pocket.

Athena frowned when he handed her the box. 'What is it?'

'An engagement ring. I thought you'd better be seen

wearing one at the press conference I've arranged for us to give this morning. Open it,' he bade her.

Her hands shook as she lifted the lid and revealed an exquisite oval sapphire surrounded by white diamonds. 'They're not real stones, are they?' she choked.

'Of course they're real. I didn't get the ring out of a Christmas cracker.'

'It must be worth a fortune.'

Athena did not know much about jewellery, but she had seen a similar ring in the exclusive shop in the hotel's lobby and been astounded by the price tag.

'I'd *rather* have a ring from a Christmas cracker.' She bit her lip. 'It doesn't seem right for me to wear this.'

The engagement ring was beautiful, and she felt that it should be a token of love between a couple who were in a genuine relationship—rather than a stage prop to fool the press and ultimately Luca's great-uncle and the other De Rossi board members that their marriage was real.

'People will expect me to have given you an engagement ring,' Luca said as he slid the ring onto her finger.

It fitted perfectly. Athena could not explain why tears blurred her eyes, making the diamonds that encircled the sapphire glisten.

'I'll return the ring to you at the end of the year, when our marriage is over,' she said huskily.

Luca gave her an intent look. 'It's yours to keep.'

'No.'

He recognised the resolute angle of her jaw and shrugged. In truth, he was puzzled. His assumption that Athena was as much of a gold-digger as Giselle did not fit with her refusal to accept anything from him.

He glanced at his watch. 'I've arranged the press conference for ten o'clock. You can leave most of the talking to me. I'll explain that we fell in love at your sister's wedding in Zenhab, but because we had both promised to marry other people we fought our feelings until we realised that we couldn't live without one another. Hopefully the story will convince my great-uncle *and* satisfy fans of romantic fiction,' he said sardonically.

Luca was a consummate actor, Athena thought later as she sat next to him at the press conference, and forced herself to smile for the paparazzi who had crowded into the room and jostled for a prime position to take photographs.

His reputation as a playboy meant that the press were fascinated by the story of how Luca De Rossi had eloped to Las Vegas to marry the woman who had captured his heart. As he had predicted, there was a great deal of interest in her engagement ring, and Athena lost count of the number of times she'd assured the journalists that she was blissfully happy and in love with her new husband.

'I completely refute the suggestion that my marriage to Athena is a sham,' Luca replied, to a question about the validity of their relationship.

'How about giving your bride a kiss?' someone called out.

'Nothing would give me greater pleasure.'

Luca's smile did not slip as he turned his head slightly towards Athena.

'We'd better keep the paparazzi happy,' he muttered. 'My PA informed me just before the press conference that my great-uncle Emilio has begun legal proceedings to try and stop me claiming my inheritance, and the only way he can do that is if he can prove our marriage is a fake.' He dipped his head closer to her. 'Are you ready?'

He made it sound so clinical. But of course for Luca kissing her was just part of his strategy to show the world that they were in love.

He had not been acting in front of the press when he had kissed her in their honeymoon suite last night, she remembered. When he had walked into the bedroom and seen her wearing a virtually see-through nightgown his eyes had glittered with desire. His hands had explored her body with the skill of a man well practised at seducing women, but his touch had been surprisingly gentle, almost reverent, when he had cradled her bare breasts in his hands and played with her nipples until they'd hardened.

She watched his darkly beautiful face descend and was gripped with panic. It was not the nervous feeling she'd had in the past whenever a man had tried to kiss her—it was a different kind of panic…a sense that she was being drawn ever deeper into a situation that was out of her control.

'I can't,' she whispered.

His face was so close that she could see each individual eyelash, and his lush mouth was a temptation she knew she must resist if she was to survive a year of being married to him.

Luca was puzzled by the fearful expression in Athena's eyes. It was the same expression he had seen on her face last night, when she had called a sudden halt to their love-making. He couldn't think of any reason why she would be afraid of him, but something had happened that had upset her. She had cried for a long time after he had left her.

'Relax, *piccola*. I'm not going to hurt you.'

His softly spoken assurance was whispered across Athena's lips. *Piccola* meant 'little one'—she had looked up the translation last night.

Luca's gentleness was her undoing, and she released her breath on a ragged sigh as he covered her mouth with his and kissed her with heart-stopping passion mixed with an unexpected tenderness that evoked an ache inside her for something elusive and indefinable.

She had no idea how long the kiss lasted. Time was suspended and the journalists with their microphones and cameras disappeared from her consciousness. There was only her and Luca. She heard his low groan as he took the kiss to another level, where there was nothing but the sensations of darkness and velvet softness and the sweet, slow throb of desire stealing through her veins.

When eventually he lifted his head, she could not say a word as she waited for him to make some witty comment to the paparazzi. But he didn't speak. He simply stared into her eyes, and a nerve flickered in his jaw when he saw the tears clinging to her lashes.

'Don't.' His voice sounded strangely rusty as he pressed his lips to each of her eyelids in turn and tasted moisture on his lips. 'You cannot deny the attraction between us any more than I can,' he said in a harsh whisper, to avoid being overheard by the journalists. 'So what was last night about?'

Athena was incapable of answering him—and was spared from having to try when Luca's PA appeared at his shoulder.

'I received a message for you from Villa De Rossi while your phone was switched off during the press conference,' Sandro told Luca quietly. 'Maria has asked you to return home urgently.'

CHAPTER SEVEN

ATHENA'S FOOTSTEPS ECHOED on the black-and-white che-quered floor of the entrance hall at Villa De Rossi. Luca's secluded home, set in thirty acres of stunning parkland with views of Lake Como and the surrounding moun-tains, was a haven of peace and tranquillity after vibrant Las Vegas. Athena had fallen in love with the villa at first sight, and after three days of exploring the house and beau-tiful gardens she felt incredibly lucky that she would be able to spend time here for the year while she was mar-ried to Luca.

But if the past few days were anything to go by she would not be spending much time with her husband. She hadn't seen him since the evening they had arrived at the villa and he had shown her to a suite of rooms: a large bedroom, en-suite bathroom and a charming sitting room overlooking the lake.

She had eaten dinner in splendid isolation in the wooden-panelled dining room, and when she'd asked the affable butler, Geomar, if the Conte—she had been shocked to discover that Luca had a title—would be join-ing her, she had been informed that he was very busy.

Whatever it was that occupied him, it wasn't to do with his work.

His design studio, on the second floor of the villa, was a huge space, which must have been created by knocking through several rooms. Athena had taken a quick look inside, and had been amazed by the dozens of sketches pinned to the walls. Luca's designs. He was obviously a gifted artist, who used bold pencil or charcoal strokes on his drawings, and she had thought how fussy her own drawings were in comparison.

Luca had not been in his studio or in his study when she'd looked. The villa was huge, and she remembered he had said they would be able to keep out of each other's way most of the time.

At least the staff were friendly—and Geomar and his wife Elizavetta, who was the cook and housekeeper, spoke reasonably fluent English. She would have to find someone to give her Italian lessons, Athena thought. The two nurseries in nearby villages where she had made enquiries about a possible job both required her to be able to speak at least basic Italian.

The late summer sunshine pouring through the front windows filled the entrance hall with golden light and danced across the portraits of the De Rossi family lining the walls. Luca's ancestors shared his classically sculpted, rather haughty features, but she noticed that none had his curious amber-coloured eyes. The two most recent portraits were of a stern-faced couple who Athena guessed must be Luca's grandparents and, in contrast, a last picture of a smiling woman wearing an eye-catching orange dress. She was very beautiful, with long black hair and slanting eyes, and she looked so vividly alive that Athena almost expected her to spring out from the canvas.

'My mother—Beatriz.'

Luca's gravelly voice sent a ripple of reaction through Athena and she spun round to see him walking into the hall through a door which was usually kept locked.

'I see you can't take your eyes off her. She had that effect on most people—particularly men,' he said sardonically.

Athena noticed that he could not seem to tear his own gaze from his mother. 'What happened to her?'

'She had an addiction to cocaine and vodka. A maid found her body at the bottom of the stairs in her apartment in Monte Carlo. It was supposed at the inquest that she had fallen and broken her neck, which resulted in her accidental death.' Luca's voice was emotionless but a nerve flickered in his jaw.

Athena drew a sharp breath. 'What a terrible thing to have happened—for her and also for you,' she said gently. Intuitively she realised that Luca had been deeply and irrevocably affected by his mother's death. 'She looks so full of life in the painting…as if she was determined to live her life to the maximum.'

'My mother was the most selfish, self-obsessed woman I have ever known—and I've known quite a few,' Luca said cynically. 'When she was a child my grandparents gave her everything she desired, and as an adult she carried on taking what she wanted without giving a thought to anyone else.'

'When did you come to live with your grandparents?'

'Just before my eighth birthday.' It had been a week before, and in the upheaval of dumping him on her parents, his mother had forgotten his birthday. His grandparents did not even know the date of his birth, and Luca had never told them. 'My mother moved in with a lover who didn't want me around. I rarely saw her after I came to live here.'

Athena looked along the row of portraits. 'There isn't a picture of your father here.'

Luca hesitated. He had long ago stopped feeling ashamed of his illegitimacy, but memories of being teased by the other boys at school about his mother's outrageous lifestyle and very public affairs with a string of men meant that he rarely discussed his background.

'That's because his identity was unknown—even to my mother.' He shrugged. 'She had a vague idea he might have been a croupier she'd had a fling with in Monte Carlo, but she told me she couldn't be sure who had fathered me.'

He grimaced when he saw Athena's shocked expression.

'My grandparents were appalled that my mother had given birth to a bastard. They believed—with some justification—that Beatriz's wild lifestyle of drugs, drink and careless sex would bring the De Rossi brand name into disrepute. And I was the living proof that they had gone badly wrong when they brought up my mother. Rather than spoiling me, they went to the other end of the spectrum,' he said grimly. 'I loved being at boarding school, because at least during term time I had some respite from Aberto and Violetta's constant attempts to suppress any source of happiness or enjoyment in my life.'

He gave a harsh laugh.

'Perhaps it was natural that when I grew older I rebelled against my grandparents' strict ways. They regarded my playboy reputation as proof that I had inherited my mother's irresponsibility—especially when…'

'When what?' Athena asked, puzzled by his abrupt halt.

'It's not important.'

Luca's jaw clenched as he remembered his grandparents' anger when he had brought his illegitimate daughter to live at Villa De Rossi.

'You continue to heap shame on the family with your immoral behaviour,' Nonna Violetta had accused him.

Even when Rosalie's illness had been diagnosed, his grandparents had been uninterested in the *bastardo's* bastard child.

The situation he now found himself in was difficult,

Luca brooded. When he had married Athena he had intended for her to live at his penthouse in Milan, as he had originally planned for Giselle. But since Emilio had threatened to try and prove that his marriage was a sham, he had been forced to bring his bride to live at the villa.

He realised he could not keep his daughter a secret from Athena for a year, but he could not forget his concern that she might talk to the press about Rosalie's medical condition. He was determined to guard his daughter's privacy, and he certainly did not want journalists hanging around the villa—or, even worse, the local hospital. Rosalie was frequently admitted there for treatment, and she had been there for the past couple of days, receiving treatment for a chest infection.

Sufferers of Rett Syndrome were prone to developing pneumonia—which was why Maria had urgently called him home from Las Vegas when Rosalie had shown signs of breathing problems. But, thank God, his daughter was okay after a course of antibiotics to treat the infection.

Relief that Rosalie was recovering from her latest bout of illness was replaced with frustration as Luca acknowledged that he had no option but to tell Athena about his daughter—sooner rather than later.

He turned his back on his mother's portrait and skimmed his gaze over his wife. She had obviously spent time outside in the garden since arriving at the villa, and the mellow September sunshine had given her bare arms a light golden tan and encouraged a sprinkling of freckles on her nose.

'You are sensible to wear a hat. The sun at this time of the year can still be very hot, and although your hair is dark you have fair skin, which would burn easily.'

The light blue cotton sundress Athena was wearing was not at all glamorous, but the square-cut neckline showed off the upper slopes of her breasts and Luca found her natural, wholesome beauty incredibly sexy. He tried to ignore the tug of desire in his gut.

'Are you settling in at the Villa De Rossi? If there is anything you need just ask Geomar.'

'I'm fine now that my luggage has arrived from England,' Athena assured him.

The villa felt more like home since her parents had sent over her clothes and personal belongings. The phone conversation she'd had with her mother about her shock marriage to Luca had been extremely tense, but now her parents were on a Caribbean cruise, and she hoped they would soon come to terms with her decision not to marry Charlie—although it sounded as if he still had not told the truth about his relationship with his best man.

She looked at Luca's darkly handsome face and her stomach twisted. She had missed his company these past few days—missed his kisses, she acknowledged.

'Where have you been? Geomar said you were busy. Was it to do with your work?'

'I had matters to attend to.'

Luca stiffened as he watched Athena lift her straw hat from her head so that her hair tumbled down her back like a river of silk. It was all he could do not to reach out and run his fingers through the glossy chestnut mane. *Dio*, she was going to be a distraction he did not need at the villa.

'Did you go to Milan?' Geomar had told Athena that Luca often went to the city. The head offices of his design company DRD and also De Rossi Enterprises were there. 'You told me you have an apartment in the city.'

He sidestepped her first question. 'My penthouse is close to Galleria Vittorio Emanuele II—Milan's famous shopping gallery. You are welcome to go and stay there if you are bored at Villa De Rossi.'

'I can't imagine ever being bored here—the house and grounds are so beautiful. But there *is* something I'm curious about. What is behind the wall that runs along the side of the house? There's a door in the wall, but it's locked.'

Luca frowned. 'The area beyond the wall is out of bounds. There's nothing much there,' he said, seeing the curiosity on Athena's face.

She wanted to ask him *why* the place was out of bounds, if there was nothing there, but he was striding across the hall towards the library. She followed him, puzzled by his secrecy about the locked door. What *was* beyond the garden wall? Luca clearly did not want her to find out.

Perhaps it had something to do with the mystery of the disappearing women!

She thought of the attractive dark-haired woman she had seen arriving at the villa early every morning, and another woman of whom she hadn't managed to get a good glimpse because she arrived in the evening, as it was getting dark. Both the women parked their cars at the back of the house.

When Athena had asked Geomar about these regular visitors to the villa he had made out that he hadn't understood her—although usually he had an excellent grasp of English.

Were the two women Luca's mistresses? Athena's imagination went into overdrive. Now that she thought about it, he *did* look tired. Perhaps he had been 'busy' entertaining his lady friends.

Her thoughts scattered when she stepped into the library and found Luca flicking through the sketchpad she had left on the table.

'Are these your drawings?'

'Yes, but please don't look at them.'

In an agony of embarrassment, she tried to snatch the sketchbook out of his hands.

'They're very good.' Luca put the pad back on the table, but continued to turn the pages. 'Your drawings of animals are incredibly detailed. Have you ever thought about becoming an illustrator?'

Some of Athena's tension eased when she realised that Luca wasn't mocking her. 'I'd love to illustrate children's storybooks.' She hesitated. 'Actually, I've written a few books for children in the five to eight age group, and illustrated the stories.'

'Have any been published?'

'No, I've never sent my work to a publisher. My father...' Athena bit her lip as she remembered her father's irritation with what he had called her time-wasting. 'He used to get annoyed if he found me scribbling childish drawings instead of studying for my exams. I really don't believe my drawings are good enough to be saleable,' she said ruefully.

'It sounds like your parents did a good job of destroying your confidence.'

Luca could sympathise with how Athena must have felt when she had failed to meet her parents' expectations. He had never fitted the mould his grandparents had tried to force him into.

'I think you should send your work off to some publishing houses. What have you got to lose?'

'Do you *really* think my drawings are good enough for a publisher to be interested in them?'

Her shy smile transformed her from pretty to beautiful, Luca brooded.

She straightened up and tilted her head to meet his gaze. 'Thanks for being so encouraging.'

'You're welcome.'

Luca knew he was staring at her—but then, she was staring at him. He watched a soft flush of colour run under her skin, suffusing her cheeks and throat and spreading down to the upper slopes of her breasts. The tip of her tongue darted out to lick her lips and desire corkscrewed inside him.

He wanted to kiss her as he had done in Vegas. Hell, he wanted to tumble her down onto the sofa and make love to her hard and fast, and then take the slow, leisurely route and satisfy the hunger that he was convinced she felt as strongly as he did.

But all *he* wanted was to spend an afternoon enjoying sex with no strings attached, and he remembered Athena had told him that she regarded making love as a physical expression of being in love. It was enough to make any sensible man run a mile.

Maybe some people *did* find happy-ever-after—Luca thought of Kadir and Lexi in Zenhab. But even if he *had* wanted a relationship with a woman that involved spending time with her on both sides of the bedroom door, it wasn't possible. He was committed to caring for his daughter, whose life was slowly being destroyed by a terrible disease, and just as important as his devotion to Rosalie was the terrible secret he carried, along with the gut-wrenching sense of guilt, which had led to his decision to remain single.

The ticking clock sounded unnaturally loud in the quiet library. Athena could hardly breathe as she recognised the gleam of desire in Luca's eyes, and she found she was mentally urging him to pull her into his arms and kiss her.

He moved towards her, but at that moment Geomar appeared in the doorway and spoke to Luca in Italian. Athena could not understand anything of the conversation between the two men, but she stiffened when she heard the name Maria.

In Las Vegas, Luca's PA had mentioned Maria. Was

she one of the women who drove up to the villa and then disappeared?

Athena would have liked to ask Luca, but he took no more notice of her as he finished talking to the butler and strode out of the library.

Ominous purple clouds obscured the mountaintops, and the air in the courtyard at the front of the villa was so hot and still that it felt as if there was no air at all. Geomar had told Athena he thought a storm was brewing when she had passed him in the hall on her way outside. She wondered if it would be cooler down by the lake and started to walk in that direction.

Her route took her along a path next to the high wall that had the locked door in it. There was probably no mystery on the other side, she told herself, just as there was probably a simple explanation for the women who arrived at the villa but she had never met. She was allowing her imagination to run away with her.

But she was sure she hadn't imagined the faint sound of a child crying during the night. And she definitely wasn't imagining the sound of Luca's voice coming from the other side of the wall.

Athena stopped and strained her ears. She recognised Luca's gravelly tones, but not the woman's voice. Laughter drifted over the wall. Luca and his companion were speaking in Italian, and again he said the name Maria. Athena felt a spurt of anger. It was true that her marriage to Luca was in name only, but it wasn't right for him to entertain his lover—perhaps *lovers*—under the same roof as his wife.

She shielded her eyes from the sun with her hand and looked up at the wall. From the ground it did not look terribly high, and the missing bricks in places would provide hand and footholds if she was mad enough to decide to climb to the top—which of course she wasn't.

She heard another peal of laughter. The mystery woman was evidently enjoying Luca's company. Damn it! What was going on behind the wall? Athena's curiosity got the better of her dislike of heights and, fuelled by temper and bravado, she began to climb.

It was surprisingly easy. The old bricks were worn, giving her plenty of places to grip while she hauled herself up. Determined to see what was on the other side, she continued to climb until she was almost at the top, and then she managed to hook one leg over so that she was straddling the wall.

Below her was a pretty garden with wide paths bordered by lavender hedges. The spires of purple flowers were fading in late summer, but even from her high vantage point Athena could smell their sweet scent. In the centre of the garden was a pond and next to it a beautiful weeping willow tree, with sweeping branches that reached down to the water.

There was no sign of Luca or the woman in the garden. Athena looked towards the house just as a woman appeared at the window. She recognised her as the pretty dark-haired woman she had seen arriving at the villa every morning. The woman looked shocked when she stared up at the wall, and quickly drew the curtains across the window.

'*Santa Madonna!* You crazy woman! What the devil are you doing?'

Luca's furious voice caused Athena to jerk her head round, and she realised that he had unlocked the door and walked through to the opposite side of the wall—where she had been standing when she had first heard his voice. She stared down at him—which was a mistake, because now she was aware of just how high up she was, and immediately felt dizzy.

'Sit still while I go and find a ladder,' he commanded.

She wanted to assure him that she had no intention of *not* sitting still, but her vocal cords, like every muscle in her body, had seized up with fear. Her head started to spin, and she gave a cry as she toppled from the top of the wall…

Luca was staring down at her when Athena's lashes fluttered open.

'This is becoming a habit,' Luca growled, reminding her of when he had caught her after she had climbed out of the window at the Fairfaxes' home, Woodley Lodge, on her wedding day.

Instead of marrying Charlie, she had married Luca—and swapped one unfaithful husband for another, she thought with a rush of temper.

'I *told* you that the area beyond the wall was out of bounds.' Luca felt a fresh surge of anger as he set Athena down on her feet. Thank God he had managed to catch her. 'Your stupid actions could have resulted in you breaking your neck.'

The word *stupid* acted like a red rag to a bull for Athena. Just because she wasn't a brilliant academic, like her parents, she had spent her whole life feeling a failure, and had meekly allowed herself to be bossed around by Charlie. It was time she stood up for herself.

'I wanted to find out *why* the other side of the wall was out of bounds, and now I know,' she told Luca hotly. 'It's where you entertain your mistresses. I suppose the room I saw is your harem?'

'*My harem?*'

Luca looked so astounded that Athena felt a tiny flicker of doubt.

'Yes,' she ploughed on. 'I've seen the women who arrive at the villa every morning and evening.'

She thought of the attractive dark-haired woman who had shut the curtains, and jealousy fizzed like corrosive acid in her stomach.

'I know you have a reputation as a playboy, but do you *really* need your girlfriends to work a double shift? No wonder I haven't seen you since we arrived at Villa De Rossi. I suppose you've been in *there*—' she pointed at the door in the wall, which led to the garden and the rooms beyond '—with your women.'

Various thoughts circled in Luca's mind—one being that Athena was incredibly sexy when she was angry. He forced his gaze up from the swift rise and fall of her breasts and narrowed his eyes on her flushed face. The slight tremor of her bottom lip touched something inside him.

'You're right,' he said coolly. 'I *have* spent the past few days in a part of the house that Geomar would not have taken you to when he showed you around.' He frowned. 'But I do *not* have a harem, and the women you have seen are *not* my mistresses.'

Athena stubbornly refused to back down. 'Well, who are they, then?'

Luca came to a decision. He was fairly certain Athena was not a hard-nosed gold-digger like Giselle—although she *had* married him for a million pounds, he reminded himself. He frowned again. He could not keep his daughter a secret for a year, he acknowledged.

'You had better come and meet Maria and Rosalie,' he said abruptly.

Athena's heart was thumping as she followed Luca through the door in the wall. He had insisted that Maria and the other woman he had called Rosalie were not his mistresses—so who were they?

Unlike the gravel paths in other areas of the villa's grounds, the paths in the garden were made of smooth stone, and the garden's beds were planted with lavender and other fragrant herbs—rosemary, basil and thyme— which released their scent as she brushed past them.

Luca led her through big glass doors into a room that she instantly realised was unlike any other room in the villa. It was like a hospital room, with a bed that could be raised and lowered, and there were oxygen tanks stacked against one wall.

Against another wall was a huge fish tank filled with brightly coloured fish, but Athena barely noticed it for her attention was focused on a young girl—it was difficult to guess her age—who was sitting in a wheelchair. Standing next to the wheelchair was the dark-haired woman, who was even prettier close up than Athena had realised when she had seen her from a distance.

Luca introduced the woman. 'This is Maria. She is one of Rosalie's carers.' He crouched down in front of the girl in the wheelchair. 'Athena, I'd like you to meet my daughter—Rosalie.'

At the sound of his voice, his daughter smiled. She was extraordinarily beautiful, with black curly hair and Luca's amber-coloured eyes, Athena noticed dazedly. But it was obvious that Rosalie had severe disabilities, which meant that she was confined to the wheelchair.

'Rosalie suffers from a rare degenerative illness called Rett Syndrome,' Luca explained quietly. 'The condition affects mainly girls, and is incurable.' He gently stroked his daughter's cheek and his voice deepened with emotion as he continued. 'A few years ago Rosalie could walk and talk. Sadly she can't do those things now. But she loves listening to music and watching her fish, and she especially loves to sit beneath the weeping willow tree in the garden.'

Acting instinctively, Athena knelt down beside Luca so that her face was level with his daughter's. 'Hello, Rosalie. I'm pleased to meet you,' she said softly. She gave Luca a rueful look. 'I don't suppose she can understand me? I wish I knew some Italian.'

'It doesn't matter. We are not sure how much she understands, but she will like hearing your voice.' He stood up as Maria came back into the room.

'I give Rosalie a drink?' the nurse said in hesitant English. She gave Athena a friendly smile. 'The weather— he is very hot. I think a storm will come.'

'You could be right.' Luca glanced outside at the sullen clouds that had covered up the sun. 'I'll give Rosalie her drink.' He looked at Athena. 'You don't mind if we stay for a while?'

'Of course not,' she assured him quickly.

It took a good ten minutes for Luca to help his daughter drink from a special feeding cup, and afterwards he lifted her onto his lap and read to her. His voice was softer than Athena had ever heard it, and tears pricked her eyes when she saw his obvious devotion to Rosalie.

They stayed for half an hour or so, before Luca tenderly kissed his daughter's brow 'I'll come and see you later, *mio angelo.*' Turning to Athena, he said, 'Rosalie will probably have a nap, so we'll go now.'

Her mind was swimming with questions as she walked with him through the lavender garden. She was struggling to equate Luca, the world-famous fashion designer dubbed a playboy by the paparazzi, with the deeply caring father of a disabled child she had seen just now.

'Where is Rosalie's mother?'

'Jodie lives in New Zealand and by her own choice has no contact with her daughter. She couldn't cope when Rosalie was diagnosed with Rett's at two years old,' he said, in answer to Athena's look of surprise. 'It's a cruel disease.'

Luca's jaw clenched.

'You don't know what it's like to watch your child slip away from you bit by bit and be unable to help. All I can do for Rosalie is spend as much time as I possibly can with her and make sure she has the best medical care. She has frequent seizures, which means that she can never be left alone. A nurse looks after her night and day, and Maria often brings her own children to the villa, so that Rosalie has company even though she can never play or run around and do all the normal things children enjoy,' he said heavily.

He looked around the garden.

'I believe she is happy here. She loves the weeping willow tree. *This is my daughter's home*,' His voice had suddenly become fierce. 'When my grandmother wrote her damned will she did not think about how Rosalie would be affected if I was denied ownership of Villa De Rossi and had to move her to a new house away from familiar surroundings.'

Athena swallowed the lump in her throat caused by Luca's emotive outburst. 'Is that why you were so determined to marry and comply with the terms of your grandmother's will?' she said softly.

He nodded. 'Being chairman of De Rossi Enterprises is not a huge deal for me, and even if I had lost the right to use the De Rossi name for my fashion label I would have continued the company under a different name. My grandmother used my love for my daughter to manipulate me,' he said bitterly.

'Why *did* your grandmother want you to marry?'

'She disapproved of my reputation as a playboy—a reputation that has been exaggerated by the press, by the way. But mainly Nonna Violetta disapproved of me, the *bas-*

tardo, and I think she wrote that will because she liked to make trouble.'

Luca fell silent, clearly lost in his thoughts. Athena wanted to ask him if he had been married to Rosalie's mother. She also wondered why he had not told her about his daughter when he had proposed his marriage deal. More than anything else she felt guilty for her curiosity and the awful accusations she had made.

'I'm sorry for the things I said,' she murmured as she followed him through the door in the wall. 'All that stuff about you having a harem.' She flushed beneath his cool stare. 'My mother always says that I act first and think afterwards,' she said ruefully.

'Why were you jealous when you thought I had a mistress?'

Luca watched in fascination as rosy colour spread from Athena's cheeks, down her throat and across the creamy slopes of her breasts showing above her dress.

'I was not *jealous*. That would be ridiculous,' she muttered, 'when our marriage is in name only.'

A low rumble of thunder rolled down from the distant mountains, and the air prickled with the approaching electrical storm.

'It doesn't have to be,' Luca said quietly.

'What do you mean?'

She swallowed when she saw his wolf's eyes gleam with a predatory hunger. Suddenly the atmosphere between her and Luca was electrifying, making the tiny hairs on her body stand on end.

'You know I want you. I made it obvious in Las Vegas. And you want me, *mia bella*. You can shake your head to deny it all you like, but your body is sending out a very different signal.'

Following the direction of his gaze, Athena glanced

down and saw the outline of her nipples pushing provocatively beneath her lightweight cotton dress. Her breasts felt heavy, and the warmth in Luca's eyes was eliciting a molten heat between her legs. Half of her wanted him to take her in his arms and kiss her senseless, but the other half wanted to run away from the powerful undercurrents she sensed swirling between them.

'I don't...' she whispered.

'Yes, you do.'

Luca saw the indecision in her eyes and decided it was time for him to take charge. She was driving him to distraction, and without giving her time to debate the issue of their mutual desire he claimed her mouth with his, intent on kissing her into willing submission.

He felt her lips open, and her sweetly ardent response had a predictable effect on his body, so that he was instantly massively aroused.

'Your body was made for pleasure,' he told her thickly as he roamed his hands over her, shaping the gentle curve of her hips, the dip of her waist and the firm fullness of her breasts. 'I can't stop thinking about you in that sexy scrap of see-through lace you wore in Vegas.'

'Your body was designed for sex and you're hungry for it, aren't you?'

Athena tried to block out Peter Fitch's voice, but he was there inside her head, saying those awful things and accusing her of teasing him just because she had left the top couple of buttons on her blouse undone. She didn't want to remember. She *wanted* Luca to kiss her and touch her breasts. But as he slid his hand into the top of her dress and inside her bra she froze.

'What's the matter?'

He lifted his mouth from hers and stared down at her,

frustration at her sudden transformation from soft and pliant to stiff and unresponsive evident in his taut features.

'*Dio!*'

Luca raked a hand through his hair and was surprised to find it was wet. He had no idea when it had started raining. A loud clap of thunder shook the ground and when he looked up he saw that the sky was as black as night. The rain fell harder, flattening Athena's hair to her head and running down her face. Luca had the strange idea that they were tears he could see on her cheeks.

'You were with me all the way,' he said harshly. 'What brought about the change?' His jaw hardened. 'Or do you get a kick out of leading men on and playing hard to get?'

'*No!* Of course not!'

Athena's teeth were chattering as she tried to hold herself together. Raindrops the size of coins stung her bare arms and Luca's accusation lashed her heart. She could not blame him for thinking she was a sexual tease. She *hated* herself for her inability to escape from the past.

'I can't,' she choked. 'I just *can't.*'

She couldn't deal with his questions. And she could see from his determined expression that he was going to demand answers. In panic, she whirled away from him—but tripped on a tree root and went sprawling down onto the gravel path. For a few seconds she was winded, and then she felt stinging pain from her grazed hands and knees. She heard the crunch of Luca's footsteps on the gravel, and the bizarre thought went through her head that his handmade leather shoes would be ruined by the rain.

She tensed as he gripped her arms and lifted her onto her feet, expecting his anger. But his voice was heartbreakingly gentle.

'I can't pretend to understand what's wrong. But you have to stop running away, Athena.'

CHAPTER EIGHT

'ARE YOU AFRAID of me?'

'No…' It was a thread of sound. Her voice would not work properly. Athena looked up at Luca and saw not anger but concern in his eyes. 'No,' she said more firmly, 'I'm not afraid of you.'

'But you are, or have been in the past, afraid of *someone*?' He had seen fear on her face moments ago when she had pulled out of his arms—the same look he had seen when he had kissed her in their hotel room in Las Vegas.

'It was years ago.' Her voice cracked. 'I don't know why I can't forget about what happened.'

Luca stared at the tears mingled with rain running down her face and felt a strange sensation, as if a hand was squeezing his heart. 'What *did* happen?' He thought of her fearful expression. 'Did someone hurt you?'

Silence, and then she whispered, 'Yes…'

Athena remembered the livid purple fingerprints that Peter Fitch had left on her breasts. The bruises had eventually faded, but the memory of his assault was like a festering wound in her mind.

Blood was running down her legs from her grazed knees. Luca wanted to find out who had hurt her—and where he could find the person so that he could mete out retribution—but first and foremost he needed to take Athena inside, away from the storm.

He scooped her up into his arms, ignoring her startled protest as he carried her into the house. His steps did not falter as he strode across the entrance hall and up the stairs, giving instructions in Italian to Geomar, who had not been able to hide his surprise when he had seen Athena, wet, dishevelled and bleeding.

Twenty minutes later her grazes had been washed and bandaged and she was sitting in an armchair in her bedroom, sipping hot, very sweet tea. Luca had dropped four sugar cubes into her cup, but she didn't tell him the tea tasted like syrup when he was being so kind and taking care of her.

Outside, the storm had passed, and the air felt fresher as a soft breeze drifted into the room through the open window. Luca was relieved to see that Athena had regained some colour in her cheeks. Her wet hair had dried into loose waves, and not for the first time he felt as though he could drown in her sapphire-blue eyes.

'Do you want to talk about what happened to you?' he murmured.

No, if she was honest, Athena thought. But not talking about it for all these years since Peter Fitch had assaulted her hadn't helped her to get over it. Perhaps if she had been closer to her parents she might have confided in them, but instead she had kept the assault a secret that had festered inside her.

Luca had a right to know why she had blown hot and cold with him. She looked at him, standing by the window. He had changed into dry jeans, and the denim moulded his powerful thighs. His shirt was open at the throat to reveal his dark bronze skin and a sprinkling of black chest hair. Even casually dressed, he was effortlessly elegant—and so utterly gorgeous that Athena quickly glanced away, her heart thudding.

She took another sip of tea and searched for courage. 'When I was eighteen I was assaulted...sexually...by a friend of my parents.'

Luca said nothing, but she knew from his intent gaze that he was listening.

'He was a university professor and my parents had arranged for him to give me private Latin tuition so that I might stand a chance of passing my exams to get into medical school.'

In her mind she was back in Peter's study. She could see the dark mahogany furniture and the brown leather sofa, see herself sitting opposite Peter at his desk, trying to concentrate on Latin verbs that might have been Greek to her.

You look hot, my dear. Why don't you undo a few more buttons on your blouse? In fact, why don't you take your blouse off, and your bra, and let me see your breasts?'

Athena remembered her sense of shock at Uncle Peter's suggestion.

'One day Peter asked me to take my blouse off and show him my breasts,' she told Luca in a low voice. 'At first I thought he was joking. But he carried on saying awful things—calling me *Aphrodite* and telling me how much he liked my body and what he wanted to do to me.' She swallowed. 'He said he knew I would enjoy him touching me because...because I looked hungry for sex, and I obviously wore low-cut tops because I liked to tease him.'

She twisted her fingers together.

'My clothes were not particularly revealing, but I was eighteen and I was starting to experiment with fashion. I suppose a couple of my tops *were* a bit daring...'

'Just because you wore a low-cut top that did *not* give your tutor the right to assault you,' Luca said grimly.

'He said my body sent out signals that I wanted sex. I was scared,' Athena admitted. 'This was a man I had known for most of my life. I called him Uncle Peter, and his wife was Auntie Jean. I tried to run out of his study but he had locked the door.'

Luca cursed softly. 'What happened, *carissima*?'

'He ripped my blouse and forced his hand into my bra,' she said tonelessly. 'He kept squeezing my breasts and saying I would like what he was going to do next. And then he…he…'

Luca's heart stopped. '*Dio*—did he *rape* you?'

She shook her head. 'He put his hand up my skirt… between my legs. I believed he was going to rape me and I felt sick. I didn't know how to stop him.'

She drew a shuddering breath.

'It was like an answer to a prayer when Peter's wife knocked on the study door. It was so bizarre. Uncle Peter was trying to force himself on me and Auntie Jean was asking if we wanted a cup of tea. Hearing her voice must have brought him to his senses. He asked Jean to go and make tea, and when he heard her go downstairs he unlocked the study door and let me go. I put my cardigan on over my torn blouse and ran out.'

'Presumably you went straight to the police?'

Luca frowned when she shook her head.

'Why didn't you? You were subjected to a serious and terrifying sexual assault.'

'Before I escaped from his study Peter warned me that no one would believe me if I reported what had happened— because he was a highly respected university professor and I was a silly, over-imaginative girl.'

'Your parents would have believed you, surely?'

'Peter was my father's best friend from school. He was vice chancellor of the university. Everyone liked and respected him. I didn't know how to tell my parents,' she said miserably. 'I tried to forget about the assault, but I couldn't—especially when I went on a few dates with guys and they tried to kiss me. I felt...*dirty*.'

Luca said something under his breath in Italian. '*You were not to blame for what this man did, piccola*—of course you weren't.'

Somehow he controlled the white-hot anger that had surged through him when Athena had told him the details of the assault. What she needed from him was sympathy and understanding. He imagined how terrified she must have been during the attack and once again felt a strange sensation—as if his heart was being squeezed in a vice.

He crossed the room and hunkered down in front of her. 'You were the victim of a dreadful crime, and the perpetrator should not have got away with it just because he is a friend of your parents.'

'That's what Lexi said when I told her about the assault a few years after it happened. She persuaded me to report Peter to the police, but before I could do so he died suddenly of a heart attack.'

Athena had been left in limbo, without the sense of closure she might have gained if her tutor had been brought to justice, Luca realised. The sight of tears rolling down her cheeks moved him unbearably and stirred his protective instincts, so he scooped her into his arms and sat down in the chair with her on his lap, just as he had done with his daughter an hour earlier.

A thought occurred to him. 'Did you tell Charlie about the assault?'

She shook her head. 'I couldn't bear to talk about it, even though we were meant to be getting married. I suppose that should have made me realise I didn't love him,' she said ruefully.

It felt good to rest her head on Luca's shoulder. Athena did not know how long she sat in the safe circle of his arms, only knew that she *did* feel safe with him. Seeing his gentle patience with his daughter had shown her a different side of him from his playboy image. She had dreaded speaking about the sexual assault, but now she felt lighter somehow—as if by bringing it out into the open it was no longer a shameful secret from her past.

They had both learned something about each other today, she mused, her thoughts turning to Rosalie. The realisation that Luca had been prepared to pay her a million pounds to marry him so that he could keep his disabled daughter in the home where she was happy had altered Athena's perception of him.

But her awareness of him hadn't changed—if anything it was fiercer than ever, and she felt desire unfurl in the pit of her stomach as their eyes met and his gaze burned into hers.

He dropped a gentle kiss on the tip of her nose. It was no more than a butterfly caress, but it evoked a yearning inside her for more. Her lower lip trembled as he traced his thumb pad over it. Suddenly she did not want to think about the past or the future, but simply live for the present and enjoy the anticipation of knowing that Luca was about to kiss her.

They both jumped when the house phone rang, and he cursed softly as he reached towards the bedside table to pick up the handset.

'That was Geomar, saying he needs to see me,' he told Athena. 'He also said that Elizavetta is about to serve dinner. Do you feel you can eat something? Good,' he said when she nodded. His eyes held hers and his smile stole her breath. 'I'll meet you downstairs in five minutes.'

Her dress had a streak of mud down the front from when she had tripped and landed on the garden path, and her knees were grazed. Athena was about to put on her jeans, but then she changed her mind and searched through the clothes Luca had bought her, finally selecting a pair of beautifully tailored cream trousers and a pink silk shirt that showed off her curves.

For too long she had allowed the memory of Peter Fitch to dictate how she lived her life, and she had worn clothes that disguised her hourglass figure. But Luca had made her see that taking pride in her appearance and wearing sexy clothes was *not* an invitation to be sexually assaulted, as Peter had told her.

As she walked down the stairs, Luca came out of his study. His unsmiling face filled her with unease.

'I've had a call from Kadir,' he said abruptly. 'Lexi gave birth to a baby boy earlier today.'

'That's wonderful news…' Athena's swift burst of delight faded and her feeling of foreboding turned to dread. 'Luca…what's wrong?'

'Apparently there is a problem with the baby's heart. It's possible he will need surgery to correct the fault.'

'Oh, God—Lexi must be out of her mind with worry.' In an instant Athena's priorities changed. Nothing was important compared to the health of her sister's newborn son. 'I have to go to Zenhab and be with Lexi,' she said frantically.

'I have already instructed my pilot to prepare the jet for our flight.' Luca ushered her into his study and handed her the phone. 'Kadir is on the line. He will be able to tell you more about the baby's condition.'

Kadir's deep voice was taut with concern. 'We have named the baby Faisal,' he told Athena. 'He is beautiful, and he has a strong cry. I'm sure he will be as feisty as his mother.'

'How is Lexi?'

'Holding up.'

Athena heard her brother-in-law swallow hard before he continued.

'She's tired after a long labour, and she is worried about our son—we both are,' he said huskily. 'Lexi has asked if you will visit…'

'Luca is arranging a flight to Zenhab.'

'What is going on, Athena? I've heard reports that you and Luca are *married*. Lexi is worried about you, too.'

That was the last thing Athena wanted. Her sister had enough to worry about. 'It's true that Luca and I got married in Las Vegas,' she told Kadir. 'I know it sounds crazy, but…' she glanced at Luca '…we realised we had fallen in love with each other when we met at your wedding, and we decided to marry in secret and tell everyone afterwards.'

Kadir laughed. 'I always suspected that Luca was a romantic at heart. Lexi will want to hear all the details of your wedding when you get here.'

As Athena replaced the phone she was conscious of Luca's eyes boring into her.

'I couldn't tell Kadir the real reason for our marriage.' She bit her lip. 'Kadir is putting on a brave front, but I know he and my sister will be distraught about the baby's health problems and I don't want Lexi to worry about me as well. While we are at the royal palace we'll have to keep up the same pretence that we married because we are madly in love.'

Luca had suggested that Athena should try to sleep on the flight to Zenhab, but she found it impossible to relax when she was so concerned about her new nephew.

A limousine was waiting at the airport to take them to the palace. The last time Athena had driven though the capital city, Mezeira, the streets had been decorated with white-and-gold ribbons for the wedding procession of the Sultan and his bride. But today she did not feel any sense of excitement from the Zenhabian people, and knew that Kadir had delayed announcing the birth of his son and heir until baby Faisal had been examined by the world-renowned heart specialist who was flying in from America.

'I know it's hard, but try not to worry,' Luca murmured. He wrapped his hand around hers to stop her unconsciously twisting her fingers together. 'Your sister will need you to be strong.'

She glanced at him, and it struck her that he must know exactly what it was like to be worried about a child's health. 'It must have been a terrible time when Rosalie became ill and was diagnosed with her illness.'

'Ironically, I only knew I *had* a daughter because Rosalie became ill.'

'What do you mean?'

'I was not with Rosalie's mother during her pregnancy.' Luca exhaled heavily. 'Do you want to know the whole story?'

Athena nodded. 'Were you married to Rosalie's mother?'

'No. Jodie describes herself as a free spirit. She's from New Zealand, and I met her when she was travelling around Europe and came to stay in a village near Villa De Rossi. I was a young man, and life at the villa with my grandparents was tense and frankly unbearable. Jodie was a breath of fresh air.'

He shrugged.

'I fell for her hard and I thought she shared my feelings. I hoped we would stay together for ever. But she grew bored and wanted to continue exploring the world. I couldn't go with her because my grandfather had named

me as heir of De Rossi Enterprises, and I was also trying
to establish my own fashion label.'

He hadn't thought about Jodie for a long time, Luca
mused. Sure, he had been hurt when she'd left him—but
he had got over it. So much for everlasting love, he thought
cynically.

'Jodie cleared off while I was at a business meeting in
Milan, without saying where she was going or how I could
contact her. She effectively disappeared out of my life, and
I had no idea that she was pregnant with my child when
she left. She later admitted that she had decided to bring
up our daughter on her own and not tell me I was a father.
She only came back to find me when Rosalie started to
show early signs of Rett's.'

Athena remembered that Luca had told her Rosalie's
mother had been unable to cope with the news that their
daughter had an incurable degenerative disease. 'So Jodie
left you to care for Rosalie alone?' she murmured.

She thought of the two women Luca had loved in his
life. His mother and Jodie. They had both abandoned him,
and in Jodie's case she had also abandoned her sick child.
It was small wonder that Luca was so scathing about love

The car drove through the palace gates into a huge
courtyard where the helicopter that Lexi had often pi-
loted before her pregnancy was parked. Kadir descended
the palace steps to greet them.

Similar in height and build to Luca, his swarthy skin
and jet-black hair made a stark contrast to his white robe
and headdress. Athena adored her ruggedly handsome
brother-in-law, who had made her sister so happy, and she
flew into his arms.

'How is baby Faisal?' she asked urgently.

'He's okay.' Kadir gave a strained smile. 'The heart specialist has seen him and things are better than was first

thought. I won't go into too many medical details, but Faisal has what is known as a hole in the heart. It might require surgery to repair it in a few months, but there is a chance that the hole will heal on its own.'

They had been walking through the palace while Kadir explained the situation. He hesitated now, outside the nursery.

'Lexi is trying to hide it, but I know she was terrified we could lose Faisal. I want to keep her as calm and unworried as possible.' He glanced from Athena to Luca. 'I must admit we were both shocked when we heard that you two had got married.'

Athena felt herself blush, and she did not know what to say as Luca slipped an arm around her waist.

'I know our decision was sudden,' he said smoothly.

He looked down at Athena's and his sexy smile made her toes curl.

'But once we realised that we felt the same way about each other we didn't want to wait for months while we planned a big wedding—did we, *carissima*?'

Luca was back in performance mode, as he had been in front of the paparazzi in Las Vegas, she reminded herself. The tender expression in his eyes was not real but for Kadir's benefit.

Kadir opened the door, and Athena hurried across the room and flung her arms around her sister. No words were necessary. The bond of love they shared was so strong that they simply held each other. But when they finally drew apart Athena was shocked to see her usually strong-willed, fiery sister looking pale and infinitely fragile.

'Kadir says the specialist thinks the baby will be all right,' she said jerkily, desperate to try and reassure Lexi.

'The situation looks a lot more hopeful,' Lexi said, and

exchanged a look of intense love and trust with her husband that brought tears to Athena's eyes.

This was how marriage should be, she thought. Lexi and Kadir were soulmates, and their love for each other was a bright flame that would never be extinguished.

Lexi leaned over the crib and handed Athena a small bundle. 'Meet your nephew—Faisal Khalif Al Sulaimar.'

Athena's heart turned over as she stared at the baby's tiny screwed-up face and mop of black hair. 'He's beautiful,' she said softly. And deep inside her she felt an ache of maternal longing.

'I *knew* you would go gooey over him,' her sister said. Lexi looked over at Luca. 'I expect you know that Athena is mad about babies? I don't suppose it will be long before you start a family.'

Athena stiffened, and then breathed a sigh of relief when Luca made a comment about them just wanting to enjoy married life for now. She glanced up and wondered why Kadir was frowning—but just then Faisal decided to demonstrate his strong cry, and she forgot about the puzzling expression she had noticed on her brother-in-law's face.

'As you're newlyweds, we've put you and Luca in the tower room,' Lexi had told Athena. But she didn't understand the significance of that, or why her sister had winked at her, until that evening, when a servant escorted them to their room.

'It looks like a sultan's harem…' she said faintly as she looked around the circular room.

The walls were covered in richly coloured silks that matched the satin sheets on a huge circular bed set on a platform in the centre of the room.

'I wonder why there are mirrors on the ceiling…'

Luca's eyes glinted with amusement. 'You *can't* be that

naive.' But perhaps she was, he thought. He could not imagine her ex-fiancé Charlie Fairfax had been an adventurous lover. 'Some people find it erotic to watch themselves making love,' he explained patiently, when she looked at him blankly.

'Oh!' Athena felt hot colour flood her face. She grabbed her suitcase. 'I…um…I think I'll go and take a shower.'

She could not forget the mirrors—or what Luca had said. Had he ever watched himself making love to one of his mistresses? A tremor ran through her as she imagined looking up to see a reflection of herself and Luca on the circular bed, their naked limbs entwined, his body poised above hers. *Sweet heaven!* She covered her scalding cheeks with her hands, shocked by the visions in her mind that had elicited a fierce throb of need deep in her pelvis.

The sense of relief she felt that baby Faisal's heart problem was not life-threatening, together with the relief she'd gained from telling Luca about the sexual assault, meant that she was now able to relax—and focus on the new feelings stirring inside her.

She spent ages drying her hair, conscious of her heart thudding painfully hard in her chest. But she could not put off returning to the bedroom for ever. A decision had to be made. She opened her suitcase and stared at her pink cotton pyjamas sprigged with a daisy motif that she had packed next to the black lace negligee Luca had admired in Las Vegas…

'Stand still,' he ordered when she walked from the en-suite bathroom into the bedroom. He was sitting on the bed, his legs stretched out in front of him and a sketch-pad in his hands. 'Hold that pose for two more minutes.'

'What are you doing?'

'Designing a new dress for you.' He glanced at her briefly, before looking back down at the sketch pad as his pen flew across the paper. 'I've decided to make you something special to wear for when we hold a dinner party at Villa De Rossi for my uncle and the other board members of De Rossi Enterprises. I've been inspired by this Arabian Nights room,' he added.

Athena's brows lifted. 'Does that mean I'll be wearing a belly dancer's outfit?'

He laughed softly. 'Only in my dreams, *mia bella*.'

Luca finished his drawing and dropped the sketch pad onto the floor.

'Can I ask you something? How are you planning to spend a million pounds? I'm curious,' he said when she looked surprised, 'because you seem uninterested in clothes and jewellery and the usual things that most women consider important.'

She hesitated. During dinner Lexi had asked her about the fund-raising campaign she'd organised for the orphanage in Jaipur. Athena had felt flustered as she'd replied that the campaign's funds had been boosted by an anonymous donation. In fact the million pounds Luca had paid into her bank account had already been transferred to Cara Tanner, who had arranged for building work on the new orphanage house and school to begin immediately.

The conversation had led to Luca talking about the charity he was patron of, which raised money for research into Rett Syndrome and other genetic illnesses. But, even knowing of his charity work, Athena still wondered how Luca would react if she admitted that she had given the entire one million pounds to the orphanage project.

'I…I'm planning to spend the money on a house.'

'That's a good idea. Investing in the property market is a wise investment.'

Keen to change the subject, she glanced around at the silk-lined walls. 'This room is amazing, isn't it? Although we have the same problem we had at the hotel in Las Vegas—only one bed. I wonder which end you're meant to sleep in a circular bed.'

'I don't think the bed is designed to be *slept* in,' Luca said drily.

Her eyes strayed to the mirrored ceiling above the bed. 'Probably not...' she murmured.

'Don't worry.' Luca took pity on her in her obvious embarrassment. 'I'll sleep on the sofa.'

He stood up and stretched his arms above his head, drawing Athena's eyes to his superb musculature. She took a deep breath.

'You don't have to.'

'I suppose it *is* a big bed...' He considered her statement. 'Are you suggesting we sleep on opposite sides of the mattress?'

'Actually...I'm suggesting that we don't sleep at all.'

CHAPTER NINE

THE SILENCE THAT followed Athena's statement was profound. Luca jerked his eyes in her direction and she saw his startled expression change to one of burning intensity as he watched her untie the belt of her silk robe. It slithered to the floor, leaving her in the wisp of a sheer black lace negligee that had definitely not been designed to sleep in.

His eyes narrowed. 'You had better be clear about what you are suggesting,' he said tensely.

She pushed her long hair over her shoulders and felt a tingle of anticipation as Luca stared at her breasts, with their swollen nipples visible through the semi-transparent negligee.

'I want you,' she told him simply. He frowned, and she said quickly, 'I won't change my mind, or freeze on you like before, I've allowed what happened when I was eighteen to affect the way I live my life for too long.'

She met his gaze, and her voice was steady.

'I'm determined to put the past behind me. I have tried to deny the chemistry that exists between us, but...but I'm done with fighting a battle I can't win,' she admitted.

'Athena...' Luca's voice was unsteady, and he could feel his heart beating faster than normal beneath his breastbone.

How ironic was it that the man dubbed by the paparazzi the 'Italian Stallion' had been reduced to the state of a hormone-fuelled youth by the most unsophisticated, unassuming woman he had ever met? he brooded. Somehow he needed to regain control of himself, but the almost painful hardness of his arousal was an indication of how turned on he was by the sight of Athena's gorgeous, ripe breasts which were in danger of bursting out of her nightgown.

'Come here, *piccola*.'

Luca's husky endearment dismissed Athena's last lingering doubts about what she was doing. What she was about to do, she silently amended as she took the few steps required to reach where he was standing next to the bed.

She had thought she would feel shy, or nervous, but she felt neither of those things as he put his arms around her and drew her towards him. The spicy tang of his aftershave intoxicated her senses, and with a low moan she pressed herself against him and tilted her head as he angled his mouth over hers and claimed her lips with a bone-shaking passion mixed with a tenderness that enchanted her heart.

Luca lifted her onto the bed without breaking the kiss and lay down next to her, running his hands over her body and leaving a trail of fire wherever he touched her.

'I have fantasised about doing this since Las Vegas.' He traced his lips down her throat to the edge of her negligee, where the dark pink tips of her nipples were clearly visible through the sheer material. *'Bella...'* he murmured, before he closed his mouth around one hard peak and suckled her through the black lace.

Athena gave a gasp of pleasure when he peeled the damp material away and bared her breasts to his glittering gaze. For the first time in her life she did not hate her breasts for being too big. Luca's appreciation of her body and his respect for her, shown by the almost reverent way he caressed her, made her glad of her curvy figure.

The realisation that Peter Fitch no longer had power over

her and she was finally free of the dark memories of the past gave her confidence to touch Luca as he was touching her. She swiftly undid his shirt buttons, as if she'd had plenty of practice undressing a man, and pushed the material aside so that she could run her hands over his naked chest.

His bronze skin was warm and silken, with a covering of dark hair that arrowed down over his abdomen. Athena traced the fuzz of hair down to the waistband of his trousers and drew a startled breath when she felt the huge bulge of his arousal.

'Now you know what you do to me,' he said thickly. He lifted his head and looked into her eyes. 'I could die with wanting you. I've never felt like this before.'

It was the truth, Luca thought. His desire for Athena was beyond anything he had felt for any other woman. Her courage in facing up to the traumatic incident in her past filled him with admiration and he knew he must not rush her, even though his blood was on fire and he was desperate to appease his hunger for her.

He stroked his hand over her sheer lace knickers and almost forgot his good intentions when he felt the dampness of her arousal.

'We'll take things slowly,' he promised—as much to himself as to Athena. 'You're trembling.' He frowned. 'You are not afraid of me, are you *carissima*?'

He assumed that as a consequence of the sexual assault when she was younger it would take her a while to relax with a lover.

'No,' she assured him, 'it's just that this is all new.'

Luca lowered his head and flicked his tongue into her navel. Her soft moan of pleasure urged him to trail his mouth lower, but his brain questioned her curious statement.

'What do you mean, new?'

Athena wished he would continue, would slip his hand inside her knickers and touch her where she longed to be touched, but Luca propped himself on one elbow and looked down at her with a puzzled expression in his eyes. She knew it was only fair to tell him the truth.

'The way you are touching me is new,' she admitted.

'Do you mean that Charlie never spent time on foreplay before making love to you?'

'I've never slept with Charlie…or anyone else.' She swallowed as she watched shocked comprehension slowly cross his face. 'I'm a virgin.'

The only other time in his life that Luca had been rendered speechless was when he had read his grandmother's will. 'But you're…'

'Twenty-five. Yes, I'm aware that I'm an oddity,' Athena muttered.

She had half assumed, half hoped, that Luca would have guessed she was inexperienced when she told him about the sexual assault. But he rolled away from her, and in the mirror above the bed she watched his expression change from shock to something she could not read as his chiselled features hardened.

'You were engaged to Charlie for a year. How the *hell* are you still a virgin?'

'He was happy to wait until we were married before we had sex.' She bit her lip.

'He must have had the patience of a saint to resist his desire for you for a year.' A thought occurred to Luca. 'You told me you discovered on your wedding day that Charlie had been unfaithful. Did he turn to another woman because he had agreed to wait until you were his wife before you had sex?'

'Sort of…'

Athena felt embarrassed by her nakedness now it was

evident that Luca was turned off by her lack of experience. She sat up and pulled the purple satin sheet around her body, wishing she could crawl away and hide.

'Charlie never desired me,' she said in a low voice. 'On the morning of the wedding I found him in bed with his best man, Dominic. He admitted he had asked me to marry him to conceal the fact that he's gay.'

'Why didn't you *say* anything—instead of allowing Charlie to blame you for calling off the wedding and accusing you of having an affair with me?'

'I had realised that I didn't love him, but I couldn't betray his secret relationship with Dominic. Lord Fairfax is an ex-Royal Marine, and Charlie has spent his life trying to live up to his father's expectations. It was one thing we had in common. I've always been a disappointment to *my* parents,' she said ruefully.

'*Santa Madre*, what a mess.'

Luca rolled onto his back and stared up at the mirrored ceiling at the image of himself and Athena lying on the circular bed. The knowledge that she was naked beneath the sheet she had covered herself with evoked a sharp tug of desire in his groin. But, *Dio*, she was a *virgin*—and he was in dangerous territory.

'What were you were hoping for when you decided that you wanted me to be your first lover?' His eyes narrowed on her pink cheeks. 'Because if you were hoping for hearts and flowers and for me to fall in love with you, then you chose the wrong man,' he said bluntly.

She flushed. 'I don't—'

'In Vegas you said that you believe the act of making love should be a physical demonstration of being *in* love.'

'I think I felt that at the time because Peter Fitch had made me feel sex was somehow dirty. In my mind I thought that if I only slept with a man I loved it couldn't be wrong.

But now I understand how I had been affected by the past. You pointed out that there is nothing wrong with two people who are attracted to each other taking pleasure in sex. I'm not in love with you,' she told Luca earnestly. 'I chose you to give me my first sexual experience because I trust you, and because I...I think you are an honourable man.'

An honourable man! For the second time in the space of ten minutes Luca did not know what to say. He had earned many accolades—a great lover, a gifted designer, a brilliant businessman—but people had always admired him for his achievements in the fashion industry, or for his wealth. Athena did not care about those things. She had said that she trusted him.

His mother had abandoned him, his grandmother had told him he was worthless so often that he'd believed her, and Jodie had thrown his love back in his face. But Athena believed he was an honourable man, and to Luca it felt like the greatest accolade of all.

Luca seemed lost in his thoughts, and as silence stretched between them Athena remembered Charlie's taunt: *'Who do you think will want a twenty-five-year-old virgin?'*

'I suppose you're put off by my inexperience,' she said dully.

She sensed him shoot her a sharp glance.

'I'm not *put off* by you.' But if he had known she was a virgin he would not have married her, Luca thought silently. 'When our marriage ends in a year's time you deserve to fall in love with a man who loves you and will propose a proper marriage.'

She grimaced. 'After running away from my society wedding and then having a quickie wedding in Las Vegas I won't be in any rush to plan another wedding.'

Her eyes kept straying to the mirror above the bed and

to the reflection of Luca, looking sinfully sexy sprawled on the satin sheets. She wondered if he was wishing he was here in this Arabian Nights room with one of his sophisticated, sexually experienced mistresses instead of her. *Of course he is*, taunted a voice in her head.

'You're too tall for the sofa, so I'll sleep on it,' she muttered, keeping the sheet wrapped around her as she wriggled over to the edge of the mattress.

He watched her awkward progress across the bed with amusement. 'You look like a caterpillar.'

'It's okay, Luca. I *know* I have the sex appeal of a creature you'd find crawling out from under a stone,' she choked.

The wobble in her voice got to him.

'You know I didn't mean it literally.'

He caught hold of the edge of the sheet she was clutching to her like a security blanket and gave a hard tug. She gave a cry of surprise as the slippery satin was jerked from her hands and unravelled from around her body.

'You know I find you incredibly sexy,' Luca told her in a fierce voice as he pushed her flat on her back and knelt over her.

His brain was insisting that this was a bad idea, that he should walk away and leave Athena to give her innocence to a man who would love her in the future. But he'd caught the glint of tears in her sapphire-blue eyes and he hated himself because he knew he had hurt her feelings.

Her self-confidence had been destroyed by the vile monster who had sexually assaulted her. Athena must have dug deep to find the courage to ask him to make love to her and now she was mortified, believing he had rejected her because he did not desire her, when the truth was very different.

He lay down next to her and skimmed his hand over

her stomach and up to her breasts. 'See how beautiful you are…' he murmured, directing her gaze to the mirrored ceiling above the bed.

The contrast of her milky-skinned body against the purple satin sheets was intensely erotic. She reminded him of a Renaissance painting by one of the great masters, with her glorious hair spilling over her shoulders and her ripe, curvaceous body so utterly perfect that a saint would be tempted by her.

And he was no saint, Luca thought with wry self-derision.

In the mirror he watched his dark fingers stroke her white breasts with their rosy-tipped nipples. He watched her eyes darken as he rolled first one nipple and then its twin between his thumb and forefinger until each peak was pebble hard.

'Luca…' she whispered.

Her breathing quickened as he bent his head and anointed one nipple with feather-soft kisses before drawing the nub into his mouth and suckling her until she gave a thin cry and he transferred his mouth to her other breast.

Athena's gaze was riveted on the twin reflections in the mirror of her and Luca. Her dark nipples stood out against her pale breasts and were swollen and reddened from where he had sucked them. She looked wanton and shameless, her near-naked body sprawled on the satin sheet for his delectation—*and hers*, she thought with a shiver of excitement as she watched him trail his fingers over her stomach and hook them into the waistband of her knickers. The sheer black lace afforded little protection from his predatory gaze, but when he slowly pulled her panties down her thighs she felt suddenly vulnerable—because Luca was the first man to see her naked.

Perhaps he sensed her slight hesitation, because he lowered his mouth to hers and kissed her deeply, demandingly, until she relaxed and parted her lips to allow him to explore her with his tongue.

He lifted his head and his eyes burned into hers. 'Watch me touching you,' he said huskily. 'Sex isn't shameful, *carissima*. It's beautiful—just as you are.'

She stared up at the mirror and her heart jolted against her ribs as she watched Luca push her thighs apart and slip his hand between them. She felt him press his finger against her moist opening, and gently, oh, so gently, push forward until the tip of his digit was inside her.

'Good?' he queried softly.

She nodded, unable to find the words to describe the sensuous pleasure that swept through her as Luca slid his finger deeper into her. She felt herself relax as her body opened for him like the petals of a flower unfurling.

'You see how your body is ready for me?' he murmured.

Athena found it incredibly erotic to watch her reflection as Luca caressed her, to see her face flush with sexual heat as he swirled his finger inside her in an exquisite dance that evoked a trembling sensation deep in her pelvis. And as she watched her body's response to his touch and saw *his* reaction—the sudden tautness of his features and the streaks of colour that winged along his cheekbones—she no longer felt shy or nervous.

Luca made her feel beautiful and powerful. There was no shame in admitting that she wanted him—no shame in showing him how much she desired him and how impatient she felt for him to make love to her.

She cupped his face in her hands and pulled his mouth down on hers, kissing him with a passion that made him groan.

'*Mia bella*, we need to take things slowly. I want to make it perfect for you.'

So much for his assumption that he would be in control,

Luca thought ruefully. Athena's eagerness was testing his self-control to its limit, and his fingers were all thumbs as he fumbled with his zip and finally managed to remove his trousers without any of his usual finesse. He pulled off his boxer shorts and, hearing her swift intake of breath when she saw the hard length of him, reinforced his determination to concentrate on making Athena's first sexual experience as pleasurable as he could.

He kissed her mouth, and something fleeting and indefinable tugged on his insides when he felt the sweet sensuality of her response. He moved lower and kissed her breasts, before trailing his lips over her stomach and lower, to the triangle of neatly trimmed brown curls between her thighs.

'Luca...'

Uncertainty edged into Athena's voice as she stared up at the mirror and watched Luca's dark head move down her body. His mouth left a trail of fire across her skin and her thighs trembled as he pushed them apart. She realised with a mixture of shock and excitement what he was about to do.

'I don't think...' she protested faintly, but he stopped her frantic attempt to close her legs by sliding his hands beneath her bottom and angling her to his satisfaction.

'Don't think...just feel,' he ordered, before he lowered his head.

The first stroke of his tongue over her sensitised flesh caused Athena to gasp and jerk her hips. But Luca held her firmly as he proceeded to use his mouth and tongue to devastating effect, decimating her inhibitions as he bestowed upon her the most intimate caresses of all and brought her closer and closer to the edge of somewhere that remained frustratingly just out of reach.

The flick of his tongue across her clitoris drove her

higher, and she twisted her fingers in the satin sheet as she tried to hold on to her sanity.

He lifted his head and she gave a choked cry as her body quivered like an overstrung bow. 'Watch and see how beautiful you are when you climax,' he said thickly.

In the mirror she saw his dark head nestled between her pale thighs. It was shockingly intimate, but she could not stop watching him making love to her with his tongue and his fingers. The pressure inside her was building, and the need for fulfilment was so urgent that she arched her hips, seeking the heat of his mouth.

And then suddenly she was there, poised on the tip of a wave's crest, before the wave broke and she was swept into a maelstrom of exquisite sensations that she was sure nothing could surpass.

She was wrong. As Luca moved over her and she felt his naked body pressing down on hers she realised that the journey had not finished—it was only just beginning.

He positioned himself so that the swollen tip of his arousal pressed against her, and then he slowly eased forward and entered her with tender care, taking his time so that her tight muscles stretched to accommodate him.

Athena found the sensation of him filling her new and wondrous. There was a brief moment of discomfort as her body tried to resist him. He immediately stilled and looked into her eyes, his own dark with remorse.

'Did I hurt you? Do you want me to stop?'

'No!' She wrapped her arms around his back to prevent him from withdrawing. 'Don't you dare stop,' she whispered.

The delicious spasms that had racked her body when Luca had brought her to orgasm with his mouth were beginning again—little ripples that intensified as he began to move inside her. She soon learned the rhythm he set as he thrust into her, gently at first, and then harder and faster, as their breathing quickened and their hearts thundered in unison.

Luca rolled onto his back, taking Athena with him so that now she was on top. She braced her hands on his shoulders and he moved her so that she was sitting astride him. Their new position allowed him access to her breasts, and he heard her gasps of pleasure as he sucked one hard pink nipple and then the other while he held her hips and showed her how to ride him.

'See how beautiful sex is...how beautiful you are,' he said hoarsely, directing her gaze once more to the mirror above them.

Her body was peaches and cream, her full breasts ripe for his mouth, and she tasted of honey and nectar. She was a goddess, and Luca was entranced by her as she moved her body in perfect accord with his and the fire inside him burned hotter and fiercer. He was losing his mind— certainly he was losing control. He wrapped a strand of her silky chestnut hair around his fingers and tugged her forward so that he could kiss her mouth endlessly, hungrily, wishing these moments could last for ever but at the same time desperate to climax inside her until he was utterly sated.

She reared above him and tipped her head back, her long hair swirling around her shoulders. In the mirror Luca watched her expression change from startled surprise to wondrous amazement at the moment she climaxed. He felt her body convulse as her muscles contracted around his shaft, and the pressure inside him exploded like a volcanic eruption.

Through the waves of his own pleasure he was determined to extend hers, and he rubbed his finger over her clitoris until she trembled and came again, sobbing his name in the throes of her orgasm until at last she slumped onto his chest and he enfolded her in his arms and held her tightly against his heart.

Was it because it had been new for her that sex with Athena had felt like a uniquely special experience for him? Luca wondered. He had found her untutored responses a thousand times more exciting than the honed skills of his sexually experienced mistresses.

But the idea that she somehow belonged to him made him realise he was on dangerous ground. He had no right to feel possessive of her because one day, without a shadow of a doubt, he would set her free from their marriage deal. That was the way it was, the way it had to be, and there was no point wishing for something that could never be his, Luca told himself firmly.

Yet he could not resist threading his fingers through her silky hair, and he felt a deep reluctance to withdraw from her when it felt so right, so complete, for their bodies to be joined. He could have stayed like that for ever, but at last she lifted her head and smiled at him, and for a split second he felt an iron fist squeeze the lifeblood out of his heart.

Athena loved the sensuous drift of Luca's hand stroking up and down her spine almost as much as she had loved the sensation of being filled and possessed by him when he had made love to her. She felt utterly relaxed and at the same time incredibly alive—as if every cell on her body was fizzing like champagne.

When he shifted position she thought he would move away from her, but instead he pulled her close, so that her face was pressed against his chest, and she fell asleep listening to the steady thud of his heart.

CHAPTER TEN

'YOU MUST TELL Athena the truth, Luca.'

Athena opened her eyes to find the tower room flooded with sunlight, and a glance at her watch revealed that it was mid-morning. For a moment she thought she had dreamed that she'd heard a man speaking, but now she heard two muffled voices and recognised Luca's sexy, husky accent and the deep tones of her brother-in-law. The two men must be in the sitting room which adjoined the bedroom where she and Luca had slept.

Not that they had done much sleeping! She felt hot all over as she recalled that Luca had made love to her twice more after the first time, and had combined fierce passion with unexpected tenderness. It had been an incredible night, but the fact that she was alone in the circular bed this morning seeded doubts in her head.

She frowned as she tried to make sense of Kadir's words. What was the truth that Luca had to tell her?

She sat up and pushed her hair out of her eyes, puzzling over the muffled conversation she had overheard, but at that moment the door opened and Luca walked into the bedroom. Athena's heart missed a beat. He looked gorgeous in black jeans and a polo shirt, his dark hair ruffled and his eyes glinting with sensual heat as his gaze dropped to her bare breasts.

It was ridiculous to feel shy after he had seen and kissed

every centimetre of her body last night, she told herself. But she still pulled the sheet up to her neck and heard Luca give a soft laugh.

'It's too late to try to hide yourself from me, *mia bella*, after the amazing sex we enjoyed last night.' He leaned over the bed and tilted her chin so that she was forced to look at him. 'And I *know* you enjoyed the night as much as I did,' he stated, with enviable self-confidence.

'If you enjoyed it so much why did you get up this morning without waking me?'

'At dinner last night you heard me arrange to go riding with Kadir this morning. We had to leave at dawn—before the desert sun was too hot for the horses.'

She did remember now, and her tension dissolved with the realisation that Luca had not left her because he regretted making love to her.

'I heard you and Kadir talking a few minutes ago.' She remembered the strange comment she thought she had heard her brother-in-law make. 'What were you talking about?'

He shrugged. 'Nothing important.'

Athena did not need to know the details of his conversation with Kadir, Luca assured himself. He understood Kadir's concerns, but Kadir was unaware that his marriage to Athena was not real.

On the other hand, he mused, there was no reason *not* to tell her the truth about himself—especially as she had met his daughter and knew about Rosalie's illness. But he had only revealed his situation to a few trusted friends, Kadir being one of them. It was surprisingly difficult to discuss a matter that was so deeply personal to him, but as he looked into Athena's sapphire-blue eyes Luca acknowledged that she was the only woman he had ever known whom he trusted implicitly.

'To spare your sister further worry while she is worried about baby Faisal we have kept up the pretence that our marriage is real while we are in Zenhab. But that has given Kadir cause for concern.'

'Concern about what, exactly?'

Luca wondered why his heart was beating painfully hard. 'There is something about me that I haven't told you—something that *if* our marriage was real I *should* have told you.'

Athena said nothing, simply stared at him, and after a moment Luca continued.

'I explained previously that Rosalie's illness, Rett Syndrome, is a genetic disorder. Most cases are sporadic, meaning that there is no reason why children—mainly girls—develop the disease apart from bad luck. Rett's usually strikes randomly, but studies have proved that in very rare circumstances a man can carry the gene mutation responsible for the disease, and he will *always* pass that mutation on to his female offspring.'

A nerve flickered in Luca's jaw.

'After Rosalie was diagnosed I had tests which showed that I carry the gene mutation for Rett's in my DNA.' He heard Athena's swiftly indrawn breath and saw the shock on her face that she could not hide. 'It is because of *me* that Rosalie's life is slowly being destroyed by a terrible illness,' he said harshly.

Athena's reaction of stunned silence exacerbated his familiar feelings of pain and guilt.

'Obviously if I had known I was a carrier, with the potential to pass a dreadful debilitating disease to my daughter, I would not have risked having a child.'

'But you didn't know. How could you have done?' Athena said gently. 'You said Jodie hadn't even told you she was pregnant when she left you and went back to

New Zealand. It must have been devastating when Rosalie's illness was diagnosed, but you can't blame yourself, Luca.'

He *did* blame himself, though, she realised as she stared at his hard-boned face and the rigid line of his jaw.

Her heart ached for him. She had seen how much he adored Rosalie. And not only did Luca have to watch his daughter's health deteriorate, but he also felt responsible for her illness. There must be implications for any more children in the future, too. Rett Syndrome was incurable, and she could understand why he would not want to risk passing on the mutated gene he carried to another child.

'Whether or not I blame myself, it doesn't help Rosalie,' Luca said grimly.

He looked away from Athena, rejecting the sympathy he could see in her eyes. His emotions felt raw, and he was in danger of admitting to her that sometimes he cried when he saw his daughter suffering—that sometimes, deep in his heart, he wondered if he *was* as worthless as his grandmother had told him he was as a boy, and that Rosalie's illness was punishment for his sins.

'All I can do is ensure that Rosalie's life is as good as it can be in the circumstances, and that she is as comfortable and happy as possible.'

He strode back over to the bed, and his eyes were hard as he stared down at Athena. 'That's the reason I married you—the reason I paid you to be my wife. To keep Villa De Rossi so that Rosalie can live the rest of her life in the home she loves.'

Their marriage was a business deal with certain rules attached. There was no harm in reminding Athena of those rules, Luca decided.

'Last night was fun.' He looked into her sapphire-blue eyes and remembered how they had darkened with desire when he had made love to her. 'But that's all it was,' he warned.

'Do you mean it was a one-night stand?'

Athena bit her lip. Perhaps, despite Luca's insistence that he had enjoyed having sex with her, he had found her lack of sexual experience boring.

He looked surprised. 'No, what I mean is that just because we've slept together it doesn't change the fact that our marriage is temporary and in a year from now we will divorce, as agreed. What I'm trying to say is that I would like to have a sexual relationship with you, but there is no chance I will fall in love with you.'

'No hearts and flowers?'

She remembered what he had said when she had asked him to be her first lover. From the very beginning, when he had proposed his outrageous marriage deal, Luca had been completely honest with her, Athena acknowledged. If she chose not to sleep with him again she knew he would respect her decision.

But why deny them what they both wanted? she asked herself. Luca had proved last night how much he desired her, and he had helped her to bury the ghosts from her past for good. He had shown her that sex was not shameful but beautiful—and he made her *feel* beautiful...especially when his eyes gleamed with a predatory hunger, as they were doing now when he looked at her.

A heady sense of power swept through her as she let go of the satin sheet so that it slid down her breasts and Luca gave a low growl of appreciation.

'I need a shower—and I need you,' he told her as he scooped her into his arms and strode into the en-suite bathroom.

She helped him strip off his clothes and he pulled her into the shower cubicle with him and turned on the tap, so that they were deluged by a powerful jet of water. They took turns to slide a bar of soap over each other's bodies— although Athena breathlessly pointed out that he did not need to lavish *quite* so much time on washing her breasts.

His low rumble of laughter turned to a groan when she took the soap and traced it over his abdomen, before circling his arousal with her hand and caressing him until he muttered an oath and lifted her against him.

'Wrap your legs around me,' he commanded, even while he slid his fingers inside her and brought her to the edge.

She cried out as he suckled her nipples, setting her body alight, and when he entered her with one smooth, powerful thrust, she dug her nails into his shoulders and clung on for dear life.

He took her hard and fast. She should have been shocked by his primal passion, but she loved how hungry he was for her, loved each deep stroke he made inside her.

They reached the pinnacle together and climaxed simultaneously in a glorious explosion of pleasure. And Athena told herself she must have *imagined* it had felt as though their souls as well as their bodies were joined.

Autumn was slipping inexorably into winter, and the last few leaves falling from the trees looked like orange-and-gold confetti, while the mountain peaks beyond Lake Como were wearing their first snowy overcoats.

Luca parked his car outside the front of Villa De Rossi and tightened his mouth with frustration when he glanced at his watch and realised that the dinner party he was hosting for his great-uncle Emilio and the other board members was due to start in less than an hour.

After a week of tense negotiations and boardroom battles in Japan in his role as chairman of De Rossi Enterprises, all he wanted to do now that he was home was spend some time with his daughter, and then a enjoy a quiet dinner with Athena before he took her to bed.

In truth, he was impatient to take his wife to bed and satisfy his hunger for her before he even thought about dinner. Five nights was the longest time they had spent apart since the first time they had slept together in Zenhab, and he had missed Athena more than he would have believed possible. And he hadn't only missed making love to her, Luca acknowledged, although he *had* found himself thinking about her gorgeous, curvaceous body at the most inappropriate times while he had been away.

It had been a new experience for him to be distracted by thoughts of a woman—but Athena was not *any* woman. During the past weeks that they had been living together properly as man and wife at the Villa De Rossi he had learned that her sweet nature hid a surprisingly strong will, and her newfound self-confidence meant that she was not afraid to argue with him—which he found a novelty, because he had only known women who either sulked or sobbed in order to get their own way.

And their few arguments had been resolved by mind-blowing sex that had left him feeling as if he had conquered Mount Everest, as if he was king of the world—because he had never forgotten that Athena had said she believed he was an honourable man, and her words had finally banished the memories of his grandmother telling him he was worthless, a *bastardo*, and not a true De Rossi.

Luca walked into the villa and was surprised to see a stunning floral arrangement on the hall table.

'Geomar.' He greeted the butler, who was hurrying across the hall towards him. 'Did you manage to book another catering company to organise tonight's dinner party?'

'Unfortunately not—and, as you know, the company I *had* booked cancelled at the last minute,' Geomar explained. 'But Signora De Rossi has organised everything. She made the decorative flower arrangements herself, Elizavetta is cooking the menu Signora De Rossi planned for dinner, and some girls from the village will be waitresses for the evening—including my own daughter.'

The butler looked rueful as a door opened and a small boy came into the hall, followed by his baby sister, who toddled after him.

'I'm afraid my daughter has also brought her children,' Geomar said. 'I have tried to persuade them to stay in the kitchen, but Signora Rossi has allowed them to play in the house. She loves to see the *bambini*.'

'I know she does,' Luca said, in a non-committal tone intended to disguise his sudden tension.

Geomar smiled. 'Perhaps before long you and the *signora* will be blessed with a family.'

A nerve flickered in Luca's jaw. The staff did not know that his marriage was temporary and that he had paid Athena a million pounds to be his wife. But it was important that he reminded *himself* of that fact, he thought grimly. Maybe he also needed to remind Athena that the reason they had married had nothing to do with love, or planning to spend a lifetime together—all the usual reasons why people got married. And definitely not because they hoped to have a family.

He had made it clear that all he could give Athena was sex and that was all he wanted from her. But lately he had caught her looking at him in a certain way that sounded alarm bells in his head. He had seen that hopeful look on women's faces before. Past experience had taught him that it always ended in tears, recriminations and hurt—and he really did not want to hurt Athena.

She was sweet and kind to everyone, and the staff loved her. And she was caring and endlessly patient with his daughter, often spending hours during the day with Rosalie, reading to her and pushing her wheelchair round the garden.

For the past few weeks Luca had felt increasingly aware that Athena deserved so much more than a sham marriage—and she definitely deserved to marry a better man than him.

He glanced towards the top of the stairs, and his breath became lodged beneath his breastbone when he saw her. The blue velvet gown he had designed for her matched the sapphire-blue of her eyes. The dress was maxi-length, with a full skirt, and had a tight-fitting bodice that displayed her slender waist and full breasts to perfection. Her chestnut hair fell almost to her waist in a silken curtain, and she looked so breathtakingly lovely that Luca felt a curious ache in his chest.

The ache intensified when she walked down the stairs, as graceful and elegant as a princess. 'I've missed you,' she greeted him softly.

He felt a sudden spurt of anger. She had no right to miss him. Their marriage was not like that and it never would be. She had no right to look at him with a dreamy expression in her eyes that was a sure sign she was weaving fantasies about him and their relationship.

Plenty of women had done the same thing in the past and he hadn't cared. The realisation that he cared enough about Athena to want to protect her from losing her pride and, even worse, her heart over him showed him that he must take action now. And if he felt a twist of regret in his gut it was *his* problem and he would get over it, Luca assured himself.

'Geomar tells me you have taken charge of organising the dinner party. Thank you.'

'It was no problem. Elizavetta is working wonders in the

kitchen, and everything else is under control. You might just want to check the wine I had brought up from the cellar. I *think* the wines I've chosen will suit the food…'

The wine appreciation-course she had gone on before her wedding to Charlie had been useful after all, Athena mused. She was surprised by how much she remembered, and felt fairly confident of her choice of wine to serve at the dinner party. It was funny how she no longer felt daunted by organising a dinner party for twenty guests, and yet it had been such an ordeal when she had been engaged to Charlie and desperate to impress his sophisticated friends.

She was a different person from the awkward, accident-prone virgin with a bucketload of hang-ups she had been a few months ago, she acknowledged. And she had Luca to thank for her transformation.

When she had first met him she had believed the image of him portrayed by the paparazzi of an irresponsible playboy. But she had learned that Luca took his responsibilities for his work with his fashion label, for his role with the De Rossi company established by his great-grandfather, and most of all for his disabled daughter, very seriously. His devotion to Rosalie was one reason why Athena was convinced that beneath his seemingly impenetrable steel shell he *did* have a heart—despite the fact that he had once told her he lacked that crucial piece of his anatomy.

Her wasn't always cool and reserved, she reminded herself. Mostly when he made love to her he was in control, and he brought her to numerous orgasms before he took his own pleasure. But sometimes his iron control slipped and she glimpsed emotions in his eyes that filled her with hope for their marriage which had begun so inauspiciously.

She smiled at him, unable to keep the news she had

received earlier in the day to herself any longer. 'I have something exciting to tell you. You remember I sent the children's books I wrote to an agent? Well, the agent phoned today and she said she has sold my stories to a major publishing company—and they have offered me a contract for more books!'

'That's wonderful.' Luca dipped his head and brushed his lips over her cheek.

She gave a playful pout. 'I was hoping for a *proper* kiss.'

Athena was disappointed when he stepped away from her.

'I've been travelling all day in this suit,' he murmured. 'I'll quickly shower and change before the guests arrive.'

'Your great-uncle Emilio is already here. He said you had asked for a meeting with him before dinner. He's waiting in the library—'

Athena's voice broke off as she watched Geomar's grandchildren run across the hall towards her. Marco and his little sister Mia were adorable, and she scooped the toddler up in her arms with practised ease after working for several years as a nursery nurse.

'Let's go and find your *mamma*.'

'You will be a good mother when you have your own *bambini*,' Geomar commented.

Luca watched Athena blush, and she darted him a quick glance that revealed more of her hopes and dreams than perhaps she realised.

It could not go on, he realised as he turned and strode up the stairs, his jaw and his mind implacably set on the course he was convinced he must follow.

The dinner party had been a great success, Athena thought later that evening, after the last guests had departed. The food and wine had been excellent, and the long table in the dining room had looked beautiful set with silverware, crystal glasses and the centrepiece of red roses and trailing ivy that she had arranged. Her only concern was Luca, who had barely spoken to her all evening.

He had emerged from the library grim-faced after the private meeting with his great-uncle. During dinner she had been aware of his amber gaze burning into her, but every time she had smiled at him he hadn't smiled back, and his hard features had been indecipherable.

At least now that the guests had gone she and Luca could be alone—perhaps she would discover what his problem was.

She frowned when she noticed a light shining from beneath the door of his study.

'I thought you had gone up to bed,' she said, after she had knocked and he'd curtly told her to come in. Her eyes flew to the suitcase by his desk. 'Are you going somewhere?'

He was standing in front of a fire that had burned down to glowing embers in the grate, and did not turn his head as he answered her.

'I'm driving to Milan tonight because I have an early meeting in the morning.'

'But you've only just come back from a trip.'

Athena's stomach muscles tightened with tension, and she wished he would turn around so that she could see his face.

'Luca, what's wrong?' she said softly. 'Was there something wrong with the dinner party?'

'No, it was perfect—thanks to you.'

She bit her lip and forced herself to ask the question that had filled her with sick dread all evening, since she had started to wonder if he had grown tired of her. 'Do you have a mistress in Milan who you are going to see?'

Luca hesitated, tempted to lie so that Athena would leave him without further discussion. But when he glanced at her and saw her scared expression he couldn't do it. One way or another he knew it was inevitable that he was going to hurt her—but he had no wish to shatter her self-confidence, and he could not forget that she had called him an honourable man.

'No.' He watched the ripple of relief cross her expressive features and hardened his jaw. 'But why would you care if I *did* have a mistress? Our marriage is not real. We made a deal.'

'I know we did.'

Athena did not know how to handle this new dark and dangerously unpredictable Luca. She acknowledged that it would probably be better if she went up to bed and left him alone, but she sensed that his black mood had something to do with their relationship.

'But I thought over the past weeks we had grown... close,' she ventured.

'We've had a lot of sex,' he said tersely. 'And it was fun. But I warned you not to hope for hearts and flowers.'

He walked across to the table, where Geomar had earlier left a tray with a bottle of Scotch for his meeting with his uncle, and poured a generous measure into a glass.

'Tonight I made a new deal with my great-uncle Emilio.' He took a mouthful of whisky and savoured its fire at the back of his throat before he looked over at Athena. 'Emilio has always been desperate for the chairmanship of De Rossi Enterprises, which is why he hoped I would fail to meet the terms of my grandmother's will, and why he wanted to prove that my marriage to you is a sham.'

'You must have given him all the evidence he needs—you virtually ignored me all evening,' she muttered.

'It is no longer necessary for us to continue the pretence that we are happily married. I have agreed to hand over the role of chairman to Emilio. In return he will not seek to prevent me from using the De Rossi name for my fashion label, and more importantly he won't challenge my right to inherit Villa De Rossi. My lawyers have managed to overturn the clause in Nonna Violetta's will which stipulated that I must be married for one year before I can inherit. The villa is mine from now, and Rosalie can live here for the rest of her life. I have got everything I wanted.'

Luca said all this in an unemotional voice, and it felt like nails being driven into Athena's heart.

'And you have one million pounds, as we agreed. You don't have to pretend to be my loving wife any more. You are free to leave and get on with your life.'

Athena tried to swallow past the boulder that had formed in her throat. She couldn't believe that Luca was sending her away. She had not just *imagined* they had been happy since he had brought her to live at Villa De Rossi, and she *had* sensed a developing closeness between them—even though he insisted that they had only been having sex.

Her pride urged her to walk away, as he seemed to want her to do. And it was what the old Athena would have done. But she had changed from the nervous mouse who had never stood up for herself, and she wasn't prepared to give up without a fight.

'I haven't *pretended* to be your loving wife,' she said huskily. 'It's the truth. I…I love you, Luca. I know you warned me not to fall in love with you, but I couldn't help it. You helped me to step out of the past and leave behind my memories of being assaulted. You showed me that it didn't matter if I failed to meet my parents' expectations as long as I met my own. You gave me the confidence to be *me*,' she said simply, 'and it is because of your confidence in me that I have been offered a publishing contract for my children's books.'

She took a step towards him, but halted when he turned away to stare back at the dying fire.

'Don't make me out as a hero, Athena, because I am certainly not one,' Luca said with savage self-contempt. 'I can't be the man you want me to be—or the husband you deserve.'

'How do you know what I want?'

'I know you want a family…children of your own. I saw the wistful expression on your face when you held your sister's baby, and I've watched you with Geomar's grandchildren. You were born to be a mother. But I can't give you children. After I found out that I am a carrier of Rett Syndrome I had a vasectomy, so that I would never have to watch another child of mine suffer as Rosalie suffers.'

He swung round to face her.

'You're shocked. Don't deny it. I can see it in your eyes. I couldn't risk having another child. Now I'm setting you free so that you can fall in love with a man who loves you and who can give you children.'

'What if I don't *want* to be set free?' she said stubbornly. 'I'm not shocked by the news that you can't have more children. I guessed as much when you told me you carry the mutant gene which caused Rosalie's illness.'

Athena plucked up her courage and walked over to him.

'I have had time to think about the fact that we wouldn't be able to have children of our own, and it doesn't change how I feel about you. There are other ways we could have a family. I also have an idea why you shy away from commitment. It doesn't take a genius to work out that, having been rejected by your mother, your grandmother and

Jodie, you in turn have rejected love.' She put a tentative hand on his arm. 'You are the only husband I want, Luca. I love you. And if you love me—'

'But I *don't*—that's the point.'

The fire in the grate had died completely, leaving behind a pile of black ash. Luca stirred the debris with the tip of his shoe, and did not, *could not* bring himself to turn his head and look at Athena.

'I appreciate your theory about the reason for my supposed emotional retardation,' he said sardonically, 'but the truth is that I preferred my life without the addition of a wife and I'm ending our marriage deal.'

Snow lay thick on the ground, and the roofs of the houses around Lake Como looked as though they were covered in a layer of white icing. People said it was the harshest winter they could remember, and Luca knew he had never felt such bitter, biting cold. It had turned his heart into a lump of ice in his chest.

Even the roaring fire in his study at Villa De Rossi that Geomar so assiduously tended failed to warm him. He felt dead inside, and brutally alone—as if Athena had ripped his soul from him when she had left that same evening he had told her he intended to end their marriage. And as the days slipped into weeks, and the ache inside became unbearable, Luca faced the truth: without Athena he would never be whole again.

Reminding himself that he had acted in her best interests when he had sent her away did not help. Being noble was highly overrated, he'd discovered. Missing her felt as agonising as if one of his limbs had been severed, and now, two weeks before Christmas, as he trudged through the crowded streets in Milan past brightly lit shop windows and the huge Christmas tree in front of the Duomo, he realised that he had to do something to try to ease the pain that overwhelmed him.

But what could he do? As much as he might wish it, Luca could not change the man he was—and he could not give Athena the family he was sure she wanted.

He remembered Athena's accusation that he shied away from commitment because he was afraid of rejection after his mother and his grandmother and Jodie had rejected him, and he admitted there was some truth in her words. He was scared of being happy with Athena in case he lost her and his happiness ended.

He was a coward, Luca told himself disgustedly, but that was something he could and would change—if he hadn't left it too late.

CHAPTER ELEVEN

THE STREETS IN the centre of Jaipur, capital city of Rajast-han, were a chaotic mix of buses and bikes, rickshaws and camels—who often added to the mayhem by lying down in the road and refusing to budge.

Luca observed the confusion of traffic and people from the back seat of a taxi. Ordinarily the sights and sounds of a new city would have enchanted him: the colourful silks in the bazaar and the astounding architecture of the majestic City Palace. But he stared unseeingly out of the window as the car joined the highway and headed out to the suburbs, where the houses became progressively more dilapidated and the sides of the road were filled with fruit stalls and bread stalls, with children running, dogs barking and the occasional cow ambling.

After what seemed like an eternity of driving along roads with potholes as big as craters, and nothing on the horizon but dry-as-dust land and a few sparse trees, the taxi driver spoke over his shoulder to Luca.

'The House of Happy Smiles is over there.'

For the first time in days, in *weeks*, Luca felt interest. He felt alive instead of feeling the dull nothingness that had plagued him day and night. And he felt a lurch of fear in his gut, so that he actually had to stop himself from retching when he remembered how he had dismissed Athena's love and sent her away from Villa De Rossi.

He looked at the square modern building. Half of it was apparently an orphanage and the other half was a school—or it would be when it was finished. Next to the new house was a ramshackle old building, with crumbling walls and a tin roof.

'What is that place?' he asked the taxi driver.

'That's the old orphanage—before the American and the English *memsahibs* came together with some Indian businessmen and raised the money to build the new one.'

Two contrasting images flashed into Luca's mind: his Christmas fashion show, attended by the wealthiest women of Milan's high society, and the waste tip the taxi had driven past further back along the road, where he had seen children crawling over the rubbish—searching, as he had been informed by the driver, for anything of minuscule value to sell so that they could buy food.

In his mind he heard Athena telling him she was going to build a house with the million pounds he had paid her to be his wife. He had assumed she meant a house for her to live in, but no.

As the taxi drove up to the House of Happy Smiles, a swarm of children ran into the compound, laughing and chattering, their big eyes wide with curiosity when they saw their visitor.

Athena was somewhere here—in this house she had built for the orphaned children of Jaipur.

'I love you, Luca.'

Dio! Luca ran his hand across his eyes. What had he done?

Athena finished feeding the two youngest residents of the orphanage and settled them next to each other in a cot. The twins, a girl and a boy, had been discovered abandoned in a cardboard box in the city. It was thought that Jaya and

Vijay were about six weeks old, and caring for them had helped a little to ease the ache in Athena's heart, which had splintered when Luca had announced he was ending their marriage.

She had left the villa and Italy immediately, and flown to India. Working at the orphanage gave her some solace, and a reason to get up every morning, but at night she could not hold back her tears. She had to accept that Luca did not love her, but she wondered if her broken heart would ever mend.

Cara Tanner put her head round the nursery door. 'Athena, you've got a visitor in your office.'

A visitor? No one apart from her sister and brother-in-law even knew she was in India.

The door to her office had fallen off its hinges a long time ago. Now that the new building was finished, Athena was looking forward to moving in to her own private flat at the orphanage. Her thoughts scattered as she pushed past the old sheet pinned across the doorway— and her stomach bottomed out as she stared in disbelief at Luca.

'What...?' Her voice was a thread of sound. She swallowed and kept on staring at him, sure he could not be real

He looked even more gorgeous than her memories of him, his body leaner, harder beneath a white silk shirt and beige chinos. But when she looked closely at his face she saw fine lines around his eyes, as if his nights were as sleepless as hers, and his hair was longer, so that he had to rake it back from his brow with a hand that she noticed shook slightly.

'How did you find me?'

'I went to Zenhab and pleaded with Lexi until she gave in and told me about this place.' His eyes moved to the window and its view of the crisp white new building. 'I like the house you've built,' he said huskily. 'Why didn't you tell me about your involvement with the orphanage?'

She bit her lip. 'I thought you might not approve of how I had spent your money.'

'It was your money to spend as you liked. But, for what it's worth, I think what you have done here is amazing.'

His smile caused a shaft of pain to slice through Athena. 'Why are you here?' she said abruptly. She froze as a thought struck her. 'Rosalie…?'

'She's okay. Her condition will never get better, but thankfully she is no worse.' He hesitated. 'She can't say the words, but I know she misses you.'

'I miss her, too.' This was agonising. 'Luca…'

He strode towards her, but then stopped. There was no sign now of his usual effortless grace. His amber eyes sought hers, and seeing his emotions unguarded for once made Athena catch her breath.

'I came to ask you to come back to Villa De Rossi and be my wife again,' he said tautly.

Athena swiftly quashed her leap of hope. 'Is your great-uncle making problems again? Do you need to convince him that our marriage is not a sham?'

He shook his head. 'Emilio is out of the picture. The other board members refused to vote him in as chairman of De Rossi Enterprises and instead unanimously voted for me. My great-uncle has retired to his vineyards in Sicily.'

She frowned. 'Then why…?'

'I miss you.'

Luca saw shock in her eyes and knew he only had himself to blame. Because—as he could see she was about to remind him—he had sent her away. He had done it for the best of reasons. He would always feel guilty that he had unwittingly been the cause of his daughter's illness, and he could not live with yet more guilt knowing that he could not give Athena children. But he did not know if she would understand or if he had hurt her too much.

'I miss you,' he repeated, his voice rasping as if he had swallowed metal filings. 'I'm asking you to come back to me.' He swallowed. 'Not for ever…' He did not have the right to ask her to sacrifice her dreams of having a child. 'But for a little while…until you decide you want to move on and meet a man who can give you…give you what you want. A family…children,' he qualified roughly when she looked mystified.

Athena ignored the violent pounding of her heart. Every night after she had cried herself to sleep she dreamed of Luca coming back to her, but now it actually seemed to be happening she felt angry—and scared that she was misreading the message in his eyes.

'*Why* do you miss me?'

The whirr of the ceiling fan above the desk suddenly seemed to fill the room. *Whump-whump*. Luca's mouth felt dry and the palms of his hands were wet. *Man up*, demanded a voice inside his head. But for moment he was eight years old, sitting on his mother's bed, holding a silk scarf that smelled of her perfume, wondering why she had left him.

His grandmother had told him his mother hadn't loved him, that no one ever would—a dirty *bastardo*. His grandmother had been right. Jodie hadn't loved him, and she had left him alone to bring up their poor, damaged little girl.

But Athena wasn't like Jodie. He had to keep telling himself that.

'I love you.' The words felt unfamiliar on his tongue.

Something hot and fierce poured through Athena's veins. It was temper, she realised with surprise. All her life she had been meek and mild, but right at this moment she felt furious.

She marched over to Luca and pulled off her wide-brimmed hat so that she could see his face clearly. The gleam in his eyes as he watched her hair unravel and slide down her back evoked an ache in her belly—but sex was easy. She wanted so much more.

'Let me get this straight. You want me to be your wife again—but not for ever. Just until I meet another man who presumably will have a medical certificate to prove that his genes are perfect.'

She saw Luca's gaze drop to the jerky rise and fall of her breasts beneath her thin cotton dress and folded her arms over her chest.

'How am I supposed to meet this man? Will I live with you during the week and go on dates with other guys at weekends?'

He raked an unsteady hand through his hair. 'I haven't thought out the details. If you want the truth, I can't bear the idea of you with some other guy,' he said grimly. 'But I have to think what is best for *you*. I'm trying to do the right thing. I won't allow you to sacrifice your desire for children.'

Athena shook her head. 'I don't want a half-hearted relationship—*or* your half-hearted love.' Tears stung her eyes. 'If you really love me, *say it like you mean it, Luca. I want everything…or nothing.*'

He caught hold of her arms to prevent her from turning away.

'I can't give you everything,' he said hoarsely. 'You know I can't give you babies. I love you with all my heart—more than I knew it was possible to love someone—and because I love you I want you to be happy. That's why I sent you away from Villa De Rossi, away from me. I felt like my heart had been ripped out when I watched you drive away, but I wanted you to have the chance to fall in love—to be wooed, to have a fairytale wedding and plan the colour scheme of your nursery. I know how much you love children.'

'*I love you more.*'

She could not see him properly through her tears, so she stood on tiptoe and reached up to cradle his face between her hands, feeling the rough stubble on his jaw scrape her skin.

'You *are* everything, Luca. You are my one love, and there can never be anyone else for me because you are all I want and I will love you until I die.'

She stared into his eyes.

'If we had fallen in love and married in the conventional way, and then discovered that for some reason I couldn't have children, would you have ended our marriage and looked for another wife?'

'*No*, of course not. I want to spend the rest of my life with you and only you.' Luca felt as if iron bands were squeezing his lungs. 'I love you, Athena—more than I can say in words. I didn't expect to, or want to, if I'm honest,' he said rawly, 'but it crept up on me bit by bit, I wanted to hurt anyone who hurt you, to keep you safe and see your beautiful smile every day.'

He kissed her damp eyelashes.

'Don't cry, *piccola*,' he whispered.

But his own tears mingled with hers as he wrapped his arms around her and kissed her face, her lips, in a silent avowal of his love that would last a lifetime.

He reached into his pocket. 'I bought this the day after I'd lied and told you I didn't love you. But for weeks I was afraid to come and find you because I was sure you'd tell me to get lost.'

Athena smiled when she saw the gold heart-shaped locket inscribed with tiny flowers on the front. 'You said you wouldn't give me hearts and flowers,' she remembered.

Luca's amber eyes blazed with emotion. 'I said a lot of things I didn't mean, but I couldn't say the words that come from the bottom of my heart. *Ti amo.* I love you, *piccola*. Will you be my wife and the love of my life for ever?'

'I will,' she promised. 'Let me show you.'

She led him by the hand into the bedroom behind her office—which luckily did have a door.

Luca glanced around the sparsely furnished room and thought that Athena asked for so little and gave so much.

'It looks like a nun's cell,' he murmured as he sat down on the narrow bed and pulled her onto his lap.

'But you *know* I'm not an innocent virgin.'

Her eyes darkened with anticipation as he removed her dress and bra and cupped her breasts in his hands, bending his dark head to anoint each rosy pink nipple with tender kisses until she moaned with pleasure. She helped him strip out of his clothes and gave a contented sigh when he covered her naked body with his and she felt the hardness of his arousal push between her thighs.

'I wish there were mirrors on the ceiling... You've corrupted my body and captured my heart, and now I am yours for ever.'

'As I am yours,' Luca vowed. 'For ever.'

EPILOGUE

THE WEEPING WILLOW tree provided shade from the Italian summer sun, and the lavender bushes in full bloom hummed with the sound of industrious bees. Luca pushed his daughter's wheelchair along the wide paths, pausing often so that Rosalie could smell the mingled scents from the herb garden.

Following him toddled a sturdy little boy with a mop of black hair and a determined chin. Faisal Al Sulaimar, heir to the desert kingdom of Zenhab, showed no sign of the slight heart problem he had been born with, and Kadir had told Luca that Faisal had recently been given the all-clear by his specialist.

'My nephew is as daring as his mother,' Athena said as she ran along the path and stopped Faisal from trying to climb into the raised garden bed. 'I think Lexi is hoping the new baby doesn't turn out as adventurous as his or her older brother.'

She glanced at her heavily pregnant sister, and back to Luca, and her smile lifted his heart as it always did.

'We're going to have our work cut out when Jaya and Vijay learn to walk. The drawback with twins is that they do everything at roughly the same time. They're double trouble.'

Luca knelt down on the rug spread on the grass and scooped his adopted baby son and daughter into his arms.

'Double the joy,' he said softly. 'Double the fun and laughter and love.'

'Oh, yes, we're doubly lucky,' Athena agreed.

A few weeks after she and Luca had had their marriage blessed in a beautiful ceremony in the local village church in Jaipur they had become the proud adoptive parents of Jaya and Vijay. They were determined to bring their children up with an understanding of their Indian culture, and planned to spend as much time as possible at the orphanage in Jaipur, helping to care for the abandoned children who called the House of Happy Smiles home.

She knelt down beside Luca and her heart missed a beat when she saw his love for her blazing in his eyes. 'Most of all we are lucky to have each other,' she whispered. 'I couldn't ask for more.'

His eyes took on a wicked glint. 'Actually, there *was* one thing missing from our lives—but a mirrored ceiling above our bed is being fitted today. I think we should have a very early night, *mia bella*...'

* * * * *

MILLS & BOON®

The Italians Collection!

  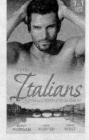

  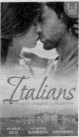

Irresistibly Hot Italians

You'll soon be dreaming of Italy with this scorching six-book collection. Each book is filled with three seductive stories full of sexy Italian men! Plus, if you order the collection today, you'll receive two books free!

This offer is just too good to miss!

Order your complete collection today at
www.millsandboon.co.uk/italians

MILLS & BOON®

MODERN™

POWER, PASSION AND IRRESISTIBLE TEMPTATION

A sneak peek at next month's titles…

In stores from 18th September 2015:

- **Claimed for Makarov's Baby** – Sharon Kendrick
- **The Wedding Night Debt** – Cathy Williams
- **Reunited for the Billionaire's Legacy** – Jennifer Hayward
- **Resisting the Sicilian Playboy** – Amanda Cinelli

In stores from 2nd October 2015:

- **An Heir Fit for a King** – Abby Green
- **Seducing His Enemy's Daughter** – Annie West
- **Hidden in the Sheikh's Harem** – Michelle Conder
- **The Return of Antonides** – Anne McAllister

Available at WHSmith, Tesco, Asda, Eason, Amazon and Apple

Just can't wait?
Buy our books online a month before they hit the shops!
visit www.millsandboon.co.uk

These books are also available in eBook format!